MW00682609

El Dorado
SHUFFLE

El Dorado SHUFFLE

MORGAN NYBERG

The publisher gratefully acknowledges the support of The Canada Council for the Arts and the Ontario Arts Council for its publishing program. The publisher also acknowledges the financial support of the Government of Canada through the Book Publishing Industry Development Program for its publishing activities.

Cover design by Bill Douglas @ The Bang

Printed and bound in Canada.

CORMORANT BOOKS INC.
RR 1
DUNVEGAN, ONTARIO
CANADA K0C 1J0

Canadian Cataloguing in Publication Data

Nyberg, Morgan

El Dorado shuffle: a novel

ISBN 1-896951-06-6

1. Title.

PS8577.Y34E42 1998 C813′.54 C98-900011-7
PR9199.3.N92E42 1998

For Lorna, Alyssa, Carl, Lawrence,
my loved ones

Contents

1

That Esperanza Fog

They suffered fog in that lofty town, and one night, some long years back, I walked through it toward the Boar's Head Tavern, to drink with English speakers. I whistled "Harlem Nocturne." To a *cúmbia* beat. And Avenida Veinticinco de Mayo, on the east ridge of Esperanza, where the fog crawls up from the jungle, was empty and still.

I passed the American Embassy and the sheet metal gates of private homes with guard dogs blustering, entered the Bore's Arse as I called it, crossed a foyer with notices of washers, stoves, fridges for sale by foreigners leaving, passed through to an area of small tables for couples or lone drinkers, and then booths of candlelit eaters. And on that night I remember one long table of American mountain climbers, the eyes placid and keen even in candlelight. I heard the names of peaks invoked: "Chinguráhua, Tingáy. "Here to partake of altitude?" I said, and the placid eyes were all keenly on me, wondering. One expatriate family. "Hi, Mac," from a kid. Kids have always fancied me, my Canuck beard. As the mom and dad sort of smiled. Missionaries. And forward into the wee bar empty except for the bald alcoholic ambassador from Panama, who was much into his morose cups and no kind of company.

"Maria Dolores, I bid you good evening. Would you be so kind as to give me some vodka. And a little ice with no amoebas."

"Mac, your Spanish is better every day." A plain, happy woman was Dolores.

"And you, Maria Dolores, grow daily more beautiful."

"Take me away then, Mac. Take me to Canada. Bancouber." A wink and her hip Latin bartender's smile.

"That's Vancouver. Bite your lower lip. Vuh. And as for your good husband and that enormous belly?"

"The husband I will leave behind. The belly I have to bring with me. The child can be yours, Maquito. Don't you want a son?"

"We won't talk about families."

"Malhumorado." Which meant, of course, grumpy.

In the dining area near the bar I saw some people leave, jacketed, even scarved, against the fog. Gustavo, the waiter, cleared their table, and a man I knew entered and sat at it and ordered fish and chips and beer.

"Arturo is here," I said. "Did you know I am teaching him English?"

"Malhumorado."

Behind Maria Dolores, among bottles, rested a petite wooden sign: BIG CATS SCRATCH. BUT A LITTLE PUSSY NEVER HURT ANYONE.

"Does Arturo pay?"

"Always. An honourable and a dangerous man. Who leaves impressive tips."

"Is it thus?"

"It is."

"In that case, another vodka. But tell me, Maria Dolores, why do you stir it? And why do you use your finger?"

"For your good luck, Mac, and long life."

"Then insert another finger, my child. Now there is a pornographic thought."

"Is it far to Bancouber?" Her wink.

"Dolores my life, what shall we name the child?"

"Mac Segundo, of course."

"There is Liz coming in, the British Council teacher."

"The skinny."

"She seems to be with a handsome Arab."

"The terrorist. He knows by heart the address of every gringo in the city."

"Thus?"

"*Sí*, Mac. A dangerous."

"But not an honourable."

"It is his *amante* who smiles behind the bullet-proof glass at the American Embassy."

"And Liz?"

"Another *amante*."

"A sad and singular city, Maria Dolores. Fog and Arabs and oil. Bananas and cops and girlfriends."

"And — what was your preposterous word?"

"CIAjerk?"

"That. CIAjerks."

"Maria Dolores?"

"*Sí*."

"Do I look like Humphrey Bogart?"

"El Bogey? Are you drunk so soon, Maquito?"

"This Bore's Arse needs a piano. We will call our son Sam, and he will be *un negro*. I will switch to beer now."

"And you will eat?"

"Soon. Maria Dolores, I cherish not only your beauty, but also your wisdom. Tell me what this country of farmers and llamas will do, with the price of oil gone, as they say in English, through the floor."

"It is said, Mac," she whispered, "*la coca*."

Damn. Cocaine.

I tried not to think about anything and managed to keep drinking beer, not vodka. I assisted the Panamanian Ambassador out into the fog, tumbled him into a cab, and told the driver for destination the vilest bárrio I could name.

Back inside, I nodded to Liz the skinny and sat me down with a well-aimed thump in a chair at the table of Arturo.

"Mac. Is good for see you again." In English, even. Arturo the brave.

"Marshal Art. Good evening." We shook hands. His soft grip. And his soft controlled laugh through clenched teeth.

"Hee hee," he said. "*Marshal Art* — this is one Canadian joke, no?"

"It is a pun, Arturo."

"I know this word. Once a pun a time."

"Exactly. Arturo, you have a way with languages. This is a new suit?"

"Yes. You like?"

"I don't lie when I say a handsome piece of cloth. But release that fake leather-covered button. You've no gut to hide."

"What is gut?"

"This." Pat pat. "But big."

"No. No gut. Only gun."

"A gun in the Bore's very Arse? I must see it. Please."

"Hee hee." He opened the coat. There was a pistol tucked under his belt.

"Maybe my English lessons have been less than first-rate. Do you plan to plug me?"

"What means plug?"

"Plug. Ventilate. Shoot. Bang."

"Oh. Shoot. You like make the jokes. But in this country we have such bad peoples. And maybe they try shoot me. Or pay money and I have to arrest." The black Indian eyes glazed almost with tears.

"Arturo, I'll never plug you. Or pay you either."

"Mac. Hee hee."

Yes, the soft laugh through the strained smile of teeth white as his starched shirt. The brightening Indian eyes, his weak handsome chin. The long forehead slope like that of some smooth volcano of the Andes. On it a wee birthmark in the purple shape of a hummingbird. His slicked hair, no brutish curls for Art. The dash of cologne.

"You are busy finding bad people for the police?"

"Please. Mac." The finger to the lips. "Is better you talk more quiet."

"For Christ sake!" I shouted. "Where is the movie camera? Don't the police know that Bogart is dead?"

"El Bogey? *Cómo?* Mac, maybe you are drink. Drink?"

"Drunk. All right, I'll whisper, then." I whispered. "What bad things do the such bad people do?"

"How you say? *Drogas.*"

"What — drugs?"

"Drugs. Yes." He buttoned his suit jacket over the pistol, showed worried teeth, looked left and right. The birthmark twitched purple wings.

"Aw, son of a fucking bitch." I felt limp. Flopped my head over the chair's back. There were threads of dust up there in the darkest cavity of the Bore's Arse. And this was a dirty, poor, and corrupt, inhuman city. And there was no glamour nor even respite. But dapper Art could handle it. Could carry a pistol, drink but little and buy a house in some steep suburb for devoted wife and daughter. "I wish I missed Vancouver. So I could go home." I saw Liz and her Arab staring down at me. The skinny. The terrorist. I had to giggle. Saved by my sorry state.

"It's winter there, Mac," said Liz. "Rain, rain, rain. Right?"

Arturo paid, leaving, as Dolores had said, an impressive tip, and stood and left quickly, patting my shoulder. A man who hates attention should not dress so well. I tried to sit up, but Jesus the chair took off over backwards. I laughed and shouted and flailed. The Arab sprang and clutched my knee and tipped me upright.

"Wow. Saved from sure death. At the hands of a chair. Give the bastards an inch and they try to throw you. Sir, thank you."

"Bloody hell, Mac." Liz almost laughed, then decided to be disgusted, or bored at least, with chair acrobatics. The British Council, super outfit, sends snobs all over the world.

Now, *patrón*, being a spectacle was not what I had intended, but merely some society, some small squirt of alcohol, an innocent evening out, no more. Innocent as an almanac, yes.

I rose and walked out to the street, where I would let my mind settle. I saw Arturo drive off in a cab, which he owned but which his cousin drove for a living. It sank into fog. Across the street, on the roof of the squat Esperanza International Hotel, tinselly letters said, Merry Christmas *Feliz Navidad*. All in a line the blurred mountain climbers went in through its door, past the doorman dressed like a native of Ichibamba, into the lobby's happy light.

From the heart's basement there rise at times sizeable bubbles of loneliness. I felt one detach and ascend, so I wheeled back into the Boar's Head before it could burst.

"Come on, then, Mac." It was Liz, inviting me to sit at her table. The terrorist eyed me coolly. How to strap a bomb to a Canadian. While he is distracted fighting a chair.

A well-executed peck on the cheek for Liz. I did not bump my nose or lose my glasses. She had a crosshatch of acne scars, which these lips of courteous greeting did not explore or dwell upon.

"Mac, this is Isman."

A handshake, he politely sort of standing, a decently dressed young terrorist in checked shirt, pressed slacks, leather shoes. Liz, as always, wore T-shirt, overalls, sneakers.

"I am going to buy you both drinks. Isman, I see by your present gin and tonic that we won't be frustrated by religious etcetera. In our quest for a fun evening in out of the fog."

"It's mineral water," says Isman.

"Ah."

"But not because I am a Muslim."

"Oh."

"It's because I have, as they say, a drinking problem. I find it's best to be frank."

"Ah." Hmm. New England accent. A terrible ease about him. Money. Amused but not bored.

"So. Not a Muslim. But you are. . . ?"

"Lebanese."

"Perhaps a Christian."

"Above all not a Christian."

If he went to the bathroom, to place a bomb maybe, I would pour vodka into his glass, hook the superior prick again on drink, make the wire connections tremble in his hands. Blow himself to Lebanese bits in some stinky rented room in Berlin.

"I'll have that gin and tonic, Mac," says Liz.

"Gustavo," I called. "One gin and tonic and one vodka with no ice and no amoebas. Lizita, I can never tell whether you are smiling or swallowing snot. However, an Englishwoman would never swallow snot but would hoik it up and discharge it expertly toward the floor."

Her mousy tufted haircut, pinched mousy face. Grey overalls on top of her skinniness.

"Bourgeois irony, yes, so predictable. Mac, tell us what your father did." The drinks came. "Cheers."

How seldom, I reflected, did nights out conform to expectations of cultured exchanges among expatriates. Rather, the poisoned mocking of drinkers. And now the memory of Jock McKnight had been called upon to add another toxic drop or two.

I took the merest slurp of vodka and said, "My poor dad worked all his life with his hands. Yes, a business executive massaging his many secretaries. Cheers. So, Isman, you're a terrorist?"

His choke and spray of mineral water.

"Oh, did I say *terrorist?* I meant *tourist*. Here, let me thump your back. I'll try again. A tourist?"

"Yes. Here for a couple of months." In the comely Eastern eyes, watery from coughing, some fear now.

"That's funny. I thought I saw you at the American Ambassador's garden party last fourth of July. With Consuelo, that stunning girl from the embassy."

"No." Amused no more. Twitch in the swarthy cheek. Good old Maria Dolores — right again. I would return to the bar and hand her a nice tip, maybe two worn-out pink bills, see her stuff them down the neck of her blouse, in next to the breasts, which expanded daily. Many years before, when Jeff was a baby, I sometimes put my mouth upon Evelyn's breast. And drank. Oh, sweet and warm and made me feel safe.

"And you, Mac?" said Isman, attempting worriedly now to be nice. "You don't seem to be a tourist. Or a terrorist. Ha ha."

His mother had not taught him how to laugh, neither with his milk nor later. Nay, had he ever known the breast except the generous money bosom? Liz' wee tit? Consuelo's splendid but milkless?

"Neither tourist nor terrorist," I said. "But I suppose a terror."

His dry ha ha.

I drank some vodka, would save enough.

I looked around. At a table at the other dark end of the place, by a window, sat Flossie Pazmiño, the principal of the American School, and Doreen Muñoz, the Whale of the Andes. My small wave of hand, their acknowledgement.

I did not want Isman to be a real killer. But I knew he was. Something about his shirt and his lingering gaze — just enough irony, especially the shirt, flaunting its absence of bloodstains. I felt nauseous.

I rotated my glass on the table, inspecting it and inspecting also, on the back of my right hand, that always embarrassing part of me that would be always eighteen — a tattoo, blue faded gothic script that said, *Who me?*

I did some spellbinding manoeuvres with my glass. The one-quarter clockwise rotate. The two-fingered slosh. I said, "What do you do for a living, Isman?"

"I'm in the meat business. Liz tells me you're a teacher. At the American School. I think I got stuck behind one of your school buses in a taxi the other morning. Is there one that goes through that posh area by the tennis club, then along Avenida Colón, República, La Prensa, and out América to the school? They sure pack those kids on, don't they?"

The bastard, he wouldn't cow me. "Gustavo!" I bellowed. "Bring me a steak! Rare!" And looked boldly at Liz. Her wispy eyebrows quizzically arched. Did she understand what was happening? Isman excused himself and went to the washroom. Liz got up to say hello to someone at another table. And by God I did it. Dumped my vodka into the mineral water of this pretty purveyor of meat.

Soberly I waited. Patient as a stone. Then I thought perhaps they had deserted me. The cowards feared the honesty and wit of the legendary schoolteacher and had slipped out into the fog. I smiled bitterly, that I was feared and legendary. Then a tear threatened. Because I was alone. I blinked it away as Liz sat down again.

"Unlike people," I said, "the best vodka has the least taste."

"You been sitting here alone working on that sentence? God."

We smiled the smiles of two happy cynics, but mine was one of anticipation for Isman's return.

Liz said, "You want a job?"

"What job?"

"I just heard about it. Tutoring the president. Pancho Perales. Everyone else at the Council is already moonlighting. I won't go near that smelly Nazi. But it's your kind of glamour. Isn't it?"

"Pay?"

"Three thousand dorados. Just conversation."

"I might. Did you think that was clever what I said about

the vodka?"

"Oh dear."

I went into the tiny bar, now jammed with lonely, loud men who spoke English, and had Dolores refill my glass. Tomás was there. Chairman of the Union of Indigenous Peoples. Raised by missionaries, it was said. Elbows on counter. Sensitive Indian face like Marshal Art's, but resentment like a cloud over it. Extravagant slouch hat of straw, yellow silk shirt, white blazer. Gleaming black hair in a braid down to his ass. Once, I had seen him unfold from his wallet a photocopy of a Stanford degree. As always his young blonde American woman, Holly, of tight jeans and loose demeanour, hung from him like a parasitic plant.

When I returned to the table Isman was there. He smiled pleasantly, which meant he wouldn't mention meat and packed school buses if I didn't say terrorist.

He squeezed a quarter of lime into his half-full glass, smiled and drank. Almost sat the glass down but, before it touched the table, returned it to his lips. With three gulps drained it. Placed both manicured hands palm down upon the tablecloth. Slowly the gorgeous eyes glazed, the smile drooped. As for a minute he stared placidly at nothing. And gradually the shoulders sagged.

I did more tricks with my glass. The vodka wobble, etcetera. Also, in honour of Isman's trance, I whistled Debussy's *Rêverie*.

"So, what's new, Liz? Think this fog's going to clear up? Personally I like to go around in a fog. Isman, what do you think about going around in a fog?"

He did not answer. His trance faded, though, and — oh! — a sudden frown of disgust. Then bitter wet eyes of resignation. Then a dry chuckle in the throat and at last his smile like a sunrise over blasted buildings in Beirut.

"I am going to have a drink."

"Isman," said Liz.

"Scotch. God, how I've missed Scotch. Waiter!"

"Isman!" Liz insistent.

"One drink. Liz, it's nothing to worry about. I refuse to be a cripple. If I can't handle one drink I may as well shoot myself. Don't you think so, Mac?"

I said, "Gustavo is busy. I'll get it."

I got up. Liz's eyes burned. I felt seared. Something pounded in my chest. I turned and went into the bar. Maybe it was my heart, maybe a trip-hammer pounding down sobs.

"Double Scotch. For the dangerous."

In Dolores' eye was a tear from her own Marlboro smoke. No tear for Mac. But, "Be careful," she said.

I handed her two pink bills, rumpled and soft as wool. "For Mac Segundo," I said. She tucked them down her blouse. Through the noise of the bar I heard the voice of Isman. Firm, controlled, desperate.

Liz quickly left when she saw me coming. No goodbye, no melodrama of last contact of eyes. She hustled out. Into fog. Liz, *feliz navidad*. Best not think about it. One more bubble to stuff into the basement. So as not to bust it, grease the skids. With good vodka. Ice. No amoebas. When I had kissed her cheek it smelled of soap and of skin.

Isman sat stonily. I gave him the Scotch. "My treat."

"Thank you."

"Goodbye."

"Must you go?" He did not look up.

I ate my steak in the bar, on a stool beside Tomás. But first I had it cooked more.

"Maria Dolores?"

"*Sí,* Mac."

"Do you ever get lonely?"

"Only when the bar is full of lonely men. I am lonely now."

"Fill my glass. Good, now stir it. If you put three fingers in we leave for Vancouver tonight. How is it that you know about such things as *la coca* and *el terrorista*?"

"I have more English than you think."

"Like Arturo?"

"No. I only understand to listen, not to speak."

"Ah, that. Then I pray you have listened well. So that I have not lost a friend for nothing." I left half my steak for her to take home.

"Tomás, what is that attached to your right arm? My God, it's a beautiful woman! Good evening, Holly. Now, Tomás, you appear to be drunk. Have you ever tried mountain climbing? I think it's exactly what we need, you and I. Leads to self-realization. Also to plummeting through space. Sheer exhilaration."

"I wouldn't worry about Liz. Good riddance to bad rubbish."

"A pithy phrase. Something you picked up at Stanford?"

"The English look down on the whole world. Bitches like Liz think this is the Em-pah." Quick ugly grin and jerk of the head with its hat. "We're their subjects. The ny-tivs." He stared resentfully at the puddled black formica of the counter.

Penthouse in Esperanza, had Tomás, and sprawling bamboo equivalent on the Rio Colorado, so they said. Lived like a nabob on what some of the poorest people in the hemisphere paid him to represent them to the government, and also on what the government, foreign diplomats and oil companies paid him to see that oil exploration on tribal lands continued.

"Tomás, in British Columbia we have a certain creature. Called a rangitang."

"A what?"

"You don't want to know. Don't call Liz a bitch."

"The jungle villages used to do it right," he said. California twang. "Some missionary comes in. Handing out comic books about a gringo with a beard walking on water. Telling us we have to stop being what we are and start being citizens. A dart. A little curare. *Pht*. No more problems. Nice blond shrunken head. Go home, little schoolteacher."

"What if a guy with a beard came in and told you you had to stop being an asshole?"

He drew from a pocket of his blazer a black spring-loaded

knife and set it on the counter and still volunteered no eye contact of common courtesy for the little schoolteacher. Holly did not move away — there must indeed have been tendrils. I resolved in future to call her Ivy. Tomás' wispy sideburn fluttered in the wind of my breath.

"Maria Dolores?"

"*Sí*, Mac."

"Maria Dolores, I am going to tell you what a rangitang is. It is a hideous creature from the frozen wastes of the north pole." The sideburn fluttered. "For pleasure it tears the arms off hypocrites and long-haired buggers who insult the teaching profession, and all black knives go right up the ass."

"Ah, that." She drew from under the counter a pistol and laid it on her shelf of bottles.

All the men stopped talking. Tomás glared at Dolores. Dolores smoked and watched him glare. He took his knife and left, and the plantwoman went too, but not without an eerie little smile of American green eyes in my direction.

Then all the men went at it even louder. Things like "Atta girl. Delores!"

Knives. An enemy who knew how to make poison darts. Cute, no? I would practise with my own blowgun. Forty feet from the end of my living room, through hallway and the open door of my bedroom, to a magazine taped to the wall. On its cover a portrait of the genial face of Pancho Perales, *el presidente*. The freckles were really holes made by darts, I was getting good.

I slid out of the bar, away from Dolores' reproaching eyes.

"Hello Flossie."

"Hi Mac."

"Hello Doreen."

"Evening Mac."

"May I join you?"

"Of course," said Flossie, without removing from her mouth a short cigarette drooping a long ash. Flossie Pazmiño was fifty and jowly and had rusty grey hair poorly combed like a boy's.

Tonight she sported a massive blue bow at her throat, lopsided and daubed with tobacco ash.

Doreen was the proprietress of a thriving whorehouse. Behind the beefy sweaty face of a Georgia sheriff and out from endless fat struggled a crumb of Southern belle girlishness. Land's sake and I do declare. Tonight the brown hair was waved, and there was a blue frock dress, but no stroke of paint on that pasty sheriff's face. She picked energetically at the wax of their table's candle. A tang of sweat always surrounded this woman. Too many deep infoldings of flesh. She melted flakes of wax, and the candle grew fat too. Phallic. I wondered about her husband, quiet Raul, pudgy chief of police — how had she gotten him? Maybe that aggressiveness of all gringas. Fat could squelch it not.

I looked around, saw solitary Isman, slouched now, head thrown back. Laughing, Gustavo took away his glass and gave him another.

"You look tired, Mac. Marking too many papers?" asked Flossie.

"Naw, just telling off assholes. Practising my blowgun. Nightly self-abuse. It adds up."

"Mac," said Doreen, "I want you to come and teach English to the girls."

My mouth, I'm afraid, hung open. "In the name of God, why?"

"Tourists. A lot of them passing through, these days. It would be good if the girls knew a little English."

"Pay?"

"How much do you want?"

"Two thousand."

"Deal."

We shook hands. And hers was larger than this one of mine and could, I am sure, pick up a hundred-pound sack of chicken scratch. And beat you with it. I had acquired two evening jobs in one night: president and prostitutes. But, *patrón*, at that moment I cared little. An internal fog had rolled in to match the fog beyond the window that reflected the fire of our candle.

Then, above me, I heard the crack of a man's voice. "Doreen, you've made that candle look exactly like a big white dick."

Jack Kelly. CIAjerk.

He leaned on the back of my chair and Doreen's, with lots of curly dark hair and his happy face leaning in. The ladies traded glances.

"Maybe one of your girls could put that candle to good use. Haw haw haw. Hi there, Mac." But in those jolly eyes was this: You Canadian flake, we don't take to your kind in these parts.

"Jack, did your son tell you he failed the Christmas English exam?"

"His report card said he passed."

Flossie butted her cigarette. The end of her bow drooped into her drink, sucked up gin like a wick. "Mac," she said, "we did discuss that. Jack, I personally reviewed Gordon's grade. His report card is correct." She butted vigorously, snatched her bow out, and said, "Damn" as she wrung out gin into the ash-tray.

"I caught him cheating," I said. "Standing up over his desk, chin hooked over Alegria Bustamante's shoulder, too obviously reading her answers."

"I talked with him, Jack," said Flossie. "It's all straightened out. Mac, we did discuss this."

"I tore up his paper, of course. Later he found me in the classroom alone. Explained that his father could get my visa cancelled. Said I had better pass him. So of course I had to assure him that his father was a pleasant harmless embassy official and was incapable both personally and technically of arranging such things. Oh, not so, said Gordon. So clear it up for me, would you, Jack. Is my visa safe?"

His hand upon my shoulder, patting once firmly. "Mac, you seem to have drunk a little too much. Maybe you better head on home."

Oh.

Flossie's face was all closed off. Not pleased, it seemed, with her English teacher. As she fished out another cigarette.

I said, "I am a genuine colourful expatriate. I like the fog, the sun, the altitude, the earthquakes and the language. Also some of the people. Maybe it's the harmless functionaries who should go home."

The hand lifted from my shoulder.

Doreen said, "Mac, I'll get you a cab."

I said, "You won't."

"Haw haw haw. Mac," said Jack, "you're a strange one, you are."

"You just want the oil. And to keep the Russians out. Ever see a Russian in Esperanza?"

"You damn right that's what we want. And if you think . . ."

"Oil and cocaine."

"What did you say?"

"Cocaine."

"Flossie, when does this guy's visa run out? There must be an American around who can teach English."

Our reflections floated in the window, above the candle's flame.

Tomás came back in from the street, with the collar of his white blazer turned up, and wearing a red scarf. He glared at us for a while, and we watched him glare. Then he left. Then Isman reeled past us on his way out. Laughing. He said, "One fifty-two San Javier."

Jack gaped at Isman's back. "What the fuck? Who is that guy? That was my address."

I left, also reeling. Across a small yard where the Boar's Head's wolfhound slept in the arc of his chain. Through a portal of mortared stones and two pots of geraniums. Perhaps the mountaineers were now in their rooms counting pitons. *Feliz Navidad*, I wanted to holler but could not. I walked away from that corner of light and taxis, the Arse, the hotel, the jailbar fence and floodlit yard of the American Embassy.

I wondered if I was falling and did not know it. A crucial piton had popped, and this was the long plummet. Faster and faster the world went past. Brighter and brighter.

2

The El Dorado Shuffle

I went to an open window, where eucalyptus smell came in on that wind they had there. "One day Poe's wife was singing," I said. "A younger person than any of you. Just singing out of pure happiness. You've done that, some of you. Yes? Singing away. Then a pound or so of blood and lung comes flying out of her mouth. Tuberculosis."

In the middle row, second seat, Alegria Bustamante said *yugh*. Fine, she would remember. Behind her, Gordon Kelly, son of Jack, would not remember. Not with his cheek flattened against the desk like that, and him asleep in a puddle of his own drool. His snoring almost as soothing as that arid Andean wind.

Out there the school buses were arriving. Old Marúchi in her fedora, with her table of candies, waiting for the bell. I turned to see if anyone was listening. It didn't matter, no one ever listens last period of the week. Unless you go the blood-and-lungs route like gangbusters. But Montserrat was. Alert and calm in her desk at the back there by the slide projector.

"In a few years, of course, she died. Poe's mother had died of tuberculosis at the same age. So Poe had a nervous breakdown. And started writing of such lighthearted subjects as being buried alive."

Dead eyes of rich students looking at wristwatches. And no one even laughed when the sleeping Gordon snorted and wuzzled. Behind Gordon, dark-skinned Lorena. Airhead deluxe. Returned from Chicago to wealth and privilege. Banana-studded acres on the coast. *Quinta* in the sierra the size of Ireland, wild bulls and condors gambolling upon its volcanoes. Gorgeous and friendly girl. Did she know what tumescence she inspired in these bulls of English 12? About Lorena even I invented fantasies. Of a kind I did not allow myself to have about Montserrat. And there was Marco Cádiz, son of a cheese magnate, in the window row at the back. Handsome, hardworking, eternally respectful. Always leaning across toward Montserrat, pretending to check her notes, even touching her arm to turn her wristwatch toward him. Here, just make a note on my lesson plan. *Get Cádiz.*

Now, in the dusty chalk of the American School, I wrote upon the board, *El Dorado*. Meaning *the gilded, the golden one*. Jeff had said something about gold that last time I saw him, in that northern place where they have winter. Where one stuck it out while the wife was alive. Watching the wee son grow. Nice, back there in the past. One's own house in the Italian district. Next door to loony Carmela, who drank home-brewed muscatel and sang spinster arias to her flowerpots.

A week in each of those few good northern summers with Evelyn and small Jeff in a tent on a Gulf Island. Oh the salt smell. And Gulf-Island sun upon the freckled skin of a person you love. World's champion scent. Must have a little lick of it. There.

"Where's Jeff?" she asked.

"Way over there. You can just see him. There by the cliffs."

We shaded our eyes against the glare of the bay. His blue inflated raft just now edging into shadows below sandstone bluffs. Stalwart Jeff rowing like Ahab.

"It's deep there, Mac."

"I know, but he says there's treasure in those caves."

"Treasure?"

"Gold."

"What if he falls in?"

"He'll swim."

"Will he?"

In Montserrat's Mediterranean eyes was that same trusting gaze as in those blue ones of Evelyn. Saying, I will carry you across all waters and there will be treasure.

Later we bought Jeff pastels, and every winter night after school he drew furiously, snatching coloured bits from the fragments spread upon his desk. An artist. Terrifying thing.

I cannot remember any of the summers after Evelyn died.

I do remember, though, Jeff saying once, "Why did God make Mommy die? Did we do something wrong?"

Another time, maybe the same winter, Carmela burst out her back door, drunk, ranting in Italian at Jeffrey and his snowman for leaning his sled against her chicken-wire fence. She slipped on ice. Cartwheeled down her steps. Broke her neck.

More and more fragments on Jeffrey's desk. Colours beyond naming. He drew and drew, painting those bleak winter nights with faces of women. It was then, of course, that I started to drink. Shall we feel sorry for ourself?

Not a pair of ears listening to my thoughts on El Dorado except those of Montserrat. I prayed no tongue had yet been in them. "Gaily bedight," I recited, "A gallant knight, In sunshine and in shadow, Had journeyed long, Singing a song, In search of Eldorado."

A certain previous night, over a clutch of straight vodkas at the Arse, I had asked Dickie Pendergast about her.

"Dickie, there's this girl. Montserrat Dávilos."

"Will you stop fucking calling me that. Your dicky is your pricky. Which you sticky. For a quicky." His bark of a Midwestern guffaw, and a challenging smile across the table. Yes, a happy and obnoxious man was Dick. Red beard, red hair sticking up in chunks, nose eternally fried by the ultraviolet wavelengths of this lofty setting. Here twelve years and still could not believe how cheap the liquor and how eager the Latin ladies to press themselves against a gringo's pasty person.

"It's not what you think, Ricardo."

"Oh no. 'Course not. Man, it must be something about the mixture of Catholicism, bubble gum and equatorial sun. Turns them into sizzlers. Green but eager."

"You've never laid a hand upon a girl student. You've got principles in spite of what you say."

"You know Lorena? Banana Lorena?"

"Yes."

"I'm still trying to get her bubble gum off my banana. But at least now she'll pass Social Studies."

One had to laugh. "Dickie, you're as big a liar as you are a lecher."

"Does Montserrat blow? Jesus, don't hit me!"

"You've no right to say that about her!"

"Okay, okay. But don't fucking call me Dickie."

"Okay."

"Jesus."

"Sorry."

"Okay. Now — Montserrat Dávilos? What's the big deal?"

"I'm not sure. Something different about her. Makes me curious."

"Uh huh. Curious about her snatch. Don't hit me, just kidding. Buy me one of them . . . what is that piss you're drinking?"

"Vodka."

"Fucking communist drink. Buy me one and I'll tell you all about her."

I did. Gustavo brought us two arctic tumblers of it, and Dickie continued.

"Old family. Rich. Her great-granddaddy was president — dictator — for a few months in the nineteen-forties. Her father, Charlie Dávilos, is head of the armed forces. House down in the

Valley. A wild and moral man, so I'm told. Davy Crockett of the fucking Andes. Apparently, all the government crooks are scared of him. Even Perales. One child, his treasure. Your Montserrat. Watch out."

"I think maybe she just reminds me of my wife. Ricardo, do you believe in El Dorado?"

"Of course. It's between Lorena's legs."

Out there at the edge of the school's playing field, perched on a chain-link fence, was a red-chested bird, a vermilion flycathcer. Edgar Allan Poe had written about a raven who lived above his door and croaked, "Nevermore." This bright little bird of the Andes, darting out to snatch a bug, settling back content on his fence, would never say such a thing. So, as a private joke on Poe I gave the bird Poe's name. And now, bumping along this ritzy school's washboard dirt road, puffing dust up around flycatcher Edgar, came Montserrat's black car to take her home.

Some stirring in the room now, anticipation of the approaching bell doing what Poe could not. A wuzzle and wuff from Gordon, and a slurp in his sleep at his trickle of drool. Laughs here and there. Lorena's like a calf in a Chicago stockyard.

I bellowed. "Gordon!"

And, wow, up he rears with an expression of terror on his face. And a long streamer of drool flies from his cheek, across the aisle into the hair of Marisol, the student council rep. And there is laughter. A lot. Even Alegria Bustamante hooting at her gringo beau.

"Gordon, would you please close the curtains."

He croaked some reply and stumbled to the window. The class all took a last look at the rescuing buses. And then, under insipid electric light, twenty-three people were all suddenly paying attention. To me.

"'Eldorado.' A poem by whom, Lorena?"

"By Edgar Allan Poo."

Loud shouts of laughter. A blush and an embarrassed smile upon Lorena's dusky face.

"Not quite, Lorena. That should be Edgar Allan Poo-Poo."

Louder hollers of mirth. Even some desk thumping. But upon Gordon Kelly's half-awake mug, only a wry smile.

"Gordon, clean your desk."

Marisol threw him a kleenex, which alighted upon his expensive haircut. Lorena's laugh like an orphaned calf. Sweet girl. Must go right home and abuse myself imagining salacious episodes with her.

Now that they were all awake there was a very orgy of glancing at wristwatches. Some fingered filthy bills to purchase suckers from Marúchi. Marco Cádiz leaned across. Took Montserrat's left wrist, drew it toward him, pretending to care about the hour. Inclined his face toward her hand. Almost as if to kiss.

"Marco."

"Yes, sir." Montserrat snatching her hand away.

"Marco, are you paying attention?"

"Yes, sir."

"Was Poe a lighthearted man?'

"No, I think he was very nervioso."

Lorena's Illinois honk.

"Nervioso. Yes, Marco. And broken-down?"

"I theenk so."

"Say think."

"Theenk."

"And why, Marco, do you think he was so nervous and broken-down?"

"Because he was buried alive."

Aside from Marco himself, only Montserrat did not laugh. Her eyes were on my face. Calm and fascinated. Yes, she was studying me. And suddenly one did not want to take the piss out of Cádiz anymore. Save all the jokes about cheese for another time. The Purloined Cheddar and so forth.

"He was in a way buried alive, Marco. Emotionally speaking. But no. Who can. . . ?"

And before I finish asking the question, comes the answer.

It is Montserrat, and her voice is eerily distinct. "His wife died. He loved her very much."

An enormous bubble lunged from the basement. I turned away from them and wrote on the board, trembling, *knight, sunshine, shadow, journey, search* and *El Dorado*.

The winter she died I tried to smile for Jeff, and he tried to paint his mother's life back. But he failed and I failed. And I drank. And darkness started to grow in him cell by cell, like a permafrost of his poor young spirit.

Another blowing, sleeting November night I was drunk and wretched and marking papers in my bedroom at my desk by the window. Jeff came in. He was eleven.

"Jeff. Come and cheer me up. What have you got?"

I stared at the painting for maybe five minutes. Finally he gave me a shake.

"Jeff, this is astounding. Where did you get these colours?"

"I have a lot of colours."

"Is that me? I look so happy. Is that you — you've made yourself tall. Who are all these people in the bright outfits?"

"They're called *Índios*."

"*Índios*. And these are volcanoes, aren't they. Must be Poland."

"Ha!" Nothing worse than the falsetto of an eleven-year-old's *ha!* in your right ear. I put on Sarah Vaughan, and Jeff and I sang along scat style and laughed far past his bedtime.

I sent my contract for the next semester back unsigned and dumped the house into the hands of a rental agent. Three weeks later Jeff and I were in Guatemala.

I turned to the class and with bogus confidence bluffed my way through knights, quests and the Holy Grail. When I asked what they knew about El Dorado they came to life and said, Ees a seety of gold; Ees a man covered in thee gold; Ees in thees country; and, Ees chust a story. I considered making a joke about all the gold in that room. Chains, pendants, bracelets and pedigrees, but said instead, "Poe had a hard life. He drank. Maybe he even used opium. What would such a man mean by *shadow*, by *sunshine?* By *journey?* What would such a man mean by *El Dorado?*

No reply, I walked to the slide projector. Someone turned out the lights. The first shots were of conquistadors. Old engravings of them in beards and armour, fighting off Indians. I made satisfactory comments, easier going in the dark. The next slides were of gold artifacts form the high Andes. Crude little gold male and female figures. Pure gold penises like stubby icicles hanging down. Pairs of gilded titties. Whispers and giggles. A snore. Gordon gone again already.

Gold man. Gold woman. Gold man. Gold woman.

How did it start — the thing with Montserrat? Simple: *Who shall I fall in love with this term?* Mere fantasy and harmless. Ask any male teacher. Dusky Lorena for lust. Montserrat for what? For *maybe?*

She had a solemn and peaceful face. Wide mouth and full lips, high cheekbones and those trusting wise eyes with no makeup. Straight dark hair heavy upon her shoulders. Strong bosoms lurking always under baggy shirts. When she wore a skirt, such fine legs. Woman's legs. Once I spied on her from my classroom, watched her there outside in the sun at lunchtime. Sitting alone on the unhealthy grass. Eating a wizened red apple of the Andes. I put on my glasses. Watched her eat. Thought *maybe.*

She was at my left hand now. My sports coat's edge of tweed touched her forearm. I pushed the electric button to urge the images on.

We lived in Guatemala for three years. There was sun, and there were *Índios*. Near our house, a mountain lake blue as blazes. Over on the other side, coffee *fincas* glued to the shoulders of a peck of postcard volcanoes. Hippies from Quebec and Düsseldorf. In the woods near town, a squat stone idol where Indians cut the throats of turkeys. I gave English lessons and lived on Canadian rent. Jeff grew tall. Too damn tall. Into puberty like a house on fire.

Samantha was forty and had wrecked nerves. Styled herself Sam. Wore tie-dye and no underwear. Blonde, attractive in her jittery way. *Born to lose,* read the tattoo on her thigh when she lay naked in the sun on lakeside gravel. She snatched up tall Jeff in his bewilderment of androgen. Showed him how to fuck and to smoke marijuana.

So I hustled him back to Canada, where we heard in the middle of another soaked and ragged December that Sam had taken sleeping pills. There was a suicide note. Jeff's name prominent in it.

He quit school. His paintings turned suddenly powerful. Portraits. All of them disturbing. They started to sell. An artist. Horrid.

I could not stand the winters for very long. Nepal next. Something about high places. Closer to the sun, maybe. Jeff came too. We met an interesting Swedish writer called Bo, who introduced my son to opium.

Yes, I remember now what Jeff said about gold. It was in that downtown room of his.

"What's this?"

"Your present. Here, open it."

Our breath made shooting plumes of steam. I wore a down jacket and leaned against a gouged table in front of his window. On it lay bent tubes of paint, a rag soiled with colour, a wee plastic envelope with his heroin. Outside, a snowstorm, and only a pathetic light to fall in upon the table, like ash. He sat near me. Pale. Hunched. Pinching at his throat a grey blanket. On a mattress in a corner slept his friend Elizabeth.

I started to open the package for him. The crackling foil made him blink.

There were paintings stacked against a wall. The top one was me, unfinished.

"I wanted to have your portrait ready."

"It looks damn good already. You stoned?"

He nodded. I stopped unwrapping, leaned back on the table, fished out my flask of vodka. Had a heavy pull.

"You going away?" he asked.

"How'd you know?"

"It's winter."

McKnight's brief chuckle.

"It's okay, you know," he said. "I'll be all right."

"No, it's not okay. But I'm going anyway."

"You tell the principal to stuff it?"

"Stories, Jeff! The poor, sweet yo-yos. Never written more than a sentence in their brutal little lives. But for me — for Mac, whom they loved — they wrote stories." I took another swig. "'But Mr. McKnight,' says the principal — nice phony smile — 'these — ah — compositions are full of sex, violence and four-letter words.' 'They have made stories,' I say — no smile — 'they have achieved something marvellous.' Case of either lose my soul or lose my job."

"Also, it's winter."

I continued with the package, careful for some reason not to tear the gold foil. "They tried to keep me out of the school. But I had worked up a damn good farewell speech. The students came up one by one. 'Goodbye, Mr. McKnight.' 'Thank you, sir.'"

"This time where do you go?"

I took the wristwatch out of the box. Black and expensive ticker, which he did not look at, but instead observed my face like a child.

"Jeff, there is no going back, is there?"

"No, Dad, there is no going back."

"It would be good, though, wouldn't it?"

"Sure. It would be a good thing . . . start over . . . try it again."

I took his wrist to strap the watch on. He released the blanket, and it slid from his shoulders. So thin he was. So pale. There could have been a light there behind his skin. Phosphorus. Uranium. I fastened the watch strap, and he did not try to hide the old scars. There were newer ones somewhere else. I heard the watch ticking, and kept holding his hand, and finally had to kiss it.

"And when you get there?" he said.

"Where?"

He smiled, reached with his free hand and slid from a pocket of my jacket the paperback, *El Dorado*. History of fools, adventurers and more fools. He stood beside me, and I put my glasses on, and we leaned over the table in that miserable light and leafed through the colour plates, shoulder to shoulder. He flipped his bag of smack out of the way. Gold, gold, gold every turn of the page. He had an ace memory for poetry. "A man saw a ball of gold in the sky," he said. Did not look up. It was a poem by Stephen Crane. "He climbed for it. And eventually he achieved it — It was clay."

I stared out the window at the storm, but Jeff went on. Turning pages. "Now this is the strange part: When the man went to the earth And looked again, Lo, there was the ball of gold."

I took a drink.

"Now this is the strange part: It was a ball of gold. Ay, by the heavens, it was a ball of gold."

I looked at my watch but could not see it in the dark. I wanted them gone. Fuck Poe. Bugger literature. In the bottom drawer of my desk waited my pint of Bellows Vodka. And that *El Dorado* paperback there too. With Evelyn's photograph among its pages, and her smile of a young woman. And with Jeff's photograph under Evelyn's. Booze and memories, please. Take a hike, Edgar.

The day before, from the school bus on the way back to town, I had seen an Indian funeral procession. Thirty brown people in black dusty suits, or best shirts, or blue velvet skirts and Spanish lace and gold and red beads and fedoras and rope slippers or barefoot. Walking at the edge of the highway toward Esperanza's graveyard. In the sooty exhaust of trucks. The coffin right there upon shoulders. The man and his son tailing the coffin. The Mrs. up there inside. But it was the god damn light! That light of the Andes that comes down like hammers upon death and life and upon all weakness.

I would try once more. I said, "So, what do you think this knight is searching for?" I thought there was at least one more slide. But when I pushed the button the screen came up white. Glaring I even threw up my arm to shield my face.

Then Montserrat said, "I think he is looking for something he has lost. A kind of happiness that is impossible for him to find again. That is why this lonely man must keep searching and searching all his life."

I dared to look down. Her face there not far from my elbow. Ghostly in reflected light. Looking up. At me. Parted lips. Eyes in shadow. But, oh, some spark there.

The bell went off like a yell. Then desks scraping and crashing, and all their voices going at it, and the door torn open, and the screen going black because someone trips on the cord, and Gordon Kelly walking across the tops of the desks. Then just me in the empty room, and out there in the hall that torrent of Spanish chatter. Fading soon enough to echoes. Like all the rest, all the rest, *patrón*.

The next Friday, parent-teacher conferences. Sign in felt marker outside the classroom door: *Sr. McKnight. English. Pase adelante.*

Señor Cádiz now. English speaker, thank Christ, and gentleman for sure in his grey three-piece suit and matching moustache. Yet a sweet person, with a smile for the gringo, concern for his Marco and not a whiff of cheese about him.

"Señor Cádiz, I think you should have a talk with Marco."

"Is there some problem?"

"Yes. Quite serious."

"Please, you must tell me."

"He leers at the girls in class."

"Leers?"

"Like this." I leered at Señor Cádiz. Let my tongue hang

out. Panted. Cádiz leapt up.

"He does that? My Marco?"

"And he rubs himself against his desk and moans."

Señor Cádiz clamped his hand over his mouth. Clenched his gentleman's eyes. All the cheese in China no good to him now.

"I've had complaints," I said.

He nodded. Could not speak. Poor fellow.

"You will talk to him?"

Nodded again.

"Perhaps some punishment?"

And again.

"Tell him to leave Montserrat Dávilos alone! He must not bother Montserrat Dávilos! Do you understand?"

I was shouting, but Cádiz took it humbly. Shook his head in despair. Turned. Left the classroom.

Now what had I done? Lies. I would be fired. Reckless. A fool. But I didn't care. The Gordon Kelly business, now this. It was like in Vancouver, when they wrote those stories. Reckless. "Then what happened, Spike?" "I kicked the fucker in the head, sir." "Write it, Spike." "If you say so, sir." A sense of fatalism, now. Game's over, jig's up. But if she fired me, would Flossie find another English teacher strolling around the Andes? Not likely. I checked that the door was shut, from the bottom drawer hauled out my vodka. Leaned back, loosened tie and placed feet upon desk.

It was late, there would be no more parents.

Ah, the vodka at day's end. Sounds like a poem. But no rhyme for the stuff itself. Plodka? Just as well. Waste of good brain cells, making fake literature. *Oh there once was a girl called Lorena. Who said sir I won't try to restrain ya. It would just be so cool If you'd make like a bool. And put the blocks to me again. Ah.*

Do they say *bool* in Chicago? No, but in Esperanza they say fool. Well anyway, another suck of the old Bellows here. Set the bottle upon the desk. Close the eyes for just a minute.

"Sr. McKnight."

Open the eyes. Dozed off, looks like.

"Sr. McKnight, I am Charlie Dávilos."

Gold braid, medals. Ribbons. Montserrat was standing beside him, in a fetching white dress, looking at me.

Feet right smartly down. Stood up. Almost saluted. "Sorry, must have fallen asleep, didn't think anyone else was . . ."

"Is no problem."

Shook hands. The required contact of eyes. And I was sure that everyone who looked into the eyes of Charlie Dávilos saw, as I did at that moment, that if you fucked with him he would rip your liver out.

A shaven head. Puggish face, yet noble. Not tall but damn sturdy. His general's hat on my desk. Next to. Oh. My bottle.

Over so soon, the game? Well, who gives a fuck? I couldn't restrain an ironic snort. The sorry joke of it all. Dávilos smiled and nodded. Montserrat watched me calmly. I would never be her lover now. They would deport me back to winter. Fine — I could look after Jeff.

Dávilos said to Montserrat, "*Espérame a la puerta, mi vida.*" Which could be rendered thus: Wait for me outside, my life.

I watched her walk to the door. Going away forever on her woman's legs. But I knew I would forget her soon, where night fell at rush hour.

Dávilos reached, his khaki sleeve so crisply pressed, and picked up the bottle. His eyes still upon me.

"You like bodka?" he said.

"See for yourself."

"I prefer escotch."

"Expensive and vile. But appearance is everything in this shit-hole, isn't it?"

"*Exacto.*" He spun off the cap and took a drink. Passed the bottle to me. No outrage yet upon his face. Fine — in for a dime, in for a dorado. I took a heavy pull. Winter could be wonderful. All a matter of attitude.

I said, "Medals. Ribbons. Pompous pricks wherever you look. Mercedes fucking Benzes. While the Indians starve."

He reached, took the bottle from me. Something new in his eyes now. What? He drank, passed the bottle back.

"Tell me more," he said.

I drank. "You people don't know how to run a country. You couldn't run a fucking errand." I laughed. This seemed to please him. "Bunch of stuffed-shirt incompetents. No one farts unless he gets a bribe first."

He reached, drank, kept the bottle.

I said, "I hope you don't think I care. I've had enough. Enough. I only wanted to do my job and have a drink or two and get away from the fucking rain and darkness and . . . But I see that's impossible. Not pompous enough. Not incompetent enough. Not evil enough." I pronounced it again and wiped my hand through the air as if smearing it around. "Not eeeeeeeevil enough." Then through my teeth I made a strangling noise and hissed, "I. Hate. Your. Shit. Hole. Country."

He drained the bottle. Slammed it down on my desk.

"Hijo!" cried Charlie Dávilos, and punched the air. *"Que cojones tienes!"* What balls you've got!

I went quiet. Had to sit down.

"Montserrat told me there was something especial about you," he said. "So I must to come and see. She was telling me about the El Dorado — what you say about it — that it is existing only in the human espirit. You are right about something else, too. This country. Everything you are saying is true. Is being run by an idiot, and everyone is corrupt and is receiving money to make the farts. But I, a patriot, say this: Please do not go away. Estay here. In this shit-hole we are needing men like you." Then he charged around the desk, hauled me up by my lapels and, with the clasp of a grizzly bear, crushed me against his medals.

3

Seduced

On a hurtling school bus as packed as any crate of chickens, would a single student of the American School ever rise and say, "Sir, would you like to sit down?" Jesus, never. The driver gunning it back to town, yanking his air horn every second, careening left into a space the size of a bicycle, then veering right into the parking lane to pass a taxi. With me catapulted forward then, onto Señorita Espinoza the biology teacher, who had prodigious nostrils and, as my skidding hand now discovered, an agreeably resilient chest. No anger upon her glacial face, with those nostrils in it like ice caves. I righted myself. Said sorry. And to put that air horn out of my head, composed this verse: *In the bower of your lab, Beneath the pickled foetus, For to grope and for to grab, Señorita will we meet us.*

You see, *patrón*, what pointless crap I come up with?

Then the circuit through the rich bárrios as the students got off every few blocks, and waiting Indian maids rushed to open their gates for them. And now, almost home, outside the American Embassy, I saw Dickie Pendergast walking, with his briefcase of Social Studies. Got off and hauled him into the Arse.

"Ricardo, I feel old."

He burped, called for another beer. "You need some diversions. Not into Montserrat Dávilos yet?"

"It wasn't like that. But that's gone too. Class like a morgue these days. Don't even hate Gordon Kelly any more."

"Aw shit, Mac. That's bad."

"I want to go home. I worry about my son."

"You're depressing me now. What happened?"

"Don't know. I make up stupid verses. Lonely old fucker of an English teacher."

"Want to go to Dude's tonight? Round up some whores?"

"Don't you know me yet, Dickie?"

A long walk through the city. Exercise at least. Inviting these clouds of the wet season to piss upon one's head. Ball of sleepiness collecting within the forehead. There is dog shit on the cracked sidewalk. Wherever there is no dog shit there is a jagged hole to fall into. At a construction site an old Indian woman in velvet, lace, gold beads and baseball cap is shovelling gravel. And here is the pizza place where I go for my amoebas. And here comes that crippled fellow across the street again. Sliding on a hip, the pants rolled up above the knees, twig legs twisted to the side. As the roaring buses speed up to squash him. But at my feet now, holding out the hand, in which I place fifty dorados.

Liz has not re-entered one's life, and just as well. Don't have the *chispa* to trade insults. No piss and no vinegar. Was the Arab stewed somewhere in this ugly Esperanza? Too stewed to get it up for Liz? An Englishwoman robbed of her entertainment in this oppressive season, and my fault. Here is the very modern pedestrian underpass, which nobody uses, because even in this wet season the reek of dried urine in there is enough to make your eyes water. Not that one's orbs do not flow over anyway with tears from time to time. You waited too long, Montserrat. Too long to see that I was gold and worth seducing. Soon you graduate. Off to some girls' college in New England. Nothing left but to invite Lorena up for pornographic pictures. Wish I had a camera.

Well into the Old City now. Around a corner, and what's this. Flames. A tire and some broken boards burning on the street. Fifty or sixty people walking back and forth. Shouts, and raised fists. A cardboard sign waved that says, *Bajo* Perales. Yonder, standing together, three unhappy policemen. Anger in this lofty town. The poverty. The corruption. Perhaps I should not be exactly here, with my gringo height and my gringo hair. Too late.

"Gringo! Join us!"

One of them walking swiftly toward me.

"I am sorry," I say. "I have an appointment."

"Join us! Forget your appointment. What is your appointment?"

"I have an appointment to teach English."

"English is the language of the oppressors. To whom do you teach English?"

"Mind your own business."

"To the government whores?"

"I teach whom I please."

"Come. Gringo. Join us. What is in your briefcase?"

"That's my business."

"English lessons for Perales and his whores? Come. We need some paper for our fire."

He reached toward the briefcase. I pulled it away. "Fuck you," I said in English. "Fuck your fire."

There was a *clank*, and my eyes stung. Tear gas. I turned and beat it.

Here in these other streets, all normal. Hopeless shoe stores. This restaurant with roasted guinea pigs toothy and oily behind its filthy window. Walk now, let the heart slow down. With this briefcase that appears to contain English lessons but which contains in fact only my bottle of Bellows.

Two guards, each with a cute little machine gun. Fish out the letter from the Office of the President's Secretary, which says, more or less, Do not shoot this gentleman he has business with

The Boss.

Gloomy place, but I suppose they think it's posh. Red carpet worn through. A bulb burnt out. Into an anteroom of bone-yellow brocade wallpaper and a half-dozen stuffed brown leather armchairs.

But strange. In one of those chairs sat a woman. Stretch jeans and a satiny green shirt unbuttoned well down the chest. Holly. Known as Ivy. Tomás' clinger. She slouched back with one sandalled foot up in the chair. That eerie smile. The green American eyes taking my measure.

"Hi," she said.

My accompanying officer opened a door. And through it and into the anteroom strode a man in a maroon velvet suit, tan silk shirt, no tie, gold chains. The officer stepped back, surprised, as the man pushed past him.

"Schoolteacher."

"Mr. Chairman. Good to see you. I was beginning to think life held no more nasty surprises."

"What are you doing here? Jesus, get yourself a suit."

"Tomás, I must. Seeing you. The dignity of velvet."

He took a quick step toward me and the chains hissed at his throat. I beamed even more than I wanted to. Felt like crying *olé!* Drowsiness all gone.

The officer laid a hand on his pistol. Some kind of clattery music burst through the door, which also made me want to laugh. Then a man's voice. Singsong, nasal and slurred. "Señor McKnight. Come in. Espeak English. You think I will going bite you?"

I went through the door, and the officer shut it behind me.

Across a dim office as big as my house in Vancouver, near a staff strained by the weight of the flag of this lofty nation, upon an ample desk of carven walnut and next to a half-empty quart of choice Scotch sat my student, Pancho Perales, President of the Republic.

"McKnight. You are *canadiense*. Is just a small country I got.

Sing. Sing in English."

Then he hunched, grimaced and attacked a small stringed instrument which he clutched to his chest. Clangs and clatters. A vague Andean flavour ringing out from blurred fingers, in spite of missed chords like splashes of vinegar.

"Sing. Is called *The Love of the Sailor for His Sheep*."

He winced, and savaged the strings again.

"'I love so much to feel my sheep,'" he sang. "'When it is rolling left and rolling right.' How you say, 'Underneath me.'"

I walked carefully toward him. Past his coat of a regal grey chalkstripe in a heap on the carpet.

"Yes, I have sheeps here. Do you visit my coast yet? Sheeps for my bananas. You like taste my bananas in Canada? You don't knowing this song? What song you like sing?"

His long hair white and waved, with a thin strip of black. White silky moustache. That look of an orchestra conductor, but now trying to conduct ten fingers. Hooked nose upon nut-brown face. Black Índio eyes and, around them, the skin madly crinkled. More interesting than the magazine cover.

"*Ship*," I said. "A person who loves to feel his sheep rolling underneath him is not a sailor but a shepherd."

"Ah. *Pastor*." He laughed, a nasal blast. "We have the songs for the *pastor* too. Later I am singing them you. Come here, McKnight. Espeak English. Tell me more of the chokes. I want laugh. Today I want sing and drink and laugh. The *pendejos*, they want — how you say. . . ?" He hooked a middle finger upward.

"Screw," I said.

"They want escrew me. Hah! They no can escrew me. I shit on them. Is good English, no?"

"Very good."

"I shit on them. I drink and sing and listen your *canadiense* chokes. You like drink?" He offered the bottle.

I shook my head. He took a long swallow, let out a growling sigh. "I shit on them. Come here. Espeak English."

He leaned toward me, intending to study, but the eyes would

not concentrate. He looked aside, tilted his behind and released a resonant fart. There was a small window. I walked past him and opened it. In the distance I heard shouting. Somewhere the demonstration had regrouped. Behind me the churrango racketed to life again.

"I know very good the English," said Perales. Then he sang. "'Juanita, is so cold These nights of the mountains. But for buy you gold ring My poncho I am selling In the market of Las Cruces.' Is a sad song of my small country."

"If you'd like, I can come back another time."

"Señor McKnight!" he shouted. "The *pendejos* want escrew me! Stay here. I want drink. I want espeak English. Okay?"

"And you want shit on them."

"*Exacto*. McKnight. You think I say, 'Dávilos, come into my office'? You think I say, 'Sit in this chair. Be *presidente*'?" He slid off his desk, took a step, staggered, steadied himself on my shoulder and gestured toward the window. "I am giving them everything. Bread. Work. *Techo. Cómo se dice?*"

"A roof."

"Bread. Work. A roof. Why they are not liking me? *Por que*?" He snarled toward the window, ran a few steps sideways, tripped over his suit jacket and fell.

The long walk had tired me. I went around his desk and sat down in his chair. Oh, comfortable. Leather.

"*Por que*?" he asked again, lying on his side. "Why they are. . . ?"

"Ungrateful bastards." I put my feet on his desk.

"I am giving them everything. Ungrateful bastards. Ai, ai, ai, is so difficult. What I can sell?" He got to his knees, and with his arms wide for balance, lurched to his feet. "Bananas," he said. "Oil. I shit on them. Tell me the chokes, McKnight. I want laugh." His hair hung over his eyes. His shirttail was out. The flesh under his eyes drooped. He came to the desk, took the bottle, drank. Not much left in it now. He offered it to me, I shook my head.

"I got the police," he said. His voice gravelly, slurred. It was as if I wasn't there. "The army . . . have their *cojones*. You think I say, 'Sit in this chair'?" He grunted. "You think I say, 'Come in. Be *presidente*'?"

Soon the bottle was empty. Perales reeled around the office, weeping. He went to the window, the empty bottle hanging in his hand. He was blubbering. "Bread," he snivelled. "Work. A roof. Is all they are wanting."

I heard shouting outside. The armoured water cannon truck would be there. Its slit eyes and pockmarking of dents from hurled stones.

"But I no can give them. Why I no can? Because my oil . . . so cheap. My beautiful oil." He sobbed so miserably that I was tempted to go and comfort him. But then he reared away from the window, flailing his arms. Stepped back. With a shout, threw the bottle. It smashed on a bar. Then I smelled it too — tear gas. I jumped up and slammed the window shut.

He stared at me, breathing hard. "I will going talk to Jack Kelly," he said. "I got one more thing. One more thing I can sell."

I shivered.

He looked stone sober. He picked up his suit jacket. Brushed it off. Put it on. Combed his hair with his fingers.

I went to my briefcase, drew out the Bellows, held it by its top, letting it swing like a pendulum. His eyes went wide, he slapped his leg, a wheezing laugh came out of him. His knees bent, he sank to the floor, went over onto a shoulder and started snoring like an ox.

I had a hit of the vodka at last, and stood staring down at him.

Good Marúchi ready with her suckers. The yellow buses ranked, ready for the race to town. Edgar, the vermillion flycatcher, watching a Phys Ed class leave the field. My grade 12 class lounging, waiting for the bell. I slipped my plan book into my briefcase. Almost reached for the bottom drawer. Too itchy for that comforting swallow at the end of labours. Itchier these days, since Perales. I'd told no one about that business, wanted for some reason to hoard it and wait for his next lesson, though weeks had passed.

The bell went.

As the students exited, essays were deposited on my desk. Spurts and plops in the direction of the Romantic Movement.

"Thank you Marisol, what a nice plastic cover. Thank you Alegria, looks like you forgot to double-space. Thank you Lorena, nice sweater. Thank you Marco, no smile for your teacher?"

Gordon Kelly walked out without giving me the assignment, confident, I am sure, that he would pass anyway, poor Flossie being terrified of losing the school's subsidy of American dollars.

I needed that drink. I tidied the pile of essays, set them into my cardboard box that said *Salsa Ají Volcán* on the side. Anticipating a soothingly empty room, I looked up. Oh. Montserrat. Still in her desk. Writing like mad.

"Montserrat, the bell went."

Grey blouse and moss green skirt. Her woman's calves. Hair wisping her hand and ballpoint as she leaned close to her paper.

"Montserrat, let's go."

Not looking up, Montserrat said, "I am almost finished."

"It's too late."

She kept writing.

I went to the classroom door, closed it, returned to my desk, opened the bottom drawer, took out the bottle. Montserrat gathered the pages of her essay, grabbed her book bag and walked toward me. She had seen my bottle before, so let her see it again. I took a drink. She stood near me, not even seeming to notice the bottle. I put it into my briefcase.

"It's too late."

"Please, can I have some more time?"

I picked up my box of essays and briefcase and started for

the door. "You lose five marks per day, my child. It is not for nothing they call me Monster McKnight." But I think my voice trembled.

Then a hand on my arm, and I stopped, and she did not take the hand away. Shockingly clear, those brown eyes. I had forgotten how they were like the blue ones of Evelyn. And what they said — *I will carry you across all waters and there will be treasure*. She was wearing makeup. Had she before today? Her lips pink, palely painted. Between us a trace of perfume fluttered like a tiny iridescent bird.

"Please," she said, and squeezed my arm. "I can finish it in the car. I will give you a ride. Okay? Please?"

Buses and a few cars waited in the dust and eucalyptus shadows. Montserrat got in the back seat of the Mercedes on the passenger side, away from the buses. I opened the door on the driver's side. But as I turned to get in, I looked up. There, in an open bus window, fifteen feet away, the red beard of Dickie Pendergast. The rains had pretty well finished, and his nose was mottled pink again. I waited for him to speak.

"Getting a lift? Wish *I* could get a lift." He twitched a smile but looked concerned.

I was afraid he would say something awkward. About stickies and quickies.

"You know those — uh — joint lessons I've been recommending?"

I knew what kind of joint he meant. The manly banana of his bubble gum lies. But he looked so serious.

He said, "I think it would be a mistake. That joint business is great in theory. But in — uh — reality" — he jutted his beard toward the Mercedes — "in reality it leads to all kinds of problems."

"We'll talk."

The outside rolled past, lubricated, soundless. Better through tinted glass. Tanker truck of molasses blasting black smoke. Girl in a torn dress and blue sweater with five goats on a gravel bank. Today, no funeral, but a new dead dog beside the highway, and a pair of vultures upon him not hopping away as we swished by. All okay as long as one sat here in Mercedes purr, looking out. One might have been drugged, the way it all did not matter.

I looked at Montserrat. Her binder on her lap, supporting a page on which she was writing. On that sorry road even the Mercedes could not stop her pen from jouncing. Such a mess she was making. But she wanted not to lose those marks. That was all.

As she bent over her paper, I studied a wispy area of chestnut hairs at the back of her neck. She scuffed off her loafers, flexed naked toes, which were pudgy and designed to be nibbled upon. By someone who was not me.

She stopped writing, waited hovering over her binder for an idea, appeared to receive none, laid her ballpoint down, straightened up and looked out the window. We were on Avenida América and passing a small slaughter yard. Dark dirt visible through a gate open in a brown wall. That morning, from the bus, I had witnessed a man pushing across the highway a wheelbarrow piled high with hunks of bloody meat. For the first time in minutes I looked away from her, and in the rearview mirror I saw two eyes. Watching me. Filadelfo, she had called him. A soldier. Upon a square head, coarse black hair. In the mirror, frigid black eyes.

Montserrat turned, and we looked at each other. Filadelfo hit a bump and we bounced softly up together. We smiled.

"So. What do you think of my country?"

"Oh, many things."

"Tell me."

"I like the Indians."

"So do I. What else?"

"I like the sun. Or at least the fact that usually it doesn't rain. I don't like the school buses."

"Maybe I can give you a ride every night."

"Oh, I didn't mean . . ."

"And the vodka is cheap, yes? Do you like that?"

A teasing smile. To spring bold as brass past polite conversation! I did not know what to say. But my prick tingled.

She turned away and for a minute looked again out at the jumbled edge of Esperanza. Walls thick with their painted words. *Pan trabajo techo*. Or slogans from the last election. At the overpass a gigantic sloping mural of ordinary working people going forward with raised fists into triumph and happiness. And someone had thrown red paint upon it.

"The truth now," she said. "You think the same thing I do. Pápi told me. That it is a shit-hole. But I love it. Here you are always closer to death. Therefore closer to life. There are primitive impulses in this air. Yes?"

"Why don't you want to be only eighteen?"

"Boring."

She worked at the carpet of the Mercedes with her toes.

Señora Maldonado sat as always on a chair in the wide door of her store, all in widow black. Not even knitting today, just watching.

"Well?"

"I'm not finished."

"Ah."

"Almost. Please. May I come up? I can't work in the car."

Montserrat did not want to lose those marks.

Filadelfo shut off the engine.

"Buenas tardes, Señora Maldonado."

"Buenas tardes, señor. Cómo está?"

I am very well, Señora Maldonado. As you can see, I am taking a female student up to my apartment. Unlock the street door. Up the bleak concrete steps. Past the frosted glass window with swipes of white paint on it. So tacky today. Never noticed it before. One, I am sure, appears calm. But cannot speak.

Unlock the top door. Must try to say some words.

"This is my deportment."

"Deportment?"

"Apartment, I mean."

"Kind of bare. Like I thought it would be."

"Did you? I have stuff, though. Masks. Stuff from the jungle. But it's all in the bedroom. I like to look at it in bed. Really I have quite a lot of stiff."

"Stiff?"

"Stuff."

"May I see it?"

"Sit here at my desk. Here, let me move these papers. This window has a good view, doesn't it? You can see Chinguráhua and part of Valle Milagro. You live there, I believe. Nice in the afternoon light."

McKnight in control. Calm as a Quaker. Not the least lathered. Montserrat desires but to finish her essay.

She sat at my desk, her back to the room and to me, and wrote.

I traversed behind her to the kitchen. Glass. Ice. Vodka. Stood against the wall behind her, watching the mountain. Too early to go pink. Maybe it will erupt. I'll just watch, in case. Her shoes off again. Toes of her right foot hooked behind the rung of my chair. Sole of her foot puckered. It has been a long time since I have tickled a foot. Or kissed one. And frankly it is a sad thing. That she will go. That I am not young like Marco Cádiz. Lovely young bodies together. I think next time Dickie asks I will go. Dude's is the place for the middle-aged and disillusioned. Doreen's whores liked me those first English lessons, although they giggled at the beard.

"Finished."

She wiggled her feet into her shoes and stood, inviting me to see her work. Her face sedate, distant. The girl at the back of the class. From the inside pocket of my sports coat came the gold glasses. I set my drink on the desk and bent over the paper,

Montserrat Dávilos' spurt in the direction of the Romantic Movement. No title page, three marks off there. One paragraph alone in the centre of this first page. Interesting.

I read.

It takes courage to be lonely. It takes courage to stand apart from an evil world. It takes courage to believe in things the evil world does not believe in, that there is a city of gold.

Not, it seemed, an introductory paragraph. Her hand reached past me and took the half-full glass and then, in a moment, set it back empty.

And especially it takes courage not to lie. You do not need to be lonely. I know how you feel. Don't you know I feel that way to? Don't you know I a door you?

Her hands crept around and took the lapels of my sports coat and tugged until the coat was half off. As I gazed out the window, all stupid. The hills beyond the valley suddenly more gold than they had ever been. And there was a flowing blue cloud like a wave breaking around Chinguráhua. Whose white tip stuck up out of it releasing a sprout of steam.

"Montserrat."

"Shh."

"Montserrat. Oh Lord."

"Why doesn't it come off."

"Oh don't. One sleeve at a time. You mustn't."

"Like this?"

"No. Now I'm stuck."

"Turn around."

I did. And, gritting her teeth, she tugged viciously at a coat sleeve.

"Montserrat, stop. Don't do this. We'll get in trouble."

"Shut up. I'm going to undress you."

"Maybe you shouldn't."

"Stop saying stupid things. Will you help me!"

I tore my sleeve from her hands. My arms were pinned back

at the elbows by my half-off coat, but I could still hold up my hands, palm out. "No. I mean it. I mean it. Stop."

She took my hands and pressed one palm against each breast. And, God help me, I squeezed. She wrapped both arms around me and groaned and reached her lips up. Pink, soft and open.

"Uh uh. Nope."

I tried to back away, but she clasped hard and came with me, stumbling, tripping faster and faster, into my dining alcove. With its one chair. And its four-dollar table from El Marin market against the window. Onto which table I crashed backward. Lacking use of my arms, I could not rise before she was up and astride, with a knee pinning each shoulder. My hands fluttered out. My glasses clattered to the floor. And still the polite Canadian tried not to look up her skirt. Her bum thumped down on my stomach. Oof. McKnight bested.

She said, "I will undress myself, then." And, looking playfully down into my eyes, quickly undid buttons and dropped her blouse behind her onto the floor. The brassiere only a hand's-breadth from my nose, thin and unfrilled and the same warm colour as her skin. She smiled. From under her skirt came a fragile muskiness. The call of the lost bird. Perfume there. Waiting. With a shrug the brassiere was gone. Nipples a darker pink than her smile. As she slid her knees down from my shoulders and reached for the side button of her skirt. And I turned my head. And saw down into the street. Where Señora Maldonado was sitting and looking up at my window, with Filadelfo standing beside her.

"Shit, get off."

"No. Ow. Stop bouncing. What is wrong with you, anyway?"

"Look."

Crouching now, below the window. She with her back against the wall. Giggling.

"How can you laugh. They saw us."

"You. Look at yourself."

McKnight not in control. On his knees and hunched, forehead to floor until she helped me out of the sports coat.

"Now. If I can get my eskirt off. Best way, over the head. You see? No panties. For you. All day at school. It was very exciting. Don't you think I am beautiful?"

"Yes."

"What's wrong?"

"I'm going to be castrated. Burnt alive. Is there a plane out tonight?"

"Filadelfo is my friend. He won't tell. I will make sure. I know some things about him. Concerning the maid. And the cook. What's wrong?"

"I hurt my ankle."

"Let me see. Such wrinkled shoes. This one? Now the sock. It hurts here, yes? I will kiss it. Now it is better?"

"You have a wonderful ass. I don't care if they saw me into pieces."

"Let's go to your bedroom. Stay down low. Where is it? Is this called waddling? Stop laughing. Oh, there is your stuff. And I do know what stiff means. You are, I think."

"Are you a virgin?"

"No. Are you disappointed?"

"No."

For reality, *patrón,* is so much more satisfying than myth. This woman in my arms who was not a pure and remote angel. But who would love me. And be my friend. This perfume between the sinews of her thighs so much better than pie in the sky. Better certainly than the idea of Banana Lorena naked on all fours, barking and whining in a toothy red mask from Salchibamba.

The only climbing I had to do was up my grubby stairs.

And a ball of gold fallen into my hands.

And it was not clay.

Yet.

I accepted no further rides home. Filadelfo would drop her off at the top of the street, or would bring her up from the Valley at night to see a movie with a friend. And if I had seen the movie I would describe it so she could report to her mother.

"Let me have another taste, McKnight."

"Sit up, then, or you'll spill the vodka. Does it warm your tummy? Let me feel your tummy. Oh, it's really warm."

"That is not my tummy."

"But it is warm. Now, a matter to discuss. Who was your lover? Or is it plural? A student? Perhaps someone I know?"

"Are you jealous, McKnight?"

"Certainly."

"But it is in the past."

"I will go back in time and punch him in the nose. Because in the past I was a rangitang."

"What is that?"

"A primitive animal with very large impulses, from British Columbia."

"Well, as a present for being jealous, I will tell you. He was a man I met when I was in Boston with my aunt for a year. A bartender. A very funny man with a big blond moustache. You would have liked him."

"Are you the quiet girl from the back of the class?"

"No, I am the Esperanza Extravaganza. Is that it?"

"Yes. And also Amazing Monzy."

"He had one of these things too. But his was on his arm. It said, *Born to Booze.* Why did you get yours?"

"When you are eighteen, sometimes you have to do something dramatic. Just to know who you are."

"Is that why it says, 'Who me?'? Another taste, please."

"All right, but leave me the ice cube. Now, another matter. Monzy?"

"Yes, McKnight?"

"Do you know anything about Mr. Pendergast, the Social Studies teacher?"

"Dickie? Oh, maybe."

"Oh. Don't ever let him hear you say *Dickie*."

"We all say it behind his back."

"Is there anything else said? Behind his back?"

"You mean like the story of Pilar Crespo? She had to go away to Colorado. She would not tell who the father was. But they say in Denver she had a baby with red hair. And a nose already sunburned."

"Oh."

"And he keeps on trying. With others. Shall we have a baby? Oh my God! Are you all right?"

"You made me swallow the ice cube. Don't ever again say *we* and *baby* in the same sentence. I wish I'd had a safe that first time. Why didn't you include one in your plan?"

"It would have been vulgar. Don't you think so? Besides, I thought all American men kept one in their wallet."

"I'm Canadian."

"McKnight, I have to leave soon. I am supposed to be at a movie. Have you seen *Missing*?"

"It's about Chile. People being massacred when Pinochet came in. Did you know I gave an English lesson to Perales? The man's a drunk. Not like me — I mean a real drunk. Bloody disturbing."

"I will tell you a special secret. Because you told me you were jealous. Pápi is going to put Perales out. He is only waiting for the right moment. Then your Amazing Monzy will be the daughter of the president."

"Holy shit! But why would he tell you such a thing?"

"I am his princess. He tells me things he tells to no one else. I did not mean to frighten you. I will soothe you, okay? Is this soothing?"

"Oh yes. Also stimulating. Monzy?"

"Yes?"

"Look under my pillow."

I put it around her neck, and she cried and kissed me on the nose and cheeks and eyes. Improvising on Poe's "Eldorado," I sang. "Now Montserrat, Do you think that A McKnight who's grown so old Has found in the Andes, Wearing no panties, A special kind of gold?" When she lowered herself upon me the little gold man spun and caught in my beard, and swung away and caught again. As grinning masks of dogs and jaguars watched us from the walls.

After school and a particularly terrifying bus race, I walked with relief upon the cobbles of my sloping street. A green plank doorway was open to show me a wee paved courtyard of cracked tiles, the sun still warming a corner of it where there were leafy plants in pots and a white dog sleeping with his snout in shade and his bum in sun. Now three boys with shouts and shaven heads and bare feet kicking the bejessus out of a deflated red ball. Rooster hooting somewhere, and *cúmbia* of accordion and cowbell playing.

"*Buenas tardes,* Señora Maldonado."

With a curt reply and a look as dark as her widow's weeds she handed me mail. Too big for my slot, the postman had said. A mailing tube. Canadian stamps of beavers and Her Majesty.

On the empty wood floor of my apartment I unrolled a painting on canvas. Weighted each corner with a textbook. And, standing above it, read the note.

> *Finished. You had to be away this long before I knew what it needed. Is your beard much greyer now? I am trying to enjoy the spring but my friend smack takes a lot of love away. I think my last ounce of it might have gone into this portrait. Elizabeth still sticks by me. I visited Mom's grave. Some black tulips have come up around it. Did you plant them?*

4

The Caca Cha-Cha

A morbid choice they seemed now, with my life in its own kind of bloom — this smouldering flower Montserrat, who so craved to bob upon one's lonely stem. I remembered — it was that winter just before I left — closing wet earth over the bulbs, but had forgotten the flowers would emerge from the earth black.

Really it must have been for Jeff that I planted those dark flowers.

"His *droga* it is the *coca*?"

I sprawled in my desk chair, back turned to the desk and the heap of marking accumulating on it, while Arturo swayed in front of my portrait. Steadying himself with my blowgun. Scrutinizing for half an hour now the eyes of me there which Jeff had put behind these same old gold glasses, with a gleam in one lens as if a small bright dream were passing.

"No. It is the *heroina*."

"We no are growing the *heroina* in this country. I think maybe you are the bad father."

"No. I love him. He loves me. And he is a phenomenon. Are you going to shoot?"

He swayed a minute longer, then shouldered the blowgun and turned.

"Ow."

"I am sorry. Is very long this weapon."

Off to the hunt, with the quiver of darts and the gourd of kapok fluff slung at his side. Soon into the living room rose the tip of one's blowgun. Arturo some distance away in my bedroom, applying himself to the other end of it, while the bark-wrapped tip felt through the air for something like an aim.

"I didn't got him."

"Arturo, can you shoot your gun any better than you can a blowgun? Come here and tell me. And drink this. It is made from potatoes of the towering Andes and will therefore make you high. Give me the blowgun and sit here. Recover from the humiliation of missing by fifteen feet."

"I don't understand nothing you are saying. Yes, I shoot so good my gun. I want be such . . . Such?"

"Yes. Such."

"I want to be such good policeman." Suddenly a grimace. Of holding back tears. "Mac. Is hard to be policeman."

"You're upset."

"Upset, *sí*."

"You keep that bottle. I have another."

"You are my friend. I think I don't got many friends. I think my friends they are saying me . . . *Cómo se dice? Mentiras*."

"Lies."

"Yes. Lies."

"A serious matter, Arturo. What friends and what lies?"

"Policemans."

"And what lies?"

"I am policeman for long time. Long time. I am working hard all the days, and now I am *capitán*. I am having a lot of the dangerous. Many dangerous. Sometimes bad people they are shooting to me. Vicente Tobar, the robber of banks, he is shooting me. *Cómo se dice aquí?*"

"Ass. Arse if your father was Scottish."

"Vicente Tobar he is shooting me in the arse. But I am shooting Vicente Tobar into the face and he is dead. In a house in Apoyán where he is counting the money. *Pum! Pum!* And it is hurting so much the arse. Ai ai ai! But his . . . *Cómo se dice sesos?"*

"Brains."

"His brains of him they are on the money, and I am so happy. That I am not dead. Many dangerous. Ricardo Guarín. Pacho Gomez the Ugly. Fat Narciso Córdoba. Paula Echevaria, who is shooting to me in the *baño* of the bus estation but is not shooting into any part of me, but I am shooting Paula Echevaria into the finger. *Pum!* And she is crying like a girl. Please, she is saying, do not shoot into me no more. Many dangerous, Mac. Because I am policeman. And then they were put me to *capitán,* and my boss he say, Arturo, you must to go for find the drug peoples. So I am catching much drug peoples. And some are rich. These drug peoples. They say, Arturo, take this money. Take this car. But I don't never take the bribes, Mac. They are not many then, these drug peoples. Federico Escobar. Juan Restrepo. The three Malo brothers. Here no is Colómbia. Not yet."

He stared glassily into space for a minute, glanced at my portrait, shook his head and drained the bottle. Then he slid down in his chair, let his head hang back and his hands down, and closed his eyes. The hummingbird on his forehead lay motionless under a film of sweat and stray strands of hair. His blue suit jacket gaped. The gun there. Stuffed under his belt.

"Christ. You'll shoot yourself." I stepped forward and bent to remove the pistol. But as I touched the white grip a hand fastened on my wrist. And the eyes now open and chilly.

"Don't never do that, Mac."

I stood back again.

"Don't never try to take from me my gun. Is my friend, my gun. I think maybe I need him." He sat up. "Because maybe now he is my one only friend."

"I'm your friend."

"Yes. Is the truth. But don't never touch my gun."

"I'm sorry. Now, Arturo. What lies?"

He set the empty bottle down, leaned elbows on knees and let his words spill toward the floor. "My boss he tells to me go here go there. Catch this man catch that man. So I am catching them. Because I am good policeman. Mac, what I am doing if I no can be policeman? How I am paying my house? How I am paying the eschool for Isabel? Or maybe I am dead and my Isabel she has no father. What I am doing then?"

I found I was tapping the end of the blowgun on the toe of my shoe. He looked at me. An answer please, Mac. But instead of trying to make a reply I started suddenly to tremble. The curtains were closed. But on the other side of them, a world of darkness. And out there in that dark world, tremendous shit being done. The *mierda* that made this country move and shake. Assassins out there. Torturers. CIAjerks more, actually, than jerks. Blood on hands everywhere. What one did mattered. No such thing as an innocent schoolteacher. On my desk was a form from the American School. *Are you returning next year? Yes. No. Don't know. Check one.* Montserrat had checked *yes* for me. I would change it and put *no.* And tomorrow at school slip her a note saying, That's all, M., it's over, goodbye. And soon go home to my son. Where I should be. Because a fool is bad for everybody. And when that darkness there is packed with virtuoso shit-skaters, then a fool is pure dynamite. Arturo being very drunk now, I hoped that he would forget his complaint. That he would ramble until we said goodnight and he drove away reeling in his yellow cab or until he passed out. Because I did not now want to know about the lies. And yet I took a deep breath. And said:

"Arturo. Please. What lies?"

"Is secret. Secret of a policeman."

I sighed with relief. "Yes, of course. I understand. You shouldn't drive. There are taxis at the hotel. I'll walk over with you."

"Mac. Is very bad the drugs. Is very bad the estory of your son. I am feeling very sorry for you."

And then I was pacing. The darts in their bark container rattled at my hip. As I listened.

"Vicente Tobar he is shooting me into the arse. And I am shooting him into the face. But he is not such . . . Such? Yes. He is not such bad man. He is only bank robber. But the drug peoples. They are the most bad. Because Vicente Tobar he is hurting nobody. Only me when I go to that house in Apoyán and *pum! pum!* But the drug peoples. Federico Escobar. Juan Restrepo. They are hurting very much peoples. Do you think that Juan Restrepo he is interested about your son? Yes, Mac. Because your son he is paying the expensive eschool of the sons of Juan Restrepo in *Inglaterra. Cocaina. Heroina.* They are equal. They are money for the drug peoples. When I am catching the Malo brothers I am hoping they are shooting the guns to me. Because I want to kill them. Is true. For what they are doing to the peoples. With the such bad lives. Like your son. But they no are shooting the guns. They are calling the lawyers. On the telephone of the wonderful car of Enrique Malo. Behind the church in La Merced. You are walking much. This talk of the *drogas* it is making you *nervioso.*"

He let out a bilious grunt, and shook his head. The hummingbird twitched once feebly.

"Are you going to be sick?"

"Womens."

"What?"

"Let's go for womens. Let's go for fuck womens. Let's go now." Missing his suit pocket twice, he managed on the third plunge of his hand to come up with car keys. And while his other hand felt for a nonexistent chair arm he slid sideways off the chair. And sat on the floor, appearing to think deeply.

"Better you go home to your wife. What's wrong? Jesus, don't cry."

He lay back, cracking his head against the corner of my desk. Threw an arm over his eyes.

"Is very bad."

"What? What's bad?"

"Elena."

"Your wife. Is she all right?"

"Yes. But I am not all right."

"Oh. Problems of the bed."

He nodded, and slid down flat on the floor. I was still sober enough to be amazed. That he, a Latin macho, would admit such a thing. And touched, that he would trust me with it.

"Arturo. Stop crying. It's because you're worried about something. It happens to every man some time."

He held out a hand, I helped him up. He tried to straighten his suit. Smiled. Then the smile went, and he stood quiet and made no effort to wipe away the tears that poured again down his face. I waited.

"Mac."

"Yes."

"You are loving your country?"

"No."

"Me I am loving my country."

"But. Yes?"

"*Exacto*. But."

"But lies. Right, Arturo?"

"Everyone. My boss. My friends the policemans. And now I know why they are saying the lies. And I no can doing nothing. Because is him. But I am loving my country. So I am like this. Very drink. Ai, Mac, it is much."

"How much?"

"A — *cómo se dice?* — a whorehouse."

"I think maybe you mean a warehouse."

"In Santa Rosa. Is fulled."

"Filled with what? Stop blubbering for Christ sake!" His shiny tie in my hand. His head flopping as I shook. But soon I let go. "Never mind. I know." He stood with his head hanging. Tears splashed on the parquet.

"But who, Arturo?"

He looked at me. Wanting me not to make him say it. I said, "It is, isn't it?"

He nodded.

I slipped a dart from the quiver. Like an eight-inch toothpick. For a very big man. Twirled a pinch of kapok around it near the blunt end. Inserted it.

One more thing, Perales had said. *One more thing to sell*. Fine, I would show him one more thing. I went into the bedroom. When I turned my back I thought I heard the dogs, the grinning jaguars, the armadillos licking their chops. So you think you can drain the love out of my son, do you? And get away with it. Now you'll see some shit-skating. This is called the smelly pirouette.

The blowgun — the *serbetana* — is all feel. Timing and judgement. On the end wall of my living room, the face still there — but richly pocked now — of Perales. Fill the lungs. Steady the weapon upon one's vodka-filled mental shock absorber. El poof. And presto. See? The president with a toothpick between his eyes.

But the caca cha-cha is no piece of cake. Not for a Canuck with a conscience. I had drunk, and if she asked me for some, she could drink too. All she wanted. Because she had to be soft. Soft as soap. I avoided the gaze of my portrait.

She arrived, and we were posthaste upon my bed and naked.

And after a while she was sitting cross-legged, sipping from time to time from the Bellows bottle. The good woman smell and smoothness. As I lay on my back, glum. For she had not gone soft. But I had.

"Would you like me to make some sexy poses? I think that would help now."

"It didn't help before."

"But I am drunk now, and I can do things that are more

wickeder. Look."

"And your English is more worser. Yes, that is extremely wicked, Montserrat. You are a limber young lady, aren't you? Don't spill the vodka."

"Nothing, McKnight?"

"Not a twitch."

"How about this?"

"Jesus, you'll hurt yourself. Look, maybe we should just get dressed. This is ridiculous."

"No. I want to be naked with you. I want to fuck. I will tell you a dirty story."

"Please don't."

"Once upon a time there was a dribbling salesman."

"Travelling. For Christ sake, give me that bottle."

"Don't shout me. Why are you angry?"

"I'm not angry."

"Because you are incompetent?"

"What do you mean — incompetent?"

"When your thing refuses to get up."

"Impotent? Don't you fucking call me impotent."

"You are shouting."

"I'm sorry. Let's get dressed."

"McKnight?"

"What?"

"I know what is wrong. It is because you are worried about something. It happens to every man some time."

So I had caught the disease of Marshal Art. Ah, night in the tropics, where life is serene. I had not given her the intended note saying, That's all, M., it's over, goodbye. That would have to wait now, left hanging, along with one's conscience, common sense, and dick that goes limp at the least whiff of moral ordure.

The walls here were as cluttered as the rest of the apartment was bare. My stuff. Comforting always, but not now. The masks. The tiny primitive paintings. The woven hangings of mythical worms, lopsided crosses, wild laughing Inca gods. There, leaning in a corner, my *serbetana*.

From Montserrat's neck the little golden man hung down. I thought I felt the bugger tiptoe on my shoulder. Shrugged him away.

"Did it happen to your bartender?"

"To Gary?"

"*Gary* is it?"

"Jealous again, McKnight?"

"Incompetent. Why not jealous too?"

"Ai, such a frowl. You look so funny. Maybe I am going to laugh."

"Frown. And don't you laugh at me."

"Why not?"

"Just don't."

She laughed, and lay on her back beside me. Took a corpse hand from my chest and placed it upon her crotch. I let it lie there limp.

"Yes, it happened to Gary. When his wife found out."

"Christ, wife now is it?"

"A shame. Because — what was your word? Suspended?"

"Splendid."

"Because his thing was so esplendid. Very big. Much more bigger than yours."

"Of course."

"You should have seen it, McKnight. As thick as your leg and as long as your *serbetana*." She laughed again, rolled toward me and threw a leg across my stomach.

"Ah," I said. "Teasing the old fellow. A bit cruel for the quiet girl at the back of the class."

"Oh, my poor eschoolteacher." She stroked my hair. "I am sorry. I love you and will not talk no more about the esplendid thing of Gary. It was not so esplendid. Maybe just a little bit esplendid. Like yours. Which wants to rest tonight. I don't care. Tonight I am your friend only. Now, McKnight! *Mi amante*. What is it you are worried about?"

"I'm not worried about anything."

"Are you lying me?"

"Jesus, I'm not lying."

"Because if you are lying me I will be so unhappy. Because my McKnight never tells the lies. In his lonely heart there is the El Dorado, and for this I love him. He is pure and angry and funny. And would never tell the lies."

"Evelyn, for Christ sake."

"No. Not Evelyn."

"Did I say Evelyn again? I'm sorry."

"It is me, *hombre*. Amazing Monzy."

"Yes. Do some more poses, okay?"

"Of course. I will do now one very good pose."

She handed me the bottle, stood on the bed and reached down a red dog mask. Held it against her face, turned and stood over me. There, in two holes, the eyes of — yes — Evelyn, but gone dark.

"Monzy?"

"I am not Monzy, señor."

"Who are you?"

"Who do you want me to be?" A distant muffled voice. Coming out of red shiny jaws and large teeth.

"Well. Be the Esperanza Extravaganza. Irresistible and wicked."

"Yes. That is who I am. And who are you, señor?"

"I am Bogey."

"I think you like me, Bogey. Because now you are stuff."

"Yes. Stiff. And thick as the bartender's leg."

"But not as long as your *serbetana*."

"I'm not finished, shweetheart. Try the armadillo."

A more or less successful coupling, though somehow she broke a tooth in the process — in the dog's mouth, not hers. From which, *patrón*, had come warnings in failing English. Not to lie her. In this anxious gut, some twists of pain. For Montserrat was ready to leave. And she was soft. But I was not.

Tonight the daughter of the future president was in baggy jeans, black sweatshirt, yellow grubby sneakers. Perched now on a corner of my desk, her rather large hands resting loose between her thighs. A young woman as sloppy as the piles of homework behind her. But more inviting. And soft now, soft as a shadow.

"McKnight."

Oh but for a different place, Monzy. And a different time and a different me.

"I have to go."

And so, then, to turn and reach across her and extract from the desk drawer a sealed envelope.

> *Dear Charlie. I have information. You do not need to know who I am.*

"What is this?"

"A letter."

"For me?"

"No, for your father."

"You forgot to put the name and the address."

> *Like you, I want Perales out. He is the lowest kind of disgusting scum. If you don't get him, he'll get you.*

"I didn't forget the address. It's a kind of private joke. He'll understand."

"What is it?"

"Never mind. Can you put it on his desk? So he doesn't know how it got there?"

> *In the bárrio of Santa Rosa there is a warehouse. It is full of cocaine. Perales bought it with government money and will sell it for his own despicable purposes. The people are depending on you, General. Rid us of this stinking sore, Perales. Though I write in English, I am a citizen. It is located in Santa Rosa, one mile past the Coca-Cola plant. Below the highway. A new warehouse. Act now while his hands are dirty.*

"But he will ask."

"Say nothing."

"McKnight, I never lie my father."

"Jesus, you're drunker than I thought. Of course you lie. Where are you supposed to be tonight? Did you tell him you're out humping your English teacher? You lie, and I lie, and nobody is as pure as they think they are. Christ. Can't I even ask you to do me a small favour, without getting a fucking sermon! Just put it on his desk, Montserrat. Okay? Can you do that? Is that too much to ask? You balled a bartender in Boston, right? You're a big girl. So if you have to lie, lie."

Her quick inhalation. The muscles of her face straining.

"Monzy, I'm sorry."

But too late. I had never seen her cry before. A black sleeve thrown across the eyes so I could not see her. Or so she could not see me. Her golden man. She slid off the desk, took the envelope, and was gone out into my dark stairwell.

"The light's burnt out," I muttered. "Watch your step."

The tape of oldies rolled on, and Doreen Muñoz sang along. She swayed in her chair, and the unplumbed valleys of her own fatness released zephyrs of body odour into the air of the Arse. That beefy face of a Georgia sheriff unusually animated this night.

I said, "Been inhaling a little something, have you, Doreen? And how is your good husband, the Chief of Police?"

But she only shrugged, too busy now singing. Under the table, someone's toes up my pantleg. Doreen's, I think, because the only other person at the table, Doreen's drinking partner, Flossie Pazmiño, sat glass-eyed and solemn after five gin and tonics, with an ash on her cigarette three inches long, and she only shivered when at last it fell down the neck of her blouse.

I did not mind Doreen's toes groping my shin. I even smiled. She would sing a different tune soon enough. Oh yaas, them blues. When Charlie Dávilos tipped toward her husband the presidential bucket of *mierda* from on high. For it was happening. And

Bogart lives.

"Gustavo, if you would be so kind. Another vodka. Ice. No amoebas."

"Mac, the girls are just dying for their next English lesson." The tape had finished. Now, only the clink of cutlery, and talk in pools of candlelight, and from the bar, laughter. Everyone happy on this eve of the event. Even our Whale, who should not have been, but perhaps did not know it. "They think you are so cute. With your beard and all. And your glasses and all. And, Lord, that funny way you have about you. Now tell me the truth, Mac. I know they are not the brightest girls in the world. And I know maybe one or two of them don't like to work too awfully hard. But Mac. Be honest now. Are they good pupils?"

Foot retreating from up my pants. Whale leaning forward. So earnest. Freckled farmer elbows on the checkered cloth. Hand that could pick up a hickory log and crush it to sawdust, resting now on my bare arm. As she chewed at dry skin on her lips and waited hopefully for my answer. Pasty face in the candlelight so close. And I wanted to say, Attend to your own pupils. Which are bright, Doreen, and large as Georgia pecan pies. Don't you know, oh Whale, whence cometh thy blow? That thy generous hubby is in up to here? And tomorrow shall be out?

But Mac the Giant-Killer said only, "Doreen you above all people must know, That the whore with a heart of gold had a head of lead."

Her tinkle giggle. "Oh Mac, you are priceless." But the hand sliding off my arm and away.

And also Flossie's laugh and cigarette hack. Aground for a moment now upon some small sandbar of clarity. "But," she said, "you're losing your number one student."

"Oh? Who is that, Flossie?"

"My God, man, haven't you heard? There's going to be a coup. Charlie Dávilos has mobilized the armed forces. Seems Perales got surprised with a warehouse full of *coca*."

"You don't say! I suppose I really should pay more attention to the news. Gustavo. *Por favor*. No ice this time."

Mac strolling toward the bar now. Greetings from eaters acknowledged with nods and winks from McKnight. If only they knew. Then there would be no greetings. Only awe. Servile fingers straining to touch the hem of my green aloha shirt, which I wore in celebration.

Up onto a stool beside Jack Kelly.

"Maria Dolores, how is young Juan Ignácio?"

"Enormous, Maquito. And always hungry. He is asleep now in the kitchen."

"If there is a small steak that he has not devoured, I will have it."

"My God, Jack, listen to these happy, inebriated voices! Will you not join in? There are Americans here, eager to feel a buddy's slap on the back. To hear his warm *haw haw*. Oh, I see. You are lost in meditation. Where might you be going next, Jack? That is, if ever you are instructed to abandon this lofty setting. Some metropolis in the Sahara, perhaps? Friend, they need you there, there are backs to be slapped. What is that you're drinking? A Cuba libre, fabulous American concoction. Jack, what say? Let's buy a round for everyone. And we'll drink to your career. Dolores, Cuba libres all around. I'll pay for the rum part. But Jack Kelly here is buying the coke. Jack, where you going? Did I say something wrong? Okay, you don't have to buy the coke. Golly. Maybe a harmless embassy functionary is not up to buying so much coke. Could that be it, Dolores?"

"Spanish, please, Mac."

"But I thought you understood to listen."

"Only the straight English. Not the crooked."

Craving further society this night of triumph, I stood scanning the eaters. With my steak on its plate, and knife and fork and beer. And was surprised to see the white blazer, black braid and blonde girlfriend of Tomás. Strange. Was this his idea of laying low till it blew over?

I set my plate, knife, fork and beer on their table and sat

down. "Why, of course I'll join you, Tomás, how kind of you. I was feeling just a tad dejected, and your company always perks me up."

"You're going to fuckin' die, man."

Strange. That morose vulnerability of Jack Kelly not evident in the Chairman. Whose goose Charlie would surely cook. And whose tune would soon enough be whistled different. Them blues, oh yaas, oh yaas.

"Have I offended you, Tomás? Some fashion faux pas, I suppose. Is it my shirt? I had so hoped you would like it. But, hey, look, it matches Holly's eyes. Which are so enchanting in the candlelight. Don't you think so, Tomás? Absolutely gorgeous. Holly, may I call you Ivy? A plant some think of as creepy. But which I love for the way it clings. And the way it spreads."

From Holly, a velvet syllable of laughter. As her lips parted to admit a spoon loaded with chocolate mousse. And the green American eyes holding mine for a second. "Schoolteacher," she said, "I can dig it."

"So Ivy it is," I said. "Tomás, can you dig it? Have you ever seen how ivy spreads? I have. My God, it is exciting. But you are an expert on such matters. Crops and such. Tropical agriculture. An actual gentleman farmer, from what I've heard. Why, you must have a lot of money in crops. Don't you ever worry about losing your investment? Gosh, I would." I thoughtfully chewed a piece of steak as Tomás glared. His face now matching his shirt, a purplish tone upon which I did not comment. But said instead, "Ivy, what is this about having to line up to see the president? Has Tomás explained it to you? All I know is that there is going to be a queue."

Holly's overlush lips parting wide to reveal fillings and release a loud and long bray. Which so delighted me that I too laughed, and slapped the table. But the table jumped toward me, and my hand went instead into coffee. As Tomás' lunge carried him across the table. And his hands grappled for my throat. And I laughed, and waved my hands theatrically. And shrieked.

Until his fingers did find my windpipe, and I felt pain and started to choke. With Tomás saying through clenched teeth, "You cocksucker, I'll kill you," as he squeezed and people stood up and Dolores came out of the kitchen Dutch door. There was a *bong*, and Tomás was suddenly down and still on the table, with his face in lemon meringue pie.

"Jesus, you've killed him," said Holly.

"Gustavo," I gasped, "would you be so good."

But Dolores now held the frying pan in position for a forehand drive. And her eyes were grim as she pointed with her free hand toward the street.

School cancelled on this Friday morning. Up early, nevertheless, with a bruised throat and, even after three cups of coffee, no feeling of joy. Rather, a sense that there were more and unexpected veils to be dropped before I would behold the naked dancing thing itself. Which is to say, McKnight's fate. But also a kind of horniness for it, whatever it turned out to be. I switched from station to station on my ghetto blaster and heard on each the same uninterrupted martial music.

Out then, to walk under a sombre sky. Here in the window of a sporting goods store, a device. Which I resolved to buy. A kind of twister bar to improve the pecs. The push-ups insufficient, it seems. Montserrat had commented, even tried to put her brassiere on me. For I had not told her to go away. I was an irresolute old man who worried about his chest, and felt he needed her, and could not act.

The American Embassy was closed, but extra sentries on guard, even a pair looking down from the flat roof, who did not acknowledge my salute.

The Boar's Head was locked up as well, Clancy the wolfhound gone from the little yard. The sign of a prancing pig playing panpipes sad in this daylight, hanging still on its rusty chains.

Out of curiosity I took a street down the hill. Here were found trees along the sidewalk, and trim walls topped with an icing of broken glass to rip the flesh, and a hungry German shepherd behind each metal gate. At 152 San Javier, though, the gate gaped wide. And Jack Kelly's dog did not charge out of it and disembowel me. Instead, an Indian man grunted under the weight of a wooden crate on his back. He wrestled it onto the bed of a flatdeck truck, and his wife in velvet and lace skidded the crate toward a half-dozen others. Wearily the man returned for another load. And beside the gate, squatting with his back against the wall, a young person.

"Good morning, Gordon. I see the family treasures are off to the airport. And you are guarding them with all the vigilance of the good old American eagle. But you seem a little downcast. Come now, what's the matter? You can tell your teacher."

Neither reply nor eye contact of basic courtesy. Ah well, the lad was feeling down, one could make allowances.

"You'll miss Alegria, I suppose. Well, you're young. I'm sure you'll find a new girlfriend wherever it is you're going. I've heard the sub-Sahara is crawling with young women. Too bad you couldn't finish the school year — it's probably going to be a bitch trying to settle in at another school this late in the term. Well, as I said, Gordon, you're young. Repeating a year will be a cinch for someone with your dedication. I must run now — I've heard they might give Perales the boot today, so I thought I'd drop by the Palace and check it out. He was a friend of your dad's, wasn't he? Maybe he's packing his bags today too, ha ha. Say hi to Jack for me."

Some bustle in the Old Town, where proprietors could not afford to close. In the Plaza de San Francisco in front of the Palace, nothing unusual, except there were no policemen anywhere — *I got the police,* Perales had said. However, the street in front of the Palace was barricaded, so I decided to hang around. I had my brogues polished.

"Can you put black around the edge of the sole."

"*Sí, señor.*"

"Will the army come?"

"Sí, señor."

I got tired of waiting and took a walk through the Smugglers' Market to see if anyone would try to pick my pocket. When I returned there were three or four hundred soldiers and two tanks. Squares of soldiers with rifles and helmets facing the Palace, and up on the portico two guards in blue coats, buttons, braids and plumes facing the soldiers alone. And though there was no wind, the plumes trembled.

I joined the small crowd, and it expanded quickly behind me. To silence her baby, a heavy Indian woman beside me heaved a breast out of her dress. And beside me I heard a familiar voice.

"Mac, I'm thirsty. Can you reach over and squeeze that tit in my direction?"

"Hello Dickie. Ricardo, that is."

"So are we going to see the asshole thrown to the wolves? Drawn and quartered and pissed on and his head on that flagpole there?"

"Ah, the optimism of you Americans. No, I think we must rest content with the knowledge that we brought him down."

"We?"

"We the people, I mean."

"Mac. Get real. This is Charlie Dávilos' gig. The people have got fuck all to do with it. But you can say *we*, I guess. Being part of the family."

He studiously observed the Palace entrance. I noticed for the first time that maybe he was taller than me. With that tuft of red hair, anyway.

"Are you still on about that business? Dickie."

"There's quite a bit of talk going around, Mac."

"There's always talk Dickie."

"A chauffeur-driven Mercedes parked near your place late at night. That kind of talk."

The clock of the Palace rang noon. The crowd hushed as eight generals filed out the Palace door and stood at attention on a colonnaded portico. The brass, but none of them smiling.

The last general out wore an eyepatch. There was no hand at the end of his left sleeve. He said a word to the two guards, who sprang down the steps, plumes waving, to fall in with the ranks of soldiers. Then he joined the line of other generals. Someone shouted, *"Viva Moncayo!"* And the crowd shouted back, *"Viva!"*

Then there was a roar from some courtyard within. A helicopter sprang up into the sky and slid away. The soldiers cheered. The crowd hooted, cursed and shook fists. Ai, Pancho, they no are liking you.

I said, "Dick, you are full of shit."

"Yes, well, that may be. Say, look at the bod on that little *morena* over there. But, I tell ya, Mac. It might be all right being part of the first family. You know what I mean? If it was all legit. No sneaking-around bullshit. Okay — marriage — why not? Anyway, if you're going to ball her, it better be with daddy's blessing. You know what I mean?"

"Isn't that Pilar over there?"

"Where? Who's Pilar?"

"Whoops, she's gone now. Young lady from Denver. Got a kid with red hair. Met her at the Arse the other night. Somehow I thought you knew her."

Dickie stared fixedly at the Palace. The sun reflected from the pink skin on his nose. And he was quiet. And not, *patrón*, taller than me. Definitely not.

Now, in front of the Palace stairs, a long black car rolled to a stop. An officer stepped forward to open the door. And, looking like the general of generals, which is what he was, Charlie Dávilos stepped out. Every soldier at attention, every person in the crowd cheering. Even the *guágua* at my elbow released his nipple and started squalling. Then Dávilos strode alone up the stairs and, except for the baby, there was silence. Dávilos walked slowly along the line of generals, looking into each face. And stopped before one and signalled to an officer, who came up with two soldiers and guided the chosen down at gunpoint. And Dávilos walked further along the line, looking into more faces.

And a second general was led away. And then he stopped and looked into the face of General Moncayo, which I could see was a roadmap of red battlescar furrows. And the one eye of General Moncayo stared back with contempt. In a minute Dávilos stopped looking into the face of Moncayo and turned to us. And he threw his arms wide, as if to embrace all of us, his children. And we shouted, *"Viva Charlie! Viva Charlie!"* Except for Dickie, who remained quiet.

5

Big RPM

In the South American edition of *Newsweek*, no mention of king-maker McKnight. Pancho, Charlie but no Mac. Fine. Same day I would give my interview. Compose the memoirs, too, among leather, books and brandy. For now, though, to bide my time. In the dreary classroom, the urine-smelling streets, the barren apartment. Waiting for veils to slip.

And of course no feeling that I had done Jeff any good. Would he read "Military Takeover" in *Newsweek* and pitch his needle? And did I feel less guilty? No, just anxious as well. And drinking more. I remember now the time I let him shoot me up, to see what it was about. Peace and a smug quiet ecstasy. Patching up reality, he called it.

I poured a little more vodka into my gullet. And did not tell Montserrat to go away. But waited. And in my own way patched.

"McKnight's famous spaghetti. Known in the better cookbooks as McGhetti. Overpriced Chilean wine for you. Nutritious spud juice for me. The intimate glow of this here candle. Admit it, amazing. It's cozy."

"McKnight. Maybe you are drinking too much."

"No. Not *McKnight*. I have an announcement. It is time for a new improved reality. Something safe and comfy. I'll call you Amazing Monzy. And you can call me Al. Al Dorado. We'll need new histories, of course, but histories can be manufactured. Like noodles. As Shakespeare himself said, what's past is pasta."

"But I like your history, McKnight. Do you have a real first name?"

"Angus."

"I will call you Angus, then."

"Sorry. Unsafe. Uncomfy. Al."

"You are so estrange tonight. I don't like this wine. Give me some espud juice. All right. I will be Amazing. Or Extravaganza. Or Extra. Or Ex."

I laughed. "That's good. That's amusing, Amazing." What fun, this improving of reality. But Montserrat did not laugh. Looked decidedly glum, in fact, as she had all evening.

"Because," she said, "I do not like my reality very much."

"Feeling down. That's not like you."

"It is my father."

She dropped her fork, took a gulp of vodka and gave me a quick, false smile.

"All he talks about is revenge," she said. "I think you call it getting even."

"I think you are mistaken, Montserrat. Charlie is not a man for getting even."

"I did not think so, either. But he has changed. Wait till you see what happens to some of the ministers of Perales. They will go to jail. Or they will be exiled. They will lose their houses. Their sons will be expelled from Harvard. Their dogs will be poisoned. Just because at some time they offended him. Did not give him money for another tank. Or made a joke about him behind his jack and he heard about it. Or looked at me like that pig Guzman did once at a party. He has gone already to Miami, and he won't be back."

"His dog?"

"I think dropped from a helicopter."

"Now about this new improved reality, Monzy. Don't you think it would be fun? I could be . . ."

"No. No new reality. If I can't have my father the way he was, at least I can have you. My El Dorado man. No more secret letters. No improved realities. It is hard enough for me to come here now, there are guards everywhere, and I have to be so snaky . . ."

"Sneaky."

". . . just to come and eat spaghetti like this. So I want my same special wonderful McKnight. No Al. And no Amazing either. Okay?"

"Monzy, I'm afraid."

"Yes. Did you think there would be no Valley of the Shadow?"

"Maria Dolores, I bid you a very good evening. Would you be so kind?"

In the dining area were two or three tables of eaters. On the ever-rolling tape, Jim Morrison and the Doors. On the silent television, the face of the President Charlie Dávilos speaking, apparently earnestly, to us his children. And on the stool to my right, nursing a beer, a burly bald man with a dark moustache and a white windbreaker over Washington Redskins T-shirt. Who watched Charlie as if afraid of missing a word, although there were no words to be missed.

"Skins fan?"

"Hometown. You?"

"Vancouver Lions."

"Vancouver — that's up in Canada." Small eyes for a second narrowed. He new in town and me the old Andes hand, but still he might as well have said it: Why you Canadian flake. And, We don't cotton to your kind in these parts. He edged his left elbow a centimetre further away on the black formica so as not, I suppose, to catch whatever it was that made me Canadian.

Even as he reached across with his right hand.

"Parker Lee. Call me Par."

The grip on him. Might even give the Whale pause.

"Mac McKnight."

"Glad to meet you, Mac. What's a Canadian doing so far from home?"

Already I did not like Par. His pig eyes, white jacket and friendly ways. But Par wanted to talk and so did I. "I teach. At the American School."

"The American School! Good man!" The left hand of Par clapping fearlessly down upon my right shoulder.

"You're with the embassy?"

"Uh huh."

"Par, I'm going to buy you a beer. Dolores! I suppose you've taken over from Jack Kelly?"

"You knew Jack? Well, not exactly taken over."

"The CIA won't corrupt Charlie the way it did Pancho."

"Haw haw haw. Mac, you're a strange one, you are."

"You won't buy a planeload of discount cocaine from Charlie. What'd you want it for, anyway? To finance some shitty little war? Or just for the joy of seeing lives destroyed?"

"Thanks for the beer."

His new beer untouched, he swung round on the stool, ran a hairy hand over a hairless head, zipped his white jacket and walked away.

"He's the Davy Crockett of the fucking Andes," I said.

"It's here somewhere."

Flossie plunged her hands into the mess on her desk. Papers slid from the edge of the heap. The lip of a chestnut-coloured coffee mug appeared for a moment, then vanished. Something lizard-like today about Flossie's jowls. At the crown of her boy's head of dry reddish hair, an incipient bald spot. The middle button of her blouse undone, a glimpse there of red brassiere. This made me feel sad, and put sinew into my resolve.

"Well, never mind," she said, "it's only a form. I don't need it. I'll remember. How come you decided not to stay another year?"

"Purely emotional, Flossie. I miss the winters. The smell of wet overcoats on the Hastings Bus. And my son has just enrolled at the Real Estate Institute. He'll need some mature guidance."

Down my black stairwell to answer my buzzer. It would not be the Naked Dancing Thing itself. The Naked Dancing Thing itself had turned over a new leaf and had lost all interest in me.

"Arturo."

I broke out the Bellows. But Arturo was drunk already. In jeans and a T-shirt with words on it saying *Hug Me*. He straddled my desk chair, crossed his arms on the back, and rested his chin.

"I've never seen you without a suit."

"The blue cheens. Is good."

"Where is your gun?"

He shrugged. "He was take it."

"Who was take it?"

"My *jefe*."

"How come?"

"What means how come?"

"Why. Why did the chief take your gun?"

He got up and went purposefully but unsteadily past me to the dining room table, where the bottle sat. "I like the vodka. Mac," he said behind me, pouring, "they make me stop to be a policeman."

I felt suddenly cold. I heard him screw the cap back on the bottle. "Now," he said, "can you hula?"

"What!"

He swung around the partition and stood in front of me. "Cañajula. Now I go to Cañajula."

"Why do you go to Cañajula? Cañajula is at the border."

"Because I will going to be a policeman of the border. Is funny, no?"

"A customs officer?"

"I will going to stomp the *pasaportes*." He guffawed wretchedly, and the blast of it knocked him backwards two steps. Then he pranced right two steps. Then left. Vodka leapt from his glass and splattered his T-shirt and my floor. The hummingbird birthmark on his forehead seemed to whir. He caught his balance again and stood there, reading *Hug Me*.

"My *jefe* is saying me is very nice at Cañajula. Is more better for my health at Cañajula. Is nice job to stomp the *pasaportes*. He is saying me no is nice job to catch the drug peoples. Is very bad for my health to catch the drug peoples now."

"Arturo. What are you telling me?"

"I am selling my house. I am selling my suits. I am selling my taxi. Isabel is quitting the nice school. Elena is angry because we must to go live in Cañajula where there is nothing and we will going to be poor and the television no is working good like here in Esperanza. Mac. I am working hard all the days. And now? Is funny, no?"

But he did not laugh. A tear instead trickled down and fell from his chin.

"This is a shit-hole country, Arturo."

"Mac. Is true."

"Fucking Charlie," I said.

"Is true, Mac. Fucking Charlie."

"You seem so interested in the scenery."

"Señorita Espinoza, I am. I count the dead dogs. It is a kind of meditation."

"Please call me Catarina, Mac."

Ah. She had liked it that time I had accidentally felt her up. And so what? There upon the sidewalk in front of the government clinic where worried-looking people were lined up for a block, a dead dog. Blonde in colour, with heavy tits of motherhood, lying in blood. On the wall of the clinic: *Down With Fascist Shits*, and *Death To Communist Whores*, and *Quique Is A Fairy*. And *Viva Charlie*.

"You are in a bad mood," she said. "What a shame. To be in a bad mood on a Friday. When we should be happy because the week is almost finished."

"Señorita Espinoza, you know what is almost finished? If you would care to take a look out this window you would see that this shit-hole country, for one thing, is almost finished. And I will be delighted to watch it go the rest of the way down the tube. Also, my tolerance for the doorknobs that inhabit this defunct tropical sphincter is almost finished. And I perhaps as well am almost finished."

There was a wind getting up. Pedestrians shielding eyes against sidewalk grit. Parade of paper litter scudding and a green fedora chased by an old woman in a pleated skirt. As the bus rocked and jarred against the air.

I resumed. "I am not in a bad mood. I am in a good mood. In fact I am in a superb mood. Don't pretend I am not insulting you. I am being unforgivably rude. So stop smiling."

"You are the type of person who gives Americans a bad name."

"Please. I will given Canadians a bad name or no one."

"Everyone knows about your drinking problem. Don't worry if the children can hear me. They know too."

"Do they know of the trysts you have with your preserved specimens?"

"What is a tryst? I think I am going to slap your face."

"Try it and I'll flatten that buzzard protuberance of yours. Yes, I can smell the corruption on you too. Under your cheap perfume. The smell of that toilet you're all going down." I turned from her and snuggled down into my seat and rubbed my hands together. "God I feel wonderful. Life is going to be such a blast from now on."

Soon I saw ahead the booths of the market and across the

avenida the chewed walls of the slaughter yard. The bus slowed. We crawled past a Mercedes stopped in the curb lane. Señorita Espinoza leaned over me to see. Breast pressed into my shoulder. Stubborn. A man in a grey suit and dark glasses was getting out of the back seat of the Mercedes. With his door open he stopped to light a cigar. In front of the Mercedes a wheelbarrow was bent and upside down. And a man face down and still. Red bloody meat everywhere. People grabbing up chunks of it and running.

"But I've got this kid from Sioux City. Fresh out of teacher's college. His letter's right here. Somewhere."

Papers gliding. One's brogues buried in correspondence. For a moment the smell of mould from in there, as ashes from Flossie's cigarette sprinkled her searching hands. My principal in a misbuttoned khaki shirt, the red brassiere again winking through, which today made me feel not sad but bullish. Charge.

"Well, he's out of luck, isn't he?" I said.

"I've already written saying he's got the job."

"Well, he hasn't got the job. I've got the job."

"Mac, you can't go changing your mind every day."

"I suddenly realized how much you need me here. I'm staying."

"Mac. Listen. Get your shit together."

"Flossie. Listen. Get your shirt together. A man can only see red for so long. Before he starts to snort and paw."

By the final bell the wind had cut loose for real. Dust blotted out the mountains and hung streaming over the playing field. Neither Marúchi nor the flycatcher at their accustomed posts. Children struggling toward the buses, arms thrown over eyes. Banana Lorena there. Trying it backward. Until the wind tossed her loose black skirt up her back, revealing toast-coloured legs and wee pink panties.

"Wow. Now that girl has got an ass on her. Don't you think

so, Montserrat? Let's invite her over some time. Have a ménage à trois. You know what that is? That's right, a zoo with three animals. My God this wind is splendid. Don't you think so?"

The classroom door was closed, and with extracurricular bottle I was circling Montserrat, with jagged stops and starts and with flourishes of hand and violent smiles. As she stood clasping her book bag to her chest and watching me fearfully.

"Plant the wind and reap the whirlwind, I always say. Don't you always say that, Montserrat? You have, after all, been planted a few times, yet never once, stout heart, did you call out that you were being reaped. For, as the Good Book goes on to say, Knock and ye shall be opened, ask and ye shall be entered. I seem to be a trifle manic. Got the wind up McKilt. Gale force zephyrs licking around the old bell clapper."

"McKnight. You're acting so crazy. Can you listen for a minute. I'm worried. I think I might be . . ."

"Worried? Well so you should be. For you reap, my child, precisely as you sow. And you have been boffing your English teacher in plain sight of God. Who is going to hand you one hell of a detention. Did you know I was the best brain in Sunday School? I could rattle off verses like nobody's business. Straight is the gate and narrow is the way. That kind of thing."

The windows went *wham wham wham*. As out there a tumbleweed bounded across the field like a ghost. I knew I was at last capable of anything. Especially of saying to Montserrat, Go away. Enough of our dangerous little game, I've got work to do, throats to cut. But. If Montserrat could somehow place my blade upon Charlie's windpipe. As she had upon Pancho's. And yet. Hell. I was in no mood for thinking. I would flip a coin.

I took a drink. "Would you like some of this?"

She shook her head. Worried, she had said. Yes, I could see that she was. And I felt a surge of joy, as I realized that I did not care.

"I have to go," she said. "Filadelfo is waiting. But I have to talk to you. Really soon."

I stepped between her and the door. "Now, speaking of plants and harvests, do you know Ivy Clinger? And her boyfriend, Thomas Aquinas? Maybe seen them at the country club? Nice folks. They farm a few acres down Rio Colorado way. Real old-fashioned mom-and-dad-type operation. Why, they probably don't produce more than three or four tons of high-grade cocaine a year. Mailing out quaint little jam jars of it to laughing, rosy-cheeked children all around the world. Well, maybe a few lives got torpedoed. Maybe one or two of them kids gets a mite carried away with his nose in that old jam jar and has himself a cardiac arrest. Now, Montserrat. Honey. The question is this. Ivy Clinger and Thomas Aquinas — are they going to reap the whirlwind?"

On my face, the encouraging expression of a good teacher coaxing forth an answer. Which was now not forthcoming. Because Montserrat appeared not to be listening, but merely waiting for me to finish and get out of her way. So I bellowed.

"You better believe they're going to reap the fucking whirlwind! They are going to rotate. I'm talking big rpm. Cyclone city. Tornadoville. Spin-dry for shit-skaters. Don't you dare try to get past me! I am instructing you on moral niceties. Oh I tell you, they are going to know the meaning of ree-gret. When their little green salads get tossed. Into the Great Garbage Gobbler. And the Schoolteacher flips the switch. Proclaiming, Let there be hamburger. And, Lo, there was hamburger. And Clinger and Aquinas were sore afraid. Because the hamburger was them. And they called out, Help us, oh Extremely High Up Government Procurer. For we did only your bidding, and now we are as chopped liver. But the Extremely High Up Government Procurer could help them not."

"McKnight."

"God damn you. Shut up and be instructed. The Extremely Fucking High Up and Omnipotent Government Whore and Procurer could help them not. Because he himself was already a stinking pile of maggot-infested *salchichas*. You take one more step. And I drive this fist up your ear. I said stand still! Oh for Jesus' sake. Son of a bitch. There goes my bus."

"McKnight, don't!"

But the bottle was already gone, trailing a streamer of vodka and hurtling toward the window. Which it went easily through, with the whole window blasting outward after it and showering the ground melodiously. Then the wind hit me. And, blinking against air and grit, I wanted to laugh. Until something big and dark jumped in through the window and I shouted in horror. It landed lightly and glided toward me but, thank God, got stuck between my desk and the wall. A tumbleweed. Then the door opened, and the wind tore through harder, and the tumbleweed strained against my desk. I turned. A man in a dark suit stood there. Filadelfo. With a hand shielding his eyes, he looked from Montserrat to the shattered window and then to me. And now I was positive, absolutely positive I could summon the good McKnight guffaw. Because surely something had to be hilarious. Yet I did not laugh, but started instead to tremble.

"McKnight," said Montserrat. "Come on. Just leave this. The janitors will fix it. I will give you a ride. Come on. Don't worry. It's the weekend, you can rest. On Monday we will tell them how that bush broke the window." Her reassuring smile. "I hear there is a good movie playing this weekend." She winked. And waited.

Filadelfo went out.

Sand pelted us. The wind tossed her hair and fluttered her skirt.

I dug into my pants pocket and came up with a twenty-five dorado coin. A disgusting thing, corroded tar-black, the noble Indian face upon it hardly visible. I flipped it high. Caught it. Smacked it onto the back of my left hand.

"Come on," she said, and continued to smile.

Until I said.

"Go away."

6

ADIÓS

Saturday now, and the air behaving itself. The day spent, however, in closing the damper upon one's own inner hurricane. Strong possibility of being straitjacketed or otherwise interfered with before I could interfere with Charlie. Further manic demonstrations not advisable. Or emotional intemperance of any kind. I practised smiling calmly into my bathroom mirror. I talked to my portrait as if it were an oilman at Dude's. So who's gonna take the National League this year. Pass the pretzels. I bought bread and Bellows from Señora Maldonado, who stocked the latter especially for me. I polished my brogues. I flexed my twisted bar. I repotted a geranium. And whenever any thought of Montserrat threatened to intrude I slammed it into the basement.

The sun went down behind the lumpy volcano that overlooked the city. In the east, across the valley, Chinguráhua went pink, then grey. And I went out with damper battened down, into the world's shortest twilight. Down the hill past white walls with their jagged icing. Past metal gates behind which dogs barked at my footsteps. Some lights coming on. The bougainvillea colourless now around windows. Close above, the day's last incoming flight roaring down to land with the day's last light. Here at the bottom of the hill the tailor's and the shoemaker's closed. On Avenida Doce de Diciembre not much traffic. But the open doors of two *tabernas* already giving out *cúmbia* and yellow light. A negro boy in ragged pants boarded a bus to try to flog his remaining half-dozen of the weekend edition. And here at the corner of Doce de Diciembre and Alfaro, one pauses. To request from a large señora in a green fedora a bowl of *fritada*. She draws her ladle through her basin of bubbling fat and comes up with potato and pork and sweet yellow plantain. And I stand eating and am well pleased. At this appearance of calm.

Down Almagro six blocks. The red lights of the radio transmitters on the volcano now visible ahead. Across wide Avenida Ruipamba, where mighty motorcycles would howl after midnight, a violent and lonely sound echoing across this city. Into Parque Colón. Across this basketball court, upon which painted white letters still visible in this dusk assure me that the ubiquitous Quique remains a fairy. Onto this dry, piss-smelling grass, where here and there young Indian couples tickle and coo. I heard ahead shouting and a ball being kicked. Jeff had played soccer when he was nine, ten and eleven. Skinny but fast he was. Dashing up and down the field in the rain of British Columbia. In three years his team never won a game. Yet stalwart Jeff never gave up no matter what the score. Until one day he knew the score and gave up on everything except art, a loser's endeavour. Suddenly there were figures rushing in this darkness. And there were the shouts of men, and I was brushed by a flying shirttail, and there was the smell of sweat. And shouts in Spanish, Get off the field. And curses in Quíchua. As across the ground a white thing came toward me, bouncing. Get ready and *Pow!* Scuffed my brogue for sure. But lookit that sucker go.

"*Chuta!* What did you do that for!"

"I'm sorry."

"Can't you see we have a game here!"

"No. Yes. I'm sorry."

"*Hijo!* The ball has gone out onto the street."

"I'm sorry. I'll get it for you."

"Estuarto is getting it. If you are so sorry, why did you kick it?"

"I got confused."

"You are American."

"I'm Canadian."

"That explains it. Well, get off the field before you get run over."

"Why do you play in the dark anyway?"

"That is our business."

"Backward fucking country."

"What. Hey, Pablo! You hear what this gringo says? He says we have a backward fucking country."

This big person looming toward me out of the darkness was probably Pablo. And those other loomers were his co-athletes and compatriots. All closing in upon the disrespectful gringo.

"Gringo, I think you had better apologize."

"I do. Please go on with your game."

"About our country."

"I'm sorry. It's not really backward."

"*Bueno*. Now get the fuck off the field."

"Sounds reasonable to me."

"So move."

"I'm moving." Through the loose circle of men cursing in Quíchua and spitting on the ground. One of them said something I did not understand. There was laughter. And what was this. Something white. Bouncing across the ground. Toward me. *Pow!*

"He did it again! Estuarto! Estuarto, get that son of a whore! He's over there."

But Estuarto was already chasing the ball again. Across the grass. Up the embankment. Onto the street. Between cars. And behind me there were many hoarse threats of damage to one's person. As in English I shouted, "There's one for our side. You pathetic pack of yo-yos." And laughed. And made the loud sound of a fart. And kept walking.

I headed along Reforma. And after some inner debate I had to admit I had handled the situation less than splendidly. Well dampered I had not been. And had paid insufficient attention to appearances. I had called them backward and yo-yos. This was wrong. This was not pass the pretzels.

But now I would make up for it. Now I would be in my element, where reason was king. I pushed an intercom button, identified myself. A metal gate buzzed and swung open. A maid in white welcomed me at the door, and I followed her down a hallway, past the entrance to a large gloomy room furnished with several mismatched sofas and, on the end wall, a weakly lit shrine featuring Jesus, suffering. Into a plain dining room, most of which was filled with a table of marred eucalyptus wood. This was my classroom. Here I would give my English lesson to Doreen's *putas*.

The maid withdrew. I looked down the battered table, drew a deep breath and felt at home. The first two lessons had gone well. There had been giggles, there had been yawns, but there had also been sentences formed in English. Knowledge had been gained. Other than carnal.

Now at the far end of the room a door opened. Doreen. She of the toes up one's trousers. Whose husband had shelved Arturo, to wither suitless in Cañajula, where the TV reception was so rotten.

"Hello, Mac. I'm awful glad you could make it. The girls have been asking for you ever since last time."

Her tinkle voice. And makeup tonight upon the pasty complexion, which made her look more than ever like a hefty cracker lawman in drag. The bulk of her. Draped in layers of some pink wispy stuff. With the ankles below like poplar stumps. And a peculiar look in her yellow eyes. Suggesting that toes up the trousers was terrific — shall we try fingers in the fly.

"Doreen. Good evening. I see you are not singing the blues."

"The blues. Heavens, why should I sing the blues? Mac, you do say the sweetest and silliest things." Her tinkle laugh, and the freckled hand laid demurely at the base of her throat.

"Music of the South."

"The South? Mac, you know as well as I do that the blues is nigger music. Can I tell you something?"

I shrugged. Smiled noncommittally.

"You are an extremely handsome man. There, I said it. Oh, I am so wicked, I am just going to burn in hell." The flames thereof already apparently colouring her cheeks as she laughed and squirmed.

"Handsome is as handsome does."

"Mac, that is so true." And, touched by my wisdom, she took a step toward me. But just then another door opened to my right, and two young women entered. "Well, here they come. Take your time and make sure they learn something. There won't be any clients arriving for two hours at least. And if they don't behave themselves, you just call me. And I'll come a-runnin'." She mimed it, ducking her head and pumping those balloon arms. Like no sprinter that ever was, but calling to mind any number of defensive tackles. Then she giggled again and spun, so that the dress billowed, parachute-like. And looked at me over her shoulder, to let me see that ol' mischief in her eyes. And left.

"Well, girls, I think I handled that well. Sufficiently suppressed. What do you think? Impressed?"

"*Cómo*?"

"*Que dice*?"

"You are Maria Soledad, yes?"

"No. I Maria Lourdes."

"Oh. And you are Maria Mercedes."

"No. *Soy* Maria Soledad."

"Of course. And here come the others. Hello, Maria Remédios."

"Hello, teacher. I am Maria Mercedes."

"Oh yes. And here is Maria Rosário. Am I right?"

"Me Maria Remédios."

"Yes, yes, right. Hello. What is your name?"

"Maria Rosário. You remember they. Why you no remember I?"

"I'm sorry."

"Pendejo!"

"And you, of course, are Mili."

"You got it." Short straight blonde hair with four inches of black Indian roots.

"From Philadelphia."

"Right on. Mili from Philly."

"You know, of course, that you don't have to stay, Mili."

"I'll stay. I get off on these bimbos trying to talk English. And besides, you're cute."

Prettily arrayed now around the table. The black hair and dusky, still makeupless skin and the dressing gowns of pink and turquoise and red reminding one of licorice allsorts. The faces all watching me. And so I turned to the small blackboard which Doreen had had installed. And the women hollered and guffawed. Oh, most crudely. And cruelly. And thumped the table when I saw what was drawn expertly in white chalk. A cartoon of McKnight. With a big head in profile with this shaggy hair and beard and these glasses. And an itsy bitsy naked body. And an extremely long and stiff organ which I was using as a pointer to indicate a word above my head. Which said *englihs*.

So. They played get the teacher here too, did they? And Doreen had not advised me of this drawing, though she must have seen it. Which only meant another yard of shaft up her. Of that final harpoon. Called retribution.

Yet I was glad of this prank. Because now I could demonstrate my self-control.

I laughed I suppose a hollow laugh and said, "Yes. That is very good."

"Yes," said one of them. "Bery good. Bery big." And they howled some more.

"But there is a mistake," I said. And I fixed the *e* and the *h* and the *s*. And erased myself and my penis.

Now a horseshoe of more awake and more serious faces regarded me. Because we had finished with preliminary fencing. Had we not. And were ready to learn. Were we not.

There was a long, new piece of chalk. I picked it up and printed *What is this*? and *What is that?* and *It is a* ________

"What is this?" I said. "It is a pen. What is this? It is a table. What is that? Look. You have to look. Over there. It's a door for Christ sake. A door. A door. Got it?" Finally, I suppose to see what I was raving about, they sullenly looked.

"Okay. Good. Mili, help me. What is that?"

And even as I pointed at the door, it opened. And a woman came through it. And Mili said, "It is a whore."

And so it was. But the dressing gown of this one was made of silk with a pattern of green tigers stalking among gnarled orange trees. And neat curled hair on her. And lips painted dark red. And round black eyes and a petite nose. And around her neck hung a pair of miniature headphones with a cord leading down among the tigers and the trees to a pocket. She sat at the top of the horseshoe and smiled a self-satisfied half-smile. And half closed her eyes. And, looking at me, she shook her head as if the sight of me was only half to be believed.

I remembered her but not her name.

"What is your name?" I asked.

"Nayng?"

"Name. What is your name."

"Nayng?"

"*Cómo se llama*?"

"Ángeles."

Ah yes. How could I have forgotten. Maria of the Angels. Those overbright eyes, that irrelevant smile. Stoned, just like last time.

"Ángeles, you have come late to your English lesson. But that is good. And there is a feverish light in your big busy eyes, suggesting recent sad and stupid goings on. Which is also good. Because both of these things, especially the latter, strain my self-control. And that is precisely what I want right now. To be tested."

"Man, I dig this English lesson."

"Shut up, Mili."

"I thought you wanted to be tested."

"Just shut up. You shouldn't even be here. So don't butt in, okay?"

"Okay. But don't ask me to help you no more."

"Fine."

"About what's this and what's that."

"Deal."

"It's a pen and it's a whore and like that."

I waited. She was quiet. I cut my losses with *What is this*, and slid into vocabulary review.

"Eat," I said. And mimed sticking something in my mouth.

"Eat," they chimed out. Fingers fluttering around open lips.

"Suck," said someone. Rowdy laughs and mighty smackings of table. Professional vocabulary. I should have been ready for it.

"Testing, testing."

"Mili, get out."

"Fuck you. I live here."

"Yeah, right. And when Doreen throws you out on your ass? Should I call her?"

"Cocksucker."

The woman recognized the word. Some of them repeated it now. Maria Soledad — I think — repeated it twice and also copied Mili's gesture of the middle finger.

But I only smiled. And held up my own middle finger. And jerked it upward at each of them in turn and as I did so looked into each pair of black impudent eyes. And when I got to Mili I saw around her eyes crinkle lines of laughter.

"Man, that's cool. But, hey, don't get so steamed."

"Steamed? My word. Did you think I was steamed? Gracious, no. I hope I haven't given the wrong impression. I couldn't be more pleased. In fact I want to thank you all. For giving me yet another opportunity to demonstrate my self-control."

I could barely hear myself over the din of Spanish gabbling, the other women having lost interest in me completely. Maria Lourdes — I think — had opened her gown, and they were exclaiming and grimacing about a thick welt that ran down the inside of her left breast.

"Now, you see?" I said. "You see what happens? When you stop fighting? When you just give up and lie down and spread your legs? It's your own fault, goddamn you. If someone takes a belt to you. I don't feel sorry for you. Not one bit. If you don't have the balls to spit in their face. Man, I'd kill myself before I let someone do that to me."

Lourdes closed her gown. Mili got up from the table and walked around toward the door through which they had entered. I noticed now that she had a severe limp.

"Fine, don't listen," I said. "Don't learn English. Don't listen to McKnight. He's got nothing to teach you. He's just a starry-eyed idealist. Well, fine, but I'm not actually the one who's going to be seeing stars. There are certain people, ladies, who are going to be seeing super fucking novas. Whole universes of them. As brains turn to phosphorescent shit. Under relentless blows from the rangitang. I am not talking bruised tits here. Go ahead and bend over and let them shove barb wire up you. But keep one eye on the little schoolteacher."

I stopped. Having heard myself at last. Ranting again. And saw that they were all now quiet. Staring at me. Concerned for their English teacher. The bitches, how dare they! I almost started again. But Mili was standing in the doorway, deeply angered.

"Everyone is a whore, man. Even you."

There was silence. Until the other door opened. Doreen smiling uncertainly there in her pink dress. A vast raspberry sherbet that spoke to me in melting Southern tones. "Lord, this does sound like one exciting English lesson." And uncertainly giggled. Then the maid entered and went to Doreen and whispered something and left. Doreen's hand went up to touch her hair. With an excited glow she bent over Maria de los Ángeles and whispered.

Maria de los Ángeles snapped upright and gave a joyous shriek.

"Charlie!"

With the green tigers writhing and leaping she ran past me in a blast of perfume. I heard her bare feet thumping madly up some stairs.

The women traded mischievous looks. And they all whispered, as if this *putaria* were suddenly church.

"El presidente."

"Es el presidente."

"El presidente está aqui."

"Si, sí, es el presidente."

Doreen left.

My bowels turned liquid, I clenched my sphincter. My fingertips tingled. The women became earnest and well behaved. So that I would not have to talk I gave them an inane grammar game, and they took their turns. As I tried to think. I rubbed my soaked palms again and again on my sports coat. Afraid of fainting, I leaned on the table. And yet I could proceed no further than a single thought.

He's here.

When half an hour had passed, the women wanted to go to brush their teeth and apply makeup. At that point I experienced a second thought: The Naked Dancing Thing had got wind of me again.

And on my left shoulder I felt a tap.

I turned.

It was Filadelfo.

He wore a blue suit and a black tie. His wavy hair was

coarser than I remembered. A restrained amusement there in the black narrowed eyes.

"Venga conmigo, señor. El presidente quiere ver-lo."

Come with me, sir. The President wants to see you.

I followed him back along the hall and up some stairs.

We came out onto a narrow gallery. It ran around two sides of the large gloomy room. There at the far end Jesus and his cross glowed sadly. And there below in an orange vinyl chair, sat Mili. Wall lamps here along the gallery faintly lit the salon below. I could make out on one of Mili's feet an enormous black shoe.

Filadelfo pushed open a door. I went through it. It closed behind me.

A large bedroom. Like a cheap hotel room where one was forced to stay for a month. A floor of uneven unpainted boards. At the far end a window with closed curtains of some purple and blue pattern. Again the right-hand wall a brown painted wardrobe missing a handle. Opposite it against the left-hand wall a four-dollar wooden table from El Marin market, like mine, unpainted. Upon that table a small television, off. Scattered audio cassettes. Scattered cosmetics. A hand mirror. A bottle of Johnny Walker Scotch, two-thirds full. Two plain glasses. A pistol. And a crystal bowl, also two-thirds full. Of white powder.

The smell of sweat and of perfume.

Maria de los Ángeles slouched on an El Marin chair at her El Marin table, facing a mirror. The tiger robe hung all open, and her two hands rested loose on her crotch. Hair wild in wings and curlicues. Red lips moving not to greet her teacher, but to sing in a discordant voice along with what she must have been hearing through her earphones.

A Sinatra song. God help me. El Blue Eyes plays Esperanza. I felt for a few seconds that Charlie had beaten me already, even though he was doing nothing but sitting on the edge of the bed just to my right, barefoot in wrinkled military fatigues, looking at me as I looked at Maria de los Ángeles. She opened her eyes, leaned forward, with a scarlet fingernail nicked a speck of cocaine, snorted it, stiffened, pressed hands hard against breasts. Hissed like an adder. Smiled very prettily. Sank slowly back into her slouch. And sang about New York, New York.

As Charlie said in English, "I am coming here for to stop being the president for a while."

I said nothing.

"Drink?"

I nodded.

"*Tragos*," said Charlie.

Maria de los Ángeles lifted one earphone.

"*Tragos*," he said again.

She poured Scotch and brought the glasses. Breasts and belly and bush. All bare. Eyes like oiled buttons of coal. Eager tight smile. "What ees thees!" she shouted. "Ees a me!" Then sat again.

Charlie and I clinked glasses. He said, "To be just a soldier again. In the bed with a *puta*. She never talks about the government and she never wants nothing."

"Except a bowl of cocaine."

"*Exacto*. You don't never go to the *putas?*"

"No."

"You should. It is right for a man."

I moved away toward the middle of the room and kept my back to him. I was glad there was no other chair — I wanted to remain on my feet.

"Especially for a man who is living alone," he said.

"Ah."

"Montserrat told me."

"Really?"

"A man has to fuck."

"To fuck."

"Someone."

There to the left of the cut-glass bowl. The pistol. A snub-nosed revolver pointing at the wall. So real and full of weight it looked, lying next to the pale drug. It would of course be loaded.

"She is yours alone, then," I said.

"To who you are referring?"

I turned to face him, tried a smile, nodded toward the woman. For an instant he looked relieved. He shrugged. Small folds of skin hung under his jaw. He drained his scotch. I drained mine.

"You will stay?" he said.

"What — here?"

"In this country. At the American School. Next year."

"Yes. I have decided to stay. You asked me to, remember? You said you needed men like me in this shit-hole."

"It is not a shit-hole now. Because I am president now."

"I see."

"That is a joke."

"Ah. Funny."

"Otro?"

"Thank you. I'll help myself." Over to the table. A tinny overspill trickled from the earphones. I did not look down at her snatch. For very long. I poured Scotch, offered the bottle toward Charlie, he shook his head. I set the bottle down and did not stare at the pistol. For very long.

I leaned back against the table.

Maria de los Ángeles sang.

"If I can make a tear, I can make it . . ."

"Anywhere," I sang softly with her for some reason. Losing just that first jot of control.

"I am tired," said Charlie. "Tired already of being the president. So I am coming here for to stop being the president for a while. And still I am tired. Are you tired, Señor McKnight?"

"No."

"You are filled with the energy."

"Always."

"To teach the English to the *putas*. For the *Ballena*."

"Yes."

"How is it that she is so fat?"

"A mystery, Mr. President."

"A mystery. *Exacto*. Like El Dorado."

"You remember."

"She was much affected."

"I'm sorry — to whom are you referring?"

There must have been a new song on Maria de los Ángeles' tape. She sang about doubt, about spitting it out . . ."

"Montserrat. My daughter. She was much affected."

"Ah. Yes, I seem to remember."

"Do you?"

"Yes."

"Much affected. You are still believing in El Dorado?"

"Yes."

"Human possibilities."

"Yes."

"Morality."

"That's part of it."

"Part of it?"

"Yes."

He looked up now. On his face a curious smile. "And the weakness of men. Is that part of it? Is the weakness of men a part of El Dorado?"

"I don't think so. No."

"La venganza?"

"No. No revenge."

He sighed. Contemplated the floor.

"Just retribution," I said. He seemed not to hear me.

The bed around him was a tangle of yellow sheet and of grey blanket, upon which I made out the design of a lion's head. I could see beside his hip a dark wool eye and white tooth. But that thing there in the middle of the bed was not part of the design. It was a knife sheath and the handle of the dagger it contained.

Ángeles sang about the end being near, about a final curtain. Her diction perfect suddenly, clear and chilling as a snow-fed creek in the Cariboo.

I drained the Scotch and, reaching behind me, set the glass down. Two knuckles touched the handle of the gun. I gave it a tap. The gun did not budge. Heavy. Real.

"Have you sold the cocaine yet?" I said.

He did not look at me, but there emerged around his eyes the hint of a mocking smile. "Soon," he said.

"I trusted you."

"I know. Thank you for that letter. You and the policeman, you were help me."

"My son is a drug addict."

He shrugged. "The world it is full of weaklings."

Something surged in my chest. I felt wonderful, released. The room went red around the edges.

He lifted his glass in tribute. "To the weaklings," he said.

Then I was standing not by the table but over Charlie. The pistol was pressing against the middle of his forehead, making a white circle in the skin. I was shouting things about the whirlwind.

But Charlie's eyes were fixed on mine. And he was laughing.

Something collapsed then. As if my heart were suddenly wet sand, and pieces were falling off it. I pointed the gun aside and pulled the trigger.

Click.

He laughed harder.

I pulled the trigger again. *Click.* And *click.*

"Señor McKnight," he said, "of course I know that your son is a drug addict. It was not hard to find out. But this is so bad. That you are wanting murder the president." He dropped his glass, reached around and took the knife sheath and slid the knife out.

I took two steps back.

He stood, barefoot, slightly crouched, holding the knife forward and low, at belly level.

"You fucked my daughter."

I took another step backward. I felt the urge to make a joke. But I only shrugged.

"You ruined my princess."

Then he was rushing toward me with his arm swept back to drive the blade in, and I was yelling and blindly backpedalling as Maria de los Ángeles bleated about doing it her way. I slammed into the table and groped behind me for something with which I might defend myself. My left hand fell on the edge of some glass object. I bellowed and swung it. The bowl grazed Charlie's shoulder, ricocheted from the wall and shattered against the brass doorknob. But most of the powder, spraying free, caught him full in the face. The dagger spun from his hand. He cried out and clasped his hands to his eyes.

"Ai!" shouted the woman. *"La coca!"*

I pushed out viciously, discovering as I did so that I still held the useless pistol. Charlie stumbled backward and thumped down hard on his ass. Upon a shard of rebounded glass, I think, for he screamed again.

I ran for the door. But as I reached it it swung open. Filadelfo stood there, looking troubled. His hand was inside his suit jacket. But before he could produce his weapon, I thrust mine toward his face. "No," he said, and sprang backward. His shoes shot up like startled crows as he flipped over the railing. When I heard his crash and Mili's screech I was already bounding down the stairs.

"Out of my way!" Canadian manners gone. Along with all Spanish words. As I collided at the foot of the stairs with a white uniform. I was outside and down the steps before I got free of her, leaving her sprawled with her linen in a border of geraniums. I dropped the gun. Tore open the gate. A street light was on above an anonymous black Mercedes. Two soldiers on guard, who for some reason saluted as I wheeled onto the sidewalk. At the end of the block I took the corner full out. But glanced back. Soldier looking down at his machine gun. Sheet hanging from it.

So. Fucked for real this time. Too late now to say Pass the pretzels. Or, Would you be so kind. As to allow me to remain alive. Across Reforma flying on a long diagonal. And who is this dark shape? Pushing himself so slowly across the street on his hip. Up comes the cupped hand, always ready for alms, God bless him. But this was no time for philanthropy. And no time to relinquish one's diagonal. I used to run the hurdles in high school. "*Por favor*," he said. I cleared him by three feet. Leaving him there with his hand extended as two lightless drag-racing buses bore down upon him. A musical horn rang out. Colonel Bogie.

In the middle of Parque Colón I stopped to catch my breath. And I realized where I was headed. My apartment. Pure stupid instinct. Goodbye, stuff. Blowgun, watch out for termites. Miles, Mingus, Monk, it's been real. Portrait, I'll be back for you some day. Hang on to that little bright dream.

On Ruipamba an early motorcycle hurtled past with a hollow snarl. All around, the black indifference of the mountains. I saw headlights bumping across the grass, and a spotlight darting. I jogged out of the park.

"Flossie?"

"*Sí. Quién es?*"

"It's Mac. Can you hear me? I'm calling from a *taberna*."

"Barely. What's up?"

"I'm calling to say I won't be in on Monday."

"Okay. Good of you to let me know. Are you sick?"

"Not exactly. Actually, I won't be in on Tuesday, either. In fact I don't think you'll see me again. Ever."

"What's that? I missed that last part. Did you say liver? Don't tell me you've got hepatitis!"

"You can keep my posters of literary terms. Goodbye. Remember me."

For hours I walked residential streets at random. The streets were named after countries, then dates, then famous dead Indians. Three times the *escuadrón volante* slowly crossed an intersection two or three blocks ahead of me. The flying squad. A new armoured pickup truck loaded with a dozen National Policemen. Looking for the Canadian who tried to murder the president.

In bárrio Santa Rosa, outside a dim *taberna* I got into a taxi.

"Schoolteacher," said the driver in Spanish, "didn't my cousin Arturo tell you not to come to Santa Rosa after midnight?"

"Take me to the bus station."

"You want to buy this taxi? I am selling it for him."

"How much?"

"For the taxi?"

"To take me to the bus station."

"For a friend of my cousin, nothing. He has a good job now. Did you know? In Cañajula. No more *pum! pum!*"

Half a block from the bus station fence I told him to wait. I dropped a thousand-dorado bill onto the front seat, then another. He said, "But Arturo's wife, *hombre!* That Elena. Such tits she has. I could fuck her until the dead stand up and salute the flag." Then he fell asleep and snored. On the car radio a woman sang sad mountain songs in a sweet voice. I remained in the backseat and watched for soldiers or police. None came. When I could distinguish the eastern mountains from the sky behind them I left the cab.

Only one bus line, Flota Oriente, was open. There was a blackboard with a list of towns I did not know.

"Pilajualli," I said.

"*Por que, patrón?* There is nothing at Pilajualli. It is just the end of the line."

I shrugged. The man shook his head and slid the passenger list toward me. There were no names on it yet. In a space designating a backseat I scrawled my illegible adiós and pseudonym. Al Dorado.

7

Everready, Aspirina and a Proper Goodbye

Everyone woke at the summit at dawn with the windows misted and babies crying from the cold. The bus stopped, and the driver took a collection in his baseball cap. I dropped a hundred-dorado bill into it, to tilt his prayer in my direction. I saw him dump the money into a container at a roadside shrine, and cross himself. Beyond him a valley of windblown grass. Then black arthritic fists of mountain. Then the sky. No, not the sky. The icy face of Chinguráhua.

We started down. Chatter now among this busload of Indians, and food coming out of bags. The driver slapped home a *cúmbia* tape with plenty of cowbell, as we swung around a tight curve. Then another curve. And I groaned and looked a mile down to a worm of river. Then I looked east, to the sun rising over lower mountains crusted with jungle. That was where I was going, please. Somewhere down there. Should have gotten a bottle at that *taberna* last night. The preferable condition in which to flee for your life down the only road toward the eastern jungle was blind drunk.

Angus McKnight, alias Anguish McFright, take one more

breath of this stuffy bus air tainted with gasoline and infant puke. Before they flag down the bus. And haul you out shitting your pants. And shoot you. And throw you over the edge. Now take one more breath.

Of course I had not slept. I knew there were routine checks just outside the city. But as I hunched down below the window a soldier had waved us through the military checkpoint. And further on, just before the asphalt ran out, a National Policeman had accepted without a second glance the driver's waybill and customary bribe. Praise the legendary inefficiency of the armed forces, oh praise it.

At the lip of the gorge now, tiny bamboo fronds. And soon on the mountainside opposite, that green dense cover, and occasional higher trees with silver leaves. Others in orange or purple flower. As we braked and swung and honked and braked around turn after hairpin turn. And windows came down. And I took my jacket off. And climbed over the small man beside me, and carefully and with soothing sounds over the fighting-rooster he stroked in his lap. I went to the front, where men were standing and passing a bottle.

"*Buenas dias, señores,*" I said.

"*Buenas, gringo,*" said the owner of the bottle, a big non-Indian with slicked hair. "Where are you going?"

"Pilajualli."

"You are a friend of Mauro?"

"No."

"Then you must be a friend of Mauro's pig. Unless Pilajualli has grown since I was last there." He brayed aggressively toward the other two men who stood swaying in our group, and they laughed too, more shyly. Indians all in white.

I said, "No, but I have tipped a glass or two with his dog."

The Indians giggled, then laughed outright. But the bottle owner only looked away. At the taller bamboo, the overgrown mountainsides, the river now close below. As the bottle went round, passing me by.

"Yes," he said, "I have heard that gringos like to fuck dogs. Would you like a drink, gringo?"

To accept his bottle I had to accept his insult. I took the bottle, drank. *Aguardiente*: raw corn liquor like sandpaper soaked in turpentine. I waited for the bottle to come round again. Behind the feet of the bottle owner stood four plastic jerricans. From the open top of one of them and through the firewall ran a flexible fuel line. We were running with no gas tank. I saw the source of the gasoline smell — the floor mat was soaked. I drank again and went back to my seat.

"Woof, woof," I heard behind me.

The rooster pecked the back of my hand.

The river we were following was the Dulce. I had travelled this way before with Dickie Pendergast, to ogle, as a newcomer must, the Oriente. Jungle rivers, reformed headhunters and so forth. But after proceeding level with the river for an hour the bus now turned off, racketed across a plank bridge and continued south on a narrower but straighter road.

We came to a village. Colourless houses of flattened bamboo. Mud everywhere, although the sky was blue. Wet, heavy heat. Half the people left the bus. While the driver refilled his jerricans I found a *tienda*. Did not bother to wake the proprietor, who was sleeping in a reclining lawn chair behind the counter. In gloom and dust I located the *aguardiente*. Took two pint bottles. Dropped a bill onto the proprietor's sweating belly.

Maybe ten people remained. We travelled for another hour, the road descending gradually. The gas fumes had long since stopped making me nauseous. Now and then we passed at the roadside a weathered board bearing a row of pineapples. More often a cluster of vultures tucking into dead potluck. When this finally pricked my appetite I knew I had fallen into the spirit of the place.

We pulled off at an eatery, which is to say a clearing, mud again, with two ulcerated dogs sniffing a black bitch. One naked toddler playing with a cigarette butt. And a smoking brazier tended by a fed-up looking woman in a sweat-blotched dress. I bought one of her miniature meat shish kebabs, washed it down with *aguardiente*.

Then a bus stopped, headed in the other direction. *Esperanza*, it said. Hope. A man got off with a bag of groceries and headed down a trail into the forest.

Then a brown pickup pulled in, and three soldiers climbed out of the back. They stretched, spat and clustered around the brazier.

The man with the rooster was walking back to the bus. I fell in beside him, ducked low, pretended to be brushing something from my knee. I sat at the very back and watched the soldiers through the grimy bottom of a window. At the feet of one of the soldiers the black bitch, pretending to sniff something in the mud, let one of the dogs mount her. The copulating pair vibrated up against the soldier's leg. He stepped back, held his shish kebab between his teeth and swung his rifle off his shoulder. *"Mira,"* he said around the meat. Watch this. Hardly aiming, he shot the male. The bitch leapt away splaylegged, dragging behind her the still linked body of the male. The soldiers danced and roared. At the edge of the clearing another soldier shot the female.

The toddler howled. The woman stood paralysed. The passengers hastily boarded, and the driver started the engine.

We rolled ten feet and stalled. There was a loud pop. The front of the bus burst into flames.

In seconds, like a well-drilled team, we were out the windows. Standing in the mud. Gaping at each other. Even a fat woman with a baby. There were scrapes, sprained ankles, torn shirts and dresses, but everyone was safe. Only the gamecock lost. Feet tied together, he had flapped into the forest. And we all backed away from the burning bus. Plenty of black smoke rolling upwards. On the side of the bus there was a painting of Mighty Mouse, winging onward. But now bubbling. And now fading to black scorch. As the owner of the rooster crashed around in the bush. And the driver walked quickly back and forth across the clearing, hitting himself on the chest. The passengers began to attend to scrapes and rips and ankles, and to lament the loss of what had been left on the bus. One of my bottles there. I did a small lament. But the other was here, in the pocket of my sports coat, which had tumbled with me out the window. From the door of the bus roared a great horn of flame. We all backpedalled. I bumped into someone and turned, polite Canadian, to beg pardon. It was a soldier. He held out his hand and said, "*Pasaporte*."

His rifle still at the ready. Vague smell on him of gunpowder. It was he who had shot the male.

I said, "*Mi pasaporte está en el carro*." My passport is in the bus. I gestured toward the blackening form of the superrodent. He squinted a long and suspicious squint, then went to confer with his sergeant.

And, *patrón*, I walked away. Heart going thudbump. Coolly past the burning bus. Sedately across the road. Into the trees. And then I ran like stink.

A path of bare earth. Only occasional pools of mud to sully the pounding brogues. Only occasionally thorn palms to snatch at the flying sports coat. Hightailing it down this trail God knows where, past this clearing and bamboo house with chickens flying up, and the hurdles again over a black pig. And on down a further path more sloping and dangerous with roots. And there ahead, spaces in the bush. A river. Narrow pebbled beach. A long dugout canoe. A person setting into the canoe a bag of groceries.

It was the man I had seen getting off the other bus. He was tall for an Indian, and bony. His T-shirt said *University of Iowa Necking Team*. As I panted, he goggled. But when I plucked from my wallet a five-thousand-dorado bill and stuffed it into his T-shirt pocket his hand shot out. I shook it.

"Can I be of some help?" he said in excellent Spanish.

"Yes," I said. "You can."

"My name is Everready."

"My name is Al. Let's go."

If the seats were softer, and if a person were anything besides a ruined and abject criminal, this river travel would be splendid. The skimming peace. Wet furnace air now soothing, and the cool flecks of spray. The hum of the outboard reassuring. One's man, Everready, stalwart there at the stern. Bliss.

No trucks of soldiers here, because no roads here, and we had so far passed only one other powered canoe and a half-dozen poled in the shallows. I began to wonder who lived back there, up those infrequent paths that led from the water, beyond the beached canoes and fringes of sugarcane. Was there room in their world for a blighted gringo?

We were not entirely out of the mountains yet. Near or distant there were rough hills. Endless broadleaf trees and creeper. Rare smudges of purple or orange flower. Sporadic thick-limbed giants dripping vines. A sense of sleep upon it all. Before we had pushed off, Everready had told me this was the Rio Colorado.

"And where does it go?" I had asked.

"Into the Zacutá."

"And the Zacutá?"

"Into the Amazonas."

"Brazil."

"*Exacto.*"

"Can you take me to the Amazonas?"

"How many of these have you got?" He tapped his shirt pocket and the five thousand.

"No more. I have two thousand dorados."

"You had better keep your two thousand. I can take you to Tigre. There I can get some gasoline to come back. And maybe some cargo."

"What's at Tigre?"

He shrugged, gestured at the trees, the water.

The river was wide but shallow. Everready stood over his motor, guiding us now in midstream, now a yard from the bank, wherever the deep water led. I had my sports coat over my head — it excluded the sun but not the breeze. But soon the pleasure of river travel passed. Charlie's a general, man. You think he doesn't know this country? You think he doesn't know how to pluck you out of this creek like a tadpole? Depressed now, I knew what was waiting for me at Tigre. Or around that next bend. I had lost my remaining bottle when I hurdled the pig. What a bloody ignorant place to park a pig.

But still I had my book. In my coat cave, sunlight dazzled on the colour plates, the gold men, the gold women. I turned to the photograph of Evelyn that I kept between the pages. I said, "Ev, I am sorry that this is what it has all come to. I owed it to you to make things turn out better." But her smile did not alter, fixed there in the past, young forever. I lifted her photograph away, and underneath was one of Jeff. I had taken this only three years ago. We had ferried together back to the Gulf Island. But the beach was now all Coppertone and ghetto blasters. We could not locate the sandstone caves where he had searched for treasure. In the picture he leaned against an arbutus tree, with his black hair hanging to his shoulders. He was so thin in his singlet and shorts, already well-addicted.

Silence.

The motor had died.

Everready gave the starter cord a few yanks, then bent for his pole. The only sound now the river's running. Then far off a dog barked. As we slowed, the heat came down like a blow.

Everready steered us as we drifted. Soon we came to a sprawling beach of white stones. I helped him pull the canoe up, and he tied it to the root of a washed-up balsa tree. He carried the motor on his shoulder, and in his hand a toolkit. I carried the groceries and a can of gas and my coat.

The sinking sun threw confusing shadows among the stones. We panted and stumbled.

"We would not have made it to Tigre anyway," he said. "We will stay here tonight. This is my cousin's place. Aspirina."

Up a sandy bank and beyond some bushes was a small house on poles. Also, shaded by banana plants, a large cage of rusted screen. Inside this cage a woman stood among a blizzard of wings. As they fluttered between perches the birds seemed to streak the moist air with colour.

We went up a notched log into her house.

A plain room missing one outer wall. A platform bed with thin mattress. On the wall a single magazine photo: Princess Di, in white. On the floor, many aluminum pots. She came in and, without saying a thing, served us. *Chicha*. A taste like beer and like yogurt. Mere yucca chewed and spat by Aspirina and mixed with river water and left for a week. Oh humble *chicha* full of chunks, the worst of drinks, the best of drunks. Lowly *chicha* steamrollered me that day like Bellows had never done. Escape I craved and escape I found. As Aspirina squatted by her pots and refilled our cups.

"I am indebted to you, Everready. More than indebted. And to your beautiful cousin. Will you thank her for me? For this very refreshing hospitality. And will she not have a drink with us?"

He said something in Quíchua or Jívaro or Waorani. She replied in a low velvety voice and looked away and smiled with her eyes.

"She says you honour her house. She will not take *chicha* now, but may she refill your cup?"

"Too kind, too kind. Now tell me, Everready, how did you come by your wonderful name?"

"It was given to me by my father who, like you, señor, was a man of noble words. He was called Chevrolet."

"Ah."

"He showed the people of these parts how to find names in the *tienda* of Doña Piedad in Puerto Asunción." He pushed the plastic bag of groceries across to Aspirina and set to dismantling his motor.

I leaned back on the mattress and thought about my

favourite painter, Gauguin. His life in the South Pacific.

"Something of a romantic, your father? Waorani?"

"No. He came up the river from Brazil. Our family name is Bizarro. He was looking for the city of gold."

"In the name of God, Everready, is it thus? I too am a seeker after the golden city."

"Was it the golden city you were seeking when you came running down that path like a hunted rabbit?"

Aspirina refilled my cup. Then she went through the groceries. Rice. Salt. Family Size Coke. Sugar. Lard. Flour. Powdered milk. Instant coffee. Potato chips, which she now ripped open with strong teeth. White yucca grinders. And held out to me. Something glad and easy in her manner. Loose white cotton blouse, and skirt of Gauguin colours. A touch of red and some wave in the unbound hair. But strange. Green eyes.

"Never mind," said Everready. "Here we know which questions not to ask."

Aspirina went around and out to another part of the house, a sort of balcony. I took more *chicha*. And tripped with negligence and grace down the notched log. Cooler now, and such peace in the air. The sun parked there on the dark sierra. No glare now on the beach of stones, but a gold light that made me shiver. I went and stood at her cage. Why did those trapped birds seem so chipper? Their song like cinnamon and ice. The forest too now full of whistle and screech, and flocks of parrots flying out and across the river.

Almost dark as I climbed back up the log. I smelled cooking. Everready was reassembling his motor. We ate by the light of a candle. A small fish each. Rice. A fried plantain.

Aspirina took the dishes away.

The food had made me sober and shy. But I asked.

"Your cousin. She lives here alone?"

He was sitting on the floor, against a wall. The candle made pronged shadows on his face. As he nodded, the shadows squirmed. "It is thus."

"No husband?"

"*Viuda.*" Widow. "Her husband, Nabisco, he was working over at La Providencia. One day he fell into the rock crusher."

"No children?"

"*Los pájaros.*" The birds.

"She sells them?"

"And the *chicha,*" he said.

"She has had a hard life. How is it that she seems so content?"

He shrugged.

"Everready."

"Speak."

"Everready, what if I wanted to stay?"

"Ah, that."

"Would it be possible?"

His long look at me. Candle glinting in his black eyes.

I said, "I'm sorry. I suppose it's not appropriate. I'll ask her myself. Sign language."

I saw myself making signs and thought that was funny and laughed, and Everready also laughed. At what?

"Señor," he said, "my cousin is a witch."

Another long look at me. Then narrowed eyes and a chilling smile. The hair on my arms stood up.

He said, "How do you think she catches the birds?"

A lightning bug dove into the candle flame. Fell onto its back with a bang.

"Señor, she will drink the fire of your substance. Every drop."

I glanced at his outboard. Ready, shipshape. Jesus, would I ever find rest? The fire of my substance. A poet yet. Why was I so ready to believe him? Because of that sense of something relentless lapping at my stubborn glimmer these many years?

I said, "Where did your father look for El Dorado?"

"Everywhere he went."

"And what happened? Finally."

"He died, señor. A soldier shot him. From the river. To win a bet."

I bent toward the *chicha*. But the sight of the aluminum pots now made me sick.

I said, "Where did they kill him?"

He gestured. "Out there. On the white stones."

I slept on the mattress. Everready on the floor. Aspirina off somewhere. I dreamt about Evelyn, about trying to touch her and I couldn't. Then I dreamt about Jeff, who shook his head and turned his back on me and walked away.

No chance to sleep after first light, with those caged finches hollering bloody murder. It was cool. I put on my sports coat, picked up the can of gas and went down the log. The rocks seemed to snatch at my feet. I slipped, stumbled, banged the gas can, swore. Something was pulling me off balance. Frustrated, I stopped and reached for the bottle in my pocket. Then I remembered it was not there. But it was. Next to my book. Not her *chicha* either, but *aguardiente*. Real liquor. The witch had gifted me. I spun the top off, sniffed, considered. If I accepted her gift, did I accept her curse? All around me, the stones, dull and difficult, a pain I could do without. Man, I didn't need this. Who knows what I would have to face at Tigre. Or around the next bend. Fuck it. I drank. I looked back and saw Everready coming with his motor. Then I went on. With negligence now and with grace. In the footsteps of Chevrolet Bizarro.

An oppressive day on the river. Vancouver clouds had come south to piss on me this last day of my life. Everready tapped me on the shoulder and with his greasy hand offered me a bun. With mine smelling of gasoline, I took the bun and ate it with Aspirina's hootch.

We kept going east. The river became deeper, wider, slower. We passed not a single other craft. There were no more fringes of cane. Soon the motor's drone was like a toothache at the back of my head, and my arse was sore. I wore my sports coat even though it made me hot. I had transferred the book to the inside pocket, where it sort of covered my heart and might interfere with the eventual bullet.

Where was this Tigre? The bun had not gone far. I wanted food and I wanted off the river. Maybe the soldier who had shot Chevrolet still cruised the Colorado, a grizzled *capitán* now, and wizard at potting human beings for bets.

The hills had retreated from the river, and trees and vegetation made a ragged barrier along either bank. Gliding near the south shore, we passed the mouth of a tributary. It curved away into the forest. Black, piranha-infested water up in there, the air humming with malaria. Headshrinkers too, maybe.

Something in a low tree ahead there over the water. A dark twined mass. I swallowed the last of Aspirina's hootch, and as we passed I tossed the bottle up into the branches. I looked back and saw the creature uncoil, droop and slide into the water.

I felt the shits, but at least I was stewed. I slipped off the seat and lay on the canoe's bottom in an inch of water. It started to rain. Cool drops hitting my face. I thought of Montserrat. That scene with her. The dust storm and my rage and flipping the coin. Bad. Maybe I didn't love her, but still she deserved a decent goodbye. I could remember something better, a better goodbye. I smiled up into the rain. Yes — that time. On my back on my living room floor, with bed pillow under my bottom and Montserrat astride. Obliging child, delighted to do the work. Both of us tipsy on spud juice.

"Let's fuck and talk," she said, as her nipples described spirals between us. "Tell me again what is a moose." Damn, I will miss her.

"Let's see. There once was a sasquatch called Bruce. Who put some stilts up his caboose. On his head wenna TV antenna. He cried, I've invented the moose."

"Is it funny?"

"Maybe not. Maybe just stupid."

"What is a sasquatch?"

"Like a rangitang."

"What are stilts?"

"Silts are *zancos*."

"What is a caboose?"

"This is your caboose."

"Squeeze my caboose. Squeeze both cabooses."

"Let's stop for a minute, okay?"

"Oh please. Put it in again."

"Soon. But first an interlude."

"What is an interlude? Something very dirty?"

"Oh, you can't imagine."

I tumbled her carefully off, and we set about inventing interludes. For example, the interlude-while-reading-excerpts-from Marco-Cadiz'-essay-on-the-*Lovesong of J. Alfred Prufrock*. The parquet under us was slippery with sweat, and in Montserrat's fingers the ink of the son of the cheese magnate seeped and smudged. "'J. Alfred Prufrock,'" she read, panting as I encouraged her, "'is a lonely man. Probably he is shy, he does not dare to eat a peach. He is afraid of women but he has heard the mermaids singing.' *Madre de Dios*, McKnight, put it in, put it in!"

I did, and the mermaids sang to me and to Montserrat, and soon we drowned together with a bellow and a screech, and when we could move we discovered we had ravaged Marco's essay beyond recognition.

Into the tape player I slipped a concerto by Mozart. We lay cuddled on the floor, wrapped in an Indian shawl.

"Amazing," I whispered, "it looks like we've done it."

"What have we done, McKnight?"

"Invented new lives. Of sex and safety."

"And happiness."

"Same thing."

"Do we have new histories then?"

"We do."

"What are they?"

"They are the histories of the golden man and the golden woman."

"Ai, that is so esplendid. Why are we whispering?"

"So our old lives don't hear us. Shh."

She was drifting off. I drifted too. Peace rolled like a slow deep river through the cells of McKnight. The only other time I had felt like this was that time I had let Jeff shoot me up.

I thought at first it was a giant bird, and hollered. Then I bailed out of the canoe. Straight up off my back and over the side. Half the Rio Colorado up my nose. A watery glimpse of Everready looking down at me with his mouth open. Submerged boulders slipped under my churning brogues as I executed something less elegant than the butterfly stroke. The panic paddle, in fact. Then up a steep bank, tearing at fistfuls of grass and clay. I chanced a look through leaves as I charged into the trees. To see the back of Everready receding. And he did not turn his head, good man, excellent man, because he still knew which questions not to ask. The helicopter made a tight circle, then flew on downstream.

I stood alone in the green light of the rain forest. Dripping. As the two motors faded. Listening. And hearing soon only the river and the hiss of rain upon leaves. And my own still crashing heart. Pumping alcohol and survival and maybe some blood. But pumping scant hope now. Of ever having another chance to offer anyone a proper goodbye.

8

The Unexpurgated Bomba

My shoes squelched as I walked deeper among the trees, until I could not hear the river. No birds either. Only that hiss of rain. I was in a clearing among shoulder-high bushes. I looked up. Large drops fell into my face. Leaves above. Branches. Trunks. Vines. And above all that, invisible, a mile of rain. I looked down. On the leafy earth a parade of ants carried a squirming orange caterpillar home for lunch. Around the forward edge of the puddle at the centre of which were my feet about a hundred enormous ants had stationed themselves, facing me. Their pincers waited open. "Oh yeah?" I said, and brought one brogue then the other down thud upon them. Then I stepped away and did fifty push-ups. Then I went on through the trees.

Now listen, *patrón*, there is a way to walk through rain forest, necessitating a bull stance, rangitang attitude, and loud cursing to keep off the quietness and the jaguars and to intimidate the headhunters. While legions of starving mud fleas leap upon the ankles. But I knew that wild animals are in their way civilized. Those that live on the ground travel on trails. If I found a trail I would make a snare from my shoelaces and catch something please God smaller than a jaguar and eat it and wear the skin as a jockstrap and soon make my own blowgun and build a bamboo hut and ferment my own yucca and by Jesus survive. I tucked my pants into my socks, removed my sports coat and persisted, sweating, in my attitude and noise. And indeed I came upon a trail. A good wide one. But was it a game trail? For the branches did not close low over it, but at a height of seven or eight feet. Tracker McKnight bent to examine the trail more closely. The dirt of it was wet. And there was upon it the imprint of a running shoe.

I stepped right smart back into the bush. Heart crashing again. For suddenly the jungle seemed a metropolis. I listened. The rain stopped. The leaf ceiling turned bright with sunlight. A few birds called shrilly. No, this was no city, but there were people in it somewhere. Who would live in this forbidding tangle except the fabled headhunters?

I stood beside the trail with my useless coat dangling from my hand. Tiny flies coasted around my face. I could feel the mud fleas tearing at my socks. Sweat ran into my eyes and down my chest. I pondered. And I remembered something. A detail from another life, it seemed. And, in spite of the heat, I shivered.

Something large dropped down over the trail and swooped into the bush. A vulture. I stepped out onto the trail, squared my shoulders and headed in the direction the footprint pointed. With a croak the vulture bustled up and away. "Stick around," I said. "I may have supper for you."

I walked for ten minutes. The trail approached the river again. But then it forked, one branch continuing along the riverbank, the other leading at a right angle into the trees. The river still scared me. I took the other path.

After three or four minutes I rounded a bend and stopped, because ten paces ahead the forest simply ended. I saw grass and sunlight and sky. I left the trail, picked my way to the edge of the clearing and peeked out between leaves. As I expected, it was more than a clearing. It was an airstrip.

And there, squatting on the grass two hundred yards away, was a small cargo plane of khaki-green. And if those two men were headhunters, they were well reformed, apparently. They wore T-shirts and yes, maybe sneakers — I couldn't tell from that distance. They came out of the trees near the plane, each carrying upon his head a bundle wrapped in black plastic. Through its open cargo door they slid the bundles into the plane. Beside the plane a soldier watched them. His footwear I could make out. Regulation black stompers. And his shooter, a machine gun. The labourers turned and disappeared back into the trees.

That goodbye I had been working on? Now this? As if all of it — the incinerated bus, the river, the witch and the panic paddle — had been just a break between rounds in a weird wrestling match. Like maybe a deranged dwarf versus a giant octopus. The octopus had been chasing Wee Angus around the ring. Now perhaps it was Wee Angus' turn.

Something stirred off to my right. There at the mouth of the trail, forty feet away — a soldier. And I had been declaiming too, hadn't I, as I came along the trail. Things about the strangeness of fate and the absence of decent drinking establishments.

I threaded my way back to the trail and hurried along it toward the river.

Minutes later I was hunkered in a bed of hollyhocks. Studying the house itself. A splendid, sprawling house it was, of bamboo and screened windows and bougainvillea. And the detail from the other life did seem to fit.

What fun, *patrón!* Bogart is back. There was a lot of greenery, most of it wild. I slipped around the house, stopping behind a banana plant to watch a boy with a basin of laundry on his head go down the steps and toward the river. Some distance behind the house was a plainer building of unpainted boards. A man in a lab coat came out the door of it, which was guarded by another soldier, held a glass flask up to the light, then re-entered. Other outbuildings were scattered beyond the lab.

I made my way back to the trail leading to the airstrip. Here I would wait until dark, when the plane might be vulnerable. I knew this would be more than a parting shot. It would not be quite like slipping Charlie's own blade up his gizzard, but it would be enough for him to send every octopus in Amazonia after me. First to ruin his princess, then to piss in the tank of his cocaine transport. Maybe a single turd down the gas tank would be quieter. I paced and muttered, needing a drink. "Al? Angus? Shall we go for it? What do you think?"

"I think you'd better stop talking to yourself, Schoolteacher."

I turned, saw Tomás standing there. And smiled. At the persistence of irony, I suppose. And at his outfit: a blue seersucker suit with no shirt, a necklace of seeds and parrot feathers, a Panama with lilac band. And mesh Adidas tennis shoes. In his hand a machete. I made a move in the other direction. But now a soldier stood there, the one I had seen at the head of the trail, and his shooter was pointed at me. And now, around a bend behind Tomás, came Holly, known as Ivy. Sporting a thin white cotton blouse. And clingy white pants. And loose demeanour. And green eyes that looked very much at home here in the jungle. She draped herself upon Tomás and, over his shoulder, regarded me with fascination. And licked her lips.

"Success!" I shouted. "I have found them at last! The legendary giant rats of the Amazon!"

They put me in a room in a building of flattened bamboo and made me sit on the floor and tied my hands behind me to a post of slivery wood. "What is this," I said, "the Saturday matinée? Hands up whoever remembers Bomba the Jungle Boy. You think I'm worried? All I have to do is whistle for my chimpanzee."

Tomás stood about fifteen feet away, outlined against a window. "I can't remember, baby," he said to Holly. "Are these the ones with the curare on?" He had removed his suit jacket and was barechested. Trim, but the pecs sadly meagre. A quiver of darts hung at his side, and he held a blowgun of Jívaro design.

Holly leaned against a wall and watched. Unlike Tomás, she had not removed clothing, although several buttons of her blouse had mysteriously unfastened. Tomás inserted a dart. Aimed. I was sure he was sighting on my nose. I said to Holly, "Tell me. Ivy, is this what they meant up at the Arse when they said Tomás was famous for his blow jobs?"

He blew.

The dart lodged in the curls of my beard just below my left ear. I snorted, sneered, but could not speak.

Holly, I noticed, seemed aroused by this business. In those green eyes a kind of predatory desperation. Her thumbs were hooked in the waist of her pants. She slid a finger along to her crotch. And for a second massaged.

Outside there was a roar. Tomás pressed his face to the window screen and watched the plane taking off. So it would have been gone by tonight anyway. So much for my plans of poo-poo polka with the plane. Tomás loaded another dart.

He said, "You'll be pleased to know, Schoolteacher, that the school will be built over there. Right next to a permanent office for the Union of Indigenous Peoples. The clinic? Maybe over there in the shade of those trees."

I found my voice and said, "Wrong, Mr. Chairman. You should know by now where the clinic goes. The clinic goes the same place as the school and the office. Directly up your ass." The dart zipped through a strand of my hair and ticked into the wall. Holly watched me intently. Another button undone somehow. Those green excited eyes drinking in my fear.

Tomás composed himself. "What kind of fucking loser are you, man! Trying to kill Charlie. Screwing his daughter. But I'm not surprised. Once a jerk-off, always a jerk-off. Fucked up in Canada too, didn't you? Turned your son into a heroin addict. Poor kid, with a father like you, an alcoholic, what kind of chance did he have? Surprised I know your ugly little secrets? Charlie filled me in. Did you really think you could sneak around behind the President's back? What a fucking loser. You're just a menace, man. The world will be a better place without you. Oh, and thanks for dropping in on us. We've got people stopping all the canoes, but you saved us the trouble. I offered to put a bullet in your head, but Charlie wants to do it himself. I was just talking to him on the radio. He's coming down by helicopter in the morning. What — nothing to say? No smartass reply?"

The Chairman of the Union of Indigenous Peoples left, and with a last eerie glance in my direction Holly followed him out the door.

Trying to work the knots loose, I only managed to get a lot of slivers in my wrists. Nothing left to do, then, but to try to keep one's booze-staved mind clear by counting the rusty nailheads in the floor. And to hope. And to work out the volume of wet furnace air in this room. One thousand, seven hundred and sixty cubic feet. Three million, forty-one thousand, two hundred and eighty cubic inches. And to hope. In a corner lay a rotting issue of *Penthouse*, South American edition. And I hoped. I prayed too. Please God, let me live to masturbate again.

But there is a limit to hope. And by twilight I was done with all clarification of the mind by counting, calculating and imagining *Penthouse* pudenda. I gave in to despair. Sad jerk-off that I was.

A soldier came in, untied me and led me outside. He indicated that I could relieve myself at a corner of the building. But I had no feeling in my hands and accidentally sprinkled his boots. You know that despair has set in when you pee on a soldier and don't think it's funny. He cursed, clipped me across the ear, pushed me in through the door and tied me to the post again.

The vanishing light was filled now with bird screech. I smelled cooking — ai! never a sadder smell there was.

And so, what would be the legacy of bold McKnight? Sweet bugger all. Maybe, though, the trauma of his father's death would somehow give Jeff the wherewithal to kick. Bah, false, that legacy, Mac, and you know it. A counterfeit of twilight. This business will only stoke his habit. He'll never lift another brush.

Well, maybe Evelyn will be waiting for me. We will be young again together and golden in eternity, and that is the real meaning of El Dorado. What a crock.

Night came.

And despair passed. And there was only waiting.

It was utterly dark. Beyond the screen, lightning bugs flashed like failed ideas. The cricket song hypnotized me. Hours passed. Maybe I slept. Then a noise jolted me alert. A nerve-withering noise like a buzz saw cutting into bone. A jaguar — and nearby, too, wishing me sweet dreams. The crickets shut up. It was so quiet I could hear termites chewing in the floor. Then the door creaked open an inch. And I knew it was the cat, hungry for a wee bit of Canadian. I went, "Shoo!" and flipped my feet toward the door.

"Shoo yourself," said a woman's voice, and the door opened wider and then closed, and the room was filled with the light of a candle. Not enough to see the green eyes. "Did you hear that?" she said. "I think it's down by the river."

She wore only a faded black tank top and white bikini panties. And gumboots. "Lot of snakes out at night," she explained. She stuck the candle to the floor and stood above me. The candle threw her shadow up through the rafters. She held a Supermaxi shopping bag from Esperanza. "Thirsty?" She reached into the bag, pulled out a full bottle of rum. "Hungry?"

"Jesus. Chicken."

My sports coat lay beside me. She spread it out, scuffed off the gumboots and sat facing me, her hip against my thigh. Red-nailed fingers held a drumstick up to my mouth. When I tried to bite it she moved it away.

"Take it nice now."

I opened. She put it against my teeth. I took it nice.

"Drink? Oh, you are thirsty. Hey, not too much, the night is long. More chicken? I knew you'd be hungry."

"Nice sauce. Freshly ground amoebas, right?"

"Some balls you got. If I was sitting where you're sitting I wouldn't be making jokes."

"I agree entirely. Most inappropriate. Could I have a little more rum?"

"Me first. Wow, that burns. Here. Let's not spill any this time. What's your name? Mick or something? Tommy just calls you Schoolteacher."

"Al."

"Not Mick?"

"Al."

"Where you from, Al?"

"I know I am not in a position to make demands. But could we forget the chitchat?"

"The night is long, the bottle is still almost full."

"From where I'm sitting, as you say, the night looks pretty goddamn short."

"You're a cool guy. But Tommy doesn't like you. Remember that time at the Boar's Head? When you called me Ivy?"

"I'm sure I called you no such thing."

"You said I liked to cling and to spread."

"I must have been drunk. I apologize. What a filthy thing to say."

A slight smile. The eyes narrowed. Considering. She gave me more rum and more chicken.

"You know, Holly, if you untied me I could feed myself."

"Do you like our place? The whole Oriente is going to be rich on account of Tommy. The whole country in fact."

"Plant the wind and reap the whirlwind, Ivy."

"What does that mean? Hey, I thought you were going to be nice."

"Fuck nice."

She leaned across me, planted her elbow on my thigh, let her forearms rest across my crotch. Her face close, studying me, hurt, arrogant. Amused. Sensational lips. Interesting incisors. Rum and Pepsodent breath. She turned away, drank, winced. Kissed me before I could react. But I would not open my mouth.

She sat back, a false smile not covering her anger. She looked toward the window.

"There's a lot of light in the sky," she said. "Dawn soon."

"You may as well go away."

"I'll decide when I go away. But I want to tell you a story first."

"I don't want a story. I want to be left alone."

"There was this French guy. This was before we got big, before we started selling to the government. His name was Roland. Young. Cute. Bought two kilos. But paid us in funny money. We caught up with him at the coast, he was going to send the stuff north on a banana boat. He gave it back to us, apologized, begged. We flew back here with him, saying we could work something out. As we were coming along the path, Tommy reached over the guy's shoulder and cut his throat. Just like that. Ear to fucking ear. Blood! I'm telling you — on the trees, everywhere! Roland staggered around, trying not to fall down. Then just for a second before he went down, he looked at me. And I finally knew what it was to have power. And I tell you, man, there's no other rush like it."

She smiled a genuine smile now, soft and satisfied. "But he got fixed up real nice. Some of Tommy's relatives back in the bush helped us out."

She reached into the bag and lifted out what looked at first like some ridiculous lapdog. All hair. Only when she pinched a strand of the hair and swung the thing like a pendulum in front of my face did I see what it was. No longer Gallic, far from cute. No bigger than an apple. The eyelids were sewn shut with coarse thread. Over the sewn lips a moustache drooped. She spoke to the face. "Power then and power now. Right, Roland?" She wiggled her tongue in through the moustache, then said, "Hey, don't be sick, Al. We've got business to attend to."

She put Roland away, let me have a long suck on the bottle.

"Now cool guy, I'm going to buy you."

She blew out the candle and stood. When my eyes adjusted

to the darkness two facts were obvious. The first was that there was indeed light in the sky. Enough of it came into the room to establish the second fact. That she was naked.

"I'm going to let you go," she said. "But first you've got to be my whore. Deal?"

"Don't you touch me. I don't want your pus on me."

She giggled. "Oo, I knew you would be upset. You don't want to be anybody's whore. Do you, cool guy? But I'll pay you well. 'Cause I've got a lot of power, see, I've got the power to let you live."

"You've got piss all. Go away."

But, *patrón,* I was lost. She did her Power Dance, there in that dimness, for her captive audience. Who, although he wanted to, could not close his eyes. Clefts, bifurcations, warm dangling handfuls, thrustings, liftings, woman smell. And I knew that I was going to live. But that I was going to live not as a man but as meat. She worked my pants down.

"Look at that," she said. "My poor little whore wants to live."

I tried not to enjoy it, but the truth is, I loved it. And hated myself for loving it.

She got back into panties and top. Taking a knife, Tomás' switchblade, from the bag, she said, "What are you?"

I did not hesitate. "I'm a whore."

"You're a pathetic piece of shit."

"Yes."

She cut the ropes. I took the bottle — there was a lot of rum left in it.

There were no guards. She led me along the path by the river. After a few minutes she turned and headed back.

"See you soon," she said.

Stiff of muscle, I trotted along the trail, hoping Mr. Jaguar had packed up for the night. Past the point of the footprint and buzzard. On to a junction. Left deeper into the woods? Or right toward the river? Right it was. Already thinking, I will reclaim my soul, I will. The noise of the river now. A high bank of dirt and roots. Sand beach. A canoe, but not thirty feet long and with a motor. More like eight feet long and with a bent pole. The man was shorter too, perhaps five feet. In white shirt, white trousers and straw hat. From one shoulder hung a woven bag. He spoke an adequate Spanish.

I said, "I would like to buy your canoe."

"I am sorry, señor, this is not possible."

I held out to him my remaining two thousand dorados. "And the clothes."

We undressed. I was elated. To see that his underwear was snowy and pristine. He was glum. To see that mine was not. We did not trade underwear, though, only trousers and shirts. My filthy for his ironed and gleaming. I could not do up the shirt, and the shoulder seams ripped the second I put it on. The pants ended at my shins. I could not button them either, they stayed up by friction. The hat, however, fit. He rolled up everything and looked well pleased, especially with the sports coat, and the wallet with its Visa card. He handed me my glasses and book. They sat handily in a pocket at the waist of the shirt.

In the canoe lay a blowgun with a quiver of darts and a gourd of kapok. He reached for them.

I said, "Leave them."

"Ai, señor!"

"Leave them."

He fingered the tweed. Shrugged. "Careful," he said, and slid out a dart. The tip of it was stained darker than the rest. He touched it gingerly. "Curare."

I twirled kapok fluff onto the dart and slid it into the blowgun.

If Holly had not humiliated me, I think I would have carried on downstream. But I had no intention now to lie down. To spread. To have barb wire introduced. I could make out the mountains clearly, like a wall against the western sky. And as I stood swaying in that little craft I felt something wonderful. The very red stuff itself: sweet rage. Oh, I knew I was drowning, that I had been down once. I had surfaced now, however. Maybe not for long, but before I went down again I would acquit myself like a knight and a rangitang. By Jesus I would. I wasn't meat yet.

Upstream! They would never guess that I would head back upstream. Toward the lofty town, where I shall dispense thunderbolts of revenge. Thank you, Holly, you made me do it. When it comes time for retribution I shall serve yours first. Polite Canadian that I am.

Sunlight crept down the sierra.

I wrapped my own hands in the torn-off sleeves of my new shirt, for they were accustomed to no greater labour than the gripping of chalk, bottle or firm young thigh, and had blistered immediately.

In spite of the hands and the warped pole, I felt I was flying. No longer stiff of joint. Scooting that overgrown pea-pod like crazy. But as the daylight increased I could see that I was not making any progress at all. Those misted mountains seemed to back away another mile with every plunge of my pole. Best not to look at the mountains. Best to watch that little bush move past at a tremendous rate of speed. Just one or two more pushes and it will finish moving past.

I kept to the river's margin. At the first sound of an outboard coming upriver or a helicopter coming down I needed to be able to step out of my pea-pod and hustle into the trees.

Into the groove and yoga of it. Poling. Punt nudging. Nothing like boredom and blisters to pacify the heart. Remove from it all bad thoughts about oneself. And images of Roland's little face. Empty the mind, as they say. And empty the bladder now, whilst gripping the pole with one's chin. With only half a litre spraying into the bilge.

The thing to remember is that fugitives and absconders invariably come to South America. Because there are so many places to hide. Butch Cassidy and the Sundance Kid went to

Bolívia. And they survived. Didn't they? But the best place of all to hide is the city of hope itself, Esperanza. Chock-full of houses, apartments, rooms and deep holes in the sidewalk. And maybe even a friend or two. Hide under Dolores' bar. Partake of any stock that might fall to hand. Listen to the nice things the customers remember about Mac. Sure miss the old bugger. Wonder whatever happened to him. Never mind, he'll be back. I hear he's got some scores to settle.

Well, wildlife at last. An anaconda, I believe. Sleeping in that low tree over the water. Twenty feet long at least. All coiled and heavy. Hell, is that only how far I've come? Aspirina's empty *aguardiente* bottle gleaming on the bank. And there, further on, the mouth of the tributary.

I poled out to midstream, where there was a sandbar, to avoid the snake and find shallow water. Then I heard it. A motor. I could see nothing downstream, nothing upstream either. Helicopter, then. Approaching low over the trees maybe. But it didn't sound like a helicopter. I was past the snake, so I poled like the devil for the shore. But suddenly I could not find bottom. I had hit a deep channel and could do nothing but drift on the current. The sound of the motor grew louder. I slashed at the water.

A long canoe shot out from the mouth of the tributary and sheered downstream. The boatman cut the motor. The canoe slowed, drifted between me and the shore. Our two boats floated parallel, twenty feet apart.

"Schoolteacher. What the fuck are you wearing?"

Tomás stood in the stern by the motor. Today he wore only loincloth and beads. Holly had been sitting in front of him, but now she stood too. The tight pants again, but the tank top of the previous night. In her eyes, delight and desperation, as if she felt the first inkling of a strapping orgasm.

"How much did you pay the guard? Never mind — it won't buy him another day alive. You should have gone left at the junction. But I knew you wouldn't. 'Cause that's not what a loser would do." He bent. Came up with a double-barrelled shotgun. Broke it open, checked that it was loaded, snapped it shut. "Charlie wanted oh so bad to do it himself. But what choice did we have? With the jerk-off trying to escape. I'm sure he'll forgive us. Besides, there's not much to do around here. A man's got to have some fun."

He swung the muzzle up toward me. But Holly, grimacing with anticipation, could not control herself. Never taking her eyes from me, she threw an arm around Tomás' neck and pressed herself against him. The canoe rocked. The muzzle dropped. Tomás' face darkened. He growled. His right arm shot back. Holly squealed and sailed ass first into the river. The canoe rocked more. Tomás waved the shotgun around for balance. In a few seconds he was steady. The eyes settled again upon me. The muzzle began again to rise. Then, for a second, stopped.

Those unbelieving eyes. To find himself staring into a Jívaro blowgun. He jerked at the shotgun. But too late. El poof. It was an easy shot. If I didn't hit his jugular I was damn close. The dart penetrated up to the fluff. The shotgun blasted, but into the water. Then it dropped into the river.

Tomás pinched and touched the shaft of the dart and the reddening fluff as if it were an unpleasant growth on his skin. He winced, and pulled the dart out, and a thread of blood wormed down his throat and across his hairless chest. I had missed the jugular.

Hands reached up out of the river and clamped onto the far gunwhale. Holly spluttered, "Help me, Tommy."

Tomás sat. His voice was perplexed and quiet. "He's killed me, baby. The schoolteacher has killed me. I'm going to die now."

The two canoes drifted.

"He's killed me. This isn't right. Oh, I can't feel it. It's not fair."

I scraped aground on the sandbar. For a minute I watched them drift in the deep channel. Tomás sitting there, forearms on knees, talking. Ivy clinging. I swallowed the last centimetre of rum and floated the bottle downstream after them. Like a signature at the bottom of a painting.

9

Alive in the City of Hope

I stood swaying in darkness, thankful for a cement laundry sink to lean against, then I managed to form a limp fist and to knock. And then to knock again, and then again. Finally a blast of doorway light and, "It's you, you fascist son of a bitch, didn't I tell you I didn't ever want to see you again!" As tears of relief rolled down my cheeks. "What on earth are you wearing? Are you okay? Bloody hell, Mac, what have you done to yourself!"

I bent to place upon her mousy cheek a kiss of courteous greeting. But there was an unexpected problem with momentum, and it was the floor that rushed eagerly up toward my kiss. Then Liz and I were dancing, or wrestling, around her kitchen, because I seemed to be determined to fall down.

"Isman! Isman, help!"

A wipe at the unmanly tears, as Liz stepped away and stared. Concern in the grey eyes, and a hand pressed upon the mouth. I smiled, but it hurt my lips, which were sunburned and cracked.

The hand of courteous greeting went out to hail the man coming through that doorway. Behind him the sound of canned TV laughter. He shambled toward me in a blotched blue sweatsuit. Stoop shouldered and pudgy and flaccid of face. In his right hand a tumbler of whisky gleaming.

"Hey," he said, "I know you. You bought me a drink. Good man!"

I remembered. The Arab. The terrorist. But now such a warm, slob smile on him. And he had learned to laugh. He ignored my attempted handshake. Wrapped me instead in an embrace and patted me with his whisky glass. "Man," he said, "you really stink. What would you like — food, bath or sleep? Please say bath."

"Sleep," I croaked.

I woke in the early afternoon in a small room with cardboard boxes, and it did not take me long to remember who I was. What had happened I recalled all too quickly. Where I was took some puzzling. But then it felt so safe and cozy that I slept some more. And dreamt that I was taking Holly on a tour of Señor Cádiz' cheese factory, and woke up remembering what Isman had said. That I stank.

No one at home, apparently. Into the shower and off with seven days of grime and goaty tang. Taste the sweat washed into the mouth. Smell the shampoo flushing out bugs and dust. Into a towel like Bomba at last, and I set to ravaging Liz' fridge.

The splendour of Andean coffee through trashed lips. Four eggs, a tomato sliced thick, these last two *salchichas* all into this pan, and a lid clamped upon it as I also cooked a stale bun on a fork over the gas flame.

And Liz too had the same four-dollar El Marin table, but hers was lacquered with foodstain over crudputty. And I was alive and I was safe. And if Liz would let me sleep in that little room forever I'd say I was swinging on a star.

A further cup of coffee, then I fetched my glasses from the Indian shirt. A little twist and they rested upon the nose at a not unacceptable angle. There was nothing in the newspaper about a manhunt for the failed assassin. Only a picture of Charlie beaming in a suit, beside a headline quoting him: *The Economy*

Is Booming.

Then Isman came in with milk and bread and eggs. Still in his blue sweatsuit.

"Schoolteacher. Smelling better? I'll get you some clothes. You're the size I used to be. But first let me have a hit of that coffee."

Down from the top of the fridge a bottle of Black & White, and a dollop of it into his coffee and into mine. My first booze since that day on the river.

In their bedroom closet, five feet of his beautiful shirts and trousers, and at the end, Liz' other pair of overalls. On the floor, a mattress and stale twisted sheets. On the wall, an ancient torn poster of Ché. I took shirt and pants.

"Nothing fits me anymore," he said. "It's the booze. Aren't you going to put them on?"

"I must sleep. If I may. I know I'm being a bore. But it seems I made a mistake when I got up. For a minute there everything was piss and vinegar. But. Yes, definitely. A mistake."

"I was looking forward to your story."

"As was I to yours."

"You won't like mine."

"Falling off the wagon."

"Jumping off."

"Landing on your head."

"Landing on Liz."

"Ah. Well, we'll talk. But I must. If you'll excuse me."

"I saw you."

"Eh?"

"I saw you. That night at the Boar's Head. I saw you pour that vodka into my glass."

"Oh dear."

"I had gone to take a leak. But there was someone in the john. I was waiting at the door and looked back. I couldn't believe it. This kind of funny and kind of hostile schoolteacher I had just met. Pouring his vodka into my glass."

"And I thought I was swinging on a star."

"The weird thing is, I didn't remember that I saw you. Until last night. As I was dropping off to sleep. Then it came back to me. You didn't hear me laugh? Around midnight? Liz thought it was DT time. All that time I had blotted out that memory. Because that night — man, I wanted that drink. But the only way I could have that drink was not to know it was there. So I didn't know it was there. Until last night."

"So your present condition is not entirely my doing."

"Does that make you feel better?"

"Worse, actually. I wanted you to be useless. Stop killing people. Maybe blow yourself up making a bomb."

"Well, I'm useless. Happy?"

"Yes."

"Come and have a drink. There's beer."

"I have to sleep."

"You calling me a killer?"

"Yes."

"Under my own roof?"

"Liz' roof. Do you want me to leave?"

"Come and have a beer."

"When I wake up."

"Who told you I was a killer?"

"The same person who told me about Consuelo, your girlfriend at the American Embassy. That you were using her."

"I don't use people, man."

"You're using Liz."

"So are you."

"Goodnight."

"It's the middle of the fucking day. Come and have a beer."

I slept another four hours. Woke to find on the bed four pairs of underwear and two pairs of Argyll socks.

He was sitting at the table, drinking beer with a Scotch chaser and listening to the radio station that played American rock. Through the window I could see the city's lumpy volcano. The sun was just descending behind it.

"Have you ever tried mountain climbing, Isman?"

"Bah. What's the point of struggling to get to the top if you only have to come down again?"

"I just think you should know that I have popped a piton. I'm going down the fast way."

"Happy landings."

"Not likely."

"Hey, look. Stay here. Liz won't mind."

"I'll have that beer now. Fine. I'll stay until I can think what to do. But I must ask you to find a different radio station. And I warn you that I might murder you — arsenic in your Black & White, maybe."

"For the things I've done?"

"Yes."

"But I'm useless now. Like you said."

"That's not retribution."

"Sometimes disgusting things have to be done, Schoolteacher. If the only weapon you have is fear."

"God, why did I come here? Do you wear that sweatsuit all the time?"

"Yes. I'm a slob now. Did you mean what you said? About arsenic in the booze?"

"I don't know. It was easier to hate you the last time we met."

In Isman's bald armchair, with a tall cold bottle of beer, there in that tiny living room, facing the silent television across a coffee table invisible under months of old TV listings and empty banana *chifle* bags, with the light coming from the kitchen along with the American rock, and with a writing pad on my knee, I wrote a letter.

> *As you know, Jeff, there is never anything worth writing about except to tell you that I love you. And you already know I love you, so I never write. Okay, the real reason is that it is just too painful, everything I feel when*

I pick up a pen and think about you. But maybe I'd better practise feeling pain, because I think I am in for some.

You may or may not be surprised to know that I am in trouble. I stuck my nose where I shouldn't have, and yes, that means between a young woman's legs, but it also means into a massive cocaine deal. With intentions on my part not to sniff but to blow. The whistle, that is. The problem is that both the dope and the woman belong to — take the wildest possible guess! you got it — el presidente himself. A formidable gentleman, I'm afraid, by the name of Charlie. You have to remember that this is a small country. And that when I fuck up I fuck up big.

Your daddy has come a long way since he left B.C. There is even blood on my hands, but it doesn't feel too bad. Are you getting an idea of the kind of trouble I'm talking about? There is every chance that I will lose my life, but I am going to try like hell not to lose my soul, although I have a hunch that that might be the roughest battle. Some pieces of said soul have in fact already been amputated.

So, my son, this is what I want to tell you. That I am going to do what has to be done. Period.

And this: You told me that smack had taken all your love. Well, take this love. This chunk of love here in this miserable letter. And put it into your veins instead of the smack. Get clean, Jeff. I ask you straight out: If you can't do it for yourself, do it for me.

Remember me.

Dad

P.S. If you write, write soon. I am Emílio Sanchez de Vaca.

All wrong. Inadequate. Miserable. But the letter would stand. Inadequacy is preferable to falseness when you're talking to your son. And is, anyway, one's inescapable condition —

no, *patrón?*

Liz came home. She looked tired. Permanently tired. She sank wearily into a chair. "Mac, I hate to say this, fascist bastard that you are, but it is good to see you." Yet she did not smile.

"You haven't told anyone I am here?"

"I haven't told anyone the time of day."

"Liz, I need joy and encouragement. I'm afraid that mournful expression on you is unacceptable. I will seek other lodgings forthwith."

"So seek."

Isman beaming. I wished he wouldn't like me so much.

I said, "Isman tells me he has retired from the meat business."

"I think," said Liz mournfully, "we won't talk about the meat business."

"Sometimes," said Isman, "disgusting things have to be done. If the only weapon you have is fear."

"What about being a disgusting drunk."

"Aw Liz."

After supper Liz cut my hair. I sensed that she was happy to be able to tend to me. Isman and I were drinking Scotch. He still sat at the table, content to watch the scissors flash around my ears.

"It's really not very long, Mac."

"It feels long. It feels like it's got the jungle in it. It feels like Tomás and Holly are nesting in it. Cut it. Cut it short. The beard too."

"So what happened next? After you shot that Tomás bloke with the blowgun?"

I had not mentioned cocaine. They thought it had all been woman trouble. And that I had headed upriver only to second-guess the woman's daddy.

"Up the lazy river," I said. "Till the helicopter caught me napping. Roared right over my head and on downstream. Didn't even slow down. But I fell in the river anyway. Touch of the old panic. Practised my terror kick for a minute. Till I found out I could stand up. But by then my canoe was gone, along with my blowgun and my hat. I didn't chase it downriver but took to the bush. That bush down there, children, is thick with trails. I don't know who uses them — there are no people. Yes, I do know. The witch sends her captive spirits out along them, looking for birds at night."

"Witch, Mac?" said Liz with her only smile so far as she lopped a forelock onto my nose.

"I saw her place across the river. I had stayed there on the way down. Now, you as a plodding material dialectician will not have the capacity to believe in witches. But Isman here, as an imaginative meatmonger, is more open-minded. Isman, do you know any women with green eyes?"

"Well, yeah. My cousin's wife in Jersey has green eyes."

"Does she have a bird? Budgie or anything?"

"I don't know. I was never in her house."

"Let me assure you, she has a bird. Has she ever bought you a drink?"

"Sure. But that was years ago. You saying Elaine's a witch?"

"That was your mistake, Isman. You shouldn't have accepted that drink. Liz, I said short, not stubble. So trails it was. With wide circles around three or four Indian houses on stilts. As their goddamn fleabags barked their lungs out at me. I got hungry. Don't ever think there is anything to eat in the jungle. Unless you like ants. Or leaves. If a trail went along the river there might be a patch of sugarcane. You can bite the tender parts and get some juice. It got dark, and I slept on a boulder by the river.

"Next day the same. Trails. Dogs. Munching cane. I saw some monkeys, hummingbirds, toucans and a pack of wild pigs who caused me to shinny up a vine. Which broke. Fortunately the sound of my fall frightened the tuskers away. Found an orange tree in a clearing and laid it waste. Of course the mud *bichos* or fleas or whatever they are were yarding the nourishment out of me faster than I could put it in. My trousers, as I am sure you noticed last night, were cut a trifle scant. Look at my ankles. Now Isman, there is meat for you."

"Ugh. Hamburger."

"That night I found a beached canoe full of crates of Coca-Cola empties. I took a chance and slept in it. Off before dawn, and spent the next day robbing gardens and throwing rocks at dogs. I saw a young woman pulling up yucca. She saw me. Barebreasted and altogether splendid she was. I pointed at her pile of yucca roots and patted my stomach, but that must mean something pornographic down there, because she threw a clod of dirt at me. Children, even a starving fugitive has dignity. Which is to say, I threw a stick back at her. She ran away and so did her dog.

"I came to a wide trail and hitched a ride in a passing donkey cart and paid the man with a stolen melon I was carrying. I think that's when I got this sunburn. At dusk I ran into the oil pipeline. Slept on top of the pipe that night. Fireflies, and things padding nearby, and twigs cracking, and the smell of industry against my cheek. Followed the pipeline west, cross-country style the next day until I hit a real road. Narrow. Dirt. But real. Well into the foothills now. Accepted a ride with a farmer and his wife on their motorcycle. I sat behind and held the baby, who kept pulling my beard. The kid's diaper leaked and I think, Isman, that it was perhaps this leakage that caused the bouquet to which you referred on my arrival. Well, bingo, we came to a highway. Buses. Tourists in rented cars. Whole two-ton trucks full of soldiers. What could I do, walk up the Andes on the shoulder of the highway, hoping no one would notice me? With my blond beard and sunburn and pants coming to my knees?

"I walked west through fields and bush along the highway. When I saw a group of Indians standing by the highway I joined them. In a crouching, squatting sort of way. Although I said nothing, they found me for some reason amusing. A new white pickup stopped. They had some trouble climbing in because of giggles. I, however, was in like a shot. And that, children, is how

Uncle Mac came up the Andes. Lying down to keep out of sight in the back of a Chevy pickup driven flat out by a guy in a stetson who looked like the Marlboro Man. With the Indians sitting well away from me. My appearance perhaps. Perhaps the tang of infant diarrhoea. But they were finished with their giggles soon enough. By the time we had climbed to maybe eleven thousand feet and cold rain was falling, we were all huddled together under a tarp the Marlboro Man had tossed into the back, pressed down like freezing leeches against the floorboards to get a little heat from the exhaust pipes.

"Over the summit of the East Range and then down. You know that road. It was getting dark and I was starving. The Indians got out at Urubamba. They each gave the Marlboro Man a hundred dorados. It was pretty well dark when I saw the lights of the National Police checkpoint. I thumped the roof of the cab. He stopped, and I climbed out.

"'*Cien dorados,*' he said. Then, in English, 'You are American.' He had a slight German accent.

"'Yes,' I said. 'Philadelphia. I'm very sorry, but I don't have any money. I was robbed down in the jungle.'

"'You look like one of those Peace Corps people.'

"'That's right.'

"'Don't you know that gasoline costs money?'

"'I'm sorry.'

"'You fucking Jew. My father knew what to do with you fucking Jews.' There was a gun lying on the dashboard. A chrome-plated six-shooter. He reached for it."

"Hey," said Isman. He looked worried.

"What?"

"Are you a fucking Jew?'

"No, but I ran anyway. I heard him laugh as he peeled off. Of course for the sake of dignity I had to fire a rock after him. Hit his tailgate. I made a wide circle around the checkpoint, through potato fields. Walked all night. Into this lofty shit-hole. Absolutely done for. Skulking around the perimeter road before dawn, and partway up the volcano to try to sleep through the day among the eucalyptus trees. Couldn't sleep because of the hummingbirds. Damn little buggers. They seemed to be attracted to my sunburn."

Isman let go a fart and a shout of a laugh and slapped his thigh and refilled my glass.

"Cheers. Down the volcano by night on a trail treacherous with used condoms. To this haven of culture and haircuts. Jesus I'm tired. Liz, let us leave the beard until tomorrow."

Liz said, "You sound more like a kind of warped tour guide than a hunted man."

"Listen, a medicinal dose of mediocre whisky can work miracles. But if I am chipper it must be because I've got to work up a charge."

"Hey?"

"For thunderbolts."

Yet as I tumbled between the sheets of that little bed I was sustained by no vision of elemental voltage. Instead, I rose helpless and thankful through soft rooms of time and was young again with Evelyn.

Two weeks in that apartment, and never further abroad than the cramped balcony with its laundry sink to look down at the chewed street and those many people going to and fro with no fear for their lives. We did not talk about escapes to Canada or to any other place. We did not discuss the future. I lived with them and was their pet and hobby, and they were glad. For Liz I was relief from the burden of her Lebanese soak. For Isman I was spice and diversion, and reminded him of adventure.

But I was not glad. I was antsy. I did push-ups four, five times a day. "Teacher, you're going to bust my shirts," said Isman. I felt I had to act while this sunburned snoot lingered yet clear of the consuming waters. I had gone superstitious since the green-eyed Clinger had said, Gimme that thing. Meaning my soul. And I was sure that soon, in some way, I would sink and sink bad. So I was antsy and felt I had to act. But nowhere, *patrón*, could I lay my hands upon a thunderbolt.

In Isman, a change. Less bad rock during the day, and less bad TV and fattening *chifles* at night. But not less Scotch. More. And more and more talking with McKnight. Telling me stories, stories I had to endure because he was my host and I was his swell new hobby.

We were, as always, in the kitchen. Momma Liz had come home the previous night with two new quarts of Black & White. We clinked glasses, and he said, "Our only weapon was fear."

"Fuck fear." Endure, yes — condone, no. But he took my every comment as encouragement, and laughed and went on.

"When the Marines were still in Beirut I arranged for this pot-head from Boise to be sold a few grams of Damascus Delight. Which is choice hashish that's been cut with the droppings of a berserk camel. Okay, not camel shit. Certain unfriendly hallucinogens. I wasn't always useless. I knew biochemistry. Go ahead, ask me something about biochemistry. Anything."

"What happens when you mix a reactive rangitang with an acidic mouse and an inert barfly?"

His slob laugh. Yar yar yar. "Schoolteacher, you kill me. But that's easy. You get a hot-blooded billygoat. Yes, I got it up last night for the first time in months. Liz had to put the light on to make sure I wasn't fooling her."

"With some clever prosthesis of Superglue and salami."

"Yar yar. It's you, you goddamn crazy schoolteacher. You're getting my blood going again. I would even go so far as to say I feel pretty damn close to almost alive."

"Ask Liz, will you, if she will accept your tumescence in lieu of my rent."

"Yar. Well anyway, the D.D. went in through the fence, and Boise and the boys lit up. I learned from a well-placed informant that there were screams of, 'Get them off me!' and, 'Ray, Ray, oh Jesus, your face is turning into an avocado!'"

Isman on his feet and laughing and doing a demented jig of ripping invisible cooties from his chest and flinging them to the floor. And I admit that I flinched when he hurled one toward me. Then he shrank in horror, as Poe would say, from my avocado face. He was right. Pretty damn close to almost alive.

Another day he came back from grocery shopping with a surprise.

"Car bomb." He was already giggling as he pulled a wind-up police car out of the bag. When he stuffed a four-inch black and red firecracker into the window of it I started to giggle too. Why he chose the coffee table I do not know. His turf maybe. He cleared a space among the old TV magazines and empty *chifle* bags and lit the fuse.

Bang, and smoke, and the car catapulted onto its back in his chair, and the two of us collapsed to hands and knees laughing. Until we noticed that the table was on fire. All that paper. Flames spreading. And now roaring.

I remembered the bus in the jungle. I shouted, "Teamwork!" We each grasped two legs and hustled the table through the kitchen, as our hair singed and stank, out onto the balcony.

"On the count of three," he said.

The sleeve of my shirt was on fire. "Fuck three." We tilted. A flock of carbonized flakes drifted away over Esperanza. The rest hurtled five storeys straight down in a single mass of flames. There was no car parked there. That parking space had been roped off because men were working. And down the open manhole sailed the conflagration. Below, an echoing scream. Then two men scrambling up into the light. Yes, that was terror on their faces, so, Isman, I suppose this must be terrorism.

Right smart back inside. Isman batted out my flames. My heart rapping like crazy.

"That wasn't cool," I said.

"Especially for those guys down the hole." He was still giggling, but now in excited spasms.

I said, "You do know, don't you, that every cop in this country is looking for me?"

"Wow!" he shouted. "Adrenalin! I haven't felt like this since we offed the ambassador. Hey, you know what? Every cop in the fucking *world* is after me. God it's great to be almost alive!"

He gave me another shirt, and we cut the singed hair off each other and swept up the flakes of carbon, which had reached every corner of the apartment. His vitality annoyed me until he brought from their bedroom a bottle of unused cologne. When he spritzed it into the burnt-smelling air of the living room, I gave in. And laughed. And even when I no longer felt it was funny I went on. Feeling the tension of my life draining so easily out. Then we really laid into the Scotch. By the time Liz came home I had trained him to sing "The Tattooed Lady" all the way through with a straight face.

We had decided to tell Liz what had happened. When we did she seemed not angry but hurt. I believe she began to feel then that she was losing him. To me. She was right, of course.

More stories. Offing the ambassador. Or a hundred pounds of dynamite in a stolen plumber's van at dawn. Elbow joints and three-quarter-inch adaptors all the way to Tel Aviv. Along with a leg or two. Then I would leave the kitchen and lock myself in the bathroom, with his yar yar just out there, and look at my face in the mirror and wonder how it was possible that I had ended up here with my life twisted beyond all recognition. And a headache would come upon me.

Oh my God. How he bribed a guard, and what the Second Secretary of the U.S. Embassy in Jakarta looked like later as he crawled around his smoking and mangled BMW searching for his hand. Etcetera in Jerusalem, Paris, Seoul. And how America was really the terrorist and he was only an inevitable part of the machine and, yes, the only weapon was fear.

So I was actually thankful for the hijinks. Inspired, he insisted, by the goddamn crazy schoolteacher. As I waited for the Avenging Angel to whisper The Plan in my ear.

Continuing the fire theme, there was the Harvard Experiment. "Methane burns," he said. "My organic chemistry prof assigned this experiment. Not to be performed in the laboratory." In the afternoon closed-blind dimness of their bedroom he lay on his back on their mattress, hoisted his legs and held a lit match to his sweatsuited rump. He bore down. I stood back. A spear of blue flame hissed across the room. For the first time in forty years I peed myself laughing, while Isman wept quietly for his lost youth and his singed asshole.

And continuing the virility theme, he said another time, "By the beard of the Prophet, Schoolteacher, I've gotten it up every night this week. Haven't you noticed that Liz is cross-eyed and smiling all the time? I'm on a roll, I tell you. You'll see, one of these days I'm going to wake up alive. Humping the world the way I used to. Hey, by the balls of the Prophet, peace be upon Him, I'm getting ideas."

"Now wait a minute."

"What the hell was her name. Cherita!" Out the door, sweatsuited into the afternoon of the City of Hope, and back in thirty-five minutes with Cherita. A teenager saucy as sin, with the laugh of a parrot and the squirm of a ten-year-old.

Isman said, "We'll flip a coin to see who goes first."

Cherita scratched my beard and pouted provocatively. But I said, "You can have my turn too. I don't approve of whores." And I wondered if I should advise Liz to cut down on his pocket money.

But yet there was no doubt that at such times I was fond of him. As usefulness began to grow in him like a dangerous yeast.

I discovered the roof. Such relief to be out of that penitentiary. One day, among hanging laundry, I gazed out upon my lost City of Hope and remembered that once I had believed there was a City of Gold. Then I opened the letter which had that day arrived addressed to Sr. Emílio Sanchez de Vaca.

Dear Dad,

Like you said once. A sad funny circus.

Yours forever,

Jeff.

Midday light beat down like hammers on the empty whiteness of the page.

Isman came up with a bottle and two glasses. I folded the letter, slid it into a pocket. He poured, then sat leaning back against the low wall surrounding the roof. His face was in shade, his sprawled legs and stomach in the sun. Dirty. But electrically blue.

"Letter?" he said.

"Routine correspondence. Now, isn't it a fine day in this picturesque city in the high Andes."

"Schoolteacher, they're all the same to me."

"Give me another hit of that execrable swill. I was sure you told me this was the day you were going to wake up alive. Humping the world. Ramming that salami known as fear up the unsuspecting orifices of international capitalism."

"Hey, give me some time. I'm just getting used to being a billygoat. *Ba-a-a-a.*" He joggled his crotch and laughed and choked and slopped Scotch down his sweatsuit.

"Time." I sighed. "Yes, time for more stories. More fairy tales." I walked among the laundry, letting my hand trail over sheets, socks, underwear. "How you blew up Cinderella's pumpkin. How you offed Prince Charming."

"We offed the fucking ambassador, man."

"Snow White and Damascus Delight. The second secretary meets the Good Fairy."

"Hey."

"What'll we do today? Ignite a fart? Hurl a burning TV guide at the American Embassy? Ah, the life of danger and commitment."

"What's with you? I thought you were my friend."

His face like a hurt child's. "Hah! Friend! I needed shelter and I needed laughs. But now I need something else, and it is not a friend. What I need is what you used to be. Have you heard the fairy tale about Mac the Giant-Killer?"

"I'm going down."

"By Christ, Isman, if you so much as get to your feet I'm

going to throw you off this roof! Sit the fuck down. And listen."

"Hey, Jesus."

"Are you listening?"

"Man, what's with you? All right. I'm listening."

"Once upon a time there was Mac. Wee Mac. And there was a giant, and the giant was — let's see — an octopus. And Wee Mac hated this octopus because it — what? Hmm. Because it ate babies. Now, this octopus had many horrible legs, and some of the legs were called Pancho and Charlie and Aquinas and Clinger. And the United States of America. Are you listening?"

"Yes, but I'm not understanding. Uh, maybe you shouldn't do that."

I saw that I no longer held my glass, and that I had ripped a pair of pantihose from the line and was tugging at the legs. "So Mac set out to kill the octopus. And by the grace of God and vodka he managed to tear off some of the stinking. Slimy. Disgusting. Legs." I jerked. The pantihose came apart. I let the pieces fall. "But Wee Mac was sore wounded. Wounded even unto death. So he hid in the Palace of the *Chifle* King. And the *Chifle* King healed Wee Mac with his magic potion called Execrable Swill."

"Yar. Well, I've got some shopping to do."

"It's five storeys down. Even that layer of booze-soaked fat wouldn't save you."

"All right, all right. What's this fucking octopus supposed to be, anyway?"

"And meanwhile, of course, that old giant octopus was growing new legs and gobbling up everybody's babies. Not to mention feeling around in every crack and corner to try to find Wee Mac. Of whom the octopus was deathly afraid. Oh yes. But Mac knew a secret." *Yes. The secret of hope poisoned. The secret of love gone to waste. The basement secret. The bubble.*

"Schoolteacher. Jesus. What's wrong? Hey, don't cry, man, It's all right, it's all right."

He got up and hugged me and patted my back with his

glass of Scotch.

I blubbered and stammered. "But Mac knew a secret. He knew where the octopus kept his treasure." I moved away from Isman and blew my nose on somebody's sheet. "Mr. Chemist," I said, "what would be the best way to destroy a whole lot of cocaine in a hurry?"

"Simple. A few drums of gasoline. A match."

"And you are the man with the matches, aren't you? Billy-goat, strut your stuff. World, bend over."

So I told him about Arturo and the warehouse and Jack Kelly. About Pancho Perales and Charlie. And my Lebanese murderer said, "Yes, the States needs money under the table to stoke some unofficial projects here and there. It appears," he said, "that they are finally getting their cocaine act together. So tell me," he said, "about the warehouse."

In the beating light of Esperanza, McKnight pranced exultant among laundry. Carving his thunderbolt. With malevolent joy he pictured Isman torching a white gleaming mountain. In an instant's flash, rendering it cinder. As Mac in the background thundered, "Wrong, Charlie. The Economy Is Toast!"

10

Commandos

Isman won't tell me what he's up to. And it's the jitters for real — ants highballing along the nerves of McKnight as if he were some jungle plant. With roots into the rot. Too true, by Jesus. But this herb — McDeadlyNightshade — has curative powers. Yes, to fix the lot of them.

And I don't care what Isman has done. As I pace the apartment and circle the roof and drench the nerves with ant-killer in the form of this Bellows Vodka which Isman has deigned to buy for his partner in laughs and havoc. Best not think about it. The dismembered children. Because there is work to be done, and he is my one ray of hope and of lightning.

He had stopped telling me stories — this was good. But it was bad that he was such an alcoholic fuck-up. Who now laughed at nothing at all, or maybe at things he imagined. His endless *yar yar yar* sent me often to the roof or to my bed, with hands pressed to ears.

At night I watched television with him. One night it was *Dr. Zhivago*, and when Omar Sharif had his coronary and fell down to die without Julie Christie, Isman went, Yar har. And wiped a tear of mirth from his eye.

"You Arab dink."

"What's wrong?"

"You just ruined my favourite scene from my favourite movie."

"Ah hng," he laughed. "Sorry. Just thinking about something."

"What?"

"Nothing."

Then Liz got up from her marking at the kitchen table and came and stood glaring down at us. Too late, Lizita. I never wanted to take your man and hurl him at the enemy. Just don't evict me until I have finished hurling.

Later at night *El Cabrón*, The Billygoat, would shake the building, and I would hear his bleatings from my bed as he perfected upon Liz what he intended for the world. But in the morning my hostess displayed not the grin of a well-fucked wife but the gloom of a widow. Frequent shuddering sighs. And suddenly things thrown. One morning, the coffee pot. I listened to the lid spinning on the floor and watched the coffee running down the wall as Liz flew into their bedroom. Isman tried to contain himself. No use. More coffee was lost as it guffawed from his mouth to drench my shirt. At which he rubbed with the sleeve of his sweatshirt while rubbing with the other sleeve at his wet cheeks. Then he slapped his thigh and squalled at my puzzlement. Hell. Frankenstein's Thunderbolt. Hurl, *patrón*, and step well back.

Then one afternoon found me occupying Isman's chair, alone at the kitchen table, contemplating my *Who Me?* tattoo. My turn at the Top 40, the *Heat Parade*, as they would have it here. Trying to take it easy on the ant-killer, I picked up a newspaper. But it was jammed with Charlie's virtuous plans. Low-rent housing here, clean water there, and jobs for *todo el mundo* and his dog. Those jungle paths had been for enterprising *Índios*. Hundreds of reformed headhunters with their kilos of *coca* paste for Tomás.

The guy I had bought the canoe from — what did he have in his shoulder bag? And now Charlie's warehouse was bursting with housing and jobs and prosperity. I gave up and hit the Bellows, and when Isman came home he found me plotzed, but pacing nevertheless.

"Schoolteacher."

"If you laugh, by Christ."

"Cheer up. Look at what just came by courier. A present. For both of us. Even if you won't tell me what you're getting out of this venture."

"I told you. Spin-dry for shit-skaters. Why aren't you laughing?"

"Look."

"Jesus."

"Five thousand. Ten thousand. Fifteen thousand. Hey yar hyar!"

Bundles of American cash thumped onto the table.

"Here you go, 'Teach. Buy yourself the world's biggest Maytag."

Money had arrived, had winged its way from where? I felt nauseous, took a long pull of Bellows. "Please don't tell me where that's from. Just tell me what it's for."

"Supplies and services, partner." He tucked a hundred-dollar bill into my shirt pocket. "Take a break. Go for a walk. No one's going to notice you. Go to the park, rent a paddleboat. Buy a woman. Buy two women."

But I went nowhere, only to the roof, where with shaking hands I set fire to the hundred-dollar bill.

The next day he came home with a case of Black & White. "Training rations," he said. Then he went out again and came home with Juan. Long and thin. Motorcycle boots. Dark drooping moustache and darker aura of violence. Juan slouched in a kitchen chair, with his legs across three-quarters of the room.

"Let me guess," I said. "This is one of your Merry Men."

"Meet Little Juan," said Isman. And laughed.

When I offered my hand Juan only nodded and went on trimming his nails with a switchblade. Then he went white and said in Spanish, "Mother of God. Help me."

He had cut himself. A drop of blood the size of a peppercorn was perched on the tip of a finger, which he gripped ferociously and from which he averted his face. I forced his head down so he would not faint.

Isman left again. I put a band-aid on Little Juan's finger and retreated to the roof. Presently, in the sudden chill of Andean sunset, I saw below in the street Isman returning with two women. Cherita and a friend. His laughs, their giggles. Supplies and services. I got cold on the roof, waiting for Juan and the whores to leave.

Isman now considered himself to be in training. The next day he bought a pellet gun, and we went up to the roof and set an orange at the base of the surrounding wall. Once, a double ricochet nicked the peeling and we cheered, but the hundred and forty-nine other shots just chewed up the masonry, and finally he swore and threw the pellet gun at the orange and he hit it and juice spurted onto someone's drying towel, and pieces of the gun flew everywhere, and that was the end of light arms practice.

However, there was still hand-to-hand combat to be dispensed with.

"But you're a terrorist," I said. "You don't need to know anything about . . . What did you call it?"

"Jujitsu. And I am a freedom fighter. So please attack me so I can demonstrate. I promise not to hurt you."

This was again in their bedroom. Venue of demonstrations. The soldier's art and the Harvard fart. We were barefoot and circling on the stale sheets and mattress. I made a feint. He fell for it. Literally. Reeled off the mattress with a Japanese shout and windmill arms, cracked his head on the open closet door and sank into the embrace of his shirts.

He avoided further training, claiming he had no time for it.

I don't know where he went or what he was up to — he wouldn't tell me. But I was left alone a lot.

I watched television, and when Liz came home at night she avoided me. Isman had hooked me on *chifles*, which are deep-fried banana slices. Cellophane bags were piling up again there on the charred coffee table. On TV this night was a Bruce Lee late movie, in which Bruce is not knocked out by a closet. I was in Isman's armchair and had negotiated a truce between my arse and a sharp protruding spring. But then from the kitchen Liz screamed, "You bastard!" and a hurtling textbook snatched the bag of *chifles* from my hand. I jumped. The end of the spring drank deep of my right buttock.

"Ow! Son of a bitch!" On my feet and clutching at my wound. With the other hand trying to fend off Liz, who was driving bony knuckles into my chest. When a fist glanced off my forearm and caught me on the chin I snatched her off her feet by the bib of her overalls and dumped her on her back on the coffee table. Cellophane bags crackled and flew. Scared, she lay in a posture of submission. On the TV Bruce Lee's hands went *swish swish*. There was the sound of someone's neck breaking.

I let her up. Her hand smacked against my face. I said, "All right. We'd better talk."

"You bastard."

"You said that. Define your terms. And if you hit me again by Christ it will be the last thing you do in this world."

"Why did you have to come here! Why?"

"Are you going to put me out?"

"Everything was fine until you came. And now . . ."

"Don't cry. Stop it. And don't lie. It angers me. Everything was not fine. He was a pathetic alcoholic blob, and you were a bitter skinny Englishwoman."

"Can't you see he's leaving me? And that it's your fault?"

"He's balling you. He wasn't before."

"So what! He thinks he doesn't need me now. Anyone can

see that. What are you two planning? Why is he always laughing?"

"I'm not planning anything. Is he? How should I know? Don't blame me for his plans. I repeat, are you kicking me out?"

"No. I'm outnumbered. You stay. I'm going."

I limped after her into their bedroom. She jerked out a drawer, inverted it over the mattress. Panties, socks and T-shirts. No brassieres. She snatched at the poster of Ché. It ripped. She tore up the piece in her hand. Fragments of Ché sprinkled her Bolivian rug, which she tossed onto the mattress as well. Oh, the bitch. The vile little bitch. She really was leaving. And without her, Isman, my only hope, would be useless again.

"Liz."

"Save it. It's too late." From the closet shelf she pulled a packsack.

"Liz. Stop. Don't go. I'll tell you what we're planning."

The Bolivian rug was half into the pack. She stopped, looked up. "All right," she said. "I'm listening."

"I promised him I wouldn't tell you. But I can see now I have to."

"I'm still listening."

"He is planning to marry you."

"What?"

Her stunned stare. "That's why he seems so happy. And also, he's got a job."

"What?"

"Lecturer in Biochemistry at the Catholic University. Starting next October."

"You're lying. Everything you're saying is a lie."

I shrugged. "Fine. Leave. He won't survive without you, of course. What a terrible shame. When he just about had it beat. I'm sure he would have stopped drinking within a month." I turned as if to walk away.

She said, "What have you done? There's blood on the seat of your trousers."

"That chair spring. You should have it fixed."

"Let me see."

"No, really, it's . . ."

"Let me see. That's an order."

"Well, actually it hurts like hell."

"Just push them down a little further. Bloody hell. I think you've severed an artery — there's pure vodka pouring out." She tore off a corner of their sheet, pressed it against my wound. Sure way to get lockjaw of the buttock. "You have a hairy arse."

"Sasquatch in the woodpile."

She got something from the bathroom, kneeled, applied it to me. I screamed.

"Fuck! Iodine!"

"Take that, you lying sod!"

"Please! No more! I'm sorry!"

"Damn you."

"Forgive me."

"You'd better take another pair of trousers."

"Thank you."

"Mac?"

"Yes?"

"How is it that you and I remain friends?"

"Beats me, Lizita."

With my failed lie I had hoped to keep Liz quiet until Isman's caper — whatever it was — got rolling. I didn't know that twenty-four hours would have been plenty.

"Okay, Isman. Time to let me in on the joke. What's with the camouflage outfit? It doesn't fit, you know. Look, your gut's hanging out between your buttons. Put your sweatsuit back on."

"Schoolteacher, I told you. The raid is on."

I chuckled, fetched the TV listings. "So, what shall we watch tonight? Let's see. *The Dirty Dozen* or *Beach Blanket Bingo?*"

We were at the table. Upon it this night, as well as his Scotch and my vodka, there were a large bottle of Coke and two litres of Trópico, the anise-flavoured grog of the masses. Also some chipped mugs and jam jars. There was a knock at the door, and Little Juan came in. He toted a plastic bag. Behind him shuffled an old man with a bushy moustache, grey pigshave and false teeth which he showed often in a huge nonsmile. At his side hung a sabre in a leather and brass scabbard that dragged on the floor — the man was short. His camouflage sleeves and pants were rolled up into thick coils.

I laughed. After all, what right did I have to expect professionals? God bless them, the raid was on!

Little Juan tugged at his tight camouflaged crotch and reached for a mug. The old man gave his nonsmile and took a jam jar.

"Best if we don't bother with names," said Isman.

In five minutes there were footsteps on the stairs outside, and another camouflaged pair entered. Definite smell now of army surplus. They were a boy of maybe fifteen, who grabbed a jam jar, and a man who looked like Omar Sharif and who gazed with cow eyes at the boy. The Kid turned, caught the Arab's look, and spat. Good, I suppose — if all else fails, spit the enemy to death. Isman and the Arab spoke at length in Arabic, then the Arab reached into the shopping bag he was carrying, took out a hash pipe and lit up.

"Muslim," said Isman. "Doesn't drink."

But the Kid did. In minutes he was sitting glass-eyed on the counter, with his camouflage ass in spaghetti sauce, as the Arab soothed him by rubbing his back. But I knew this youth! He was one of the shoe-shine boys from Pepe's sidewalk restaurant. Black shoe-polish fingers gripped the jam jar.

The Old Man started making disgusted faces and complaining to Isman about the Arab *maricón*. He added his spittle to the Kid's.

Next the Hood joined us, and the Student. The Hood in long slicked hair, gold teeth, and rings heavy on hands that gripped a shopping bag. The Student thin in wire glasses, trembling, pale, pimpled, gripping no bag but only a book, whose title read *Las Moscas*. The Flies. The Hood was into the Trópico like gangbusters. The Student accepted a toke from the Arab, who now abandoned the Kid and set to cheering the Student with his back-rubbing routine.

"Isman," I said, "did you really off the ambassador? Or did you get the shine-boy to polish him off?"

"Funny."

"Listen, are we done with the secrecy crap now? Who is it that you work for?"

"Schoolteacher, you deserve an answer. I work for who pays."

"I thought as much. The freelance meat business. And who is paying for this?"

"Ah, but that's a secret."

"I thought it might be. And are you finished as of tonight with being a useless slob?"

"It seems I am."

"Then I don't think I'll be able to be your friend anymore. After tonight."

"Wrong, partner. After tonight you're going to love me."

No, it was Isman who was wrong. He was no more than a tool to me now. Even if I could accept his new self, I could not let him be more. Because failure was in the air — could I send a *friend* out on this fiasco?

One chipped mug remained on the table. The second litre of Trópico was half demolished. The Student had stopped shaking and was reading *The Flies* and ignoring the cow eyes of the Arab, who was pouting in a chair. The Kid had puked in the sink and was now watching *Beach Blanket Bingo* and eating *chifles*. The Old Man worked his dentures viciously, as if needing to bite something, jogged his crotch and said to the Arab, "*Maricón*. Do you want to know what the cudgel of a man tastes like?"

The Hood cackled.

"Grandfather," said the Arab, "what you call a cudgel would

taste like what it is — a boiled noodle." He stopped pouting and looked evil.

The Old Man said, "Let us go outside, and we will soon see who is the man and who is the *maricón*."

"Grandfather, it is cold out there. You will get rheumatism in your cudgel."

There was laughter, and wild denture-flashing, and a gilded sneer from the Hood, and distant cellophane crackling, and the Student flipped a page. I leaned against the door and gazed upon these persons with a sagging heart. The Septic Six. Then the door swung open. I was knocked aside. And in strode the last commando. The splendid seventh. And boy did her camouflage outfit ever fit. The Student started to shake again.

"So these are my *compañeros*." Her voice was strong and clear. She threw back her head and laughed. It was like a run of Charlie Parker eighth notes. "So this is the gringo." She looked at me earnestly. Full, unpainted lips made an O and smooched me loudly on the nose.

Her energetic eyes again took everyone's measure. Again she laughed. She had straight black hair tied in a tail. Upon her head there was a black beret, upon her feet a pair of greased combat boots, upon her chest a pair of dusky breasts that struggled uncamouflaged against her largely unbuttoned shirt. On her hips nothing but the fit of those pants. In her hand a plastic shopping bag.

She blew a kiss to Isman. He winked and passed her the Trópico bottle. She took three long swallows, wiped her mouth with the back of her hand, whooped, and crashed a combat boot against the floor. And I knew what it was I really wanted. I wanted to be a raider. Doomed outlaw love with the Woman in far-flung camps in the mountains. I wanted to be Ché.

Isman stood and said, "*Bueno, hombres*." They formed a line along the counter and one wall. Even the shine-boy, with his bag of *chifles*, stood warily next to the Arab.

"Your weapons," said Isman. He faced Little Juan. From his

Supermaxi bag Little Juan lifted a gun, an angular, ancient-looking thing. He worked the action of it for his *jefe*.

Isman moved on to the Hood. The Hood took out his gun, a six-shooter like that of the Marlboro Nazi who had given me the ride up the mountain. I wondered if this was what they called a Magnum. But why did it have a thick red rubber band running back to the hammer? And why did it say, in raised letters there above the trigger, *Lone Ranger*? I see. Not a Magnum. A cap gun, fixed up to shoot bullets. Good Luck, Kemo Sabe.

The Arab went out to the landing and brought in a scarred rifle. He slapped and jerked unsuccessfully at its mechanism until Isman moved along to the Kid. If he was still drunk, he did not show it. He had no shopping bag, but from a pocket came a slingshot. Store-bought, even. The stretchy parts made of surgical tubing. Wrist brace. Snipe a dozen soldiers before the Arab got his relic loaded.

"Your weapon?" said Isman to the Student. The Student shrugged. Isman slapped him twice — forehand, backhand — flung *The Flies* across the room, jerked him away from the counter, snatched a bread knife from a drawer and jammed it under the Student's belt. The Student stood at attention. Blood flowed from his nose onto his camouflage shirt, the first blood of the night. Isman trod on the Student's glasses and remained on them in front of the Woman.

As the Arab continued to rattle his relic the Woman extracted from her bag a marvel. A machine gun, but compact as a box of After Eight Mints. There were whistles of admiration. She waved it over her head, laughed, gave it a kiss and returned it to the bag.

The Old Man next, at attention, his hand wrapped around the sabre's handle, eager to present arms. He pulled. The sabre remained in its scabbard. He pulled again. The Arab had at last mastered his fowling piece and could afford to chuckle at the old fool. The Old Man heaved at the handle. The blade screamed through the air. Isman, nimbly for a fat man, skipped aside. But still a tuft of his hair was left suspended in the slipstream. Before descending to the *en garde* position the blade swept a cobweb from the ceiling. And we all watched in fascination as a spider ascended its thread toward the tip of the sword. Until the Woman's hand shot out. With a pinch she killed the spider. And popped it into her mouth. And took two quick steps to the table and washed the bug down with a belt of Trópico, and whooped and stomped and laughed.

The Old Man slammed his sabre home and stepped forward. "Mother of God, señorita," he cried, "I would leap laughing into my grave just to frolic for a moment in your magnificent grotto!"

"Is that so, grandfather?" she laughed. "Well, I have seen one of your weapons. Does your other one drag on the floor too?"

"Fight me toe to toe, my pretty, and you will see how my weapon behaves."

"Ai, que guerrero!"

"Soy guerrero de amor." I am a warrior of love. "Let me battle between your thighs."

Little Juan and the Hood shouted, *"Eso! Eso!"*

The Old Man laughed at last, and he and the Woman spat on their hands and smashed them together. And I thought, By Jesus this is the real thing. This is actual Hemingway.

And when everyone had quieted I said, "Please. I must say something. You are the strangest and most wonderful army that has ever walked this earth. Well, I suppose there was the Children's Crusade. But what I want to say is this. That I don't know who you are, except for *el chico*, who used to shine my shoes at Pepe's and *el commandante*, who now gets his hair cut at home. And I know, of course, that you are not doing this for me. But yet I want to say thank you. And I want to say that no matter what happens tonight, I will never forget any of you."

There was an embarrassed silence.

"Spin-dry for shit-skaters," said Isman in English.

I said, "Hallelujah, brother."

"Tornadoville."

"Amen."

He nodded to Little Juan, who took from his Supermaxi bag a folded camouflage suit and held it out to me.

Isman said, "We need you."

Ah.

They. Need. Me.

Damn cute. What could I do — refuse? Obviously, if this was anybody's fight, it was mine. *Patrón,* I sighed. With relief. That at last my fate was clearly displayed. We were all going to die. Game over. But I would not die, as I had feared, with paying customers playing with my snatch. I went into my safe little room for the last time and came out looking exactly, I'm afraid, like one of them. They admired the figure I now cut. In the Woman's eyes an undeniable erotic glint.

Then the door opened. And there stood Liz. Clasping her bag of marking to her chest. She looked at the commandos, at Isman for a long time as neither of them said a word, and then at me. I knew what she felt. Betrayed. Simply done for. No iodine truce this time. And by God I didn't care. There were larger matters on the agenda. She went into the bedroom and closed the door. I didn't hear the light switch. She was standing in the dark. Alone.

Isman said, "Let's go, gang."

11

McShite

I had laboured up these stairs five weeks before. I descended them now in the company of commandos, with the night air of the Andes crisp in my nostrils. I smelled eucalyptus smoke. Behind and above me I heard the Old Man's scabbard bumping down the stairs.

In a straggling group — shopping bags swinging, the Arab's rifle on his shoulder — we walked three blocks behind office buildings to a dark lane bordering a stonecutters' yard. There was no moon, but I could make out well enough some scattered chunks of granite. Like gravestones. And here were parked three trucks. Two-and-a-half tons each. Canvas over frames hid whatever cargo they carried. But even the darkness could not hide their defects. The middle one lacked a door. They were motley with cannibalized body parts. I heard the slow drip of oil.

We stood together for a minute, quiet. Then, among us, there was a light, pulsing and phosphorescent — a firefly, rare in this lofty town. To insects, at least, we were Nemesis. The hand of the Kid shot out. He cracked the bug between his fingers, then ran a finger across his forehead. A line glowed faintly there, like the warpaint of a ghost. There were hisses of indrawn breath. The Kid said, *"Brillo, señor?"* Shine, mister? I had not grown less superstitious. Lightning was lightning. *"Por favor,"* I said. I smelled shoe wax as the Kid made a cross on my forehead.

We drove through the night in the outskirts of the City of Hope.

"Man," I said, "you almost hit that tractor! There it goes into the ditch. Maybe you should put the lights on."

"No lights. And shut up. I'm driving fine. Just give me a hit of that exceptional swill."

"Execrable. Which it certainly is not. And you don't get a hit till I get a weapon."

"You'll get your weapon. Later."

"When later?"

"Later. Don't worry."

"Okay, here. Hey, save some. For the Woman. Woman, would you like a hit? Ah, so you do understand English."

The three of us in the cab of that truck. More seat springs up me arse. I was hollering over grating noises and rhythmic thumpings from the motor. As Isman, by wrenching the wheel, tried to dodge the geyser of steam that poured from under the hood and into the cab through the hole where the windshield should have been. My glasses and my beard dripped, and the whole world smelled like rusty steam and hot radiator hose.

Behind us somewhere were the two other trucks, also lightless, running other farm machinery off the road.

Waiting for Isman under the dashboard had been a revolver. On the lap of the Woman rested her After Eight Mincemeatmaker. And as she drank now from the bottle her left thigh pressed tightly against my right. And as Isman fumbled for the stick shift I prayed he would not seize my erection. For I was already in overdrive. Señorita, don't let that toothless codger frolic in your grotto. Let me. Before my piton pops.

On a rutted road we skirted the bárrio of Santa Rosa until we came to a highway. The Pan-American. We waited, idling.

The radiator, having boiled dry, stopped steaming. In Spanish I said to the Woman, "Did you know that if you wait here long enough you will see either a polar bear heading south or a penguin heading north?" She laughed and pushed her arm behind my back and gave my buttock, the unwounded one, a squeeze. Could I in truth kiss someone who had eaten a spider? I lifted the beret from her head and wiped my glasses with it.

"Schoolteacher," said Isman, "I have some bad news. But I also have some good news."

"The bad news is, we're not going to get out and walk, right?"

"Such a pessimist. Pass the swill. The bad news is, there is no weapon for you. A hng."

"No weapon! Jesus, why are you laughing? Hey, what's this about? I thought you said you needed me. What good am I without a weapon?"

"Hee. And the good news is, you won't need a weapon. None of us will. We've been watching the warehouse for a week. There are no guards. Not one."

"Oh sure. How do you know it's the right warehouse?"

"We saw a delivery."

"No guards — I don't believe it. God knows how many millions of dollars worth of cocaine is in there."

"Right. And who would you trust to guard it? This place is secret, man. No one knows who doesn't absolutely have to know."

"Sorry. It doesn't make sense."

"You'll see. Hng. Hyar."

"So we just walk in and torch it and split."

Behind us there was a volley of backfiring. I looked out the rear window, and through an opening in the canvas flap saw the shape of a truck and the gleam of the Old Man's dentures. I could not make out what cargo our vehicle was carrying. We drove across the Pan-American onto an unlit paved road that led down into an area of warehouses and assembly plants.

I asked, "All three trucks are carrying gasoline? That's a lot of gasoline."

We stopped. Isman said, "There it is."

Off by itself a few hundred yards away in the darkness I saw a concrete façade with a big square red door in it. From the roof two floodlights glared down.

"Isman, who sent you the money?"

"The money? Oh, Uncle Giuseppi. My cousin Elaine's dad. Charming man. From Sicily originally." We started rolling.

"You bastard!" I howled. "We're empty, aren't we? We're not carrying any gas!"

"Yar yar! Yes! We're empty. Empty! I told you you were going to love me after tonight. You goddamn crazy schoolteacher — I'm going to make you rich!"

"No! I am not a whore!"

"Bullshit! Everyone's a whore if the price is right!"

I lunged across the Woman for the door. But her gun swung up and walloped my cheek. I sat back, stunned. She let the muzzle of the weapon rest in my crotch.

We were picking up speed.

In English the Woman said, "I am buy the swimming pool most big in the world. And I am fill it with the champagne. And I am go for live in the Canada, where all the mans is so pretty like you, gringo."

Isman shouted, "You're going to love me, Schoolteacher! I promise! I promise!" He pitched the empty bottle out the window.

I grabbed at the steering wheel, but my timing was bad. We veered left into the entrance to the warehouse property, and I was tumbled back against the Woman. We coasted down a long paved drive. A wire mesh gate was wrapped over the hood of the truck. Through the mesh I watched the wall with its red garage door grow larger. Over the door there was a plain sign. *Productos Sanitários Aguilar S.A.* Ten feet from the wall we stopped.

Isman put our headlights on, and the Old Man and Little Juan came around into them. Little Juan gave us the thumbs up. The Old Man bent for the handle of the door.

I said, "Why isn't there any padlock?"

The red door floated up. And inside the warehouse I saw bright light, a smooth concrete floor and the cocaine, there at the far end, stacked to the ceiling in cubes covered in black polythene. A dozen of the cubes, though, were arranged on the floor. Making a stage. Upon which danced a fat pale woman in black panties and military boots, and a dark skinny woman in nothing. The skinny woman held a bottle of Trópico. Over the grinding of our motor I could not hear the music to which they cavorted. But I saw its source: a two-bit portable radio. It lay among scattered playing cards on a folding card table there on the right. I saw the card players too — seated on black cubes and looking at us — four soldiers, one of them bootless in khaki socks and ready to slap down a card. The rest of the soldiers — six or eight — lounged on the floor in front of the women, who now stopped dancing. The fat one folded her arms shyly across her breasts. The bootless soldier wore a pistol at his hip. He stood, flipped his card away and drew the pistol.

Over our motor I heard the Old Man shout "*YAH!*" His false teeth sailed out of his mouth. The skinny woman fell back against the stack of black cubes, laughing. The Old Man turned to run. Then he turned back and hustled into the warehouse after his dentures. The soldier fired. As the Old Man pitched forward, his reaching hand scooped the teeth backward. Up and out through the warehouse door they flew. And in through our glassless windshield. And down the open shirt of the Woman. At which she now tore. And there were her tits. And there were the teeth.

Gears shrieked as Isman fought for reverse. Then he remembered the clutch, and we rocketed backward until we piled into another truck and stalled. The two dancers were scampering now, looking for shelter, of which there was none. The soldiers were diving for their rifles. Behind us I heard a bang — not a shot but a backfire — and suddenly I could hear everything. Soldiers shouting. Dancers screaming. The song on the two-bit portable. Not one of the truck motors was running. And there in our headlights Little Juan stood facing us. His hands pressed over his ears, his weapon stuffed under his belt. The bootless soldier shot him in the back. He took two floating steps and sank out of sight.

Then the Kid was there. He drew his surgical tubing back to his ear. I heard *POK* as the rock connected with the bootless soldier's skull. Then one of the soldiers at the card table stood up, reared back and lobbed something toward us. The Kid skipped out of the doorway and ran for darkness.

It was a long way down to the ground. I landed on the Woman, but my face hit asphalt. Up and after the Kid. The grenade bounced under our truck. Running, I looked back. When the Woman tried to follow she could only limp and hop. She sprayed her mincemeatmaker into the warehouse. The Old Man was trying to rise. But he dropped again, felled by his own *compañera.*

I made the corner of the warehouse just as the grenade went off, and stopped to look back again. Our truck was burning. I could not see the Woman, but I saw her weapon on the ground between me and the truck. I saw Little Juan, too, who was on his hands and knees, moaning. And I saw the Arab. He was just at the far edge of the doorway, aiming his fowling piece. He shouted something in Arabic, *Allah Is Great*, I expect. Then his rifle exploded in his face. He screamed and pirouetted into the warehouse. There were more shots. I sprinted away, out of the pool of light, into blackness.

I ran blind. If that big yard was empty I would run out the entrance. If the yard was not empty, however, but was used to store piles of hard jagged objects, I would soon find out. These old eyes so slow to adjust. But now I saw on the ground scattered white shapes.

I hit hard but clean — a long dive terminated by earth. Began to get to my feet.

"Schoolteacher."

I cowered against the grass.

"Schoolteacher. It's me."

"Isman? Where are you?"

"I'm right here. You want these?"

One of the white shapes just there, three feet away. A hand emerged from under it. In the hand, my eyeglasses. The left lens was missing. But with my right and best eye I could now look for the entrance, which I at that moment remembered was located at the end of the driveway. As I rose again I whispered, "What is that thing?"

"What thing?"

"That thing you are under."

"A urinal."

"Is that what I tripped over?"

"No, you tripped over a toilet. Get down."

The hand that had handed me the glasses pointed back toward the warehouse. A soldier ran crouching past the trucks and down the drive. We were probably halfway to the fence and a hundred yards from the driveway. Among bathroom fixtures.

Isman said, "There's one more at least. Maybe out on the road."

I crawled twenty feet to where three toilets were piled. Pressed myself into and around them. Looked over a rim toward the warehouse. The shroud of our truck was burning vigorously. The floodlights were almost obscured by dirty smoke. A soldier darted out the warehouse door, turned the corner and disappeared, heading for the back of the building. The door of the third truck opened. And the Student climbed down. He raised his hands over his head. In one of them was his book. He walked briskly into the warehouse. The instant he disappeared inside, there were shots and something small flew out the door

— *The Flies*. Then four or five soldiers ran out and started firing into the trucks. The door of the third truck opened again. And the Hood climbed down. He had his gun in his hand. The soldiers ran back into the warehouse. He stood for a second looking out toward us in the light of the flames, with his gun hanging at his side. Then he raised and aimed. At his own head. He dropped before I heard the bang.

I left my toilets and crawled close to Isman.

"Isman. I guess we've had it."

"Fuck you. Have you got a drink?"

"No. Listen. Let's do this right."

"Do what right?"

"Dying."

"Fuck you. Don't you have a flask or anything?"

"Were you going to leave Liz?"

"Shut up. They might hear us."

"Were you?"

"Yes. Shut up."

"And did you ever kill children?"

"What the fuck are you talking about?"

"With bombs. Listen. You won't have another chance to come clean. So, did you?"

"Sometimes you have to do disgusting things. If your only weapon . . ."

"Shut up."

"But I thought you wanted to know . . ."

"Shut up. Did you know my son is a heroin addict?"

"Look. You better be quiet. I think we still have a chance."

"You're killing him. Just like Charlie and the others."

"You asshole. This is cocaine. Get away from me. Go hide somewhere else."

"It's on you, then."

"What is?"

"Everything."

"Schoolteacher, there is nothing on me except this reject

pisser. And that is only until it's safe to run for it. Shit."

I looked where he was looking. Mounted above the windshield of the third truck — as sad a pile of scrap iron as the other two — was an adjustable spotlight. Whose long snout of light was now sniffing here and there around the yard. Resting for three or four seconds on a buckled sink, on a sagging commode, on a trio of urinals leaning together like drunks. Working its way from one ceramic artifact to another. I crept back to my fort of toilets.

The spotlight came to rest upon Isman's pisser, which was squirming slightly as he settled it over himself. But it was no use. He was fat — there were six inches of Isman between his shell and the grass. Also, there were those expensive Portuguese loafers pointing skyward. And the pink and yellow Argyll socks.

The first bullet smacked into the ground between us. The second hit the back of the urinal. When Isman tried to retract more of himself under it, it broke in half. The third shot zinged over my fort, an accident — the spotlight was still on Isman. The next shot knocked a jagged chunk out of the side of the urinal. I thought he had been hit — he wasn't moving. But then he shifted again. And the urinal separated into three pieces.

He said, "Maybe I'd better not stay here."

He sat up. The pieces of the urinal fell off him. He looked like an insect bursting out of its chrysalis. To his feet right nimbly. But then sitting again. I heard the bullet hit and I heard him grunt.

He said, "Help." And sat there.

Three shots missed, but the next one knocked him onto his back. He moaned and kicked his feet. But he managed to say, "Schoolteacher, they're killing me. Your son. I'm sorry. Everything. Help."

Then I was standing just outside the circle of light. Around me in the air there was a lot of whizzing. I think I was going to try to help him. But something warm had splashed into my left eye, and the remaining lens of my glasses was splattered too. I flung the glasses away, heard the lens shatter against some sanitary product. And I saw that Isman had stopped moving and that he was quiet. One of his eyes staring. The other, gone. A black coin of blood there instead.

I turned, took a bead on where I thought the entrance was, and ran. There were no more *productos sanitários* to hide behind. I cruised through blackness. Behind me the guns still banged at Isman. I thought I saw the driveway — blacker than the rest. A soldier would be lucky to hit a running figure in this dark. But what was that? There, right in front of me. Best stop. Stand still. Damn, a mistake. One should run. Always run.

POK.

I saw the person fall. Yes, a soldier. Over whom I now leapt. Kid, I think you must have remembered that time at Pepe's when I left half my hamburger on my plate for you. Hope you didn't get amoebas from it. I did. I think just now I caught a glimpse of your warpaint. Little Chief Firefly, are you all that is left of my lightning?

There was a sound. Maybe a soldier sort of laughing. I saw a shape. Too late. *Wham!* Tackled. Down and flailing to get free. Then I realized I was not being held. And that there was a stink. And that caught between my lips was some fleshy part of my tackler. A nipple.

"Gringo. Mate-me."

The Woman. Saying, Gringo, kill me.

"Por favor. Por favor. Mate-me."

Pushing off her, I could see. Enough. She was on her back. Yes, the breasts. But her abdomen. Open. And spilling out what could only be intestine. I touched it. It was warm. Pieces of dried grass were stuck to it. It ran down her leg and circled a combat boot.

"Por favor, gringo, por favor."

I wrapped her throat in both hands and squeezed. She lay still for a few seconds, then she started kicking, which I couldn't stand because of the intestine over the boot, so I squeezed as hard as I could. Then her hands reached up, slippery with blood, and they clawed at my face. Damn her! Wanting to live! I glimpsed figures outlined against the fire, advancing toward us.

"Die, damn you!"

They could not have been more than a hundred and fifty feet away. Yet her nails dug. Finally she locked her fingers into my beard and pulled. I snapped my head back, leaving her reeking hands full of my whiskers. Then I let go and ran.

Behind me I heard her, gasping air. A sound like a dry pump. Then I heard the soldiers' voices, exclaiming over their find. I listened for the shot. There was none. Only the sound of those men. Laughing.

Out the entrance and up the road. Right up the middle of the sucker, I didn't care. My lungs and legs could not handle this. But by Jesus they would. Because no way I was going to die. And because that pure Andean air was all that McShite had to wash the smell from himself.

12

Rat's Last Splash

On the edge of the soap holder — the words *Productos Sanitários Aguilar*, written in uneven green. Hands trembled on the taps. I stepped out. Stood outside the bathroom door, towel-girded but with no illusions of Bomba. Before last night I had a cozy little room where I was safe. I should have stayed there. Now I was in a different little room with the hot water finished, and it was not cozy.

There was a window high up, barred against burglars. There was the army cot I had slept on, with its churned blankets. There was a wooden desk with a few papers, a small television and a geranium on it. There was a door locked from the other side — I had tried it before my shower. And on the walls there were a dozen masks — jaguar, bear, dog, bird — too many for this cramped room, and all looking at me eagerly. I heard a key scrape into the lock, and the door opened.

She had lost none of her ability to fill a doorway.

She wore her usual tent dress, a yellow one now, maybe for good morning. And just for a second I thought I was back in the snug past, that I might even say, Doreen, how about we take a stroll up to the Arse later? But I had no clothes. And she kicked the door shut behind her and said in her belle's tinkle, with a shy smile, "Land's sake, you sure do know how to make a towel look good." It was not the snug past.

She carried a tray, which she set on the desk among the papers. On the tray there was a plate with scrambled eggs, a fried plantain, a roll, butter, red jam, a cup, a pot of coffee, a quart of Smirnoff Vodka and, hanging over the edge, my laundered and pressed camouflage outfit, which she handed to me.

"You see — I remembered you drink vodka. Mac, I am so glad you decided to come to little old Doreen for help. But you know, you didn't have to smash quite so frantically on the gate last night. A little wee poke at the buzzer would have done the trick." She giggled and gave a little wee poke at the air between us. "And if you could have found some place just a little less conspicuous than the front hall to throw up? Several gentleman callers had to step over it before Carmen got it mopped up. But don't you worry your pretty head, everything is going to be all right now." And a hand like a cluster of liverwursts descended to rest for several seconds on my moist pectoralis major. Her sweat smell. Her massive face just a foot away, with yellow skin around the eyes to match her dress.

She said, with hands on oildrum hips, "Has that Charlie Dávilos been chasing you ever since that night you lit out of here like a jackrabbit? Some people just don't know when to quit. Old Charlie must be some mad at you, son. What did you ever do to him, anyway? Well, never you mind, you're going to be safe here, Mac, and you're going to be comfortable."

She turned to leave but stopped at the door.

"I'll be in from time to time to use the desk. You won't mind, will you? And sometimes I'll want to pop into the shower. Say, you could scrub my back for me, make yourself useful. Little bit of the old give and take. You give and I'll take." More giggles, and the hand demurely to the throat. From the sausage pinkie a ring of keys dangled. "Lord, Mac, the way you are hanging on to that towel, a person would think you felt insecure."

I stood holding the camouflage gear with one hand, strangling the towel with the other, and said nothing.

"And we'll talk too. Why, sure we will. Did you know I was a college graduate? Economics. You want to know what economics is? Economics is this — you scratch my back and I'll scratch yours. That is, if you're fool enough to turn your back on me." She laughed, even squirmed, very pleased. "Oh Lord, that is funny. But maybe I should say wash, not scratch." She unlocked the door and went out and — *snap* — the latch shut.

I ate, and the meal, like the shower, was too short. Next meal I would cut the pieces smaller, and I would also spray the shower more slowly. I reached out, pinched a withered leaf off the geranium. I was behaving like a prisoner. Was I a prisoner? Or was I safe? Or was I both, or was I neither? Maybe I would ask her.

Oh Jesus, Isman — your eye! My shout was still pouring from my mouth as I leapt up from the cot. Doreen stood inside the door, with her hand on the light switch.

"Now you stop that, Mac. You scared the daylights out of me."

The room pitched and kept pitching. I sat. The window was dark. On the desk there was the tray and a plate with a few French fries and the remains of a steak in rose-coloured grease. It seems I had eaten. I had definitely drunk — the bottle on the floor by the cot was two-thirds empty.

"If you puke you clean it up yourself this time. Use the toilet."

I did. Vomited wretchedly into another Aguilar Sanitary Product. When I came out of the bathroom the office was almost dark again. Doreen sat at the desk, ghost-like in the light of the television. I stood behind her, looked over her shoulder and patted my shirt pocket for my glasses, which of course were not there. But I didn't need them. What was on the screen was plain enough.

It was a shot, from a fixed camera apparently, of a bed, seen from the foot and slightly to the right. As if from across the bedroom. The bed was empty. Doreen punched a button on what looked like a large calculator on the desk in front of the screen. The channel changed.

Another room, another bed. On the wall above the bed, a magazine picture. Bambi. Oh, didn't they love Bambi in this City of Hope. And on the bed below Bambi a couple were hard at it. The man at least was. Pudgy, mostly bald, with his hairy back to us, naked except for one dark sock, up on his knees pumping and grunting, buttocks very white for this part of the world, ballocks swinging like the bells of St. Clement's. Or oranges. Or lemons. For her part there was only wiggling at Bambi of stiletto heels, and whimpers that probably signified discomfort. I could not see her face.

Doreen said to the TV, "Maria Soledad, I would say that *el señor* seems to be enjoying your company."

Maria Soledad? Ah — closed-circuit technology in the House of the Whale. I glanced toward the locked door.

"Lord, I am just tickled pink about my new electronic toy. Sound and the whole bit. There are certain customers, Mac, who pay very well to sit in my office and watch television. But maybe we'll just tell them it is temporarily out of order. So that our guest of honour is not disturbed."

She switched channels.

Mili. I knew her right away — her two-tone hair, more of it black now. Sitting in bra and skirt on the edge of her bed, with a small man with slicked hair and moustache kneeling naked in front of her. Holding her bare foot, which was twisted and hooked downwards. Kissing it. Taking the toes into his mouth.

"Mili, you are a treasure," said Doreen, and changed channels again.

More fucking, plain and uncontorted. Anonymous buttocks rising and falling between spread knees.

"The good old garden variety is more common than you

think. My bread and butter, actually. Mac, witness supply and demand. Oh, I declare, this country is ripe for economists. I came here with an aid project, then helped myself to the Chief of Police. These machos are no match for good old American know-how, by which I mean pure female aggression. Held him down with one hand and tore his pants off with the other. Sweet little Raul, what a godsend he's been. Because demand is demand, but certain kinds of supply need a close friend in a high place. Carry on, Mercedes, you're doing great."

She changed channels as she went on.

"Oh, I suppose it's power too. I suppose it is. What I trade in here. Customers have told me this is the best house in the Andes. Well, I'm sure it is. And that's because I understand the fundamentals. Sex. Economics. Power. The gentleman callers' power over the girls. My power over them both. Okay, boys — no pay, no lay. Okay, girls — no lay, no pay, excuse my French, Mac. And of course that's how the world works too. Why, of course it is. Lay and pay. And those of us who understand that principle tend to become successful. If I do say so myself. Except of course if you're smart like I am, you get paid and someone else gets laid. Oh Lordy, that is funny. I must remember that. So, Mac, you see, this is the world in miniature. And that is why everyone feels at home here. Why, didn't you feel — I don't know — just real comfortable the second you came through my door? In the South we have a word, and it means a lot to us. That's right — *hospitality*. Now, sleep tight, you hear? And don't use all the hot water in the morning."

She turned on the light, unlocked the door and left. But the latch. I did not hear it snap. When I checked, yes — the door was maybe four millimetres short of latching me prisoner. I pulled gently on the door handle, looked out through the crack. No one else knew I was there, even though Carmen the maid had mopped up my vomit. So I opened the door and walked casually past that staircase on the right, and then across the empty entrance hall toward a big white door. If anyone saw me they would think I was a customer, my special kink being to frolic in soldier camouflage. While clutching, perhaps, my bazooka. And there was the door to the salon, where I had seen Mili and Jesus that other night. There was recorded music coming from it, a saucy female voice known, I think, as Madonna. And male voices loud with drinking. Maybe here to smooch the clubfoot.

Carefully I shut the white door behind me. Hurried along the walk where last time Carmen went into the geraniums. Now the tall sheetmetal gate, its spring-loaded bolt. And whether I had been a prisoner or not, I was not one now. As I stood alone on the sidewalk in the night of Esperanza. No sound but the snarl of a motorcycle echoing from the mountains. There was no danger now of Charlie. I was safe, definitely. Charlie's mind doubtless on other matters. The warehouse business. Whereas, in Doreen's office, *patrón*, the vibes were so very bad.

A person was approaching. I decided to loiter by the gate until he passed. As he drew close I saw by the light of the streetlamp that he was a northerner. Blond, bearded just like me but with his granny glasses still intact. Then, half a block behind him, another man turned the corner from Reforma and walked toward us. Damn, a policeman! Best head along in the opposite direction, maybe fall in beside the northerner, offer a pleasant word or two. But now there was another problem. Approaching from that direction, the red pimple on its roof barely visible, was one of Esperanza's eight patrol cars.

So I did not fall in, but turned to scan the gate for a device to open it. There was none, only the button and the intercom. As behind me on the street the police car stopped, and a voice said, "Señor McKnight." The doors of the car opened, and there were steps on the sidewalk. The policeman approaching from Reforma now also drew near. And the same voice said at my back, "Señor McKnight, you please to come with we." As I hammered at the intercom button.

Then the northerner spoke. He said, *"Vil du talla med mig?"*

And Doreen's voice came from the intercom. "*Quién es?*"

"*Soy yo.*"

"*Quién?*"

"For Christ sake, open up."

"Mac!"

I slapped my hand over the speaker. They hustled the Swede into the patrol car, as he protested even in a voice like mine, "*Det mosta bli orãtt.*"

And now I know the truth — that if you ever see your double it is a sign that he is going to get the shit instead of you. The gate buzzed and swung open, and before I slammed it in his face the foot patrolman just had time to say, "*Disfrútese.*" Which means, Enjoy yourself. And Doreen welcomed me back into her safe haven of whores.

I could not pour more alcohol into myself. Yet I could not sleep. There were sounds of the House all night, and I felt I was a little boy in a submarine in hell. Music, and loud male laughter sometimes, and sometimes curses, or Doreen's voice. And no one else knew I was here, safe and damned in the dark nerve centre. I heard a woman crying just outside the door, and once a scream. From the salon I heard Ray Charles and *cúmbia* and glasses clinking.

I grabbed the bottle and reeled into the shower and stood under hot water in the dark, and drank until I passed out. I came round with cold water pouring down on me, and I crawled into the cot with the House all silent.

I slept through the next day in wet sheets, and woke with dying afternoon light in the window and breakfast not hot but still edible on the tray. And a new quart of Smirnoff. Soon there were a few joyless female voices in the House, and the aroma of coffee at this the cockcrow hour for *putas*. A radio came on, panpipes and churrango. Carmen's broom scratched above me on the stairs. I lay on the cot, drinking, looking up at the masks as it got dark.

And eventually, conscious that self-respect is founded upon discipline, I put the light on and dressed. In the bathroom I used the new toothbrush waiting on the sink. Next, push-ups. But I got no further than lying face down on the floor. I was still there when Doreen came in with my next meal. I watched her feet move as she set the new tray down and picked up the old one. Blue strappy sandals. Popsicle-pink toenails. Ankles like culvert pipes. Up under her dress I could see it. Swirling around the summit of her colossal thighs. Unfathomable darkness.

Soon again there were drunken voices of men, and heavy feet stumbling up the stairs. I sat on the cot, refusing to put the television on. From the screen the reflection of my face blinked back at me.

I sat listening to the sounds of the House. When they finished I slept. I dreamt I was teaching my grade 12 English class. I was small and I was naked, but I decided to be nonchalant. Continue the lesson as if nudity were indispensable. "Now do you understand," I said, "what I mean by El Dorado?" The class all replied in unison, "Poo-poo. Poo-poo."

Awake to the smell of coffee, and one of the whores singing an Indian song of the hills. I remembered it, Perales' English attempt. *Juanita, is so cold These nights of the mountains. But for buy you gold ring My Poncho I am selling In the market of Las Cruces.* I dressed and washed my face and combed my hair and my beard and brushed my teeth. Then I sat on the cot and waited. And in a minute Doreen came in. With no tray.

I said, "Where's my breakfast?" A prisoner's query.

She said, "You want your breakfast already? Why, aren't you the hungry boy! Don't worry, Mac, if there's one thing I'm going to make sure of, it's that you have plenty of energy. Breakfast shall appear. But not just yet. First we are going to have us a real nice talk. Nothing like a stimulating conversation to work up an appetite."

Today, a tent dress of red froth. And black stockings and high heels, on which she swished and pivoted gracefully, astounding as a Gulf of Georgia killer whale tap-dancing on its flippers. She skipped and dipped around the office, stoked on the *coca*, surely, of Charlie, the other economist in my life. And her little blue eyes sparkled like Yukon ice as she lectured.

"Now Mac, if you think economics has anything to do with money, you're as wrong as two left shoes. Economics is the study of the supplying of man's physical needs. And when we say man we mean man and woman too, of course. Because if women don't have physical needs someone sure forgot to tell me."

She giggled lark-like, spun, curtsied and carried on.

"So the best economist is the person who does the best job of getting their needs satisfied. And, as I said before, I've got a dee-gree, son. As for the person who does the supplying without getting his own needs terribly satisfied, why there's a name for him too. Loser. So the losers supply the economists, don't you see, and the world goes on turning for all its worth."

She paused, sighed.

"Lord, it was a pretty sunset tonight. Chinguráhua went as purple as a darkie's dingdong. So, Mac, is the economics of your present situation becoming at all clear? Don't get me wrong — you're not a prisoner. If you want to leave, just ask. But you didn't seem to enjoy your brief visit to the world out there, night before last. If you choose to keep on enjoying my hospitality, however, it should be obvious by now that you'll have to play a little part in the great web of supply and demand. I am a big woman, Mac, and I have big physical needs. So don't go away, you hear?"

She gave a final spin, and the hem of her dress floated up and touched my lips. Then she went into the bathroom, and I heard the shower running and her singing a song, something about American pie.

It is true that I had begged to be let back in. If that Swede had not come along, Charlie would now be playing stick hockey with my scrotum. Or I would be falling, falling into the deepest canyon in the universe, where the cliffs are thick with the orchids of death, and Charlie's voice echoes for eternity, *Happy landings, gringo, see if you can ruin a princess now.* Life out there, I finally realized, was out of the question. The more you fight, the more you sink in smelly substance. If that was the price of being a man, then I'd pass, because the whole goddamn game was rigged. And worse things exist than wormhood. And worse things than life in a submarine. I knew the rent was high, but *patrón*, I was plumb wore out. The time had come to bend over.

I shuffled around the office, crying quietly. Then she came out, borne forth in steam, a cheap special effect. Around her head was wrapped a black towel turban. Around the rest of her was wrapped nothing but an epidermis the size of a parking lot. On high heels she swayed toward me. Blue eyes flashing in the steam. Monster breasts swinging. And a girl's nipples tracking me like little searchlights. She had managed almost to sluice away her body odour. But the furrows in her fat were deep, and even here in the safe submarine I smelled the orchids of death. She lowered her mass onto the straining cot, and her thundercloud buttocks billowed over the edge. I looked down upon the moist, pink, surprisingly petite and almost hairless genitalia of the Whale of the Andes. Who said in a breathless belle's tinkle, "Breakfast has arrived."

But a drowning rat saves his best splash for last. Doreen dressed and left, and — *snap* — the latch shut. And with the taste on my tongue of a worm's breakfast I tore open the drawers of her desk, mumbling, "I'll take my chances with Charlie." And I found precisely what I needed: a credit card. In view of the act I had just performed I wished the card had not been Diner's Club. But it did the trick. I slipped it between the door and the doorframe, and after ten minutes of struggling I got the latch to release.

I looked out, and it was the same. White door waiting. This time I wouldn't fool around. Just point myself north and scram, the five-thousand mile dash. Out, then, and with bold stride toward the white door. Which, before I reached it, opened, and there were uniforms of soldiers. And I found myself leaping up the stairs and hurrying along the upstairs gallery. In the salon below I saw Jesus and some of the whores. And now the voices of two laughing officers and Doreen were coming up the stairs behind me. I looked down at the shrine in the salon and said, "Lord Jesus save me." And he did. I was beside a door. There were sounds coming out of it, early merrymakers — the officers would not be going in there. But I would. There was a mask on the wall beside the door. I almost left it where it was, because it mocked me — a wooden pink beaver. But I needed a shield against Doreen's closed-circuit technology.

Happily, I was met by no shout of outrage. The bed, on the far side of the room, was almost hidden by four people on chairs. A woman, a man and a woman along the side that faced me, and a man at the end. They were Watching. As a couple, lit by the glow of a bedside lamp, performed. I never did see the faces of the performers, and I could not identify them yet by the conformation of their loins, which pumped in a gap between the Watchers, nor by their exaggerated Spanish moans, and certainly not by the plunging and oversize male organ, for it was false, attached to the upper set of loins by leather, but itself a Dayglo orange and made apparently of some sturdy penis-textured polymer, obviously imported.

The officers went loudly past the door. The man at the side of the bed turned to face me. He was a boy with messy blond hair and a face mauve with acne. Through thick lenses he peered at me. "Cool mask," he said.

I said, "Thank you."

"You Peace Corps too?"

"Yes." Schoolteacher's voice muffled by wood.

"You want to watch? It'll cost you four dollars U.S."

"No. I'll just wait here. You guys go ahead."

"I don't know, man. We all had to come up with four bucks. What do you think, Bernie?"

Bernie shrugged. A long, slouched lad in a reddish fuzzbeard at the end of the bed. He did not even look up from his Archie comic book.

The Castillian endearments became keener. The dildo blazed like a radioactive frankfurter. The two female Watchers had spared only a glance for the Man in the Mask, because they, at least, were digging the performance.

Mauve Chops said, "You're just stalling so you can watch without paying, aren't you? And how come you go around in that mask anyway? Say, are you really American?"

I heard footsteps outside the door. Doreen going downstairs? The performers squealed to a credible climax. Fuzzbeard flipped a page. I opened the door, stepped out. And on my shoulder settled a hand like a bag of yams.

13

The Visions of Captain Kaput

What I saw became my world. Even in the early evening before the men arrived, I watched. The cameras and their microphones must have been hidden behind transparent mirrors, for the women looked directly at me as they put on their lipstick and fiddled with hair or fretted over various parts of themselves. And soon I knew those features, figures and particularities better than I knew my own. The worrying progress of the pimple on the chin of Maria Rosário. Maria Remédios' caesarean scar, which she fingered with an expression of gloom. Maria Mercedes' partial upper plate, which she removed for oral delectations. I learned that Mercedes and Soledad were lovers. And that the first thing any of the Marias did when she came into her room with a man was to cross herself.

I forgot about push-ups. Like the rest of the whores, I slept during the day. I showered, but only out of habit. I ate what appeared on the trays. At night I drank, and offered to the TV screen the vodka-inspired commentary of a dead soul.

"Is that your tape player I hear, Mercedes? Come now, girls, you cannot do the *merengue* to Willie Nelson. That's better —

nothing like your basic honky-tonk grapple for Willie. And don't forget to put your teeth in, babe. And let's see who else is in. Hello, Remmie — will you leave that scar alone! I said don't touch! — this is your captain speaking! Life is loss, kid, so get on with it. Wisdom from Captain Kaput."

On the next channel Lourdes was hauling out of her closet the only costume in the place, a nun's habit. And on the next, Mili smoking a joint as she sprayed cologne on her clubfoot.

However, when the men came — mostly liquored, mostly loud, but sometimes silent and shifty — they didn't give a hoot for aesthetic niceties. The garden-variety of gent set to plowing forthwith or had his implement otherwise attended to. The rest performed more or less imaginative rituals of humiliation upon the women or themselves or both. Into this category fit most of the army officers. Such, *patrón*, was prime time on the Hospitality Network.

Doreen would surely have switched off the camera in the room of Maria de los Ángeles when the office was occupied by paying voyeurs. But now it was only me in the submarine, and she let it roll. Not even the President was immune from communication technology. So there was Charlie, right there, in those wrinkled fatigues, with that knife at his hip, and that pistol. Soldier Charlie, whoring like some young *capitán*, having a break from being prez, with a posy for Ángeles and a refill for her new crystal bowl. As I watched I felt no fear and no hate. Charlie just another gentleman caller. Maria of the Angels performing on that far television shore with tasteless enthusiasm. Once she dared to ask Charlie if he would buy her a house. He did not answer, sprawled there on the bed in unpresidential post-coital peace. Another time I watched him watch himself give his third-Friday-of-the-month speech to the nation on Ángeles' TV. And he never mentioned to her the warehouse. Or Tomás. Or Montserrat. Or me. And if he had I wouldn't have cared, because it was only The Box.

He made her a gift not of a house but of a VCR and a pile of videos. When the other women were hard at work she would be watching a movie, at ease in an armchair (another gift from Charlie) with her bare feet on the table and the bowl of cocaine in her lap. Her television sat in front of the mirror, and I could only see the back of it. But from her expression and from the soundtrack I could guess the action. She liked Bogey best. And how alive his dead voice sounded! "Shmile, shweetheart," that voice seemed to say, "we got a shwell shubmarine here. You and me, kiddo."

Casablanca. Even Ángeles could say, Play eet again, Sam. *African Queen*, too. Her toes always curling during the leeches scene. I often watched her watching. It was at least as enthralling as anything else on Eternity TV.

Rosário's pimple faded. But then some Colombian *pendejo* punched her and broke a tooth. On Channel 4, always Remédios and her caesarean scar. A little child gone where?

And one night who should I see on Channel 5, following Mili as she limped into her room, but Dickie Pendergast. Perpetual cowlick of the Crested Finch of Kansas. Nose gleaming where skin had recently fried and peeled. Absurd beaming smile. Just there on the far shore, almost real but not quite. "What the fuck is with your hair?" he said.

Mili said, "It's my hair, for Christ sake. Black."

"You mean all this time you've been a wog? I thought you were American. An expatriate like me."

"Ricardo, I am an international *puta*."

"Come on — wog or not?"

"I'm a fucking Indian, man. Born in Rio Chumbo. But I'll tell you something. This thing here between my legs — you know what it is?"

"I have a pretty good idea. But tell me anyway."

"Apple pie."

Dickie's laugh as he undressed. "Mili, I always knew you were American where it counts."

I hoped he would sooner or later say a word or two about his colleague Mac McKnight, who had mysteriously disappeared. However, Dickie uttered only a lot of ardent breathing, a few grunts and a strangled squeal of joy.

I changed channels. And there were the Peace Corps kids, blowing off steam after another month among the peasants. Yes, a month gone. I saw that the two *putas* were Soledad and Mercedes. Mercy humping Solitude for the benefit of International Aid.

At dawn, when I was tired and the TV smelled hot, I would sleep.

Meanwhile, several times a week Doreen came to collect the rent. In high heels of some tawdry hue. Froth dresses, b.o. and a beach towel. "I tell you, there is nothing like a nice hot shower to start your day. Or should I say night." Her tinkle laugh. Such was her usual way of saying, Cough up, Kaput. And sometimes she would say, "Come on, Mac, there's room for two." I would squeeze into the shower with her, and wherever she wanted to be soaped, I would soap. Wondering as I soaped if I would be able to come up with today's rent. For a thoroughly drowned ratworm is not a creature easily aroused. As Doreen sang with gusto and nostalgia the songs of Buddy Holly and Elvis.

I had tried to recall Montserrat — her adolescent zest. I had tried Evelyn — the good young years of our pleasure secrets. I had even tried Miss Paddle, a colleague at Trudeau High in Vancouver. But such memories were useless here in the submarine. To get hard I had to picture none other than Holly, whom I remembered as my Naked Dancing Thing. That night in the jungle. The very first night of my whoredom. Cavorting in the darkness as if she had always been waiting for me in that shed. And now helping me earn another day in the office.

One night Doreen was in a filthy mood. "I can put you out any time, you know," she said.

"Please don't."

"Don't what?"

"Please don't put me out."

She stepped closer and, with a hand like a backhoe, pressed my face into her belly. Dark. Warm. Deeper and deeper, until my ears were blocked by soft corpulence. I heard a voice, borne not upon air but upon the truer medium of fat. "Now it is time for love." So, there within fat I conjured my fate, The Dancing Thing, the Clinger, in a shed almost as dark as that belly, dancing the Power Dance against an indigo square of window. Saying, Look at that, my poor little whore wants to live. I struggled to remember the ruinous pleasure of being bought for the first time. And was relieved to find, when Doreen stepped away and I could breathe again, that my penis was standing up.

"Love always makes me feel better," said Doreen.

On the floor between the cot and the desk she spread her damp beach towel. It was green, and there were big bright tropical fish on it, chasing little, not so bright ones. She got down on her hands and knees. Like that, she no longer resembled a person. Perhaps a giant amoeba. The Sheriff of amoebas.

Once, she hit me. A backhand on the ear with her weaker, left, hand. I skidded on my shoulder into the bathroom. Encountered the base of the toilet with my nose. Lay listening to sirens and watching lights go pop and whiz. Felt blood trickling down my throat. She stood straddling me, adjusting the shower. Distant dim eyes peered down past the bulge of her equator. She said, "You liked that, didn't you? Soap me." I soaped her.

Once I dreamt I was wandering in a city of hills and curving streets. There seemed to be no houses or people, only rust-coloured walls and inconsequential shortcuts. But, fading in the day's last light, was a distant bridge. I heard a voice. "What would you like — food, bath or sleep? Please say sleep." It was Isman. He was in his sweatsuit, and he wore what was maybe an eyepatch but could have been just a hole.

I said, "I seem to be lost, old friend. What is this town?"

"Yar! Some schoolteacher you are! Don't you know? This is Lebanon, man."

"Hell, I thought it was Vancouver. Show me the way to the bridge, okay? They're waiting for me on the other side." I pointed to it. It was closer now, but barely visible in the dusk.

"Oh, hey," he said, "don't go over that."

"Why not?"

"That's the *Productos Sanitários*."

I woke.

Another night, I dreamt about Evelyn. We were, I think, in our house in the Italian district. Except that what I saw out the kitchen window was not our weedy back yard but an ocean, which spread to the horizon, winking flashes of gold up at us. Evelyn and I were unpacking a bag of groceries onto a counter. She was wearing that dress I liked so much, of loose white cotton. Her black hair was tied back, but a wisp hung over one ear. She said. "Let's see, is there anything we've forgotten?" I looked out the window. The ocean was gone. Instead there was a vast field of sunflowers. Miles and miles of gold faces, all turned towards our window. And a person wandered there, a young man. Only his bare pale shoulders and long black hair were visible above the sea of sunbursts. He would never find his way. I reached out to touch Evelyn, but she was gone. I was alone. On the counter there was nothing now but a black tulip.

I woke from that dream in a state of panic. I felt as if from a great depth I had been floating toward a surface. And now, with my first glimpse of the weak light that filled the office, I seemed to inhale a kind of electrical and corrosive oxygen. God help me, I was alive again. I grabbed for my vodka, knocked the bottle over, splashed a good bit down my chin and chest and finally managed to swill two or three ounces. Then, shaking, I waited. And it was as I feared. Nothing happened.

Doreen found me still not dressed. Pacing. Running my

hands through my hair. Panting. She had her shower. I swigged more vodka. No use. I sat naked on the cot, feeling the panic seethe. Doreen came out in her black turban and her customary negligée of steam.

"Now, Mac, you can't be drunk again already — you just woke up. Or have you gone back to sleep? Didn't you hear me call you to wash my back?"

I didn't look at her. Couldn't.

"You going to get sick on me?"

"Oh God."

"Ah. So that's the kind of bad you feel. Well, see here, son, I'm not having it! As my daddy used to say, you want to cry, I'll give you something to cry about. Snap out of it, Mac! Unless you want to try crying on Charlie's shoulder. Maybe he'll be more understanding than me. And now it's time for love. Love always makes me feel better."

"Oh God."

"Move your feet. One good thing about being fat is a person doesn't need a mattress. I could use a block and tackle up there on the ceiling, though. This getting up and down business is for the birds. Come on, buckshot, earn your keep."

"Fucking alcohol. What am I supposed to do now?"

"Okay," she said. "Help me up."

"I just wanted to stay dead. Even that was too much to ask."

She rose unaided. A fist like a sandbag whumped into my left temple. I flew off the cot, into the corner. A rabbit mask fell and broke an ear against my right eyebrow. The momentum of Doreen's swing carried her down again. Under the fluid mass of her the cot collapsed. Not satisfied, she came lumbering toward me on all fours, snorting like a bull. Then she stopped and, breathing hard, looked down for a few seconds at the one-eared rabbit mask and the toppled bottle resting between her hands, and at the puddle of spilled vodka in which she was kneeling. She heaved herself up. Got into her garter belt, magenta shoes and the rest. And left.

The blow had knocked some of the panic out of me. I got up, staggered into the bathroom, rubbed a circle of steam off the mirror, looked. My left temple had swollen already and was a milky blue. But it was the face that interested me. The vile fact that it was mine. With the hair longer now. And the beard that, after two months, resembled a mass of dry mould.

As I felt my left eye begin to close with the swelling I pushed the mangled cot and the bottle and the mask out of the way. I wrapped a sheet around myself and sat on the floor with my back against the wall. I was surprised to find that I felt calm now. Even clean. It got dark. I sat. The television submerged the room in its comfortless light. I listened to the sounds of the house. Men laughing. Tapes playing in the salon. I knew I was waiting but not exactly what I was waiting for.

The night finished. I waited into the next day. The house was utterly quiet, and I listened to the cheep of sparrows near my window, the rattle of traffic out front, buses backfiring on Reforma, footsteps on the sidewalk, voices approaching, fading. I felt no desire to sleep. When the afternoon light began to weaken and the first toilet flushed upstairs I realized I was smiling.

I had a shower and combed my hair carefully and cleaned my nails and got dressed.

The light had gone golden. I moved the chair over to the high window. Climbed up. I saw a tiny courtyard a foot deep in weeds and yellow wildflowers. Tiny moths fluttered, and dozens of snails crawled on the weeds. From the back garden of the neighbouring Venezuelan restaurant a billow of vines with brilliant orange blossoms hung over the wall, and two long-tailed hummingbirds whirred and hovered among them. In the distance the setting sun blasted at me from the glass of Colón Towers. And just there, on a telephone wire, his colour intensified by the reflected sun, sat a vermilion flycatcher.

I said, "Jesus, Edgar, boldly ride you said in your poem, and you meant it, didn't you! But what a sneaky place to put El

Dorado! Those bastards thought they had us beat. They thought this was third time down for McKnight. Third time lucky, is what I say. Not to mention, He that loseth his life shall find it. I win after all, you sad bunch of doorknobs!"

I confess to having a metaphysical inclination. But I think what I was experiencing was not grace or nirvana or El Dorado. I have since read about similar cases. Let's call the phenomenon the *Light of the Suicides.*

I stepped down, moved the chair to the middle of the room and opened the drawer of the desk. I had noticed the plastic twine before. Now I took it out, a modest coil, and unwound it. It was about six feet long. Enough. I climbed back up on the chair. A heavy lighting fixture must have hung once from the ceiling. Now there was only a bare lightbulb on a cord, but the hook that had held the former fixture was still in place. A limerick came to me. I recited it as I tied the rope to the hook. *Oh, there once was a bold mountaineer Who had dangled from peaks far and near, But to save best for last — The ultimate blast — He swung from the shandy-o-leer.*

I made a noose, opened it wide, and held it with both hands above my head, forming a halo which, for a few seconds, I admired. Then the door opened, and closed. Doreen barely glanced at me. "You are beginning to be a bit of a bore, Mac. More than a bit." No froth dress today. A simple tent in a sober print. She switched channels on the TV. I heard a piano, and Sam. Sam from *Casablanca.* Ángeles was watching a video. "Get down off that chair before you fall and hurt yourself."

I got down.

"Here is your last lesson in economics. If you are involved in a losing proposition, get out." She looked up at the noose. "I see you may have come to the same conclusion. But I'm not talking about you, I'm talking about me — my losing proposition. Which is you. You've stopped producing, and I need the TV for paying customers. You have become a drag on my economy, sir. In fact, you have become a drag, period. So I am going to divest, and I do not mean clothes. The deal is this. You arrived here yesterday. You don't tell him how long you've really been here, and I won't tell him how you paid your rent."

Him could only be one person. And in fact there he was, on the TV, standing behind Maria de los Ángeles, who was as usual sprawled in her chair, with her feet on the dressing table, tiger gown hanging open. As both of them watched Sam sing about fundamental things and their application, Doreen opened the door for me. "'Bye now."

I went through the door. Two soldiers with machine guns stood there.

When Charlie opened the door he did not at first step aside to let me enter the room, but stared with disbelief. Then he stepped back, and I went in. Today, he wore not fatigues but a three-piece charcoal pinstripe suit. He gestured toward the bed. I sat. It was neatly made, the lion blanket hidden by a white spread. He closed the door. Ángeles tied her gown closed and turned off the VCR and sat primly watching us.

"Trago?"

He handed me Scotch.

"You look like the hell," he said. "You have one shiner in the eye, and your hair and your *barba* they are like Jesus Christ. What's the matter, you don't can talk no more?"

I was waiting for the Scotch buzz. It didn't come. There was no point in saying anything. But just to see if I could speak, I said, "Hello, Charlie."

He winced. And started pacing aimlessly. And talking. "Well, I am find you, Señor McKnight. The *Ballena* she was telephone the *palácio*. I think maybe I like that *Ballena*. She say, Mr. President, I have something for you. This is you, Señor McKnight. Is one estrange way to talk, no? Sometimes I really like you gringos. I will going to make sure my generals and my ministers they come here for fuck the *putas* and she gets more rich. But you no are gringo, you are *canadiense*. Not like the *Ballena*. This is good too, because, *hombre*, she is smelling bad. I think the *canadienses* they no are smelling so bad. They are looking bad, with the shiner eye, but they are smelling okay, no? This is my joke. You no are laughing. *Otro Trago?* What's wrong? — I was think you are the big drinker *canadiense*. I hope you still got your *cojones*. You will going to need them."

He stopped pacing to look at me again, made a face and shivered. "Because I am chasing you you look like this? Like one dead man? What is that uniform of the soldier? You think it make you to hide more better? You are one funny man. The last time I was see a uniform like that it was on some Arab *pendejo* who wants try esteal my *coca*. But my soldiers they were shoot him in the eye. Then the eye of that Arab *pendejo* it look even more worse than your shiner. You need the pitch. Is the pitch? No, the patch. You need the patch. Like General Moncayo." He began to wander the room again. "I think Moncayo he was lose that eye from looking where he should not look. And maybe he was lose that hand from putting the fingers into estupid places. And I think that maybe soon he will going to lose his *cojones* from fucking with *el presidente*. But now he no can put his other eye and his other fingers into my *coca*, because my *coca* she is went. Much money for the economy, and a little money for me. Maybe I will going to buy for my Ángeles one apartment near the *palácio*. Sí, Angelita?"

"Sí, Charlito," said Ángeles, and continued to sit demurely.

He took more Scotch. "You like *el Bogey?*"

Was this all part of his pre-execution drill? To ramble on about shiners and apartments near the *palácio* and Humphrey Bogart?

"Ángeles she like *el Bogey*. She . . ." Suddenly he wearied of his chitchat. He sagged. Tossed back his Scotch. Stood silent in the middle of the room. "God damn you, *hombre*," he said quietly. "God damn you." He handed his empty glass to Ángeles and came and sat on the bed beside me. Laid his arm across my shoulders. "The life she is full of tweet and turns, no?" I could smell his cologne, but also a tinge of nervous sweat. We looked steadily into each other's eyes. There was some strange desperation in his. Mine were, I'm sure, like the wicks of extinguished candles. "I have one mess," he said. "Because of you." He squeezed my shoulder. Then he stood, and with his back squarely to me, cleared his throat. "My Montserrat she is no stop crying since you go away."

I felt a stirring, like when a leg has gone to sleep and then the blood begins to return. I looked down at my glass. Empty. Damn. Buzz or no buzz, I needed a drink.

"She say she want you back. She say . . ."

He was silent for a full minute. I stared hard at the back of his head. He went to the table, poured more Scotch, drank it off, leaned against the table where I had also leaned that day when I had fingered his pistol.

"I will just must say it. My princess is — *cómo se dice? Embarasada.*"

Charlie grimaced at the word. Ángeles went moony and melty and clapped her hands.

And I was on my feet. The room seemed to pulse and flash. On Ángeles' gown the jungle cats squirmed. And now the Scotch hit. My body joyfully realized that once again it was blotto. And — most strange of all — a smell rocketed up through twenty years of memory. Baby powder. And although I did not want to be, I knew that I was. Beaming like a bloody fool.

"You will going to be a father." As if he had rehearsed this part, Charlie came toward me with his hand extended. Robot-like. To squeeze this trembling one of mine. "Señor McKnight, I invite you to marry my daughter. You understand, of course, that you are not having no choice."

14

The Ministry of Strangers

A soft push, and how obligingly the window swung open. In unaccustomed pyjamas I looked out from a second-storey window, beholding on a fresh morning of blue sky and birdsong what now belonged to me, Mac.

Fat short pineapple palms with trunks dripping white roses and nasturtiums. Taller palms, sober and grey. Fig trees, a mango tree, an avocado tree. A purple-blossomed Jacaranda. Orange trees. A banana plant propped with bamboo. Shaded beds of calla lilies, sunlit beds of brilliant something. For contrast, a towering cactus and one spiky *agave*. Formal herb garden. Tiled benches. Gazebo of white wrought iron and screen — there were mosquitoes in Valle Milagro — burdened with bougainvillea and honeysuckle. Hummingbirds going whiz and whir. Two grackles attacking fallen avocados on the grass. A barefoot Indian, Alejandro, raking the grass. There was a lot of grass. And there was a lot of shade, to shield a person from the light of the Andes.

I blinked out upon my real estate through a new pair of gold-rimmed glasses.

Behind me, she spoke.

"Did you sleep well, darling?"

"I don't know. Um, don't call me darling."

"Isn't the garden so beautiful? You like flowers, don't you? I remember you had some in your apartment. They died, but Pápi made them bring all of your other stuff. Your *serbetana*. That estrange painting. Your cassettes. The masks. Wasn't that nice of him?"

"I don't know."

"Let's go for a walk through the town today. I want to — *cómo se dice lucir?"*

"Show off."

"I want to show off my husband and my estomach. And if I see some ladies of the town I will invite them to take coffee. Oh, Maquito, it is so good to be married. Don't you think so?"

"I don't know."

"Don't lie. You were married before, and I know you loved it a lot. And now you have me, and soon our child, and also this beautiful house that Pápi gave us, and your new and so important job."

She came up behind me. Her stomach touched first. Then her hand slid around and inside my pyjama shirt. She had done something like this before, that first night in my apartment. Tearing my sports coat from my body. Life was fun once.

"This weekend let's go shopping in Esperanza, okay? You can help me choose some furnitures for the baby's room. What is it that is so interesting out there in the garden? You need your breakfast. I will cook it myself. Now know everything about the breakfast *canadiense*. Eggs and bacon and flopjacks. Doesn't that sound good?"

"Monzy?"

"What, darling? Is something wrong?"

"I don't know."

Later we took her estomach through the town. When ladies stopped to say to the President's daughter, "I am so happy to meet you at last Señora McKnight and when is the big day," I could not help but smile. Because my child was in there.

When we got back home I trounced our chauffeur, Roosevelt, in three straight games of ping-pong.

"Señor Mac, you are too skilful and too powerful."

"You must learn to hate the ball more, Roosevelt."

"I will try, Señor Mac."

I also had a squash court, but there I played alone, driving the ball against the wall until the echoing bangs forced every thought out of my head.

I no longer did push-ups.

After lunch I puttered in the garden. This seemed to make Alejandro uneasy. He was a stern, bony fellow missing half a left ear. The remaining half went red as I set to yanking weeds among the snapdragons.

"The señor likes my garden."

"My garden, Alejandro. Yes, I like it. And I like this work. Therapy."

"*Terapia*. The señor has more Spanish words than I, a humble gardener." He began to rake the weeds I had tossed onto the grass.

"What happened to your ear?"

"A machete. Someone wanted what was mine."

"A woman?"

The ear went a brighter red.

"Look at this lovely worm here, Alejandro. The worms shall inherit the earth. Do you know why? Because they have never learned to fight and because they eat shit. Go forth into the darkness, my friend, and multiply." I sprinkled protecting earth upon it.

I had a study, or library. A room. There was a walnut desk and a green leather couch. I sniffed the leather. As I thought, Dog. Gone now. The house had belonged to one of the generals that Charlie had imprisoned and ruined. Roosevelt told me that the ample bookshelves had been crammed with leather-bound pornography but that Charlie had had it removed so as not to offend his princess. Now my dozen jazz cassettes, to which I had no desire to listen, were lined lonesomely on one shelf. Montserrat had suggested that I fill the shelves with fake books, which could be purchased from the United States by the yard. In this room was also located my liquor cabinet. It was time, I felt, for the day's first drink. I was having another shot at temperance. Was the sun over the yardarm yet? Best not start with the nautical references. Captain. Just throw open the doors. And thar she blows. Five shelves of vodka. Like ranks of pale gladiators. Mac's knights. Ready to die to the last dribble. Fighting whom?

In this room I hung Jeff's portrait of me, and my masks.

For supper the cook, Maria Cristina, had done trout from a lofty mountain lake. But Montserrat allowed hers to get cold, for she was engrossed in *Star-Glamour*, the South American edition.

"Monzy."

"Yes, darling?"

"You changed your hair."

"I changed it before we got married."

"Is it, um, permed?"

"*Ondulación pemanente.*"

"*Permanente?*"

"*Sí. Permanente.*"

"Monzy, do you still believe there are primitive impulses in the air?"

"Darling, what are you talking about? Sex?"

"Well. Yes. Among other things. I suppose."

"Maybe after the baby, okay?"

Jesus, she didn't even know I was impotent. I hadn't had a hard-on since the last time I conjured Holly and clambered upon Doreen.

Such, *patrón*, was McKnight's new setup. The wife. The real estate. The staff. The stuff. The lack of stiff. I found none of it wonderful, of course. But I was alive, sort of, and was possibly more sane than I had been at Doreen's. Suicide not contemplated now, at least. Because inside Montserrat was my child. The trick was to endure. Dig in the garden a lot. Smash the squash ball. Trounce Roosevelt. Don't think.

The period before we started work we called our honeymoon. I don't know why — we didn't go anywhere, there was obviously no sex. Then I started my *so important job*. I had the title and the salary of Second Deputy Minister in Charge of Emigration at the Ministry of Strangers. My job was to sign certain passports.

My office was in a converted mansion across from Colón Towers. At eleven a.m. or so I would exit my black Mercedes and send Roosevelt back to the Valley. I would then turn down the walk and pass a guard and a beggar. The guard would salute, the beggar would thrust at me his tin bowl, into which I would drop fifty dorados. He would kiss the coin and say, "God reward you." I liked this beggar, a creased, toothless and happy man. On into the building. More salutes and phony smiles and, "Good morning Deputy Minister." Then through Ms. Nieves' outer office and into mine. Ignore the dozen passports waiting to be signed. Look out the window for a minute into the little chicken yard maintained by the *guardián*. "Dig deeper, girls, there are worms." Then pick up the phone and say "Ms. Nieves, I will have my coffee now."

Ms. Nieves was I would say fifty. She came through the door with a tray bearing a mug of coffee and a French pastry. Ms. Nieves wore a plunging white transparent blouse over a black well-laden brassiere. Tight skirt above knob knees above teetering heels. Hair reddish and with *ondulación permanente*. Lipstick loud. Eyelids cobalt blue.

"Thank you, Ms. Nieves."

"Your favourite pastry. Am I right, Mr. McKnight?"

"Next to you, Ms. Nieves, this is my favourite cream tart."

Her laugh. Fingers fluttering around the cleavage. "Oh, Mr.

McKnight, what a breath of fresh air you are."

"Hardly fresh, Ms. Nieves. Where did you learn your English?"

"In Miami. I was the secretary for Lopez Brothers. Scrap metal dealers to the peninsula." She picked up my phone, said into it, "In copper and brass, Lopez gots class." Set it down. "That's how I used to answer the phone. Their English wasn't so hot. But if you're the scrap metal dealers to the peninsula, who needs English. Right, Mr. McKnight?"

"And if you're Second Deputy Minister in Charge of Emigration at the Ministry of Strangers, who needs Spanish. Right, Ms. Nieves?"

"Oh. Such a breath of fresh air."

"If only you knew how stale. This is good coffee."

"Thank you. Mr. McKnight, I know stale. You could never be stale in a million years."

"Hey, it's not so bad to be stale. I deserve my staleness. I've worked hard for it."

"Come on. You can't fool me with your straight face. I know when you're pulling my leg."

"Ms. Nieves, I would never pull your leg nor any other limb or appurtenance. Stale, I say. Dry. For recent events have sucked out one's juices. The piss. The vinegar. But stale, as I said, is okay. It's the other thing that worries me. I can't quite make sense of it all. I don't sleep well. This is, I think, yesterday's cream tart."

"Sense of what all?"

I gestured. The long dim office, the flag heavy on its staff, my desk with its tray. My three-piece pinstripe outfit of what they called here *cásimir*. My repatriated secretary sitting on the corner of my desk, offering a glimpse of rippled thigh and black garter-belt snap.

"I have my own gardener. Does that sound like sense?"

"You deserve the best of everything."

"He only has half an ear. He lost the other half fighting for his honour."

"They're big on honour here."

"Better to be stale. But it's not so easy."

I could have spent my working days at the Esperanza Golf and Country Club or sleeping on the grass at Parque Colón, no one would have cared. But, except for escorting my wife's estomach through the posh town of San Jacinto, I was not ready for any kind of public. Specifically, I feared running into Dickie, Dolores, Flossie, even my former students. I would have had to explain. And if I saw Doreen? No, not ready.

Ms. Nieves took the tray away, and I closed the shutters upon the clucking hens and their trumpeting cock, and donned the earphones of my Walkman. Formless turn-of-the-century music now. Debussy. *L'Apres-midi d'un foreigner*. *Zut* and fucking *alors*, for the worm in his latest turning. As the thoughts and the images paraded and did not get any better.

Schoolteacher, they're killing me.

Mate-me. Mate-me.

My friend smack takes much love away.

My friend smack.

My friend smack.

And as I listened to the music, I would fold paper airplanes from the letterhead of the Ministry of Strangers and launch them into the dimness.

In the evening, at home, in our living room redecorated by my wife, of white walls, deep white carpet and white engulfing furniture, I would watch soothing video documentaries. One night Montserrat was beside me on the couch, reading a book of baby names as I watched *The Canadian Tundra*. A place, it seemed, in another solar system. Watching the box did not generally remind me of the Hospitality Network. But suddenly now I was drowning again. And my heart did the panic paddle. Because Montserrat had taken the remote control, missed *pause*, and hit *TV*. And there was Charlie, in his general's uniform, delivering his third-Friday-of-every-month speech to the nation.

"What are you doing? I don't want to watch this."

"Did I press the wrong button again? I am such a — what is it? — airhole?"

"Airhead. Put Canada back on."

"It's only Pápi. Isn't his uniform so beautiful?"

"It was just getting to the exciting part. The ptarmigans."

"You can watch it again. Listen. If it is a boy, how about *Carlos*, for his grandfather."

"My father was not called Carlos. He was called Jock. I can't watch this. Give me that thing."

"No. You never want to discuss names with me."

On the television Charlie said, in Spanish, ". . . continuing growth . . ."

"Well, turn it off at least."

"Never mind the television. And if it is a girl, don't you think that *Maria Soledad* would be nice? Why are you laughing? Why do you look so estrange?"

". . . opportunity. . . ," said Charlie, ". . . stability . . ."

"All right. If it's a girl — *Evelyn*. If it's a boy, let's see — *Kenneth*. Now, give me that thing."

"Kenneth. What's that? Is it a name? Are you joking me?"

". . . war on drugs. . . ," said Charlie.

"And Evelyn. That was your wife's name."

"It wasn't."

"It was. You told me. Why don't you think of me instead of your wife? She is dead. I am alive."

"You could have fooled me. And don't you ever again say she is dead."

"But she is. Ai, Maquito! Don't hit me!"

My hand was indeed raised. I let it fall.

"Where are you going?"

"To get another drink."

"Darling, don't you think that you are starting to drink too much? Come back, darling. I only wanted to talk about names."

". . . peace and prosperity for every citizen of our beloved country. . . ," said Charlie, behind me.

I think it was that same night. In our bedroom. Montserrat propped upon the bed, reading a new *Star-Glamour*. Me at the window, not looking out, for it was dark, but at my reflection. I had been rescued from the submarine, yet I was adrift. But there was beckoning in the darkness a distant light. Float, Angus. That's the idea.

"Monzy?"

"Yes, darling?"

"You are going to breast-feed, aren't you?

"What, let the baby suck? Like an Indian woman?" I saw her reflection too. She dropped the magazine and picked up a nail file from the bedside table. "Don't you know what would happen? My breasts wound hang down like *salchichas*. Haven't you seen those Indian women with their breasts hanging down to their knees? Would you like me to look like that? Darling?"

"What."

"Where were you before you came back to me?"

"I'll tell you some day."

"Were you being bad?"

"I don't really know."

"Do you know where I would like to go?"

"Tell me."

"Disneyland. Pápi took me before. When I was fifteen. On my way to Boston. We will take our child, okay? How old does it have to be? Six months? You can take us on all the rides, Maquito. Oh, I remember. It was like magic. I liked the *palácio*. What is it called? — the Palace of Snow White. Do you think Pápi could get them to make a Disneyland here? I am going to ask him. He likes to make me happy."

Best get a drink. Sleep is out. Or maybe just tell her. Maybe she would care. Once, you were her Estrange McKnight. There were impulses. She was Amazing. And now she is, after all, your wife and your life's companion. If not her, then who? Is one to be totally alone?

"Monzy," I said, my heart thumping, "I may not show it, but I am suffering. I have been through — well — more than you can imagine." I turned from the window, ready to tell her everything. She was asleep, head flopped back, mouth gaping like an oyster, a noodle of drool garnishing her cheek.

I went to the bed. Eased up her pyjama shirt so I could address the bulge.

"All right then. It's just you and me. Her? Well, it's obvious, isn't it? The idea is going to be to ignore her. Don't worry, she's easy to ignore. As for me, I'm just going to bob on the waves. I think you know about that. In there in your little ocean."

I bent and kissed the belly button. Felt a twitch there. Hi, Daddy.

And not long afterwards, in our bedroom again, this:

"You don't look happy, darling."

"I'm happy."

"Don't you want to go?"

"I want to go." Buttoning my shirt. Montserrat sitting on the bed, waving her red talons to dry them. "Why do you paint your nails? You look like a fucking secretary."

"You are grunchy."

"I'm not. I'm bloody happy. And it's *grouchy*. Maybe if you had stayed in school you could speak English."

"How could I stay in school with my estomach? Anyway, they let me graduate. And if you don't like my English, you can speak Spanish."

"Ugly goddamn tongue."

"My tongue is ugly? First my hair, then my nails. Now my tongue."

"You know, to call you an airhead is a compliment. That skull is pure adobe. Don't cry, I'm warning you."

"You have been drinking already."

"That, at least, is perceptive."

"It is only dinner. Do you have to drink to have dinner?"

"With President and Mrs. Charlie, yes." Out the window,

below, through foliage, I saw a car stop. A man in a dark suit got out and walked with a rolling limp toward our front door. "So Filadelfo is still around. I thought he'd bought it when he went over the railing."

"What railing? Bought what?"

"Didn't you say once that he would never rat to Charlie, because you had something on him? Buggering the stable groom or something?"

"Darling, could you say that again, in Spanish?"

"Yes I could. You heap big adobe skull. Me go drinky quick one, chop-chop."

And greeting us presently in the entrance hall, rising now so very courteously from his chair, was the president's chauffeur himself, my last view of whom had been the soles of his oxfords as he backflipped into Doreen's salon. I whipped my hand toward his nose and shot him with my finger.

"Pow!"

Life still had its small rewards. As he had at Doreen's, he shouted.

"No!"

And as he had then he now also leapt backwards. No railing and plunge now, but at least he tangled in the chair. And as he smashed into the wall and went down he dragged with him a hanging from Pastosa which, struggling with the chair and with his dignity, he tore. This pained me, but I said nothing about it, for I had something else prepared. I helped him to his feet and said in Spanish, "Forgive my childish games. I should have realized how difficult it must be to keep your balance with a mangled leg. May I ask how it happened? A fall of some kind? Am I wrong, or have we met before?"

Filadelfo drove us past palms and verdure and high walls and jewel swimming pools, while under a reading light Montserrat read *Beauty Tips of the Stars*. I had bought a silver flask. I slid it now from the inside pocket of my suit jacket. Had a heavy pull. Spud juice and silver.

During dessert I said to Montserrat, "You know, I made a vow to ignore you." My silver flask was by my plate, and my wineglass was brimming with vodka. "But reading at the table offends even my rude Canuck sensibilities. Put that execrable piece of trash away right now before I send it crosswise up your bunghole."

I grabbed for my wineglass. Knocked it over. Señora Dávilos nodded coolly to a servant in native dress, who approached to assist me. I waved him away. "That's all right," I said. "I have more." I refilled the glass.

Oh, Mamita, even if you spoke English what could you say that was not already in that look of clench-mouthed hate? I said, "They gave the good teacher dessert. They said, See, it doesn't hurt. Did you know your princess is married to a poet? Charlie, would you be so good as to translate for the Señora?"

Charlie did not translate. He sat on my left, tieless in a pink sweater, tapping his flan with the back of his spoon, transmitting a Morse code of suppressed rage. Too late for gutspilling, Papito. But look at the control on the bastard. Those steady eyes that had stared down every scheming plenipotentiary prick in the country. Lord, I have imbibed overmuch. And I am insulting my wife and her gracious parents. And enjoying it. And don't feel like stopping.

"Charlie, you're right, as always. Who needs translation when there is this magic. Called love. Gluing us together in familial whatever. Even this dull Canuck can feel it. In the deafs of my soul. Jesus, can you say that? Dep-ths. Excuse me, I have imbibed overmuch. Bet you can't translate that. Well, perhaps this is an opportune time to do the thankyous. Let me just sluice out the pipes with a nibble of flan and a slug of this here self-service sodie-pop. The wedding — we'll start there. The honour guard was like out of sight, man. If I seemed less than eager, maybe it was all those swords over my head, speaking of which, thanks for the nice haircut, too. As for the house, are you quite sure that General Jaramillo doesn't mind our using it while he's in prison? You better ask him if he wants his book back. *Bedrooms of Barcelona,* I think it would translate as. Splendid nineteenth-century engravings of tremendously engorged Spaniards doing sport in diverse settings. Oh, and thank you especially for my swell job and my swell secretary, Ms. Nebulous, of high heels and low blouse. I like her. I must recite for her my dessert poem. And I do love the Mercedes. Now I can look like an authentic government gangster. Anyway, put them all together and sho-nuff they spell Papito, saviour of the republic and Davy Crockett of the fucking Andes."

As I raised my glass to toast Charlie I saw that Montserrat had looked up from her magazine. She was staring at me and biting the long red nail of the little finger of her right hand. By God, there was even upon her pretty and pregnant-chubby face a look of puzzled worry. One was making progress here.

"As for your daughter there, do you know that she says she is not going to breast-feed? Look at those tits! They're like *melones!* Yet she will deny the milk of life to her own child! Has she ever told you how we frolicked? Yet now she is afraid to sully her snow white *tetas* with the lips of her own blesh and flood."

Señora Dávilos was on her feet, saying something to Montserrat in Spanish, which I didn't get. My head was suddenly reeling. I felt sick. Montserrat stood. Two tears rolled down her cheeks. She left the room with her mother.

Charlie had the servant take coffee into his study. He steered me in with a hand on the shoulder. The President's room was impressively modest. A desk, a liquor cabinet, a fireplace, a handful of books looking unused on shelves, a small table with the coffee, many maps on the walls, a leather couch and chair and, on the couch, a dog. The dog was small and ugly. Shit-brindle and black. It breathed with effort through a pug nose reminiscent of Charlie's. Two fangs curled up around its top lip. Charlie bent and scratched the mutt's head. When the servant left and closed the door, Charlie straightened.

And presto, *patrón*, I was flat on my back on the floor. There was a brown blur pinwheeling around my head, and a shattering noise of *yak! yak! yak! arf! yak!* Then a pain in my right arm. God's teeth, not only had Charlie punched me, but the mutt had bitten me! My glasses had gone, but I could not miss the pink mass of sweater hovering above me. I was pulled up by the shirt front. Then there was a blizzard of spittle in my face and, along with the mutt's hysterical *yak* and *arf*, a flood of incomprehensible Spanish.

"Speak English, God damn it!" I shouted. "Can't you see I'm drunk!"

Charlie released me. My head thumped against the floor. He kicked out, the brown blur went flying. The yakking stopped.

After several attempts, I stood. I tasted blood. My lip was split. Charlie faced me, with his fists clenched and again ready. He said, "I was hope maybe you are the good — *cómo se dice yerno?"*

"Son-in-law. Fuck you."

"I was hope maybe you are the good son-in-law. But tonight you show me I was hope wrong."

"So get out your knife, you murderous prick."

"No. No knife. Not yet. I wait and I see. My *nieto* he will going to need one daddy. This is you. Ai, *hombre*, is like one bad joke, no? But I wait and I see. And if you no are being the good daddy, then maybe the knife. You understand me?"

"You hypocritical bastard. You're still selling it, aren't you?"

He unclenched his hands. "Oh, so this is why."

"We're living on fucking drug money."

"This is why you are behave so ugly in my house."

I swung at his pug nose. He dodged my fist, grabbed me as I stumbled, and set me up straight again. Our faces were a foot apart. I sucked saliva onto my tongue.

"No. Do not espit. Even my patience it has an end."

He left me tottering, fished under his desk and handed me my glasses. Then he went to the little table and poured coffee for himself.

"Mac. I will going call you Mac now. Mac, I was tell you before, the *coca* she is went. Much money. Enough money. The *droga* she is one big problem. One big problem of the — *cómo se dice sudor?* — is sweat, no? One big problem of the sweat and the worry. So I start build the eschools and the hospitals, and I make some jobs, and everybody is happy, and soon I will going make the election. Me? I got enough. No more *droga*. She is one big problem. I know about your son, okay? But you no are living on the *droga* money. So relax, *hombre!* Relax and be the good daddy."

He poured coffee for me, but I didn't accept it, because I felt a wave of nausea. Perhaps even a permanent wave. I bent and threw up on the leather couch. The mutt jumped up and sniffed at some morsels of undigested roast beef.

So Papito appeared to forgive me. Yet it was three years before I was invited back for a second family dinner. Three years! Not everything happens wham! bam! in the life of A. Dorado. There are, thank Christ, periods of uncertain respite. But relaxing, like being stale, was not so easy. Tumescence continued to evade me. I fiddled so obsessively in the garden that Alejandro finally learned to ignore me. I gave Roosevelt fifteen-point handicaps and still murdered him. For hours at a time I lambasted the walls of the squash court.

At work I listened to Delius and Ravel, and I tried to write to Jeff. Fountain pen poised, I would grin down at the paper and imagine how happy he would be to know he was going to be a big brother. Then, with nothing but the Ministry of Strangers letterhead and *Dear Jeff* on the sheet, I would fold it and send it drifting down my office into dimness. I never actually said to myself, Get real, Angus — he's lying! Because what I needed most was for Charlie to be telling the truth. The *coca* she is went. Nevertheless, I couldn't write to Jeff, even to share the one particle of joy that kept me going. Captain Kaput was still aboard somewhere, and the Captain knew the score.

It was early one Saturday evening before supper. I was alone, as always, in my snowy running shoes and snowy cotton shorts, barechested and trim from gardening and ping-pong and from punishing the ball in my squash court. The almost-darkness soothing. Like when I was seventeen, out behind the house in late autumn, shooting baskets before supper. The ground too uneven for dribbling. Glad that it was dark so I could not see the chicken shit on the ball. It was like that here. *Wham. Wham. Bang.* But now the shit was out there. In here it was clean.

Then the door opened. And Montserrat was silhouetted against the twilight, her loose white dress draped over her pumpkin stomach. The little ball hit one, two, three walls, then ricocheted softly off her forehead. "Darling," she said. "It is time to go. Ai!" The *ai!* was not for her forehead but for her stomach, which she gripped with both hands.

"Oh Jesus! Just stay calm. I've done this before. I'm a veteran. How far apart are the contractions? Where's Roosevelt?"

"He has gone home."

"Gone home! Oh my God, no! Can we call him?"

"Darling, please do no escream. He does not work at night. You know this."

"Christ, you're right. What the hell are we going to do now! Never mind. I can do it. There's just some business about the umbilical cord. Damn, what was it!"

"You do not have to eswear. Never mind the cord."

Hanging from her fingers, a set of car keys. Which, calmly, she offered me, then nodded toward the little grey suitcase at her feet.

I booted the Mercedes up the squirming mountain highway toward the City of Hope.

They took her right into the delivery room. I sat for a few minutes in a waiting room, with two other waiters. One of them, a smooth and groomed man in a three-piece suit, stared at me for a long time, then said in English, "Señor Deputy Minister, this your first children is?"

And suddenly I was striding down the hall. Running shoes going *eech eech eech* on the tiles. But there was a lookout: a nurse, draped in hospital green. Whose instructions, I am sure, had been, Watch out for that gringo with no shirt. Her little hands against my determined Canadian pecs. With her shouting a lot of Spanish phrases all of which meant, No you can't go in there. And me shouting in English phrases such as, "Do you realize that is the President's daughter in there? By God, I'll have your job for this! You'll be selling oranges on Avenida Colón!"

Then the lookout's backup, a second nurse, was at my side with an armful of green cloth. They both helped me into a gown, cap, mask and shoe covers. Just as, twenty years before, two nurses had helped me in Lion's Gate Hospital in North Vancouver. Through the swinging doors now. And the doctor not even looking up. From Montserrat's gaping vagina. In which there rested a little slimy dome.

"Jesus, he's coming!" Yes, I said that. He. Montserrat heard my voice and looked toward me. And I said, "Come on, Ev, come on, he's almost out."

Twenty years before, in the Lion's Gate delivery room, a pair of smiling nurse eyes had handed me a wrapped bundle to hold for a minute so that tears of joy could spill down my face. Now several green arms swung to indicate to me the swinging doors, and no one handed me anything. So I stepped forward, and from Montserrat's cradling arms I myself lifted the bundle. Muttering green forms hovered around me as I made several turns around the delivery room, but I ignored the green forms, and I ignored the red fingernails that on my third pass reached toward me from the delivery table, because I was talking to my son.

"Well, Kenneth, this is it. This is the world. What do you think? Pretty cool, huh? I'm your dad. I'm Mac. Canadian guy? Beard? Oh yeah, now you remember. Hey, we're going to have fun. You like racquet sports? Only one thing you've got to remember. One thing. This time we do it right. Okay, Kenneth?"

15

Ondulación Permanente

"You see this new bowl, Ms. Nieves? Keep it full of ice. For my Scotch. I intend that the execrable taste of the stuff will keep me temperate. My son has begun to notice things. As has, I think, my liver. Yes, it is an unusual bowl, isn't it? Ken helped me chose it. Mickey Mouse's ears are actually handles, you see. Since he and my wife got back from Disneyland he has become a bit obsessed with cartoon characters. But here, try a little in your coffee. Ruin a cup of Colombia's best."

There have been a few changes to my office, *patrón*. No scrapheap of paper airplanes now, for I have filled the whole expanse with rain forest plants and racks of Gro-Lites. A vine called Devil's Holiday hides the flagstaff and seems to be ingesting the banner itself. Ferns do slow battle to hog a spot of artificial sunlight. Plants are stupid and elemental and determined. I prefer plants to worms now. While Ms. Nieves gossips with her sister, Engrácia, in Fort Lauderdale, I water and prune and fertilize. Hidden among the foliage are high-fidelity speakers, which offer me daily sustaining doses of bebop, for I have abandoned fin de siècle impressionism and am back into jazz. The orchids all dig Sonny Rollins.

There are a few leaves mashed into the carpet, and a sprinkling or two of spilled soil which the janitor has chosen to ignore, the results of my bringing Ken with me up from the Valley at least one day a week and letting him rampage on his tricycle. Ken likes only old rock 'n' roll. His most-requested number is *Rock It, Robin*. Deedly-tweet.

The Ministry has supplied me with a coffee table, and there are two leather chairs in which Ms. Nieves and I recline to enjoy our morning and our afternoon coffee breaks. The present is our afternoon one.

"The pastries are very nice today." Ms. Nieves' voice is like cracked brass. I have always liked her voice.

"Thanks, but I'll stay with the *chifles*. Scotch and *chifles*, my new regimen. In honour of a man I once knew. A terrorist. Blew people up. They called him the Harvard Fart."

Ms. Nieves laughing. Flakes of *chou* pastry sprinkling like snow down her cleavage. "Mr. McKnight, the stories you tell! Terrorists! Pancho Perales! A witch called Tylenol and her cousin, Flashlight!"

"Aspirina. Everready."

"I don't know whether to believe half of what you tell me."

"Ms. Nieves, perhaps some day I will tell you the other half. Which is truly unbelievable."

More crumbs down the bodice. "Oh, such a breath of fresh air."

"And what of your stories, Ms. Nieves? It's your turn. For example, was there never a Mr. Nieves? In Miami perhaps?"

"Oh yes. There were. Three. And all in Miami. But not Nieves. Mr. Snoozer. Mr. Loser. And Mr. Boozer. Mr. McKnight, why didn't you go with Señora McKnight and little Kenneth to visit Disneyland."

On my feet now. Plucking nervously at the yellow fringe of a leaf. "Here is another story for you not to believe. If the Second Deputy Minister in charge of Emigration at the Ministry of Strangers had applied to his own department for an exit visa, he would not have received one. But he didn't apply. Because the Second Deputy Minister would rather stay home. Where there will be no further nasty surprises in his life."

Float. Try to bob a bit. On this permanent wave that has borne you forward in unrelenting seasickness of the spirit these two-and-a-half years. "Oh Christ, look! See how they're all drooping. Damn! The droop is back. Now I'll have to spray."

"I thought maybe you would have taken the opportunity to visit your other son. The one in Vancouver."

"God damn you! Are you going to sit there stuffing your face all day! Go file your nails! Go show your fat legs somewhere else!"

Gone then. As I stand alone in my drooping jungle. Listening to the speakers hiss like a steady rain.

Once I had seen Dickie Pendergast from the open window of my car. Walking along Reforma with his briefcase of Social Studies. He saw me and shouted and waved. I looked straight ahead and ignored him.

But someday there would be peace, I just knew it. For I had already learned to go for walks by myself. Not just through the posh town of San Jacinto with Ken, but alone upon the cratered sidewalks of the City of Hope itself. Not the main streets yet, where I would have run into people whom I used to know and to whom I would have had to explain. When I had managed to explain first to myself, then I would walk on the main streets. On this day the back streets were adequate. In the afternoon glare of white walls. While several blocks behind me my shouts about fat legs still echoed in my office, and poison spray dripped from the leaves of my plants.

I turned a corner, and there on a wall was old paintbrush graffiti that said *Dávilos presidente*. The election long past now. Charlie the boss of a democracy. And as I walked back to the Ministry mansion I wondered yet again if I had written to Jeff when Ken was born. I must have. Surely I must have.

To be a driver is not just to drive. It is to make human sounds as you purr down the western range into Valle Milagro. Sentences in easy Spanish which your employer in the back seat can understand.

"You went for a walk, Señor Mac."

"As is my custom, Roosevelt."

"To the stonecutters' yard again?"

"Did you know they fill the water cannon there? At a hydrant just across the street. An ugly thing. The metal of it is rough from bricks and stones."

"And bullets."

"Is it thus, Roosevelt?"

"It is, Señor Mac. The trouble has returned again. Every day. *Manifestaciones*. You know this. Look."

"Jesus."

Roosevelt steering with his left hand. In his right a pistol. "Do not worry about the *terroristas*. I, Roosevelt, will protect you." He lowered the window. On the shoulder of the left-hand lane lay a dead German shepherd. As we cruised past. Roosevelt poked the gun out and fired. The dog bounced off the shoulder and into the ditch. "One dead *terrorista*," he said.

"Never do that, Roosevelt."

"I am sorry, Señor Mac."

Marshal Art had told me once about a room in the basement of the police station. The smell of excrement and vomit absorbed forever into the cement walls. Ropes and pulleys and an electrical device with clamps. Time to open this amazing little cupboard behind Roosevelt's seat. With its glass and decanter of Glenlivet.

I should have been happy that the trouble had returned, that Charlie had resorted to torture and murder to keep the lid on. Because it meant that Charlie's *coca* she is went, and the country was poor again. But happy I was not.

"What you told me, Roosevelt. That *coca* is everywhere in the city."

"It is thus, Señor Mac."

"Where does this *coca* come from? Have you heard?"

"It comes."

"The other chauffeurs you talk to don't know?"

"It comes."

I put my glass away and from the seat picked up a toy Ken had left behind. A hand puppet. A toucan. Orange and green and yellow. I put it on my hand — my toy, I suppose, as much as Ken's. And as I made its mouth move I thought about Montserrat. How she seldom seemed to mind anything I did. My drinking. My insulting the red-nailed airhead she had turned into. My unceremonious proddings and gruntings in the middle of the night whenever the urge took me. McKnight's ardour derailed no longer by memories of the Hospitality Network.

Between borders of pink and white roses, and under bougainvillea, into the carport. I walked around to the back entrance and, as I prepared to mount the steps, I heard a voice.

"Darling."

There behind honeysuckle blossoms and the screen of the gazebo, two figures. I crossed the grass and opened the gazebo door and went in. Montserrat and another woman were seated at the little wrought-iron glass-topped table we kept there. They had coffee cups. Montserrat in shorts and sandals and a loose striped blouse and permanent wave. But the other woman was in a black glitter T-shirt, with hair in a chewed spiky style imported late from America.

"Alegria Bustamante," I said. I put Toby the Toucan in my pocket. She stood and shook my hand.

"Hello, sir," she said.

"Sir!" I had to laugh.

But she just went white and sat down and glanced at Montserrat.

Montserrat said, "Would you like some coffee, darling?"

"No. What's wrong?"

"Alegria has brought a bad news." Then I noticed that

Montserrat's eyes were reddened and moist. Through the glass tabletop I saw clutched in her hand a handkerchief. "Do you remember Marco Cádiz?"

I looked at Alegria. "They found him in his father's factory," she said. "In the morning, when the workers came in. He was sitting in a pile of cheese. On the floor by his feet was the needle."

"I see. Heroin?"

She shook her head. "Cocaine. They think his heart exploded."

"He used to take your hand, Montserrat," I said. "To look at the time."

I found my son digging with a wooden spoon among some snapdragons. His *niñera,* Trinidad, sat in a folding lawn chair nearby, in lace and beads and velvet, reading a newspaper. I saw the picture on the front page. The water cannon, spraying people who were falling and running. Ken's roar and laugh and leap up to be squeezed against his daddy's chest. Such a wild wee rangitang. Trinidad came running to brush the dirt of Ken's shoes from my suit, but I turned away and walked toward the gate. Red-faced, squirming, kicking, snot-nosed, wild hair and pissy pants as I squeezed the bejeesus. And when I stopped squeezing he showed me that he had a yellow snapdragon blossom and, with great concentration, how it could bite my nose.

I set him down. His face lit up. "Toby!" One of the words he always got right.

"Hi, Ken," squawked Toby the Toucan as my right hand flapped his beak. "Where you going?"

"*Paseo.*"

"*Paseo?* What's that? Oh, you mean a walk! Hey, can I come?"

"'Mon, Toby."

He took my left hand and led me and Toby out the gate.

Across the paved road and along a gravel one. Walking backward in front of Ken now, so that he and Toby can talk, through the original San Jacinto, here before property values, palm trees or petroleum. Here is the store marked only by a 7-Up sign, with the dark air inside full of grain dust and where sometimes I buy two homemade popsicles of frozen milk, first checking for the legs of insects.

Now the barber shaving someone in his nameless shop of unpainted adobe. Now the tailor's son sitting on his doorstep, stitching. Now the crumbling Spanish church and the square for Thursday's market and the vacant lot where on Saturdays they sell the meat of grinning barbecued pigs.

"Where's your dad?" squawks Toby.

"Deh."

"Where? I don't see anyone."

"Deh!" Tugging the knee of my pants to show the stupid bird.

"What, this funny-looking guy? This is your dad? I don't think this is your dad. This is a monkey. Look at that hair on his face."

Ken shouting with laughter and jumping up to take swipes at Toby. Then two Indian girls pass us going the other way and burst out giggling and run off with hands clapped to mouths and long skirts jouncing. Then I step in some dog shit. And Ken watches with interest as with a stick I scrape the sole of a new black brogue.

Best walk frontwards. As Ken forgets about Toby and scampers ahead and starts scuffing up dust storms and saying, "Duss. Duss. Duss."

The setting sun is perched there ahead, just on the tip of Volcán Tingáy, and the coppery light makes my son's hair flame and his shadow long as now he chases a blue butterfly back and forth across the empty road. My son's eyes, although not blue but *Índio* black, are round and Scottish. Away yersel', Jock, and I hope that's all you handed down to your grandchild. For you were not — as I lied that time to Liz — a business executive but a used car salesman in the town of Clover Valley, who called Canadian lager the "best beer in the wurrrld" and who drove your wife away at the age of sixty with your rages and your weeping and who finally went for that fishing trip in the Cariboo, where you left your aluminum boat bobbing empty in the middle of Lac La Hache.

And there across the road is that abandoned old house in its yard of weeds and deadly nightshade. And once I saw a strange thing. A black horse standing on the porch.

Now he has found a stick, a piece of eucalyptus branch, and with it he is slapping at a particular purple pebble.

Hand-in-hand now, eucalyptus stick dragging, down the road in the deep light of sunset.

Newer stores and a crossroad. A Mercedes passed us, the driver of which waving because he must know I am the Son-In-Law. We cross the street to Manolo's ice cream shop. It is full of rich kids. A quick check for students, then in.

"What flavour, Ken?"

"Buh-guh."

"Good choice." My favourite too. Bubble gum.

Then next door with Ken and his cone to my destination.

"Vodka, please. Two cases."

"Esmirnoff?"

"Yes. Please deliver it."

And so I walked back along the road, carrying Ken now, and his stick and his cone. Not minding the blue ice cream on my lapel. Because Marco Cádiz was dead in the cheese factory. His heart had exploded. And the sun had gone behind the volcano. And it was cold. The light was disappearing fast. I needed to feel my son's weight and warmth and to put my nose into those golden curls.

16

The Nun's Tale

The next morning I didn't even make it in to see if my plants had recovered. Ms. Nieves stopped me at her desk.

"The President's office just called."

"What — Charlie!"

"You're supposed to go over there right away."

"While I am gone, would you think I was cruel if I asked you to prepare some exit visas?"

And, though the previous day I had shouted "fat legs," she said, "Mr. McKnight, you could never be cruel in a million years."

"Leon Marques de Herrera."

"But he's on the *No Salir*. He's not supposed to leave the country."

"Give him his visa. And the others."

"Everybody?"

"While a little light remains, Ms. Nieves. Before the black depths claim what's left of us."

I walked. Along Avenida América in the exhaust of trucks, past ashes on the road where the previous night a barricade had flamed. Up the hill of Calle Chile, left past the central post office, where two urchins were kicking a spent tear gas canister. Right, to the Plaza de San Francisco, where on that day of the coup I had silenced Dickie Pendergast with a reference to a red-haired little Dick in Denver. Inside the Palace someone would hand me a document to sign, and I would sign it. Then I would go back and take Ms. Nieves to lunch, because I should not have said that to her about the black depths.

I had seldom been to the Palace since the day Charlie had made me a citizen and had me sworn in as Second Deputy Minister in charge of Emigration at the Ministry of Strangers in the same afternoon. But I knew there was a shortcut through a parking lot. So I flashed my government I.D. card and walked down a dark driveway. But strange. That burly bald man with a greying moustache, who passed in the gloom, then stopped and turned and looked, as did I. I remembered. Par Lee, CIAjerk. I turned away and went on, into a big courtyard. It was from here that Perales, on that day of the coup, had beat it in his helicopter. Now it was filled with many black Mercedeses. I walked across the courtyard toward a guarded door.

But strange. That one car. So extravagantly out of place. Low and red, like a coal smouldering in the heart of this botched city. I would walk past it and touch the hot insolence of its rear end. To such, *patrón*, had my sense of adventure been reduced. I let my hand slide along the lacquered roof, and when I got to the door I bent to see inside. The window was down. And a face was smiling there. A woman. Who said, "Well, hi there, Schoolteacher."

I laughed. An empty black laugh. And the green eyes of the woman laughed even blacker. As she said, "So how's my little whore?"

Her hand reached out, and she pinched my expensive lapel. "Surviving quite well, by the looks of you." She licked her lips. She whom I had last seen three or so years ago in the Rio Colorado. Hanging like a rag from a drifting dugout. Now here in the Palace parking lot, doing her Power Dance from the passenger seat of a Porsche. "A whore knows what it takes to survive," she said. And winked a green eye.

Someone led me down hallways. Everything looked now like a tunnel in a dream, which would come out where? There was a whooshing in my ears. Through doors and more doors, until there he was. In the middle of the tunnel. Rising behind his desk, in a soft grey suit. Indicating with a gentle smile a chair, in which, thankful, I sat, for my bones were sawdust, and the sawdust was burning, and I was choking on the smoke.

Charlie did not sit, but ambled amiably around behind his chair as he talked to me.

"The life she is good, no? Your important job. Your much money. Your so beautiful Kenneth. Your wife, my daughter, who is loving you for always. I think you are one lucky gringo, Mac. My favourite and my one only son-in-law. The life she is full of tweets and turns, but sometimes at the end is waiting the El Dorado. Once you were teaching this, no? And now here it is. A life of gold for my Montserrat and my Kenneth and my Mac."

He leaned on the back of his chair and looked at me, seeing, it appeared, no suffocating gases of fear, but something satisfying. "And you, my Mac, are no more not the *canadiense loco*. You are *tranquilo*. Yes, I think it is time for you to come again pretty soon to dinner." He ambled again. "At the Ministry you are making a good job. I think maybe is time for give you more money. Yes, is time. I will going to give you much more money."

And I thought, Where could she have hidden, these years, on Esperanza's sombre streets, with that Porsche pulsating so red and those green eyes beaming evil? But she is not the one who has been laying low, Angus — you are. And she was in the passenger's seat, not the driver's. And who was the driver, then? And why was the CIAprick visiting the Palace? And now Charlie loves me and is saying I deserve much more money. Is it back then? The Naked Dancing Thing?

Finally he sat, but turned his chair sideways, as if we both should look away into some golden haze he was fashioning in the air of his office. "Your son will going to have a good life, Mac. He will going to have the best life and the most happy life that is possible in the world. There will never going to be no problems in the life of your beautiful Kenneth."

Then up again, looking out between the bars as he talked.

"For me this good life she no was been so easy. When I was a general, and in this office was that *hijo de puta* Perales. I come to here one time, and he was been drinking all the day, and he was throw up right here where I am standing. And I say, Mr. Presidente, I have here the report you are asking, and Perales just say, Bring me a *puta*, bring me two *putas* from the house of the *Ballena*. So I go and I was bring him two *putas* and he was fuck them on top of my report. Then he say, Go away, Dávilos. But I do not kill him. And I do not say to my army, Put him out. Because the people was elect him and is no so good to put out a president who the people was elect. I am tell to myself, Later it will be better. Wait. There will going to be a good time. To wait it was so hard. But what I am telling you? — the life she no is easy. I wait. Then one day is very very easy to put him out. It was hard to wait but it was better. Hard. But better. Understand?"

His quick glance over his shoulder to ask this.

"Always I am wanting to do one thing, but is better that I should to do something else different. This I don't like, Mac, but this is the politics. So I was put out Perales. I was put him out before Moncayo can to put him out. Because General Moncayo he was hating Perales too. And he was hating me, and today he is still hating. This *hijo de puta* with one shit hand and one shit eye. So I was put out Perales, and then I am thinking, Now is better that I should to put this Moncayo in jail. Like the other *generales* who were kissing the *culo* of Perales. But Moncayo he no was kissing. He was hating. And all the army they were loving their General Moncayo. So I no was put him in jail. And now Moncayo he is boss of all the army. And now he watches me like I used to was watching Perales. This is the shit, Mac. But who is in this office, Moncayo or Dávilos? Me, Charlie Dávilos.

I am in this office."

He sniffed at the air of the outer world that was drifting in through the window. I smelled it too. Tear gas. And there were far-off shouts.

"But Perales he was teach me something. He was teach me is better the democracy. Because when the people are electing you, is no so easy for these *pendejos* to put you out. They can to shout *bajo Dávilos* all the day. Moncayo he can to look me with his one shit eye all the day. And to me it doesn't matter. Because this is the democracy, and they all must to wait and to vote. I hate the democracy. Is much trouble the *congresso* and so much talking for to do every little thing. But I was spend some money, and they elect me, and now I am here, and they can to shout, and to me it doesn't matter. And maybe soon I must to spend some more money, and the people they will going to elect me again. I hate the democracy. But I like very much this office. And I like very much that my beautiful grandson Kenneth he will always going to have the wonderful good life."

He swung the window shut, came and sat in his chair and leaned toward me across his desk. He said, "Sometimes is necessary to do some things which they are not so nice. Because without we do these things, the wonderful good life she is went. There exists a word for this in English, no?"

I tried my black laugh but couldn't put it together. So I said the word.

"Compromise."

"You got it, Schoolteacher."

The voice came from behind me. I turned. He rose from a chair in a dark corner where the open door had concealed him when I entered. He came slowly down the office toward me. White linen suit. No tie, but half-a-dozen gold chains shining against a pale blue silk shirt. Hair pulled back into his braid.

"Compromise," he said. "Eat shit today to eat caviar tomorrow. Or maybe forget about getting even with assholes if forgetting about getting even with assholes is what it takes to get what you want."

He stood above me, smiling down. Then he tilted his chin up so I could see his throat. It looked as if some animal, a horse maybe, had taken a bite out of his neck and it had healed into rough scar tissue.

"Thay said I would have died if I had been a monkey."

Then he bared his teeth and made a chatter and a screech and an *oo-oo-oo* in my face, and scratched at his ribs. His chains hissed. He smoothed his already smooth hair and sat on the corner of Charlie's desk. Preliminaries done, business meeting called to order.

"Here's the deal," said Tomás. "We're expanding. Buying from Peru and Bolívia. Selling only to governments who need money quick. Several clients from Eastern Europe. Like, there is some heavy financing going down, and it's probably a good idea to bury it."

"So Moncayo he no can sniff with the nose," said Charlie.

"And so that CIA asshole Par Lee no can sniff with the nose, either," said Tomás. "And his Drug Enforcement Agency jerk-offs. Think they're big time undercover cops 'cause they manage to get a couple of gringo bars shut down. Shit, if Loser Lee only knew what that jerk-off Jack Kelly before him was into. Anyway, we've got all this new business, so we thought we'd better do a little burying. And you're going to be the shovel. Dig?" He threw his head back and laughed. The blotch of his scar gleamed like mother-of-pearl. "Charlie's made up a new bank account for your department — what is it? — Ministry of Pathetic Creeps? It's easy. You bring money to me or Holly. You bring money to Charlie. You accept receipts and you issue receipts from the Ministry of Pathetic Creeps. Just to be official if anybody ever checks, which they won't. There will be money out and money in, and everything will balance real pretty. Except, if there's anything left over maybe we'll buy a bicycle for your kid. Or maybe he'd like a little office tower in Montreal, like me and Charlie are buying."

Charlie said, "Is best to keep this business inside the government, Mac. And inside the family. Where is hard to sniff with the nose."

"It's only accounting, Schoolteacher. Interim financing."

Charlie led me to the door.

"You will going to come to dinner soon, yes? You and Montserrat and our little Kenneth."

I should have put pants and shoes on him, of course I should have. I should not have just scooped him up from his excavation among the delphiniums. With Trinidad and Alejandro gawking as I ran with him and our two passports toward the Mercedes. And now I was here at the General Patrício Santos International Airport too early. A bearded gringo in a beige suit carrying a beautiful blond boy with a bare ass.

I sweated the big drop and waited for the delayed flight to Miami. An hour walking around that little airport building with Ken in my arms. This way I could cover his bare bottom with my arm, sort of.

"Ken! Now Listen! Be still, damn it! Hey, wanna hear a story? No? Let's see — wanna hear a song?"

"Downg! Downg! Downg!"

Pushing away from my chest. Hanging over backward.

"Rock It, Robin. Deedly-tweet."

"Downg! Downg!"

"Hey, let's go and look at this shop. Wow, Ken, look at all the stuff."

"Downg!"

"See this? This is a shawl from Pastosa, dyed with plant juices."

With one hand and my teeth I managed to give the shop woman some money. Then I set Ken down and restrained him as I wrapped and tucked and knotted.

"Hey, does this look cool or what!"

A hand-woven ethnic diaper. And there went Ken. Chasing

those other little kids. Roaring at them. Scaring the bejeesus out of them in his blue and yellow bulging breechclout, as they ran to hug the knees of their mothers. Maybe now, though, no one would realize he was mine. Maybe they would think that I was another of those solitary businessmen returning home. Home. Where there would be no Tomás back from the dead, and no Charlie and no drugs. Where Jeff, when he had kicked, would take his brother Ken camping on the Gulf Islands.

The main lounge was almost empty now. Everyone had gone through that doorway and past that soldier into the International Departures Lounge. Because at last the flight was ready. In a minute the passengers would board. Therefore, anyone just arriving would be processed through fast. A trick Isman taught me. Only, in my case it was not my luggage that I didn't want them to have time to check, but their *No Salir* list.

First, then, scoop up Ken again and hustle around the corner, panting as if I had run from a taxi, to the wicket where departing tourists were automatically given their exit visas. The old Canadian passport was the key. That much I had thought out. I had stayed three years beyond the date on which my work permit expired, but that was okay. I would merely have to pay a fine.

I now noticed, however, that the passport itself had expired one year before. No problem. The man at the wicket would never catch that.

I held Ken prominently in my arms, which is a trick I had learned by watching the pickpockets at the Smuggler's Market. The idea is to appear innocent. And as the man handed back Ken's passport with no questions about why my son did not have a Canadian one like me, and as he now flipped through mine and as — with Ken perched in his breechclout on the ledge of the wicket — I filled in the visa form, the idea was to appear calm. Calm as glass.

The man said, "You have to pay a fine. A big one."

"All right. Do you think you could hurry? I have not bought

my ticket yet, and I just heard the last call for my flight."

"Fifty thousand dorados."

I paid him. The heart started to beat light and fast.

He held his rubber stamp above the form. But he did not press it to the paper. He swung it. Like a pendulum. As his moustache was bent by a sort of smile.

"I do not have much time."

"Wrong, señor. You have too much time."

"My flight is leaving."

"Too much time." The stamp swung in his fingers.

"Yes, I know. But I paid the fine. Is there something else?"

"Yes. Something else. Too much time."

I stared at him. "I do not understand. Do you speak English?"

"Too much time," he said in Spanish.

I forgot the calm bit and looked wildly left and right, expecting to see Charlie and Tomás watching me with their arms folded.

"Downg," said Ken, and held out his arms.

"What do I have to do?"

"Dwong. Downg."

"Too much time."

"In the name of God, you said that! Please, just tell me exactly what the problem is and what I have to do. I am going to miss my plane!"

Ken whining now. Jesus, I was not going to get out of the country.

"What exactly do you mean when you say too much time?"

"Señor, your passport has expired."

I stared. The rubber stamp swung. Then, suddenly, I knew. My wallet appeared again, and a handful of bills flew in through the bars. *Bam!* — the rubber stamp came down. And I was running — with Ken in my right arm and my stamped exit visa paper in my left hand — toward the ticket counter. In my uncalmness I had almost forgotten the first rule of travel in the

Third World: When in doubt, bribe.

In less than two minutes I had two tickets to Miami. And as, with Ken's hand in mine I walked with composure toward the International Departures Lounge, the heart again tripped light and fast. I was free. The only irony was that it was so simple. Just hop on a flight, McKnight.

Beside the door to the International Lounge a soldier stood behind a small counter. But I felt no anxiety. Because my papers, as they say, were in order. I handed him our tickets, passports and exit visa, and as I waited with Ken beside me for the soldier to hand them back I gazed out the window of the main lounge. The passengers were walking across the tarmac toward the plane. The ones at the front were already climbing the stairs. I could see a stewardess at the top saying, "Hello," and "Welcome."

I turned back to the soldier and reached to receive the tickets and passports and visa. But that was not what he was holding. He was holding a long, wrinkled sheet of paper. It looked like it could be a list of some kind. Also, he was frowning and shaking his head. And now Ken was laughing. To him I must have resembled something from Saturday morning cartoons, the way I had jerked the soldier toward me by his shirtfront and was screaming into his face something like "Don't you know who I am!"

Another soldier appeared, then another. They restrained me. They probably would have shot me if they hadn't realized I was the Son-In-Law.

I looked down into the sun-baked chicken-run to see what poultry could teach me. I called Ms. Nieves. She came and stood beside me.

"I gave them the last bit of my croissant."

"Mr. McKnight, you have a heart of gold."

"The rooster took it all. When the hens came near, he pecked them."

"He's the boss, all right."

"The person at the airport. The one who gives out the exit visas. Does he work for us?"

"I can find out."

"Fire him."

"What?"

"Fire him. I want him gone. Today."

"Well, I'll see what I can do, but . . ."

"No. You won't see what you can do. You will get that son-of-a-bitch OUT!"

Ms. Nieves hustled for the door. Damn, I had shouted again.

There were passports. These people all wanted to leave the country, surely a reasonable aspiration. I picked up my pen, opened each passport to the page where someone in the outer office had put a large stamp of blurred purple ink with words to the effect that the bearer's balls were not worth clamping, and I began signing. But strange. One passport was American. Why should a *yánqui*'s request to go home require special scrutiny? Especially when the *yánqui* lacked handy bits for the electrodes, being, as I saw by the photo, a woman. And being, moreover, a nun. Sister Louise Walker Forrest. What could this delaying of her visa be except a tactic to punish a bride of Christ who had perhaps been irritatingly insistent about some matter of human rights?

"Shoo, Louise Walker Forrest," I said. "Go home." I signed her blurred stamp.

And, flipping back to her photo again, I saw that she was smiling. Nice, to see a nun smile. I could almost hear her say, "Have a nice day, amen." A woman in her mid-forties. Gold-rimmed glasses exactly like mine. Eyes of blue Northern ice. Bony sturdy face. More, actually, than sturdy. Masculine. With a bold black spot beside the nose.

On a corner of my desk lay a little suitcase, one of those shiny metal jobs a safecracker might carry his tools in. It had been waiting there on the desk when I arrived at the office. It was full of money, with a manila envelope containing a note that said, "Schoolteacher. Hotel Esperanza, Thurs. 8 p.m." I opened the case again, took out the manila envelope, tore some tiny shreds from it and placed the shreds upon the smiling cheeks of Sister Louise. Then I bent and studied my wobbly reflection in the mirror surface of the open lid, above the stacks of American bills. I pressed my beard flat and tried to remember what I looked like without it. "Hey, Louise," I muttered. "Shweetheart. You goin' my way?"

I took a sheet of the letterhead of the Ministry of Strangers and wrote.

Dear Jeff,

Of course you understand that if I didn't write, it was because I couldn't.

Things have not been clear. Will that do for an excuse? There have been confusing events. Didn't I write to you a long time ago about a struggle of my soul? Jesus, if I had only known! But it's over now, Jeff. And, miraculously, I'm writing this letter. And more miraculously, I'm coming home. To be by your side where I should always have been.

I will tell you about the confusing events when I get home, perhaps over dinner at the Dai-won — how does that sound? And if you say, 'Dad, what a sad, funny circus,' I'll shed a few tears into my wanton soup, and laugh, and say, 'Jeff, as always, you're right.' For now, though, here's a teaser. I won't be arriving alone. There will be a rather short person with me. He has never tried Chinese food, but my guess is he'll be partial to almond chicken. He has your nose.

If I say that so much has gone wrong for both you and me, I'm sure I won't hear an argument from you. But hear this from me: That chapter is finished. Now it is time for healing. My short friend, by the way, is an accomplished healer. I'm sure you remember that poem by Yeats, the one about Crazy Jane and the Bishop, where

he says, 'Nothing can be whole That has not been rent.'
Maybe that's what it has all been about.
Till soon.
Love.
Dad

The flight, of course, late. And me without my flask. As I waited to get on the only airplane willing to tackle at night the meagre atmosphere of the lofty capital and the linebacker shoulders of its volcanoes. I squinted past the edge of my left hand, which was cupped against my face as I pressed myself into a corner and pretended to look out the window.

So many people, so brightly lit. Mostly families tonight. Good. Families don't care about the rest of the world. The usual businessmen, scattered in sober suits among the families. Fine, businessmen don't care about the rest of the world, either. What worried me were the two nuns. Standing way back near the coffee shop. Nuns care about the rest of the world. And they were watching me. Maybe I would just turn around for a second and get a better look. Yes, God damn it! Leaning toward each other and whispering behind their hands. Talking about me. I just knew it — there was something wrong with my habit! But the guy at the costume shop had assured me it was authentic in every detail. Or maybe they were working up their courage to come over and say, "Hi, we haven't seen you around the convent." And, "What are your views on the liturgy?" Only one thing to do. Turn around again and give them a quick but lethal Louise Forrest Walker scowl, masculine as hell. That did it, they were off into the coffee shop. Try the grilled amoebas, girls.

I saw no other students. And no one from the Ministry. And no one else was looking my way. But jeez I felt conspicuous without my beard. All Ken had wanted to do on the way to the airport in the taxi was feel my face. But I couldn't let him, because he might have smudged the makeup. The black spot especially vulnerable. Thank Christ he was still happy, zooming his friction car up my leg. If he got crabby later, I had Toby. Right there in the pocket of my habit, along with Louise's passport and his, Louise's ticket and his, purchased from an obscure travel agency by Louise's friend the Second Deputy Minister. We would sit in the smoking section because smokers are less observant. They would not notice when I returned with Ken from the washroom. Wearing trousers and a quiet plaid shirt and finding different seats. There would be many empty seats because no one flew Air Dorado if they could help it. Especially at night. In my shirt pocket, for presentation in Miami would be the passport which Charlie had given me along with my job and my citizenship. On page seven of this passport was a stamp, the same kind the soldier at the door of the International Departures Lounge was going to put in Ken's passport and Louise's to show that they had left the country. I had prowled in the outer office after work and, sure enough, in a cupboard there was a little box of stamps that said *salida*. Supplies for the airport. Also in the pocket was Ken's exit visa paper from three days before. It would still be valid. Louise had the big purple stamp signed by the Second Deputy Minister, saying her balls were not worth clamping, so she did not need a piece of paper.

Lights moving out there in the darkness. An Andean flying machine, full of fuel and freedom. Now the call for passengers for Flight 371, and businessmen bestirred themselves, and milky breasts were tucked into bodices, and black grannies were helped creaking up out of their seats, and there was a general movement toward the International Departures Lounge. People passed behind the tall nun in the floor-length black habit, who was so interested in seeing what was out there in the night. And I prayed. That no one would stop to chuck Ken's chin and say, "What a handsome child!" as he zoomed his car along the window. Because they loved their beautiful kids in this country. And they loved their nuns. They called them Sister and were oh so polite and phony, trying to get an in with God. Try it with me, you bootlickers, and you'll get a devil of a surprise, the Sister

Louise snarl. Send you scampering to say your rosaries.

"Well, Sister, what made you decide to fly Air Dorado?"

Jesus, Mary and Joseph, someone was talking to me!

"Kind of like tempting the Lord thy God, don't you think?"

Son of a bitch, there was a person right beside me saying Sister and God! Probably expecting all kinds of nice nunny chit-chat. Something just had to go wrong, didn't it? Well, I was ready for it. A one-two punch for this situation. First a mannish black God-fearing glower to make this meddler sore afraid. Then turn my tall back on her and walk away. But there were so many people, and it was so brightly lit. Best just ignore the person. Give her the cold black shoulder.

"Did you know that the wreckage of Flight 308 is still sitting on Tingáy? Just below the crater. Six years it's been up there. Condors still getting fat on the corpses. The cold preserves them."

Something chillingly familiar about the voice of the woman.

"I always drink a lot before flying Air Dorado. No offence, Sister. Couldn't get on the plane without it. Thinking about those birds ripping out mouthfuls of me for the next six years. And me almost ready to retire."

I peeked around my hand. And gasped as I saw a face I knew. Flossie fucking Pazmiño! Almost bald now. With her blouse buttoned wrong and a burgundy brassiere conspicuous. Once when she was my principal she had said, Mac, *get your shit together*, and I had said, *Flossie, get your shirt together*. Now she was saying *cold* and *corpse* and *condor*. But at least she was drunk and short on awareness and would never guess that I was not a nun but Mac, the English teacher. Also she was smoking, and that, too, was bad for awareness. Good. Maybe Mac would even say hi later, in the smoking section. Meanwhile, if I just ignored her long enough, she would go away.

"Actually, I'm in a bad profession for drinking. Lot of drinkers in my profession. Teaching. I'm a principal. Get a lot of dinking treachers. Excuse me, can't talk right. Drinking teachers."

Yes, like that Canadian. What was his name — Mike McKnack? Tall guy, broad shoulders, just like you, Sister. Up so soon, the jig?

"My friend Doreen Muñoz finally persuaded me to go home and take the Cure."

The Whale too, invoked to witness my final humiliation. How bloody appropriate. But by God I was not giving up yet. I was keeping my nose to the glass. Because I knew she had to beat it some time. If only I wasn't so hot! My trousers and shirt underneath for the quick change in the airplane john. And that goddamn brassiere so tight! Montserrat's stretchiest. Cutting off my circulation, my arms going numb. To stuff it perhaps I should not have chosen the two grapefruits. Because I felt that if I moved at all quickly they might pop out. So I decided to continue to stand still, maybe even to meditate, looking out into the night, where thank Christ I saw them now driving the stairs up to the plane. When Flossie saw that, she would leave me and stagger into the International Departures Lounge with everyone else, hungry for the Cure.

"Either I fly Desperado and connect right away for Baltimore and get in at five a.m., or I take it easy and fly out of here in daylight and overnight in Atlanta, but I'm not going to sleep anyway, so why blow the hotel money? I'd be fine if I could stop thinking about those birds."

Scrabbling in her bag. In my sideways squint I saw her spin the top off a pint of Canadian Club.

"Don't suppose you'd like a drink, Sister?"

Sister Louise's hand shot out to accept, but snapped back to hide her face.

But I could not hide my face all night. My disguise was perfect. And Flossie was in no condition to recognize anything. For example, she had forgotten to remove her cigarette from her mouth before drinking. And, whoops, the cigarette now dropped down her bosom. I lowered my left hand, not to take the bottle, but because I suddenly realized that I should cover my right hand with it. However, Flossie poked the pint toward me with some urgency. She needed both hands to go after the cigarette. Nuns care about the rest of the world, and will always lend a hand in emergencies involving holding a pint for a principal. First, barefaced, I looked around. Everyone had gone into the International Departures Lounge. Right, then. A quick deep pull. Oh, Canada! Land of distilleries. Confidence blossomed in the stomach of Louise Walker Forrest. Yea, though I walk through the Valley of the Shadow of Death, and through the airport also. With Flossie now bent over with her shirt open, shaking. Which Ken found hilarious. What a sweet clear laugh he had. As he zoomed his friction car up the leg of Flossie's slacks and across her fat behind. Barefaced, I looked down. The wrinkled white cleavage. The big wagging things in burgundy. Verily, this was a country of fuck-ups. Like the former Second Deputy Minister, forced finally to invent his own Cure — cure for his septic fate — not with flaming tobacco down his front, but rather with fresh citrus fruit. Never mind, soon it would be the northern lights and family trout fishing. Yea, the courage of Canadian Club was upon me.

They were starting to cross the tarmac toward the plane. Flossie squashed her cigarette against the floor and re-misbuttoned her blouse.

"See what I mean, Sister? I need that Cure. I do that at least once a day. And a burn there hurts. You can imagine. I gotta strop dinking. Or my boobs are gonna be charcoal. Get away, kid."

She retrieved her bottle and swatted indecisively toward Ken, who then punched her in the ass. At the door to the International Departures Lounge the soldier at the little counter was watching us. Waiting for Flossie to rip her shirt open again, I suppose. Not the least interested in the tall black nun and her short blond companion.

There were only two people waiting to be checked past the soldier. I took Ken's right hand in my left. And I plunged my right hand deep into that commodious pocket which perhaps was not an authentic monastic detail, but the soldier would never catch that. And now I slid calmly away from Flossie and toward the soldier.

Ken had punched Flossie in the ass — it was past his bedtime and I hoped he wasn't getting crabby. I walked slowly, because the brassiere was so tight that it was beginning to slip down over the grapefruits. Flossie's mammary display had been grisly enough. The thought of my own nun's udders being revealed for what they were was certainly very much less than titillating. But I was comforted by the rod and the staff of Canadian rye and, Lo, calmness was upon me. And in my overactive imagination, nothing now but glass. Moonlit snowfields. Sleeping lakes. Yea, as Sister Louise Walker Forrest glided sedately toward the soldier, the same soldier as three days before, she was as calm as a virgin who had never told a lie.

But great, just great! Flossie was shuffling beside me, and now holding my right arm for dear life. Needing religious instruction on how to walk straight. Never mind — a blond kid in a sailor suit on my left, an old drunk gringa on my right — suffer them all to come onto Louise. It would distract the soldier from that bit of stubble which was so hard to shave, above the Adam's apple.

"So why you flying Desperado, Sister? Couldn't get a better connection? I'd've thought you were connected pretty good. With the guy upstairs." Her bark of a laugh ending in a long cough. A sound like wet marbles tumbling in her lungs. There might have been a spot of phlegm on my right sleeve, for Flossie was wiping at it with a nicotine-stained finger. The soldier glanced past the person he was checking through, and I knew what he was thinking. He was thinking, That is no fake nun, *hombre*, that is a real nun, look at how she is helping that old drunk gringa who just coughed on her sleeve, maybe I will go to mass tomorrow, but *caramba!* that was funny with the cigarette and the *tetas*.

"So where you heading? Get a convent Stateside? Who's the little fella? Taking him north to be adopted? You won't have any trouble, not with that head of hair. You work in an orphanage? The one down in El Marin?"

Like all drunkards, Flossie was lonely. She wanted Sister Louise to speak to her. But Sister Louise did not want to say anything. Sister Louise was a tall silent type of nun. Not only that — Sister Louise was ready. I released Ken's hand, reached into the other commodious pocket of my habit, felt among passports and boarding passes, and handed my former principal a three-by-five card. So ready was I, in fact, that the three-by-five card had even been plasticized. On the card were printed the words, in Spanish and in English, *I have taken a vow of silence. Have a nice day, amen.*

Flossie seemed baffled by this message. She frowned over it as we approached the entrance to the International Departures Lounge. At last she shook her head and whispered, "Man oh man. A sow of violence."

Then we were in line, behind a man in a black leather jacket, whose papers the soldier was checking. And calmness was no longer upon me. Calmness she was went. So, to stay *tranquilo,* I meditated upon the sprinkle of dandruff on the shoulders ahead of me. Dandruff on black leather is almost as good as fields of snow in the moonlight. Fuck, it was hot. Does makeup dissolve in sweat? Jesus, maybe nuns weren't supposed to wear makeup! Maybe the soldier had a sister who was a nun and who never wore lipstick, even when she flew. The main thing, Angus, is to remain silent and under no circumstances to scream, *Don't you know who I am!* It was no use. I could not concentrate. The brassiere. It was cutting off the blood to my head. I was going to faint. Flop right over on top of the soldier. I turned around to collect my wits, look back into the soothing emptiness of the main lounge.

"Ah!"

There was someone behind us. Those two nuns. And I had

shouted. A masculine syllable of terror. Now, as the leather man walked ahead and out to the plane, I heard them giggling behind me. Merciless bitches. And everything fading. In a second I would fall down. They weren't wearing makeup. Their habits were grey. And shorter than mine. And didn't have any pockets. Now I heard them trying to choke back their laughter. I remembered where else I had seen a nun's costume. Maria Lourdes had used one at Doreen's. I should have learned from her: First you dress up like a nun, then you get screwed.

But I did not seem to be fainting, after all. Okay, passports and boarding passes onto the counter. Best just look down at my feet. My brogues were sticking out. The nuns had not been wearing brogues, they had been wearing Nikes. Maybe if I wiggled my ass a bit the habit would shift and cover my shoes. Lord, now snorts and guffaws behind me. The soldier looked past to see what was funny. Maybe he thought we were together, all us nuns. Mother Louise and her two minions. In which case it would be best to get in on the act and give a silent giggle or two. Salvation through mirth.

"Ca me!"

Blast, Ken wanted to be carried! Reaching up, putting on his most pained and crabby expression.

"Ca me!"

Couldn't wait till we got past the soldier. And this was the crucial moment. The soldier looking at Louise's photograph. Now looking at me. Now at Louise's photograph. Now at me. And I saw what it was about Louise's photograph and about me. The spot. It was on the wrong side of my nose. I decided to create a diversion.

"Toby!"

The puppet was on my right hand. Ken was beaming to see his old friend. The nuns were shrieking with laughter. And, most importantly, the soldier was not interested in Louise's passport any more. Toby opened his beak to say, Hi, Ken! But stopped just in time. And everybody waited for the puppet to speak.

"Talk Toby!"

Best just flap the beak around a bit.

"Talk, Toby!"

Suddenly Flossie was tugging at the soldier's sleeve and shoving the three-by-five card in his face and babbling in Spanish. Good, Flossie! The soldier looked baffled, and somewhat afraid, as his eyes went form the card to Toby to me. The nuns peered around Sister Louise's shoulders to get a better look. They smelled of incense.

"Ca me!"

Back to this again!

"Daddy, ca me!"

"Ha! Did you hear that, Sister!" bellowed Flossie. "He called you daddy! What a cute kid!"

"Daddy, daddy," giggled the nuns behind me.

And I really should not have reached so quickly to put my hands over Ken's mouth. Because there went one of the grapefruits. Shit, better move Toby around like crazy. With everybody laughing except me and the soldier. I didn't think they heard the grapefruit hit the floor. Best hunch over, so the soldier wouldn't see that I had lost half my chest. And yes, kind of make little nibbling gestures toward him with Toby. Be familiar and sassy. Bring him into the joke. As I kicked the grapefruit away to the left. And began suddenly thinking better, as blood got into my brain. Why was the soldier not amused? Why was he squinting? At my spot. Now at my Adam's apple. The guy was smaller than me — better make a fist inside Toby, even if it did make the beak look weird. Because I could see what I was going to have to do.

The soldier opened his mouth. I got ready to drive him before he could call for help. But then he was looking down again. And not at Louise's passport. There was a little hand reaching up. To place upon his counter. A grapefruit.

"Aw, isn't that nice," said Flossie.

"Gay-foo."

I wound up to drive the soldier.

"Grácias, niño." He reached over to pat the golden curls. Opened his drawer. Set the grapefruit on top of his wrinkled list.

Oh, limp, limp as a chewed rag. But free, *patrón*. As Ken and I walked across the tarmac toward the plane, with our stamped passports in my pocket. I took long strides, not caring who saw my brogues. In its hammock of Montserrat's twisted bra the remaining grapefruit tapped a pacifying rhythm against my chest. There were many people still filing toward the stairs up to the Air Dorado 727. Suddenly I realized that I would be home before my letter to Jeff. I would work on a surprise, teach Ken to say, Hi, big brother.

"Ca me!"

Yes, yes, my golden one. Up, and let me know the meaning of your weight and your warmth. I could feel the bad things fading already. The guilt, the horrors, the whoredom, the whole El Dorado shuffle.

"Hermana!"

That meant sister. A man somewhere behind us, calling. It would be a family-type sis he was wanting, surely. Not a religious-type. Probably something wrong with somebody's sister's papers. But it wouldn't hurt to pick up my pace a bit. Kind of jog along. Pass a few of the slowpokes.

"Hermana!"

Closer. And the sound of boots going *clop clop* on the tarmac not far behind. What if I ran? Like this. I wondered if my trousers were showing as my habit flapped out. The idea was to do an end-run around those passengers and dart up the stairs two at a time. Hell, there went the other grapefruit, right under their feet. A businessman fell with a shout, papers flying from his attaché case.

"Hermana!"

It was me he wanted, all right. But he was saying *hermana* — he still believed I was a nun. I stopped — he had caught up with me anyway. No choice but to turn around and fake my way through.

It was the same soldier. Walking the few remaining yards between us. Holding something out to me.

"Toby!"

Yes, Ken, it was only Toby the Toucan, which I must have dropped somewhere back there. The nice soldier had run after us to return it. When in doubt, lavish grapefruits upon the military. I realized that in spite of everything, I was going to miss these people. I smiled, and nodded thank you, and reached out with my right hand to receive the puppet. But the soldier did not release Toby. There was a small tug-of-war. Why was he not smiling now, but looking down at my hand? Before I could release Toby the soldier's other hand clamped on my wrist. He brought his face down close. I saw it now, too. The thing that interested him. The faint gothic script.

Who Me?

17

And When His Strength Failed Him at Length

"Shut up, why don't you? Just give me the money."

"Cur. Scum. Whoreson. You like whoreson?"

"Listen, you can't drink if you're going to do this, okay? There's too much at stake here."

"No, you listen. To this. There once was . . . No. They call me . . . Yes, let's see . . . They call me a creep, scum or whoreson."

"Man, you're too much."

"A scurvy and vulgar impureson."

"So recite. But hand over the case."

"One does fret at times. At the thought of one's crimes."

"Schoolteacher. You kill me."

"But a pull at the flask reassures one."

"So pull. Meanwhile, give me that."

A room in the Esperanza International Hotel. Green-eyed Holly smiling down at the open briefcase, and the money seeming to smile back at her. A cute couple, Ivy and Lucre.

"Ivy the Clinger. Power me again."

"What?"

"That night — remember? You enjoyed it. I enjoyed it. Let's

do it again. But no ropes this time."

She came away from the bed and stood facing me. Tonight, for the cash injection, she was dressed respectably. Heels. Hose. Hair in a blonde bun. Black pleated skirt, white soft blouse open enough to show a green stone on her chest, the size of one of her evil eyes. Perfume too.

"I thought you were a family man."

"Don't lie. What you thought is that I was a pathetic creep."

A finger rose to stroke the stone as she considered, then fell to the top button of the blouse.

"You're too drunk."

I was wearing my dark blue suit. "Oh yeah?" I said. I undid my trousers and pushed them and my underwear down. "Look."

"Are Canadians all this subtle?" She undid the button, and with her other hand took hold of my engorged Canadian subtlety.

"That night in the jungle," I said. "The way you danced. Do it again. Now. Make me your whore."

"Why?" She undid another button. There was no brassiere. She reached in and slowly massaged a breast.

"Because it's fun down here in the dirt."

I bent to kiss her, but she stepped back. "Come along, Schoolteacher."

"Hey, pulling is fine. But not off."

"This way, please. Don't trip on your pants."

"Where we going?"

She undid another button, and there was the breast. "Come on, then." She backed up.

I followed, laughing.

"Look," she said.

Above the dresser, a big mirror. Once, on a blackboard, the girls at Doreen's had drawn my penis as long as a pointer. Now I saw that it was no more than a handful for Holly. And that the purple thing was attached to a stranger, a cleanshaven, grinning man in blue suit jacket and bare white thighs.

"See what I mean?" I said to the stranger in the mirror. "Life is good. Always someone ready to give you a hand. Hey, where you going? Aren't you going to power me?"

She buttoned her blouse and closed the briefcase. "No challenge, man. No fun. You've got nothing I want. Power your fucking self."

"It wounds my heart. It wounds my soul. To see you like this. I am going to die of shame. You whore. What about honour? Do you not ever think about honour? What am I going to do now for honour? You shame me. You shame our family. Whore!"

I laughed richly and thumped my fist upon the table. Paco doing it again tonight, saying the same words to his sister, the same exact Spanish words coming out of his sweaty stubble face and droopy moustache. As across from him his sister Inés nestled into my chest. Paco spat on the floor.

"Paco!" shouted a man at another table. "Give your honour a rest. Inés has got her gringo, and everybody is happy. Go and call someone else a whore."

"I call *you* a whore and a son of a whore, too."

"Paco, you poor *paisano*, do you think anyone cares about your insults? Gringo, *salud!*"

Now, all around this *taberna*, glasses raised and heartfelt shouts of *salud!* And the laughing gringo in the beautiful suit — who has as usual been buying drinks for everyone all night — raised his own glass graciously to return the toasts of these his loyal friends, the buddies and belles of the Bar Urubamba, into which he had glided one night recently by way of not giving a fuck about anything anymore, and which now reserved a nightly table for him near the door.

There was blaring *cúmbia*. Cowbell, accordion, handdrums, and a guy singing about coming home blotto and finding himself locked out. A couple sprang up to dance among the tables.

"Our mother is going to die of shame. Will you be happy then?" asked Paco.

Beer on some of the tables, but mostly Trópico or rum, because the gringo was buying. Every chair was occupied, and even the five places at the bar were full tonight, such was my fame. The owner, fat César, hustled behind the bar.

"Paco, have some *chifles*," I said.

He took some.

"Would you like a little more Trópico?"

"*Sí.*"

I poured some into his glass and into his sister's and into my own and added Coca-Cola to theirs. I poured nothing into the glass of Luis Enrique, who was resting his head on the table. Perhaps he felt slighted, for he objected with a groan. I saw a flea hop out of his hair and make a vulgar display out of drowning in a puddle of something. We clinked glasses and drank. Then Inés pulled my head down and kissed me.

The kiss of Inés is a cavern of mystery, a sunless sea tasting of Trópico, of Coke, of lipstick and *chifles* and the paradisal milk of promise. But, oh, such grunting in front of her brother. Such a greedy tongue, too, with everyone watching. And were it not for this one missing tooth, Inés, you would be beautiful indeed.

"Whore," said Paco.

I laughed again and walloped the table, making Luis Enrique mutter. I called for more *chifles*.

"You are confused, as always, Paquito," said Inés. "You do not understand about love. You see a woman with a man, and the only word you can think of is *whore*."

"That dress. Showing your tits. Inés, I beg you, think about your mother."

"Don't you ever talk about my *tetas*, or *el Mac*, this gentleman that you will never be, will break you into two *paisano* pieces and feed you to the dogs!" She jabbed a chipped red nail at her brother, her voice so loud and saucy, her dress so low, the tops of her *tetas* so very smooth and brown. I took off my suit jacket and flexed my biceps, and there were cheers.

"Wait till you get home."

"What if I do not come home? What if tonight I go to Canada with *el Mac?* Ha! You did not know, did you? You did not know he is going to take me to Canada. Well, how does it feel to learn something?"

Finally Paco glanced at me.

"*Otro?*" I asked.

He nodded. I refilled his glass. Inés kissed me again. Best leave soon, not for the True North strong and far away but for the Mercedes, waiting just outside with Roosevelt, who worked nights now because he knew the way to a deserted wood, where for a well-earned bonus he would wander off to smoke and leave his boss to frolic in a backseat the size of Alberta.

"Nobody breaks me in two pieces," said Paco.

"No?" said Inés. "Then how about a hundred pieces? Less work for the dogs." She laughed, slapping the table. I stopped looking down her dress to admire the gap in her dentition.

"*Viva* Inés!" shouted someone.

And we all answered, "*Viva!*" Except Paco.

César brought the *chifles*. He poked Luis Enrique. "Hey, *hombre*, time to go home." Luis Enrique didn't budge. I saw that the flea who had abandoned ship was still making slow circles in the lagoon of whatever it was.

"César," I said, "if you would be so kind as to make sure that everyone keeps on getting even more drunk."

As the free drinks were distributed I stood and tried to overpower the throbbing *cúmbia* with the song President Pancho Perales had taught me. *Juanita it is so cold These mountain nights.* When I finished they called out, "*Viva gringo!*" and Inés kissed my hand.

Paco's chair was empty.

I put my mouth to the ear of Inés and whispered, "Do you like my car?"

"*Mucho, mucho, Maquito.*"

"Would you like to go for a ride in my car?"

"*Sí, mi vida*, let's go for a ride."

"To the woods?"

"Yes, to the woods. Let's go now."

All the same to me, my plum. Those woods filled with the smell of eucalyptus and with our animal cries. This loud low bar where my money is famous. Paco with his pride. Montserrat in her snow white lie. Everything part of the same funny darkness.

"Mother of Christ!" screamed Inés. "He's pissing!"

Inés scraped her chair back and leapt to her feet. Sound of water trickling. Luis Enrique sighing with relief. Deafening guffaws everywhere in the Bar Urubamba.

"You bastard!" My Spanish suddenly gone, as I stood and wrapped my hand into the filthy hair of Luis Enrique and jerked his head up, then smashed it down, and then smashed it down again, and then once more. Inés standing well back from the table or from the pool under it, looking afraid. Then her eyes went wide as she saw something behind me.

A shout. "Nobody breaks me in two pieces!"

With a roar I let go the hair and grabbed the Trópico bottle by the neck and swung it wildly backhand.

"Where's your honour now, you contemptible cockroach!"

Paco just inside the door, on his knees, his eyes out of focus, both hands groping up for protection. I kicked his empty chair out of the way and swung again but this time only hit his shoulder. I lifted the bottle again, but something red was in the way. Inés. Throwing herself on her brother, crying, "*Ai! No, Paquito!*" Kissing his bleeding head. From the hoisted bottle, Trópico ran down my arm.

"Christ," I said. "I'm drunk."

Then Inés attacked me. A jaguar snarl, and my field of vision suddenly nothing but red fingernails. The bottle fell. I grabbed her wrists and pinned them behind her back. She spat in my face. I spat in her face. I held her wrists with one hand, took a handful of hair with the other, twisted her head back and kissed her. I released her wrists, and she pulled my head down, kissing and crying. Then I pushed her away and she stood there, in her satin dress and one high-heeled shoe.

On hands and knees Paco crawled out the door.

I turned to the belles and the buddies, and all the faces were silent, and there was not one that did not appear terrified. The only sounds were the *cúmbia* cowbell going *tonk tonk*, and Inés' loud sobbing. I had to laugh. But I didn't. I shouted.

"God!"

Because one face was not turned toward me. There at the bar. A white shirt on narrow back. Black hair in waves on his shoulders. As I moved toward the bar I stopped hearing the music and Inés. I smelled oil paint and the tide in False Creek. "Oh, Lord," I whispered. "You've come." Something let go in my stomach. As if a blossom of peace had been dormant there. The enormous one I had been keeping for last and for best. Opening now. I laid my hand on his shoulder.

"Hello, Jeff."

He turned. Showed me a face like a walnut with an occluded eye and a flash of gold in a drunken smile. "Gringo! What happened to your face? You are bleeding."

I stared at the white-eyed walnut, and all at once my legs were weak. From laughing. I spun around, snatched someone's shot of Trópico off their table, tossed it back, smashed the glass on the floor. There was a fat woman in an orange dress. I pulled her out of her chair, and we danced wildly, crashing into tables. Everybody shouted, "*Eso!*" And the *cúmbia* guy sang about his wife, who was so ugly he got her mixed up with his dog.

"But I thought you are going to stay at home tonight. With me."

"No."

Montserrat standing in the middle of our white living room, in an apron with a pattern of strawberries.

"I am cooking your supper myself. A nice steak, with garlic."

"Yes. I know. Have you seen my green silk tie?"

"Please stay."

"I hope I haven't lost it. Maybe it's down here inside the couch."

"Mac."

"How could I lose a tie?"

"This the first night you are home in two weeks."

"Don't give me grief, Montserrat."

"You are tearing the furnitures apart."

"I'll tear what I want."

"Darling."

"No grief, okay! Listen — where's my fucking tie?"

"Please don't shout me, Mac. It makes Ken afraid."

Looking at my wife now. With the furniture cushions spilled across the floor. "Don't you dare tell me how to raise my son!" Fear in her eyes. Under them, dark bags of sleeplessness, which made me more furious than the tie. "Do you hear me! What do you know about raising a son! You . . . you teenager! Shit, the day you can cook a steak, I'll celebrate."

"I am twenty-one."

"Well, you look bloody fifty. Have you tried looking in a mirror recently?"

"You know why I am not sleeping."

"Oh do I?"

"Where do you go every night?"

"Are you accusing me? By God, woman, if there's one thing I hate, it's being accused." Shaking a fist in her face. "I'll come and go as I bloody want!"

Up the stairs two at a time. Her plastic apron scraping up behind me. Following me into the bedroom.

"I am making you a steak."

"Stick your steak."

"Don't you care?"

"Look at this. Half my ties are gone."

"And the rest of them smell like perfume."

"What?"

I stood at the closet, my hand wrapped around cravats.

"Perfume. Very cheap. Like your hair when you come to bed in the middle of the night. At least you could buy her some nice perfume."

She came close to me. I clenched my teeth and glared into the closet.

"Cigarette smoke, too. Cigarette smoke and cheap perfume. But I was so happy tonight when I thought you want to stay at home with me. Because I thought maybe you still love me. A little bit. Please. Don't go tonight."

Her tentative hand on my shoulder, which was bunched hard as concrete.

"Don't be pathetic," I said into the closet.

"I can forgive you, Mac."

"Forgive!" She stepped back as I spun to face her. "Damn you! Don't you ever try to forgive me! Don't you ever try it! I won't be accused, and I won't be forgiven! Not by the likes of you and not by the likes of anyone!"

Crying finally. And I was glad to see that her bullshit composure was gone, and her bullshit accusing and her bullshit forgiving and her bullshit about love.

"Stop crying," I said. "It's bullshit. I hate it." I continued fingering ties.

"Okay! Hate it! Hate me too! Because I hate you!"

"Don't shriek, darling. You'll make Ken afraid. How about this pink one? Think she'll like it?"

"Do you hear what you are saying? What has happened to you? What terrible thing? What made you to change? Do you hear how cruel you are?" Her voice calmer. But her sobbing — I couldn't stand it.

I said, "I think you'd better go away."

"No, darling. It is not me who should go away. It is you. You should go away from me. And you should go away from Ken. I do not know what is wrong with you. But you are destroying us."

In front of me the clothes in the closet and the ties of many colours dissolved into a pool of blackness whose edges were tinged red.

"You destroyed your last family," she said. "And now you are destroying this one. Why don't you bring her home? Wouldn't you like Ken to meet her?"

Neckties flew like snakes through the room as my hand streaked out of the closet. In Montserrat's eyes, shock. That I could strike her. That I could be what I was. I slapped her again. Her eyes went blank as she staggered back against the bed. Jesus, her face so helpless and old and hurt. I couldn't stand it. I hit her again. She fell over a corner of the bed onto the floor.

"Mama."

Ken. In the doorway. In his soft blue sleepers. Beaming because he thought his mother wanted to play, crouched on the floor like that, making funny noises. Two strides and I scooped him up and we were hurtling down the stairs two at a time.

"Whee! Down we go."

He dug a hand into my hair and shouted with fear and with helpless laughter. At the bottom I tripped and sprawled onto my elbows. Ken went rolling, scrambled to his feet, caught his balance and looked around, dazed. Montserrat rushed past me, fell to her knees on the white carpet and hugged my son against her apron.

"No llores, no llores, mi doradito. Tu pápi lo hizo sin querer. Shh, shh, todo está bien, lo hizo sin querer. No llores, no llores."

I ran out the door. Oh Lord Christ, she was forgiving me. And in a goddamn foreign tongue. Your daddy didn't mean to do it, my golden one. Walking to the carport, I felt for my wallet. Thick with cash it was, for the buddies and the belles and the funny funny darkness.

I stood one afternoon in the rain at the corner of Reforma and Doce de Diciembre, watching the buses rattle past, wondering as I inhaled the diesel fumes of each whether or not I should step in front of the next. Watching also my tan brogues go black with wet.

"Schoolteacher. You ever heard of an umbrella?"

Tomás. Speaking to me out the window of a car that had stopped. I got into the back seat. A man in a blue suit was driving. I recognized him, pudgy Raul, Doreen's husband, the Esperanza Chief of Police. The car was an old grey Toyota with a differential that growled as we headed along Doce de Diciembre. Whenever the police force found a stolen car, they would drive it for a few weeks before informing the owner.

I slid the briefcase over the back of the front seat to Tomás. He opened it, took out a bundle of money, reached across and tucked the bundle into the inside pocket of Raul's suit jacket.

"Sit still, Raulito, I'm not trying to feel you up."

Raul held out his hand to Tomás. Tomás took from a pocket of his own cherry-coloured leather coat a plastic bag tied with a twist-tie and half full of white powder, about two cups' worth. He gave it to Raul, who slipped it into another pocket.

We drove through the rain, with nobody saying anything. Raul turned corners at random, and soon we were heading along the perimeter road that skirted the volcano, toward the Old City.

"Stop," I said.

"What's wrong?" said Tomás.

"Just stop."

"Fucking basket case, man — an alky who gets carsick."

I got out and told them to go on. Along the side of the road opposite the volcano there was a collection of squatters' shanties. Jumble of corrugated metal, sheets of black polythene, odd lengths of lumber, cardboard drooping from the rain. The Toyota pulled away growling, as from gaps in the walls of the hovels a few faces watched me throw up.

It was different when Charlie had me flown down to Tomás' place on the Colorado once, in his own helicopter, with a cash injection to pay off some of our suppliers. In an unpainted workshop Tomás and I watched an old Swiss guy in a lab coat weighing stainless steel buckets of cocaine on a supermarket scale.

I said, "So how's the hospital coming along?"

"Next year, man. The looks of you, you're going to be the first customer. You given up eating, or what?"

"Mr. Chairman, the less I eat, the more for the starving millions. Like you, I am an altruist."

"Shit. I can't see why Charlie uses you. You're just a liability."

"And what about the school? You going to be needing an English teacher?"

"What I need is you the fuck out of my life."

"Ah, Mr. Chairman, and who does not?"

The Swiss guy — Heinz, his name was — sprinkled a scoop of cocaine. Minus the weight of the bucket, one kilo on the button.

"Tomás, there are few memories I cherish. But one is of you in that canoe. Remember? With my poison dart six inches into your throat? You are an evil and despicable man."

"Schoolteacher, you should've let me blow your head off. Don't you know you would've been doing everyone a favour?"

"I like your hat."

"You're fucking pathetic."

"Panama?"

"Yeah."

"And the feather?"

"Macaw."

"I must have one."

"Excellent coffee. Absolutely splendid."

"Thank you, Mr. McKnight. But aren't you going to eat your pastry?"

"Ms. Nieves, I would be grateful if you would have it."

"You never eat your pastry anymore."

"I don't?"

"You're thin as a snake."

"Excellent simile. Splendid. But I'm not, really. It's just the poor light in here."

"You never listen to your music anymore."

"Same old stuff. I'm tired of it."

"Your plants are all dead. Look at them. All black and rotting."

"I thought they were just dormant."

"Dead, Mr. McKnight. Dead as a doornail."

"Dede as stoon."

"What?"

"That's Chaucer."

"And why don't you bring little Ken up to the office anymore?"

"He's happy in the Valley."

"I miss him."

"You are a lovely person, Ms. Nieves."

"You know, Mr. McKnight, it's really not necessary for you to spend so much time in the office. I can run things pretty well. If you came in for a few minutes every couple of days, that would be enough. Just to sign the passports."

"I know. But, you see, this is a kind of refuge."

"This office? With all those pots of dead plants?"

"I'm sure they are only dormant."

"They don't smell dormant."

"Is that what that smell is? Ms. Nieves?"

"Yes?"

"Are you going to abandon me?"

"Abandon. . . ? I don't understand."

"Now, don't cry. Look, you've spilled your coffee."

"But, Mr. McKnight, I'm worried about you."

"Here, take my handkerchief. Ms. Nieves, I saw something bad today. A dead person."

"Oh no."

"You know him, Ms. Nieves. Our beggar. The one who waits

by our gate every morning."

"Teodoro? Teodoro is dead?"

"Is that his name? I didn't know he had a name. The guard was gone. The beggar — Teodoro — he was lying on his back across the sidewalk. Staring up into the rain. It's the only time I've ever seen him not smiling."

"I always gave him something."

"His bowl was beside him on the sidewalk. There was only one coin in it. Yours, I guess. And rain. It was half full of rain. Funny. I felt like taking it. The coin. I felt he had left it for me."

"Oh, Mr. McKnight, I'll never abandon you. Not in a million years."

Much fawning over Ken in his high chair. Señora Dávilos even smiling toward me once, in appreciation of the fact that I was not being horrible. Although Montserrat looked haggard, and I looked I suppose gaunt and deranged, it was a relatively successful tri-annual Sunday dinner at Charlie's and Gramma Eugénia's.

Holding Ken's little hand, which was mucky with chocolate mousse, I said, "Home and family." I lifted my glass. They all joined me in the toast. Even Ken, who, instead of a glass, hoisted his silver spoon.

The next day I received a letter.

Dear Dad,

I'm not feeling so great so Elizabeth is writing this for me. You remember her. When are you coming? Who is the short person? I hope I have a brother. Why do you want to come here to this ugly place?

Love,

Jeff

P.S. The Dai Won went belly up.

18

Nevermore

The scab there on the right side of Paco's forehead, angling down out of his hair. I leaned across the table and studied it and shook my head and smiled. Brother Paco back at our table, pretending to be the beaten obedient cur. One of the pack once again. But Inés had said that now he carried a straight razor. Fine. When he cuts my throat I will hold him down and bleed into his face until he bloody-well drowns.

"Inés, I think this is a new dress."

"Sí, Maquito. You gave me the money, remember? Do you like it?"

"No. It is too high. I cannot see your *tetas*. Luis Enrique, would you honour us with your opinion."

"Too high, Inés. Senor Mac wants to see your *tetas*." Luis Enrique, on the verge of passing out, had as usual no idea what he was saying.

"Now, Inesita," I said, "that money was to buy a front tooth for yourself. A nice gold one." I raised my voice. "Absolutely necessary. So that I can see it gleaming in the dark, Inesita. And know which end of you is up."

None of the other Bar U drinkers laughed except Paco, to whom I said, "Who told you to laugh!" He shut up. And put his hand into his jacket pocket. And oh aye, there were any number of these buddies and belles who would slice a guy's gullet and get blood on his tie. Because we're bored with his money. Because the *pendejo* gringo buys drinks and asks no questions, and we can't put up with that any longer. Hurts our wee Latin prides.

"I have enough bad blood to drown the lot of you!"

"*Español*, Maquito."

"I am tired of *español*. I am tired of everything. Paco, I want to see your razor."

"I have no razor." Took his hand out of his pocket. The round brown face and empty eyes of Inés' brother. Never saying anything now about honour. Just always watching me and pretending to be the cur.

"Inés says you have a razor."

"I have no razor."

"Would you like to come along tonight?"

"Where?"

"To the woods. We invite you to watch. It is lonely with just your sister and her honour."

He shook his head, as if he could not understand my Spanish.

"To whores and honour!" I shouted.

Luis Enrique hoisted his glass. "Whores, honour."

César's *chifles* having done their work, someone had farted. The never ending *cúmbia* too, more like a smell than music.

"Did you buy perfume, Inesita?"

"Sí, Maquito."

"That and the dress instead of a tooth."

"I will get the tooth."

"A gold one."

"If that is what you want."

"And did you put the perfume where I said?"

"Sí, Maquito."

"A gold tooth gleaming. And perfume there. So I can tell the top from the bottom. In this my very special darkness."

"In Canada it is light for six months. Is this not true?"

"There is no Canada."

I heard laughter, and somewhere in the Bar U others said it. *There is no Canada.* And I saw fingers dialling screwy circles around ears. As long as they thought I was crazy they would not kill me.

"I am not crazy," I said, and the laughing stopped. "And to prove it — no more free drinks for anyone."

A man's voice said, "It is your money, gringo."

"Maquito," said Inés, "sometimes I think you are not going to take me to Canada."

"There is no Canada."

"And what if I do not go with you to the woods?"

"Then you will never find out which is your head and which is your arse. For in this country only I know top from bottom. And what I know is this. It is all bottom."

"What?"

"Drink up, drink up, my plum. It is all the same."

"You are married, aren't you?"

Mac's splutter of Trópico. "Do not be ridiculous."

"And you have a child. I saw a toy in your car. A bird of cloth."

Coal eyes flashing. Crimson lips clenched defiant over tooth hole. The peach wisp of moustache. Beneath the tabletop a stiffness stirred.

"I can find another man, you know."

"One with money?"

"Of course."

"One who makes jokes?"

"Of course."

"Fine." I stood and leaned into Inés, propping myself against her shoulder with my erection, and reached over her head toward another woman. Blonde and sturdy at the next table.

Gripped the meatiness of a bare upper arm. "Excuse me, Señorita. Would you like to go to Canada?"

A manly olive face of Indian bones and amused interest. Open-knit white sweater over black bra and big belligerent chest. Whiff of woman's sweat.

"But, señor, you said there was no Canada."

"But there might be. We could explore. Do you like to explore?"

She laughed. A full set of teeth and a sound like a VIA Rail air horn. The man at her table, with a wild moustache and stubble cheeks and hard blue suit and a shirt with many-coloured cars on it, stared at me and sucked his teeth loudly.

Inés shouldered my boner aside. I sat down. "Tell me, Inesita, do you think she will fit in the backseat? There is more of her than there is of you."

Over several tables heads leaned together and whispered.

"Señor Mac," said Luis Enrique, "the bottle is empty. Buy another one."

I went to the bar myself, tickled to find that I could not walk straight.

"Gringo, watch where you are going."

"Go home to your wife, gringo."

"*Hijo de puta!* Look what you have done! On my new dress!"

At the bar I said, "César, another bottle of Trópico. And more drinks for everyone."

But behind me, voices said, "We do not want your drinks, gringo."

As he gave me the bottle César looked sad but he sounded relieved. "It is time to pay, señor."

The woman in the white sweater was gone.

Back at our table I shouted, "César! Bring some more *chifles!*" Behind the bar he shook his head.

At the next table the man in the car shirt had turned his chair to face me. He sucked his teeth steadily and the squeaking noises cut through the *cúmbia* like darts.

I said in Spanish, "Common courtesy demands that a bowl of *chifles* be brought to my table so that the members of my party can fart with the best of you."

Squeak, went Car-shirt, as if he had a mouse in his mouth.

"César! I said I want some *chifles!*" I stood. The *cúmbia* tape finished.

"Fine," I said. And wrapped my hand around my glass. And wound up. And winged it. Behind César a bottle shattered. Pieces of glass and a shower of rum fell upon César and the bar and the people sitting at it and some of the drinkers beyond. César straightened. Slivers sparkled in his slicked hair. On the bar he laid a machete.

Inés stood beside me. And squeezed between our table and the knees of Car-shirt. And went out the door.

There was no more music. No more talking either, or even tooth-sucking. Only the sound of all those eyes on me. And now César tapping the back of his machete on the bar.

I sat down. "Paco," I said. "I told you. I want to see your razor."

"I do not have a razor."

The woman in the white sweater came in the door. She slid past Luis Enrique and stopped behind my chair. A hand was placed upon my shoulder. Her chest touched the back of my head.

"Did you notice my car?"

"Sí, gringo."

"Do you like it?"

"Mucho."

I reached up and took the hand that was squeezing my shoulder. Looking into Paco's eyes, I kissed a finger.

I refilled my glass, saluted Car-shirt, and drank.

Luis Enrique said, "Señor Mac, this time you have gone too far." Then he slowly lowered his forehead to the table and started to snore. I stood.

"Do you know the woods, señorita? The ones near Floresta

Alta?"

"No."

"Come."

Inés was outside, leaning against the wall beside the door, crying. And there was the Mercedes, with the rear door open and Roosevelt in attendance.

"Roosevelt, you are a treasure."

"Quickly, Señor Mac."

I was holding the hand of the woman in the white sweater. I extended my other hand toward Inés. "Come, my plum." She drew away. From inside the Bar U I heard the scraping of chairs. A dozen men strolled out onto the sidewalk. One of them went around to the side of the building and pissed loudly against the wall. The rest stood silent, watching me. César there, with his slicer. A bus pulled up behind the Mercedes. I didn't recognize the name of the district on the sign above the windshield. I hauled the woman behind me.

"Where are we going, gringo?"

"I don't care. Some dark place."

Again she laughed. We stumbled up the stairs of the bus. The dozen men, except for César, followed. I sat in the middle of the back seat, and the woman sat sideways on my lap. She kept on laughing, not in the air horn register now, but in half-stifled giggles that came out of her in snorts and noises like bullets ricocheting in old western movies. Paco sat on one side of us. On the other side, behind the woman's back, sat Car-shirt. I don't think she saw him. His squeaks were lost in the yelps and rattles of the decrepit vehicle itself. There was plenty of room but he chose to sit tight up against me. The bus had been almost empty when we got on. The dozen men sat scattered here and there, with heads turned and arms resting on the backs of the seats and eyes resting upon me. Halfway up the bus I saw the back of Inés' head.

"How much do you weigh?" I said to the woman.

"Sixty kilos."

"I mean all of you, not just your chest."

Her air horn, and a blast of anise and *chifle* breath. I was happy, with this good-natured broad stopping the circulation in my legs, the rattling dim bus full of vigilante eyes, the driver's stretched tape of Kenny Rogers making sounds like doom. As we headed east along Doce de Diciembre, bound for the dark place.

There was a flash of lightning. A pack of dogs raced along the sidewalk. I saw a house I recognized. A mansion. The door was open and a man was standing there in the light, watching us. I was sure it was Teodoro, the beggar who had died. It started to rain.

I kissed the woman on the ear, which caused her to squirm and to make the ricochet noise. There was another flash of lightning. The bus stopped to let a man get on.

The new passenger stood at the front, looking down the aisle. He wore a toque with a pom-pom, and a poncho. The moment the bus started moving he reached down the neck of his poncho and placed something white over his mouth and nose. A dust mask. He screamed, "Your money! Your jewellery! Your watches!" There was a gun in his hand.

The driver hit the brakes. The man backpedalled but did not fall. He whipped the gun backhand, cracking the driver's head. "Keep this bus moving!" But the bus jerked once, and stalled. With a groan the driver settled against the steering wheel. The man started down the aisle. "Quick! I will shoot everyone!"

He had a shoulder bag. A watch went into it, handfuls of crumpled bills. He swung the gun left and right. Heads flinched away from it. Hands reached, and dropped more bills. "Your rings!" he cried, but there were none. He made everyone push their sleeves up so he could see if they had watches. He was halfway down the bus.

The woman was shaking, and squeezing me so hard I couldn't breathe. Even when I stood up I had to pry her arms loose. I pushed her on top of Paco. The man shrieked. "Do you want to die!"

The gun was levelled at my face. I walked quickly up the aisle. *Patrón*, I had not done any push-ups for some time, but Christ I landed a good one. A right cross. My fist hurt only for an instant. And together we proceeded up the aisle, me throwing right and left hooks around the gun, which poked annoyingly about my Adam's apple.

At the front of the bus he fell. His loot spilled out of his bag and down the steps. He was on his back, with the mask over one eye, and his teeth shiny with blood. I knelt on him and continued to pound his face. There was a flash and a shattering bang and spray of pain in my cheek. I stopped swinging left and right, but gripped the neck of his poncho with my left hand, pulled his head up out of the stairwell and drove him in a more piston-like fashion. The driver reached unsteadily down and took the gun. With his other hand he hooked my right elbow. I stopped punching.

There was a racket of feet, and I was jostled by passengers exiting the bus. Some stopped for a second to snatch property off the steps. The woman in the white sweater ran away in the rain. Car-shirt too. Paco. Except for the creaking sound the robber made as he tried to breathe, and the doom of the driver's tape, there was silence. Then I felt soft hands on my cheeks, and I smelled perfume.

Inés.

"Maquito."

I stood and pushed her away. With our feet the driver and I shoved the man down the steps of the bus, into the gutter.

There was lightning another day too.

The outing with the Urubamba bunch had addicted me to riding buses. I would get off in disreputable bárrios, places adorned with the names of saints and the odour of urine, and wander into tiny dark bars, saying, with rangitang persistence, "All right, you pack of degenerates — I am buying!"

On this day, just to see how drunk I was, I had performed a running dismount from a bus. And as I rose laughing from a sidewalk of what I believed to be the bárrio of San Bartolomé I saw a strange thing. Above a door a faded sign said, Dental Clinic. Yet in the window a chicken was turning on a spit. By the heavens, was this not a marvel!

A car stopped behind me, a battered white Porsche Carrera, and the driver sauntered around to the sidewalk. A grimly handsome young man of prettified hair, dark suit, open red shirt, chest hair and chains. He held a three-foot length of plumbing pipe.

I gestured toward the window and said, "Some clinic."

He leaned on the pipe and looked at my face for a few seconds. "Excuse me," he said, "I have some business with the proprietor." Then he walked over to the window and smashed it. Inside I saw shapes plunging under tables. A few shards of glass were left hanging. With the end of his pipe he poked them out. Then he pounded the spinning chicken. Glowing coals bounced across the sidewalk.

This destruction seemed to make him happy.

He stepped back to admire his work. Then he turned, smiled and said, "*Brillo*, señor?"

"Ah. It is you, then. This is indeed a day of wonders. I still have bad dreams. Do you?"

He studied me, noting my bandaged hands and the powder burn on my cheek, results of the Encounter at the Dark Place, and shook his head and said, "Dreams. Fuck."

"You have learned some English. I knew you were ambitious. And where is your slingshot?"

He held open a pocket. I saw the butt of a pistol.

"You were wonderful. You put lightning on us. That night. The war paint of ghosts. I remember that we believed in something. Am I not right? What do you believe in now?"

"Ghosts? Fuck, man."

"Come and drink with me. You saved my life."

"Life?" He hawked and spat and tossed the pipe in the window of his car. "Fuck." He got in his rusty Porsche and drove away.

Little Chief Firefly.

"You shouldn't have come in."

"Sanctuary, Ms. Nieves."

"Mr. McKnight, I think I'd better call a doctor. You look like you should be in the hospital."

"Hands all better."

"No, I didn't mean your hands."

"A little ringing in the left ear. That's all. Sort of Eeeeee-sharp. A hell of a note, as my father Jock used to say. Drownded hisself — did you know that? Perhaps I should sit down."

"Yes, sit here on the couch."

"Ms. Nieves, is this my sanctuary?"

"As long as I'm alive, Mr. McKnight, this is your sanctuary."

"This is not the sanctuary I remember."

"I had the plants taken away."

"Oh. Do I like plants?"

"Yes."

"Tulips probably."

"No, not tulips. Mr. McKnight, would you let me take you to lunch?"

"Will I have to eat, Ms. Nieves?"

"Of course."

"In that case, thank you but no. I shall just sit here for a while and listen to my ear. I was in a fight — did you know?"

"Yes. You told me."

"An Encounter at the Dark Place. Hurt my bloody hands. Gun, too. Do you know how loud a gun is? Bloody loud. Did I tell you I saw Teodoro!"

"Yes, you said that."

"God, he looked great! Remember we thought he had died?

God. He looked great. Are you crying?"

"I'm sorry."

"Women like to cry when they're around me. Did I tell you about Inés?"

"But Mr. McKnight, what about your lovely wife?"

"Her too. She cries too. I think she is unhappy about some of my behaviour. Do you think that could be possible? People so bloody narrow-minded sometimes — don't you think so, Ms. Nieves? Wives. Everybody. Not you. Do you want to know what I did? God, it was funny. I woke up in a room in El Marin. Can you believe it? Just recently. Maybe this morning. And whose room was it? In God's bloody truth, Ms. Nieves, I don't know. I woke up on the floor of an empty room in El Marin, and I went like this, AHHH! Because there were fur things. All over the floor. Fur things scampering. In the right circumstances a fur thing is fine, Ms. Nieves. But this was a horror vision for sure. Perhaps I scared them. Because they ran out the door when I did. There was a street right there, and a bloody cold dawn. I hope they find the guinea pigs. I should go back and leave money. But there is no going back, is there, Ms. Nieves?"

"Will you have some coffee at least?"

"No going back. No passport to that place. Did I tell you I was in a fight?"

"Oh, Mr. McKnight."

"Bloody splendid. Pow. Ms. Nieves, do you think I could lie down?"

"Here, just stretch out on the couch."

"Room seems to be spinning. Whee."

Rain every day now, and one day I was walking through it for no reason. It was siesta time, with all the shops padlocked and the streets empty. Shreds of cloud tore along above the roofs. And here, huddled against a wall away from the rain, a ragged mound of earth-coloured cloth. No, two mounds, a woman and a wrapped baby. I stood looking down at her and shivering.

"You too," I said in English. "There oughta be a law."

Those eyes as green as spring grass. Once I had imagined that with her I could be Gauguin.

"You made good *chicha*," I said. "Lowly *chicha*. Full of chunks. What happened to your birds? Did you leave the poor buggers to die in their cage?"

She held out her hand and said an English word. "Money."

"Aspirina. Did you curse me?"

"Money." She tugged at the knee of my trousers. Dirt under that thumbnail black as a crow feather.

"Did you drink the fire of my substance?"

She let her hand fall.

"Someone did. Every drop."

I should have known what was coming. Seeing Aspirina and Little Chief Firefly should have alerted me. Now the chickens muttered outside the window, and in the dimness of the office my ghosts made themselves comfortable.

"And then what did you do, Spike?"

"I kicked the shit out of him, sir."

"Write it, Spike."

"I just wrote things for you, sir. Cuz you let me write the swear words and everything. These days I don't write no more."

"What do you do these days, Spike?"

"Stickups, mostly. Grocery stores. Garages. You don't get much, but it's easy."

"You're good at it?"

"Fuckin' right."

"That's what counts. Spike, will you join me in a drink to your success?"

"Jeez, I would, but I can't. Like, I'm not exactly real."

"Well, I can't blame you for that."

"Sir, can I ask a dumb question? Where am I?"

"This, Spike, is the Ministry of Strangers."

"I fuckin' believe it. Well, catch you later, sir."

"Later, Spike."

Ms. Nieves, I suppose, listening in her little office. Crying, I suppose. I think maybe I made some noise crashing into things, too. To keep these ghosts in focus one had to reel around a lot. And wave the bottle of Smirnoff.

"Oh my gawd, it's Mr. McKnight!"

A bawl of laughter like a slaughtered calf. From the darkness of my office a dusky airhead face emerging.

"Lorena! Banana Lorena! Just in the knickers of time! Do you remember my fantasies?"

"Wowee! Do I?"

"And Edgar Allan Poo-Poo?"

The calfy bawl. "He wrote that poem!"

"What a priceless creature you are! Come and let's fuck before it's too late. Show me everything you know about bananas."

"Have you heard about José Banana . . ."

"Ha ha! Are you literate after all?"

". . . Who plied his trade in Havana? On his whopping, hirsute And magnificent fruit, The ladies would holler, Hosanna!"

"More! More! Hey, don't go. I need your poetry. Where are you?"

"'Bye, Mr. McKnight. Everything rhymes if you look long enough."

Once I had imagined her naked on all fours barking and whining in a toothy red mask from Salchibamba. How had she learned limericks and philosophy? A marvel. Life was good. That one's students should amount to something. And if the Second Deputy Minister in his blundering about his office should crash hard into his desk and spill vodka upon the telephone, would another ghost be called up? Oh yes, indeed. A rattle of churrango, and there he was. Sitting on my desk in shirtsleeves, wincing again over his vinegar chords.

"President Pancho Perales."

"*Sí*. Is me. You are the *canadiense*, no? If you tell me one *canadiense* choke very funny I will sing for you one song of my country."

"I am helping to sell cocaine."

We laughed until our tears streamed. Then his fingers blurred upon the strings of the churrango. He sang. "In the sky a man he sees one ball of gold. He is climbing for it. And pretty soon he was get it. It was. How you say?"

"Clay, by God! Clay! *Viva* Perales! More!"

But the blur that was his hand shot up his arm, and he disappeared. "Wow!" I said. "What talent!" And, infected by the whole glad business, I started in on "The Tattooed Lady." "I came to town to see . . ."

"You goddamn crazy schoolteacher."

He was climbing in through the window from the chicken yard. He closed the window and stood there chuckling. His belly jiggled in a gap below his electric blue sweatshirt. Behind him rain started to bang on the glass.

"I should have known you couldn't stay away from a party."

I stared fixedly past his accusing eye hole to the water rippling on the window glass.

"Rain, rain, there's a bullet in my brain," he said.

"So rhyme. Am I supposed to be impressed? Is that your idea of literature?"

I looped and dodged around the office. Couldn't lose him, though. He followed. So I tried to turn and face him. Tripped. Cracked my head on my desk. Pain, something real. I saw that I still held the bottle, and drank. Isman sat on the window sill. I could see all the way through his eye hole. A silver dollar of wet daylight. "I've got a golden guy," I said. "Doing it right this time. Happy in the Valley. Fucking mansion. Did you notice my car?"

"Life is good. Perfection. Erection. An endless bloody cash injection."

I managed to get to my feet. "You bugger. You know everything, don't you?"

"Your Guatemalan lake blue as blazes. Samantha there to show him how to lose. The dust of Nepal."

Shaking my fists at him. "I am the Second Deputy Minister in Charge of Emigration at the Ministry of Strangers! You are not real, and I did not invite you. Get out of my office!"

He sprang off the window sill into a martial arts crouch. "Come on! You think the old freedom fighter has forgotten his jujitsu?" As he bobbed and feinted the day flickered through his eye hole.

I stared at him, trying to make him disappear. I couldn't. I whined, "Please. I'm scared. Why are you here?"

"Because I'm dead. And my only weapon is fear."

I screamed. "Fuck your fear!" And charged. And would have pitched through the window if he hadn't vanished. I stood leaning on the sill with my forehead against cold glass.

There below was the chicken yard, all mud. Slick and black. The rain making pocks that lasted each the merest instant. Because of its high shit content this mud could resist any amount of cleansing. Worms down there in it, right at home. Drowning. Third time down for everybody.

Best go home. Ms. Nieves could phone Roosevelt. I turned to call to her. "Oh blessed Jesus."

"I thought I'd just drop in for a minute, see how my Mac is doing."

A woman. Standing there quietly. A breeze from somewhere stirring the hem of her white cotton dress. "I wore it for you. It's the one you like. Well. Aren't you going to say hello?"

"I . . . I never thought you would . . ."

"Surprise." A smile in the blue eyes. And the thing I had forgotten. Love.

I said, "Is this a miracle?"

She shrugged. Her black hair was tied back loosely, but stray wisps hung over her ears.

I fished my glasses out of my inside pocket and put them on. "You're young!"

A laugh clear as water. "And the picket fence still needs fixing. And Carmela sings Verdi to her flowerpots. Can't you hear her?"

I nodded. "May I touch you?"

"Best not."

"I'm glad you came."

"You should let your beard grow again."

"Okay. Evelyn? I had forgotten, you know."

"Yes. I know."

"Not you but . . ."

"I know. Us. This. Feel nice?"

"A miracle."

"My little giftie for Mac."

Suddenly I was fidgeting, sloshing the half-inch of Smirnoff in the bottle, trying to stroke my absent moustache. I drank the last half-inch of vodka.

"Did he grow up to be handsome, Mac?"

"I think you know. Don't you? You know everything."

Her eyes returned to me. "You can't keep a good miracle down. Did he go to university? Has his heart been broken yet? Does he have his own apartment? Tell me, Mac. Tell me about our son."

"That smile of yours. It's only a mask, isn't it?"

"Everything's a mask if you look long enough. My love."

"Thank you for coming, Evelyn. Go back to the past now."

Her laugh, no less sweet. "You haven't changed. You still get angry when you're afraid."

"Tell me what you want so we can get it over with." I glared at her.

"Have you been a good father?" Irony in the soft eyes.

"Fuck you."

"Have you taught him to be strong, Schoolteacher?"

"Don't call me that!"

"Or does he live with his heroin in a dark room over False Creek, patching up reality?"

"I've had enough of you dead people! Go away! Go away! Christ, I've got to rest." I looked down, a tear dripped from my nose and splashed on a shoe.

"Don't cry, Mac. Just give me what I want, and then I'll go."

"I have nothing you could want."

"One thing."

"Take it, take it, take it." With the back of the hand holding the bottle I wiped a tear from my chin.

"You did what you could. Now it's my turn."

I looked up. I expected the mask to have fallen, but there was nothing changed about her face. In her hands, however folded at her chest, she now held a bunch of black tulips. "I want Jeff," she said.

"NO!" I threw the bottle. She vanished as it touched her face. The bottle bounced from the upright of a coat rack that stood near the door, and rolled back to my feet.

I waited. But it was finished. For there could be no ghost worse than Evelyn. But what was that? There, fitted over a prong of the coat rack. One of my carved masks leering? Or was it Toby? Had I put Toby there? So that he resembled now no cloth toucan, but a darker bird, one presiding over these proceedings? I laughed for a minute, shaking, and the tears still trickling. Then I levelled a finger and in a terrible voice commanded, "Take thy beak from out my heart, and take thy form from off my door!" With a flourish of wrist I offered Toby his cue.

"Quoth the Raven . . ."

Did Toby not know his line? I tried again.

"Quoth the Raven . . ."

No. So I hissed the word myself.

"Nevermore."

Then, stillness. No more ghosts. The party was over. Through the door I heard Ms. Nieves blow her nose. So dark now in the office. Best just stand here. Listening to the downpour. A sound like nothing, like nevermore. A good sound. Then I heard Ms. Nieves' phone. And, "Yes. One moment," she said in English. Then my own phone went *Brrrt*, and I turned to look at it. A tiny light flashing. Reflecting in one of the ears of my

Mickey Mouse bowl.

Brrrt.

No way I could be Second Deputy Minister. Might be Ken, though. Hi, Daddy.

Brrrt.

The receiver for some reason wet. Vodka.

"That you, Ken?"

"Mr. McKnight?"

Oh.

"Yes, but I'm just leaving the office. Terribly sorry."

"I don't know if you remember me, Mr. McKnight. Elizabeth? Jeff's girlfriend?"

The office went suddenly brighter. "Yes! Yes, I remember! My God! This is wonderful! How is Jeff? Is he there? Can I talk to him?"

"I had a hard time tracking you down. Finally the American School told me where to call."

"Oh Jesus. Something's wrong."

"I'm sorry, Mr. McKnight."

"Don't cry, don't cry. Please. Just tell me. I'll be fine."

"Jeff died yesterday."

I must have wandered through the streets for hours. I recall only finding myself in the stonecutters' yard, off the road where we boarded our trucks on the night of another calamity. I stood among half-formed blocks of granite, soaked, wondering what had happened to make me behave so strangely. The stonecutters waited out of the rain, in the door of their hut, watching me. After a while one of them, a fellow in an Indian outfit, came and took me into the hut and made me drink some coffee.

19

The Foul Rag-and-Bone Shop of the Heart

"I didn't think you'd let me in."

She shrugged. "Drink?"

As she poured rum I surveyed the room. Tidier now. Pile of marking on the table, and a coffee mug, but no crudputty. Almost a different place. I had been afraid it would still be a room that could welcome a squad of doomed raiders. Yet I wished that Liz had changed more. Her hair a pewter grey now but still cropped; her face chubbier but still acne-scarred and still mousy; and over a British Council T-shirt, the eternal overalls.

She handed me my drink. "What's it like out?"

"Night fog. Wet air up from the jungle."

"You look like hell."

"Older."

"You should grow your beard again."

"Yeah. You still go to the Arse?"

"Not much."

"We should go some time."

"No."

End of small talk. I leaned against the door, she stood in the doorway to the living room, almost as if blocking my way. The television was on. For a second, wondering if somehow Isman was in there, I felt dizzy.

"Something wrong?"

"No. I'm fine."

She left the kitchen and came back in a minute with a white Indian shirt. I remembered it. So. She knew why I had come. She dug in the shirt's pocket, found the book and tossed it to me. Some of my drink spilled as I caught it. *El Dorado*, swollen and brittle from that Rio Colorado dip years ago — but still it fell open to the photographs. The two were stuck together, and for fear of damage I didn't dare try to separate them. The one of Jeff on top, perfect.

In his tank top.

Under the arbutus tree.

"Liz?"

"What?" Now, without warning, the hurt shrillness. "You got what you wanted, didn't you? Power. Money. Gorgeous child bride to wash your socks." She gulped down her half-glass of rum. "You've got a fucking nerve, coming back here!"

"Jeff died."

She looked at me steadily.

"My son," I said. "Up north. Heroin."

She didn't look away, didn't even blink. "That's what happens to people you care about, isn't it? They die. Get out."

Carefully down the dark stairs, shivering in the fog. Clutching the book against my chest as if it were not just another cold thing.

A cloudy afternoon in San Jacinto. On the top step of the derelict house that Ken and I passed daily on our way to buy ice cream or booze, sitting in jeans and sweater, with my bread. Behind me a long gallery porch and the empty house itself. In front of me the big yard or pasture with its many thornweeds and bushes of deadly nightshade. Beyond the yard the road to the town centre. From behind, smells of darkness and dust. From in front, smells of growing green and horse dung. I had tried to breathe without smelling anything. Impossible. I had even cupped my hand over my nose, but the smell of my own damp palm had been worse than all the others. When a hummingbird had made the mistake of darting up close to investigate my red pullover it had received a swat: There is a hair-trigger aspect to ruined nerves. The bird hunkered in the grass for a minute then whizzed away.

Patrón, on television have you ever seen Bulgarian weight lifters attempting to outstare the thing at their feet, before attacking it? That is how I now tried to dominate the piece of white bread in my hand. I eyeballed it. Opened my mouth. Then closed it. No use.

So I took a breather from my labours, and groaned freely for a while. Then, as I set to subjugating the bread again, the black horse who lived on these acres came around a corner of the house, saw me and approached. It stepped over the piddling splash of vomit I had managed to produce an hour before, placed two unpared and curling hoofs on the lowest step and wriggled its lips toward my bread. God's teeth, horse smell.

"Easy for you," I said. "You're not trying to stop drinking." I let him take the bread — an improvement on thornweeds, I suppose — then I stood, placing a shaking hand on his shoulder for support, went down the steps, and walked gingerly toward the road. The horse followed, nosing my elbow, wanting more bread. "Horse," I said, "once I had a ladder. It didn't lead anywhere, because it came in a bottle and was not exactly real. You with me? And now that my ladder's gone I must lie down where all the ladders start. In the foul rag-and-bone shop of the heart. That's Yeats. Look over the fence, horse. You see that? That is the road to the ice-cream parlour. It is no longer the road to the liquor store."

"Excellent, Ms. Nieves, excellent."

"A custard tart, a napoleon, and they didn't have any éclairs so I got a slice of cheesecake."

"Now, don't cry. We're finished with crying, the both of us."

"It's just that I'm so happy for you. And so sad too."

"Here, take my handkerchief. You must try a bite of my cheesecake. Pardon my plastic fork. Best blow your nose first."

"One in a million, Mr. McKnight. You always have been and you always will be."

"Ms. Nieves, brush those flakes of pastry from your impressive declivity, and we shall get back to work. You have found all the figures I wanted?"

"Most of them. Gee, I had no idea so much money came in to this department. Zillions of dorados. Where does it all go?"

"Paper clips, envelopes, a two-hole punch. Supplies, services, surprises. Have you found Clinger Ventures yet?"

"Yes. Fifty million dorados. What on earth did they do for us?"

"A holding company. With whom we had relations."

"I don't know why that should be funny, Mr. McKnight, but it sure is good to see you laugh. I mean, a healthy laugh. Not like before."

"Productos Colorado? Premier purveyors of paper clips?"

"Uh huh. Found the file. That's one hell of a lot of paper clips. Why haven't I seen any of them?"

"Waiting in the warehouse with the rest of the surprises. And the other companies?"

"I'll have all the figures for you this afternoon."

"What a godsend you are. Ms. Nieves, would you accept a gift from me?"

"Why, Mr. McKnight!"

"I'm sorry — it's not the kind of present you gift wrap. I would be honoured if you would let me send you to Miami to visit your sister. For a month. No, two months."

"Oh my God. Are you serious? You are! But what about. . . ?"

"If I become nostalgic for the sound of nails being filed I will call in a temporary secretary. I'm sure she'll soon get the hang of it."

"Let me get this straight. Are you offering personally to pay for me to go for a two-month trip to Miami?"

"Personally."

"Oh, Mr. McKnight, I couldn't possibly . . . Anyway, don't you remember? I said I would never abandon you."

"Just show me how to do the coffee and give me one last glimpse of cleavage, and I will fear no evil. Now stop staring, it makes me feel like taking a drink."

"Okay, what are you up to? All that money going through the department. All those companies with the strange names. And now you're sending me away. No, don't lie, I know you. Why don't you want me here? What's going to happen?"

On Reforma there was a good deal of noise. All the traffic was halted, and there was an uproar of horns blaring. As the men hanging out of the bus doors strained up on tiptoe or skipped down and over to the sidewalk to see what the problem was. Noise is tolerable if you do not resist it. Except for those musical horns playing "El Condor Pasa" and "Pop Goes the Weasel." And now I saw that the jam was caused not by the usual collision, but by two men who had by some daring means stretched a banner between them across the street. Balding, determined-looking men in moustaches and black leather jackets. It was a well-lettered banner of paper which said, DOWN WITH THE GOVERNMENT OF HUNGER. I took advantage of the halted traffic to cross the street.

And as I walked soberly along a street which ran off Reforma, I saw in the weak light from the sign of a Venezuelan restaurant a certain green metal gate. The forbidding portal, *patrón*, of Hospitality House.

But, across the street, a rescuing sight: a *fritada* woman in fedora and pleated skirt, and her bubbling basin. And at this cockcrow hour for *putas* another woman there too, stocking up on greasy calories for the hard night's work head. Red dressing gown, a built-up black shoe for her clubfoot, Indian hair still cut short but no blonde dye in it now.

"I didn't know which one it was going to be. I'm glad it turned out to be you, Mili."

"You got it, man. Mili from Philly. But I ain't started work yet, as you can plainly see. Unless you got a thing for hot lard." Such a frank American grin on the Inca face. "Hey, do I know you? Hey, are you that schoolteacher? That Canadian? Fuck, you are! Shaved off your beard. Man, we heard you made it big. Married the President's kid or something. Is it true?"

"Does he still come here?"

"What — Charlie? Hey, how'd you know that?"

"I don't suppose you remember a certain English lesson?"

"What's your name? I forget."

"Mac."

"Mac, I remember that lesson like it was my address. Haven't laughed so hard since."

"I said I would die before I'd bend over and let someone shove barb wire up me."

"And I said everyone is a whore. Even you."

"And you were right. And as you know, Mili, the head of a whore is full of other people's secrets. So — does Charlie still come here?"

"Yeah. Hey, are you all right?"

"Yes. Yes, I'm fine."

But she saw that I wasn't. She handed her empty bowl to the *fritada* woman. Then she reached, firmly drew my head down and kissed me on the cheek. Her breath stank of sleep and grease and tenderness. "Come on." She took my arm and, her limp causing her to rock against me, we walked slowly down the block. I told her my whore's story. She understood everything.

"Nowhere to go but up," I said. "Nowhere to start but here."

"Schoolteacher, good luck. But what do you want from me? I can't do nothing for you. I'm just a whore."

So I told her what, because she was a whore, she could do

for me, and she said, "Yeah, I can do that."

"You're not as young as you used to be, Mili. You can't last in this business forever. Wouldn't you like to go back to the States? Let me send you, help set you up in a legitimate business of some kind. You could import — let's see — Indian shirts. Or frozen *fritada*."

"Frozen *fritada* — yeah, sure. Naw, I don't think I could live in the States any more. Look, Mac, I don't want nothing."

"But you'll be taking a chance."

"Listen, I know what it's like in with the rags and the bones, man. I live there. I don't know if there's any way up for me like there is for you. But maybe it's time I put this twisted goddamn thing on the first step."

"Mili, there are false ladders, and there are real ones."

"Still got to be the schoolteacher, don't you? I know what's real, man. Now it's time to get ready for work. So. See you round."

"Soon, Mili."

With my briefcase of photocopies I continued through the city toward the Jesuit church, to wait under the painting of sinners roasting in hell, where General Moncayo had said he would meet me.

"Amazing?"

"Yes, my estrange McKnight?"

"Have you loved me all along?"

"Yes. But you must know this."

"Even when you told me to go away?"

"Especially then. And also I remember something else. I remember the night I wore the blue lion mask from San Jorge. And we invented new lives of sex and safety."

Lying on our white bed, she in a flannel nightgown, me in a new pair of blue pyjamas. Leaning on elbows, nose to nose. Her cheeks firm and young again. As McKnight's cheeks glowed too, with new silver stubble.

"But there have been many lives since then. A multitude."

"Yes, Maquito. *Una multitud*. The lonely life when you ran away. And still I do not know where you went or why."

"I'll tell you some day."

"The nice life of being a young married airhole."

"Painting your nails. *Star-Glamour*. I didn't expect that. But not much has happened that I did expect."

"It was in my blood. Being an airhole. Just waiting for a chance to poop out."

"Pop."

"Then when Ken came. That was a life. Oh such a life."

"And?"

"When you drank and hit me and went with other women."

"That was a life?"

"A death, Maquito."

"Ah. And now?"

"Now you have lost your son, your Jeffrey, and you do not drink anymore, and you are so calm and so gentle, and of all my lives this one is the most sad and the most beautiful. And soon it will be time for our next life, which will be beautiful but will not be sad."

"Yes, I think the next life comes soon."

"And maybe then you will tell me?"

"Tell you what?"

"Why you ran. Where you ran. Why you drank. Why you hit me."

"Yes, in the next life I will tell you."

"Maquito, I see tears in your eyes."

All still in that big house. Outside, crickets and a moon.

"Remember something else," I said.

"From very long ago?"

"Yes, please."

"Something naughty and esplendid?"

"Oh, by all means. From the time of sex and safety."

"Before you ran."

"Yes. Before I ran." I rolled onto my back. My collection of masks was mounted in that other room, which I visited now only to be alone with the portrait of me that Jeff had done. To wonder about that gleam he had painted into one lens of my glasses. That small bright passing dream.

She said, "Do you remember how to fuck and talk?"

"An impossible thing, surely, like patting your head and rubbing your belly."

"Rub my belly, Maquito. Under my *camisa de noche*. That is not my belly."

"I'll rub it anyway."

"I want to rub something too. Where is your belly? What is this thing in the way? Sticking out of your pyjamas."

"Pretty close to belly. Rhymes with it."

"Ai, you and your rhymes. Is it your Botticelli?"

"It does look like Venus rising from the waves, doesn't it? But no."

"What, then?"

"It's my umbrelly."

"Ah. And you are expecting rain?"

"No, but I go around with it up anyway."

"Up where?"

"Anywhere you would like."

"All the way up?"

"Absolutely."

"Ai, Maquito, is esplendid your umbrelly. Now we can talk about the different kinds of weather."

"Tornadoes, Monzy."

"And *huracanes*."

"Twisters."

"Yes. I think we should discuss the twisters."

Under the twin hammers of midday light and sobriety I waited in my gardening clothes. On my feet, my squash shoes, to tread stealthily. Across the street the gate opened with a buzz. I picked up the athletic bag I had bought the day before at the Smuggler's Market, and crossed the street.

The house was silent. Doreen not there yet, the whores asleep. I went up the stairs. Mili was standing in her doorway, teetering with sleepiness, in her dressing gown. She leaned heavily on my arm as we went into her room.

"You got the thing?" she whispered.

"In the bag. Where's an outlet?"

I slid the thing under her bed, plugged it in, attached the cable and showed her which buttons to push.

"Maybe I'll go to the States after all. You still for it?"

Down and out and around into the little overgrown courtyard. Wading through the weeds. A cloud of white moths flying up. As I stepped up onto the chair that Mili had provided. House walls were hard in that lofty stone, concrete and adobe town. Best to run wires not through them but down the outside. And indeed I saw that several converged there outside Doreen's office, and that they went in through a hole. The last window, said Mili. That one up there, was it? Which meant that this was the wire of Maria de los Ángeles, who alas never did get her apartment near the *palácio*. There is a device called a splitter, which is easy to put in place provided you have practised it once or twice. It is not for nothing that they call me the HandyMac. And now, snaking down from Mili's window like a hotline from God, a sufficiency of 75 ohm coaxial cable. Through which, sometime soon, electrons of retribution would course. With the speed, *patrón*.

Of lightning.

He twists in my lap and tries to stuff a remaining bit of cookie between my lips.

"Ope." Determined, he resorts to the flat of his hand, and pushes. "Daddy, ope!" Until with a growl the daddy mouth snaps open, showing large teeth, and goes after his fingers. His shout and laugh, and the bit of cookie flies away, and his elbow hits the mug, and juice sluices over the glass tabletop. But now he is overcome, as he seems often to be, by the sight of my stubbly beard. His mouth hangs open as he strokes it.

"Beard," I say.

"Nice," says Ken.

The breeze of Valle Milagro stirs the honeysuckle leaves that shelter us here in the gazebo. Blades of sunlight tremble on the wet table glass and on Ken's hair. I smell cookie and honeysuckle. And? "Hey, what's that smell. Did you do something?"

"Fart."

One of the words he gets right.

We left the gazebo. There was a grackle on the lawn, pecking an avocado. Ken chased it, offering his best rangitang bellow, but it only hop-flapped ahead of him, keeping its eye on the fruit. While I hid behind the agave.

And now he ceases his pursuit of the grackle. He turns. His dark eyes look left and right, but there is no daddy. He spins in a circle, but in the circle of what he sees he finds no father. He stands still. Between the thorns of the agave that frame his blond head I see a kind of blankness settle upon the eyes. For a second he wonders if there ever was a daddy. Then comes fear. The corners of the mouth turn down. Then the lips part in a grimace. Oh, of rage. Because the Golden Guy does not care for this fear business. It makes him furious. "Daddy!" he screams, gnashing his teeth.

"I'm here, Ken." I stepped well away from the long thorns of my cover and let him tug me to the ground and belabour my shoulder with his little boy fists until he was laughing again.

He took my hand and led me beside a border of touch-me-nots. "'Mon, Daddy." I was happy enough to be led.

The touch-me-nots ran out, then there was just bare dirt and the place where Alejandro burned rubbish. Ken led me through the ashes. In the broken adobe of the wall there was a hole. Ken stuck his hand down into it.

"Jesus, don't do that! There could be scorpions."

He began drawing treasures out of the hiding place. The first was Toby the toucan, who was dropped without ceremony to the dirt. Next, a eucalyptus pod. "*Huele*," he said. Smell it. I did, and it was my turn to say, "Nice." The seedpod fell beside Toby. Now, the shell of a rhinoceros beetle. Ken's round Scottish eyes aglitter at this prize. Now came a chunk of volcanic rock, pitted with violence. The last treasure was a rock also, flattish and gleaming with mica flakes. "Gold," said Ken, but restored it to its hiding place before I could get a good look.

We walked again. Here, tall hollyhocks going scrape against the wall. Here the orange climbing thing with a single blue blossom. Which was not a blossom after all, but a long-tailed hummingbird. Here Alejandro had pruned a peach tree to grow against the wall. Because of its crucified appearance I called that peach tree Jesus. My fruit is better than gold, saith the Lord, but Jesus produced peaches that not even the grackles would eat.

Recently I had not gardened much. Gardening was for floaters, and I had some time back given up floating. In order to sink. And now I had given up sinking and taken up thunderbolts again. But even in my own yard the sun was hammers, and dead people were hanging from me as if I were Jesus the peach tree and they were my vile fruit.

"'Mon, Daddy." Through this open door, into the soothing plainness of Man's works. My squash court. No more *wham bam* these days. Ken kept his tricycle here, and while now I sat with my back against the wall, he barrelled around the floor, cutting two-wheel turns. A good sound, rubber rolling on hardwood. I was even moved to compose a couplet. *Don't roll out the barrel of blossoms in bud. Just roll me in peace like a piggy in mud.* Ken almost vanishing in the obscurity beyond the baseline, highballing back into view in the open door's light.

Out again, along the side of the house to the lawn in front. "A-pay." Still couldn't get that word right. He lay on his back spread-eagled, half in, half out of the shadow of the house, and I took a wrist and an ankle.

"Getting too big for this, mister."

"A-pay."

Around we went, in and out of the light. There was no way of avoiding it — I would always be at the hub of some whirlwind. Ken, maybe your circle would be safer if I wasn't in it. But without this grip on you, what would anchor me to anything?

A day crisp and bright in the City of Hope. There was snow frosting the mountains around Esperanza, but I felt no northern tingle. As I tried to make sense of an unfamiliar bárrio. Cross this plaza of packed dirt and one blooming rose, and let's see what happens if I turn left. A dead end, with an impressive view over a wide ravine with a dozen vultures gliding.

I found a taxi. We went up a hill. I got out in front of a jailbar fence and, in the three-piece suit of a Second Deputy Minister, flashed my letter. I was led past dark eyes and ready machine guns, down halls and up stairs, and was shown right in. And was pleased to see that this was a working office and not, like mine, a bullshit one.

"Look out there, Señor McKnight."

"Spectacular view, General."

"Spectacular but ugly. I hate it. Because in the bottom of that ravine many men and a few women are sleeping the long sleep. Do you know what it is you have put into my hands?"

Hands was metaphorical, because he only had one. The left sleeve was folded neatly back at the elbow and pinned.

"I know exactly, General."

"What you have put into my hands, Señor McKnight, is death. Treason. Vulture bait."

He sat behind his battered desk. The eye that was not covered by the patch studied me for some time, in the same way, maybe, that Charlie's had perused Moncayo's own face — that roadmap of reddened scars — on the day of the coup.

"These papers that you gave me, Señor McKnight."

"Those papers indeed, General."

"These figures that you have so considerately circled in red."

"Yes, General, those figures."

"Represent government money used to purchase cocaine?"

"Borrowed and later repaid. *Inyecciones de dinero*."

"These companies."

"Clinger Ventures. Productos Colorado. San Tomás Personal Services. Transportes Blanco."

"Only shells?"

"As hollow, General, as the smiles of a father-in-law."

"Of course you realize that this alone proves nothing."

"Perhaps a warehouse full of cocaine would prove something. And government-protected processing facilities on the Rio Colorado."

General Moncayo standing again, looking out his window at the circling vultures.

"And this *Índio* — this Tomás — is his partner?"

"*Exacto*. Are you thinking, General, that maybe Charlie Dávilos should join the others down there sleeping the long sleep?"

"No. But you are, Señor McKnight. Are you not?"

"Most certainly, General."

He faced me. "You do not have the appearance of a killer. Except for the whiskers."

"Well then, pay attention to the whiskers."

"Deputy Minister, I am disturbed by your confidence."

"It helps to have done this before."

"The Perales business. Yes, I know. The daughter, the letter. If you are as careless this time as you were then, we'll both end up down there, nourishing those birds."

"Fuck you, General — you have been more negligent than I ever was. Letting the *coca* be bought and sold right under your nose like potatoes in a market. *Hijo madre*, he even uses your soldiers to guard it!"

There was a sawed-off artillery shell on his desk, full of pens. I flicked them noisily back and forth and stared out the window, across the ravine to the snowy sierra.

"Understand one thing, Señor McKnight."

"Yes, yes, I know. That you are a man of principle. But if it becomes necessary in order to save yourself, you will throw me to the dogs, right?"

"I would have said the vultures." He sat again. "You see this horrible face? This is the face of a man who refused to close his eyes when he saw something that needed to be done. And this hand that is not here is the hand of a soldier who took hold of that thing that needed to be done. Where are your scars, Deputy Minister?"

"General, like the scars of all killers, mine are invisible."

And so, he was satisfied. The remaining hand of General Moncayo reached across the desk, gripped this right one of mine. Squeezed. Pumped once.

He took from a drawer a bottle half full of rum, and two glasses. While he poured a shot into one I laid my hand over the mouth of the other.

"Health, Deputy Minister."

"Health, General." I touched my empty glass to his non-empty.

"Let us discuss details, then. You will not be surprised to know that I have maintained certain key elements in a state of readiness. Like a pot of soup bubbling over a fire. For example, I am on very good terms with the owners of the *Diário de Notícias de Esperanza* and of *Canal Cuatro.*"

I nodded, smiled and drew from my briefcase its lonely cargo. "Not the best newspaper and television station in the hemisphere, but then quality is hardly the issue here." Leaned my lonely cargo against the artillery shell.

"A videotape cassette?"

"Wrong, General. This is not a videotape cassette. This is spice. This is *salsa ají*. Try some in your soup."

20

The Blazing Blue Bullet of Mac McLightning

"Cold, General!"

"Even for a Canadian?"

"No one hates the cold more than a Canadian. Are you going to get on with it?"

Standing on boggy ground among clumps of coarse grass up to our knees. Snow falling steadily. Bare fisty peaks all around, but in this snowcloud seldom visible. Not much alive here in this *páramo* valley except this stubborn grass and the General and his hundred soldiers and me.

"You should have worn a heavier coat, Señor McKnight."

"It was necessary to wear this one."

Of shapeless tweed. Hauled from the depths of my closet. The tang of the piss and vinegar of roomfuls of adolescents still caught in its nap. The sports coat, *patrón*, of an English teacher. Who took shit from no one. I flipped the collar up and pinched the lapels together.

"The warehouse . . ."

"Yes, General?"

"Soldiers. Just as you said. So sloppy, though — no sentries, nothing. Not a proud moment for me. Betrayal is inevitable, of course. But incompetent betrayal. . . ?"

"I know what you mean. If you are going to whore for the enemy, at least show him what you have been taught."

"A painful metaphor." The general sighed. This operation, this crowning day of his career, appeared to be giving him little joy. "Because there were. Right there in the warehouse. Whores."

"Women! No — was it really thus?"

"It was. Two."

"Dancing?"

"*Dancing*? Why do you say *dancing?"*

"Not naked, dancing, wearing the soldiers' boots?"

"*Hijo madre*, you have some strange ideas, you North Americans. Naked, yes, but dancing? — certainly not. As a matter of fact they were sleeping. Curled up with a pair of young privates."

"Ah. Not dancing. So what did they do?"

"When we arrived? They ran around shrieking and looking for their clothes for a while. Then, when they could not find them, they did the same thing the soldiers were doing."

"Which is?"

"They stood to attention and saluted."

"I suggest you recruit them, General."

And those other two, the fat pale one in black panties and boots, and the dark skinny one in nothing — maybe they would have been happy to salute, too. But I suppose they had been finished by the Woman's mincemeatmaker. Now they hung with her on my death tree and twisted in the steady wind of memory.

Behind us, parked on the grass, a dozen army trucks were going white. The hundred soldiers shuffled around smoking or muttered in groups or sat in the cabs with the motors running for warmth. General Moncayo, in battle gear even flimsier than my tweed, checked his wristwatch. Then he looked up into the snowcloud. For a minute lacy flakes settled upon the eyepatch and among his scars. Then in the cloud a tremendous roaring passed from west to east.

"Thunderbolts, General?"

"Three antiquated jet airplanes, which I have sent to make sure that the man you call Mr. Chairman will be warmer than we are. Did you know we have napalm, Deputy Minister?"

I said in English, "The Lord sent thunder and hail, and the fire ran along upon the round. I hope he remembered the weenies and marshmallows."

"One of the things that this hand that is not here never had the courage to take hold of is the English language. Will you translate?"

"It was from Exodus. Exodus is the part of the story where everybody gets their exit visas."

"You know the Bible?"

"This is my Bible. But I do not believe anymore." From a pocket of my English teacher's sports coat I took the book that the English teacher used to believe in.

"Ah. That. It is good that you no longer believe. Because El Dorado is an idea invented by fools so that they can do the kind of damage that fools like to do. And these pictures? Your family?"

"My first wife. My first son. My second wife. My second son."

"Why do you keep the book if you no longer believe?"

"Can you not make those clowns walk faster?"

"They are not clowns, Señor McKnight. They are explosives experts."

In the distance two soldiers walked slowly toward us, each holding an end of a stick upon which two large spools were unwinding. A third soldier followed, carrying a toolkit.

I said, "I think perhaps you find me amusing."

"Oh certainly not. You are far too dangerous to be amusing. This . . ." — waving his one arm into the snow, toward the approaching soldiers — ". . . is not amusing. That cassette of yours — it is not amusing either."

"Certainly it is."

"Ai, dangerous, dangerous. Merely standing this close to you makes my scars itch."

"I am only a mild Canadian who is good at talking."

"And good at knocking down governments."

"Will you let me throw the switch?"

"No, Señor McKnight. You have done enough already."

The two soldiers reached us and set the spools down among the whitening grass. The third soldier took wire cutters from his toolkit, snipped off the two wires, stripped the ends, wrapped the bare copper around the terminals of a detonator that rested at the feet of General Moncayo, spun butterfly nuts down snug, and stepped away.

"I don't know what it is about this country," said the General, looking off at the distant plastic pyramid. "Everything so violent. Politicians dancing on the dead bones of the poor. Murders in every town every day. These mountains themselves, with their eruptions and shaking and knocking people's own homes down on their heads. Is that what it is — that there is the violence of fire not far below our feet, always looking for a weak spot to get out? Whatever it is, Deputy Minister, it is above all primitive. Primitive and ugly. Perfect for a soldier." And as he bent toward the detonator he did finally look — scars and all — perfectly happy.

He threw the switch. The black pyramid of plastic-wrapped cocaine disappeared in a searing white instant that lit up the snowy air around us. Then there was a leap of orange far up into the snowcloud, and a ripping blast. The ground bucked. The soldiers cheered half-heartedly and started climbing into the trucks.

It seemed as if the air had inhaled the drug in a single fiery snort, and if any cocaine remained now it would soon dissolve and seep back down into the soil that had fathered it.

It was night when Moncayo let me off outside the Boar's Head

Tavern and continued on his way to look into the face of what had to be done. Upon the City of Hope a light rain was falling.

Clancy the Irish wolfhound scrambled to his feet to wag not only his tail but his entire large person, so that his feet skidded around under him, and he whined with joy.

"Have a sniff, Clancy. Oh aye, isn't that sweet? Printer's ink. First copy off the press, the General's gift to yours truly. No — here! — don't eat it. This is dessert, Clancy. Dessert. Main course first."

Stood for a minute, peering into the candlelit dinner-hour darkness of expatriates. And.

In.

And what have we here? A long table of what I judged — from those Yankee vowels and fair heads — to be American mountain climbers. "Here to partake of altitude?" I asked them, and the placid eyes all keenly on me, wondering. "Enjoy your meal. And may your pitons never pop."

And on into the bar.

"Dolores, my life, would you be so kind as to give me a glass of your best mineral water, with a quarter of lime and no ice and no amoebas."

"Mac. I have missed you. You do not want vodka?"

"Maria Dolores, I have missed me too. No, just *água mineral*. But tell me, why do you stir it? And why do you use your finger?"

"For your good luck, Mac, and long life."

"What are you waiting for then — insert another finger. Insert two."

Her tilt of a grin, the blowing out the corner of her mouth of Marlboro smoke, and the hip Latin bartender's wink.

"And how is our young Juan Ignácio?"

"Ah, that. What was your preposterous Canadian word?"

"In the name of God, Maria Dolores, no! The boy is a rangitang?"

"Thus he is, Mac."

"Then I will drink to his health. *Salud!*"

"And your son, Mac? I have heard that you have a beautiful one."

"As always, Dolores, you have the best ears in Esperanza. But at this moment I do not think we will talk about families."

"Grumpy."

Behind her, among bottles, the wooden sign petite as ever. BIG CATS SCRATCH. BUT A LITTLE PUSSY NEVER HURT ANYONE. Which prompted this greeting to the mousy person on one's left at the counter. "Damn it, Liz, when are you going to put some weight on?"

"Bloody hell — right back in form, aren't you? What happened — get fed up being the minister of whatever? Gorgeous child bride get tired of washing your socks?"

"We will discuss neither of those topics."

"You quit drinking?"

I nodded, turned, leaned back against the counter. The wee bar full at this dinner hour. Oilmen from Dallas or Calgary with their potbellies, beards and baseball caps. *Esperanzeños* in suits and moustaches, and their high-heeled girlfriends.

"Mac. When you came to get your book. What I said. About your son. I'm sorry. Jesus, what's wrong — you're shaking."

"Dead people hanging from me, Liz. Must be trying to shake them loose."

"Whatever are you talking about — Isman?"

"Among others. But listen now, and I will tell you about Isman. Isman was bad. Isman was not faithful to you. When he was still a suave, sober Arab, Isman used to pump — literally — a certain gorgeous Consuelo, a United States Embassy employee, for information. Later, when he was finished being suave and sober, Isman used to bring a thing called a Cherita back to the apartment. A weakling and a drunk was Isman. Also, incidentally, a murderer, and he did not think that this was wrong. Isman died because he as a shallow, weak, selfish, murderous, inhuman drunk. And I want him and the Woman and the dancers and the fucking Harvesters and everyone else the fuck off me!"

Hell. Shouting. And, looking perhaps savagely at Liz, I saw that her pinched face was creased and old. Twisted now too in a grimace, as she tried to hold back tears. And could not. With a trembling hand I pressed her face into my chest, and I felt warm tears through my shirt. Conversation died, and the faces of strangers looked on with concern. An oilman with a baseball cap that said *Calgary Flames* offered a pressed white hankie, which Liz accepted. I eased her away and checked my watch. One minute to nine.

I looked up at the television on its wall bracket. Men in short pants running desperately after a ball. The television was not on Canal Quatro. Therefore I pushed my glass aside and, retaining my newspaper, climbed up on to the counter.

Gosh. All those faces gaping up at me. Like an English class, sort of. More people paying attention, though. And all waiting to be instructed.

I felt a tug on my trousers. "Mac," said Dolores, "that was mineral water, not vodka. Get down."

I ignored her.

"I have stopped drinking," I said.

"I'll drink to that," said the *Flames* fan. There were laughs.

"And I had to lie down in the foul rag-and-bone shop of the heart, among many sad and ugly things."

"A million empties, right?" said Flames.

I bent toward him. "You shut the fuck up!" An English teacher's best bellow. He staggered backward, and a number of *Esperanzeños* and their girlfriends were crushed against the wall. A Stubbs print of horses and hounds fell. Its glass broke against the head of a girlfriend, raining shards upon her bare arms.

"Ai, Mac," said Dolores.

"I have something important to say, and I would like you all to be quiet." I waited. And, except for the bare-armed girl, who was whimpering and peering down her décolletage, they were quiet.

"I had to lie down in the foul rag-and-bone shop of the heart." Blond heads appeared in the doorway. Mountain climbers, unable to avoid the scent of danger.

"And what a stink, children! Maybe you know it — the smell of the things you've done that you wish to Christ you hadn't, so you turn your back on them and leave them there to rot? But soon you notice that certain particularly nauseating odours appear to be the fruits of persons other than yourself. What then? Why, then, children, it is time to settle accounts." I waved my rolled-up newspaper, and among my audience there was a general leaning away, out of striking distance. "Yes, I mean revenge. I mean retribution. You make a stink in somebody else's rag shop, and it is only right that you should pay and pay big. You plant your vile little wind if you like, but don't be surprised when you find yourself reaping the granddaddy of all bad smells. Let there be no doubt, I am talking shitstorm. A turd-twister of considerable rpm. Because it is time to hoover the old rag-and-bone shop. The little schoolteacher has decided to clean house."

I laid my newspaper on top of the television, which was at my shoulder, reached around to the channel selector, poked a button, turned the volume right up and heard the stirring chords of the national anthem.

I pinched the end of one of Dolores' shelves of bottles and leaned out so I could see the screen. There it was, the flag, waving against the stainless sky of the Andes. I gave an encouraging nod to my audience and tossed them a salute.

The anthem finished. The flag faded in a slow dissolve. And there was the grey suit, pug face and shaven head of President Charlie Dávilos. He was seated at that walnut desk in his office, pen in hand, studying some document. As the camera moved in for a close-up he laid the pen down, looked up and folded his hands on the desk.

"Democracy, is not easy," said Charlie. "Freedom is not easy. Freedom means being free to make wrong choices as well as right ones. Sometimes we make the wrong choices, and when we do not like the consequences of those choices, we blame it on the system."

Yes, well, Charlie, you'll know any second now what it is like to make a wrong choice, which is to say to fuck with Mac McLightning.

Dolores tugged at my pants cuff again.

"I assure you," continued the President, "that there are those who are only waiting for the opportunity, the right moment, the moment when we tire of bearing the responsibilities that come with democracy."

Oh oh. Would the camera now pull back to reveal, mounted on the presidential flagstaff, the dripping head of General Moncayo? But as Charlie opened his mouth to continue, the screen flashed a clutter of magenta and green. The image disappeared and the screen went to snow. But not for long.

I snapped upright again. Mac McHeight. Did not now need to see the screen — I knew by heart what would follow. "Ladies and gentlemen," I said, "this is a little home movie I threw together. I call it simply the Blazing Blue Bullet."

I heard Sam, playing it again.

"Yes," I said. "The fundamental things and the ways in which they are applied. First, as if the camera were a mirror, we have a shot of three people looking into it. A woman, the President and the President's penis. What the woman is applying to the President's penis is not, however, a fundamental thing, but a refreshing glaze of cocaine. Visually this is a good move, because, as you see, it cuts the glare somewhat."

Strange — no one paying attention to my commentary. Below me the woman in the low-cut dress crumpled to the floor, but her beau did not notice. Through the many shrieks and shouts of outrage or disbelief or joy it was hard for me to hear Sam's lyrics and, thus, to know exactly at what point we were in the minidrama.

"Now, as you can see, ladies and gentlemen, a kiss is most certainly still a kiss, especially when applied to that part of the presidential physiognomy. We're back to the glare problem, though."

The President had a drink in his hand. His shirttails drooped, and his pants were around his knees. As naked Maria of the Angels expressed her devotion to the rod and the staff that comforted all of us. Charlie sang along with Sam about it being the same old story.

Right, and Mac will have his glory, you murdering prick. You see this? This is the Shitty Shimmy. In which these wrinkled brogues that I have owned since Evelyn was alive do a kind of shuffle-skim, twist, slam! on the puddled formica of Dolores' counter. And when I also beat time to Sam's song with my rolled-up *Diário de Notícias* it is called the caca cha-cha.

There were shouts of disgust. Female groans of nausea. From oilmen — who perhaps did not even understand whose willy that was up there — earnest comments on the technique of Maria de los Ángeles. Mountaineers used elbows to advantage as they gouged their way into the bar, which was wild now with the smell of sweat. Grey-headed Liz there, still crying — or was she laughing? Dolores too, jostled and jarred and looking up sadly at her President being fellated.

Through the tumult I heard Charlie leave off singing and begin to moan, "Ai, Angelita!" The oilmen took up his anthem, chanting, "Ai, Angelita! Ai, Angelita!" Then someone tried to climb up onto the counter, reaching toward the television. I recognized him from years before. Mr. Oates, a missionary. I placed the sole of my shoe against this forehead and pushed. The downed girlfriend grunted as Oates landed on her.

"And so, children," I shouted, "the airwaves went out unto the multitudes. And, Lo, the multitudes beheld the pictures of the President's penis, and were much diverted. There was mirth in Tigre. And in the mud huts of Salchibamba grandmothers took this vision of Charlie's penis to be a portent, and many chickens were sacrificed. And maybe even the subject of this minidrama, the President himself, has seen our presentation and is even now seeking out the director to bestow honours upon him. My friends, I must away."

I reached around and turned off the television. The chant of the *petroleros* petered out. Oates rolled off the girlfriend. There was an uneasy silence.

I climbed down. They made room for me. All those eyes, *patrón*. As uncomprehending as those of sheep. This was surely what Jesus must have seen on his way down from the Mount after the Sermon. Then Liz squeezed toward me. She lifted her sheep's lips, and I kissed them. The tip of her little English tongue touched the tip of my Canadian one. Meaning goodbye. Then Dolores came and kissed my cheek and gave me a whiff of Marlboro breath to remember forever.

"Well fucking hoovered, man. You take care, now," said a voice.

"You too, Flames," I said. The climbers let me pass, averting their eyes.

The dining area was empty, but the crowd flowed out behind me from the bar. People returned unsurely to their tables, and there was conversation. I heard a *petrolero* voice. "Man, I love these foreign parts. I ain't *never* goin' home." Above candle flames faces watched me. "Class dismissed," I muttered, and took a step toward the door. Then I took a step back. As two people came in.

She wore diamond earrings, a rain-spattered grey silk blouse unbuttoned almost to the navel, and black leather pants. He wore a Panama with a green parrot feather, a white double-breasted suit, a green silk shirt and chains. They were both bright-eyed, having perhaps run a few yards in the rain from their car. So I said to them, "I see you don't know about the Blazing Blue Bullet yet."

"Schoolteacher."

"Or the napalm."

"You better get off that booze, man. Your brain's had it."

"Gustavo!" I called. "Champagne for the Chairman and his

gorgeous sidekick! On my bill!"

Tomás shook his head, walked past me and sat at a small table. "C'mon, baby, leave the schoolteacher to his DTs."

Holly said, "You've put on some weight. Your whore's outfit not fit you any more?" She touched my wilted tweed.

I followed her to the table.

"Beat it, man. We don't want your champagne," said Tomás.

I sat down, placed my rolled-up *Diário de Notícias* on the table. "Haven't heard from the plantation today?" I said.

"The plantation can take care of itself."

"Seen tonight's headlines?"

He looked away in disgust.

I said, "That scar on your neck clashes with your shirt, I hope you know that."

Holly laughed and leaned forward. Her own shirt buckled. I glimpsed a nipple. Gustavo came with champagne glasses and lit our candle. "Señor Mac," he whispered, "don't you think you should. . . ?" He nodded toward the door.

"Bring the champagne," I said. And to Holly, "Well, Ivy, as I always say, it don't mean a thing if it ain't got that cling."

She smiled steadily, watching me watch the way her blouse bent, until I said, "Hey, you still got that shack where I stayed that time?" and winked. Then her smile trembled. She sat upright, taking the slack out of her shirt, and started playing with her empty glass. The semi-twiddle. The one-eighty rotate.

"What fuckin' shack?" said Tomás.

"You know — the whore shack."

"Talk English, man."

The champagne came. I lifted my glass and said, "A toast."

Holly started to lift hers but set it down again.

"Yes. A toast to toast. Which is to say, to that which — whore shack included — is now nothing but one big smouldering clinker in the jungle. Is that English enough for you?" I tilted my champagne into the ice bucket. "Hey, has the little woman ever showed you that trick she does with Roland's shrunken head? I didn't think it was possible, but I was forgetting the way Ivy can spread."

Tomás' neck scar glowed a dirty magenta. His hand slid down to the pocket of his suit coat. Watching that hand, Holly leaned back from the table.

"My son is dead," I said, unfolding my newspaper.

Behind me there was a bustle of someone rushing in from the street, and a man's American voice sang out to the clientele at large. "They's tanks all round the Palace. And about a million soldiers. Look's like Charlie's goin' down. And look what's on the front page of the paper. Special edition."

Tomás paled as he read, over my shoulder, the six-inch headline, *DÁVILOS VENDE COCA*. So I did not bother to show him the front page of my own *Diário*. Instead I spread the newspaper across the table — lifting the candle clear, pushing the glasses off the edge — and opened it to page two. They did not notice the champagne in their laps, so I pounded the table to get their attention. Slowly their eyes fell to the slightly smaller headline, which referred to the fire-bombing by the National Air Force of a cocaine-processing facility on the Rio Colorado.

"I may have mentioned him to you before. His name was Jeff." I set the candle on the newspaper.

Holly's shoulders sagged and, again, her shirt. She turned to Tomás and stretched a hand toward his face.

"You can keep the paper." I stood and turned to leave. There was a smack, a yelp, a crash. Holly down. Her head under the table of an *Esperanzeño*, who took his candle from the table and leaned over, illuminating her. A fat tendril of blood slid out of her nose, down her cheek and into her ear. A breast had escaped the shirt. She lay there and cried.

Then a mass of newspaper, table, and white suit spilled toward me. In Tomás' hand was a gun. But he pitched forward over the fallen table, and as his hands shot out to break his fall the gun spun away. It landed on the newspaper which, having come to rest with the candle, now started to burn.

As he scrambled to right himself two things fell out of his jacket pockets: his switchblade and a set of keys with a leather tag. With one hand I scooped up the knife and snapped it open. With the other I grabbed Tomás braid. Thick it was, *patrón*, and strong. I jerked it forward and down. Some part of his face engaged the edge of the table. With half a dozen strokes of the Chairman's shiv, I cut off his braid.

My left foot was stuck in his Panama. There were flames going up my pantlegs. I didn't want any more dead people hanging from me, so I tossed the knife away, swung my leg over him cowboy style and sat on the back of his neck. His throat bore down on the table's edge. Noises came out of him like the ones a straw makes when the milkshake is all gone.

I saw Holly crawling toward the door, among the feet of diners. In those leather pants her ass was like an evil black heart beating unsurely. But beating it for sure. I jerked up Tomás' head, and when he gasped for air I jammed his braid in his mouth, then sat again. The *Diário de Notícias* was still blazing. I wanted the braid to ignite like a wick. But as Tomás clawed at my legs there was only a small stink of singeing. I dismounted the Chairman, kicked his Panama off my foot and started again for the door.

"I'll take those." With a bloody smile Holly held up to me the bunch of keys. She also tried to take my hand. And she said, "Please."

Then I heard Clancy bark. There were footsteps in the alcove, *tiptap*, someone with a limp. I stepped aside into the door of the men's john. And in a second I saw between me and Tomás a dark suit and the back of a head. Filadelfo. Obviously here looking for me. Charlie not happy to see his big thing on the small screen. But what Filadelfo now faced was not the Son-In-Law but Tomás, kneeling beside the toppled table, reaching into flames, with his braid hanging out of his mouth. When Tomás extracted from the fire his pistol, how was Filadelfo to know that it was not him that this berserk *Índio* intended to plug?

Filadelfo fired first.

The braid popped out of Tomás' mouth. He lowered the gun, looked with scepticism down at the red blotch on his breast pocket. Fell sideways onto the dwindling flames of the newspaper.

Outside I passed Holly. She was still crawling, and Clancy, unhinged by the sight, was whining and tugging at his chain. I spotted the Porsche across the boulevard, under a streetlight.

Seconds later a German motor shrieked, along with smoking rubber, as I drove my foot down on the accelerator, spun the wheel and dented the roof with my head as the car bounded over the boulevard divider. Ahead of me on the sidewalk, aiming his gun, was Filadelfo. I carried on, between two parked cars, up onto the sidewalk. There was a low wall. And a vision from the past returned to hearten me. As Filadelfo's shoes flew up like startled crows. And he plunged over the wall backwards, Mac's gift to the guard dogs.

I lost a headlight against the wall but was able to thread down the sidewalk, back toward the Arse. Bloody and bare-chested, Holly waited at the entrance. For a second she looked hopeful. But she just gave a forlorn wave as I skimmed past. Then I booted it and shot back onto the street.

I stopped twice, first beside an Indian girl selling roses, then in front of the Bar Urubamba. I waited a few seconds, double-parked, listening to César's *cúmbia* slide out the open door. Then I lobbed the flowers. Some of them made it. Inés, maybe we were fun and maybe we were rot, but this at least I know: You sure would like my new car.

Outside the city, on the Pan-American Highway, heading north, I took time to wonder where I was going and what I intended to do when I got there. But then the highway pitched down into a ragged valley and fog. Better. Concentrate on immediate narrow shaves. Sudden hairpin curves. Headlights jumping toward me out of nowhere.

Through a mile of bottom land smelling wetly of dirt, across a narrow plank bridge at seventy-five miles an hour, then twisting up the far slope, out of fog and into black air bristling with stars. And now, on this first stretch of the northern highlands, my one headlight swept white graffiti on a cliff face: *Quique is a fairy*. Reassuring. That some things endure.

With mountain peaks just beginning to show against the sky, figures appeared ahead on the highway. A roadblock. Probably set up by Moncayo, but I couldn't risk it. Besides, I made his scars itch. There were two soldiers, one waving a flashlight, the other a machine gun. No barricade. So I just slowed down, then tromped it. Shouts, and a flashlight clubbing my fender. Then a sound that could have been a shot. But I was gone.

I stopped in predawn light, got out, stood in the middle of the highway. In a brushed-choked valley below the road birds were singing. The high air still and transparent. "Pecs could use a little work, there, Mac," I said as I pushed. I lost sight of the car right away, but I could hear it crashing and bounding. A cactus keeled over. And there two startled vultures flapping up. A red roof for an instant bobbed above the brush. Then I noticed farther down a column of smoke. Someone's house.

I walked down the highway, and soon I saw not far away the Cañajula bridge, with a box-like building at the near end. The customs office. When I reached the building I stood for a few minutes watching sunlight crawl down a mountainside. Then, as I turned to enter I noticed something — upon the tip of the flagpole of the customs office, a bloodred bird. The bugs were up, apparently. The vermilion flycatcher fluttered out, snatched one, and back to his pole.

"So where's the gold, Edgar? Did I take a wrong turn somewhere?"

Feeling tired finally, I went through the open door into the cool dark interior of the building and across to a wicket. Hearing my steps echo. With planning I could have done a Sister Louise again. But to plan it is necessary to know everything that you intend. And sometimes that is not a good thing to know. Too late now.

"Hee hee. Mac. Is you."

Echoing in this dismal place, a voice I knew.

"Marshal Art?"

"I was wait you."

"You was?"

"Yes. The *presidente* he was telephone me himself. He was say me the gringo must not leave the country."

Patrón, everything comes to an end but strangeness. There in the dimness beyond the counter, a grey uniform, and slicked hair and smooth *Índio* face. A wine-coloured hummingbird that twitched a wing as Arturo's smile cut through my fear.

"Christ. You work here."

Our hands clasping. His soft grip. His soft controlled laugh.

"I am working here four years. Hee hee. Mac. I have here a little rum. We have one last *trago* for to say goodbye, no?"

"Well, well. Marshal Art. You were always a good friend. Never ever anything but."

"*Sí*, Mac. A good friend."

"And you remember your English lessons."

"For you, Mac, I remember. The rum?"

"No, but thank you. You are not going to keep me, then? I have no exit visa."

Wham! his stamp came down upon my passport.

"Did you know you were working for my department? Until today?"

"*Sí*. I know this." His smile faded. He looked away. "Why you are say *until today?*"

"Because I am now nobody's boss. Also, Charlie is out and General Moncayo is in. With these two eyes, Arturo, I saw him blow up the *coca*. Remember the *coca*? So finally we have won. I suppose. And now you can love your country again. And if you talk nice to him, maybe you can be a real policeman again and catch the bad peoples."

"Moncayo? *Presidente?*"

"Wouldn't you like to get your old suits out of the closet? Send Isabel to a decent school?"

"These are the good news, Mac. These Moncayo news. But I think maybe I will going to stay here. Is nice. Is peaceful. Elena and Isabel and my new son Marquito, they are happy. We are live in a house in the valley near to here. We have the garden. We have the chickens."

"You say your house is down in the valley?"

"Yes. Maybe you was see the smoke from my fire of wood."

"Ah. Yes, Arturo, I saw your smoke. And do you happen to like fast cars?"

The first warmth of sun on my face as the guard at the near end of the bridge glanced sleepily at my passport, handed it back and nodded me on. Then the metal roadway going *clong clong* under my brogues as I passed beneath a sign that said *frontera*. Below, a ravine and creek and garbage. And now a guard from a different lofty republic, with a cleaner uniform and polished machine gun and wide awake, handed back my passport and said, "Go ahead."

But I stopped for a minute, to turn and look back and see this last sight of what it was I was leaving. One soldier scratching his ass. A highway, the customs building. Some mountains and blue sky.

Then I heard something. A small purr. It got louder, and there was a spot above one mountain. A helicopter. Maybe a-comin' for to carry me home. But being beyond the sign that said *frontera* one did not care. Pah! I spat on the bridge.

The helicopter landed near the customs building in the dirt parking area, with a storm of dust until the rotors stopped. Then a door of the helicopter opened and a man stepped out. Army fatigues and a gun in holster, and the shaven head. Next, out the same door, a woman in a loose white dress, stepping more carefully because she was helping a child, a boy in short pants and the green shirt with the dinosaurs.

"Charlie, not this," I muttered.

He stood at the end of the bridge, with a hand on his holster, saying nothing, beside the guard, who was frozen in a salute. As the soldier of this other republic held a bead on Charlie's chest. And Ken saw me and hollered.

"Daddy!"

He came running. But just as he got to the span his mother caught him. He tried to push free, shouting, "Daddy! C'mon see the helicopter!"

Montserrat shouting too as she held him. "Mac! What are you doing! What have you done!"

Then, from somewhere, there was a jeep making more dust as it skidded to a stop near the helicopter. Four or five soldiers surrounded Charlie, with guns. My father-in-law gave me one last sinking look as the soldiers marched him off to the customs building.

And I shook as I looked at my wife and my son there. In that other country.

"You stay there, Ken, okay? You stay with your mom."

"Daddy! Where you going! I wanna come!"

"Mac, how can you do this!" Oh Lord. Screaming. "Go away! I hate you! I hate you!" And now shrieking in Spanish. As Ken twists around in her grip and his little fists strike out. And he cries.

"Don't shout my dad!"

Montserrat released him. Her hands tore at something around her neck. With a snarl, throwing. A teeny flash up in the air and in a second a hiss on the bridge metal at my feet.

I bent. Picked it up. The chain broken. But there he still was. The golden man.

Ken not struggling now. Just standing beside Montserrat. His eyes all full of the truth. As I did a silly hop and a hip. And, in spite of or because of everything, managed at that last moment to sing.

"Rock It, Robin."

And damned if his little boy's voice, cracked with a laugh or with a tear, didn't dance like a bell in that transparent air.

"Deedly-tweet."

And I turned.

And the guard of this other lofty republic said, "That you go well, señor."

And I went away.

21

Now This Is the Strange Part

One Saturday afternoon not so very long afterward I looked out a train window, across rice fields, to a distant hill, where I saw a fiery gleam. It was no golden city but only the sun grazing the gilt eaves of a temple. Nevertheless, it pained me. I leaned well out the window of that slow-moving train and closed my eyes so that the warm Buddhist breeze they had there might cleanse me of such unproductive longing. We were coming to a town — I could smell the garbage dump. Opening my eyes I saw two boys with no shirts and in short pants lying on their backs among the plastic bags of the dump. Hands behind heads, looking up into the sky. One of them, with knees crossed, waggling a bare foot. Good lad. How to be surrounded by rot and not give a damn. Now drab cement walls of buildings. Now a row of houses with no fronts, colour televisions flickering inside as a monk in a saffron robe walked past, looking in at the cartoons. Streets of bicycles, motorcycles, and trucks with chrome and bright curlicues. We creaked to a stop at a station. Vendors beside the train jabbed cooked chicken up under my nose. Here the amoebas were Buddhist, so when you got dysentery, people just smiled and said, Karma.

Patrón, one lived now in an infamous Asian city of grinning procurers. Sin and smiles on every corner as we all sank together down the commodious drain to Nowhere. And the first thing one did upon arrival was to procure a person to remove one's tattoo. Once, you'll remember, it had said *Who Me?* Now it said zip.

We rocked across rice plains and irrigation ditches. Not far to the west were lumps of twisted mountains. In an hour we would arrive at the coastal town that was my destination. There, at the waterfront I would stroll past racks of drying squid, and further on at the beach I would listen for the thumps of fishermen's dynamite far across the water and would walk among hundreds of coloured fish washed up dead. My recreation.

They did not believe in coincidence here. Instead, lights flashed and bells went ding on the pinball machine of karma. And suddenly I had the strangest sensation. The emotional equivalent, maybe, of *TILT*. I turned away from the fields, and in the seat facing mine I saw an amazing thing. Red hair sticking up. A nose mottled pink. A beard.

"God," I said. "Dickie."

"So where's your fucking Mercedes?"

And the former Second Deputy Minister had to splutter for a second and to blush for another before he could say, "One travels by public transport now. In this less lofty republic."

Some restrained but prolonged chuckles as we observed each the other, and much shaking of heads in amused disbelief.

"Well, Dickie. Or must I say Richard? Ricardo won't work here, obviously."

"Call me Dickie. They all do. I know you're going to anyway." He coughed.

"And who is *they?*"

"My students. At the American School."

"Good grief. Social Studies again?"

"English. Your old turf."

"American Lit.? Poe?"

"Started him last week."

"Christ. 'Eldorado'?"

"Nah. Lousy poem, couldn't stand to teach it."

"A wise move, Dickie. And do you like it here?"

"No." He coughed. "Do you?"

"No."

There was no joy in the voice that had once been so lusty and keen. Rather, now, this phlegmy cough and a ragged resignation.

I said, "I'm with the British Council. Teaching English language."

"Managing not to be seduced this time?"

I did not answer. Outside, pale fields floated past like empty pages. Unwritten letters.

"But they are pretty, aren't they?" he said. "The girls."

"Dickie, I can't deny it. And should I ask why you left your paradise in the land of the condor?"

The sun seemed to be gliding along with us, not far above the tops of the twisted mountains. Its weary light reached in through the train window and touched the face of Dickie. And I saw that there were drooping crescents dark below his eyes, which were bright but tired, and that above his beard the skin hung on his cheekbones. The Goddamned light. Follows you around the world like a homeless dog spreading, *patrón*, these fleas of the Apocalypse.

"There was a thing," he said. "With a girl. Like you."

"Ah."

"Parents kind of upset. Flossie not too happy either. Gave me the boot in fact." A twitch of the red moustache in a sneer.

"Well, I can't really say I'm surprised. Someone I know, perhaps? Lorena?"

"Banana Lorena? Mac, Lorena graduated years ago."

"Yes. Of course. Years ago. Another student, though?"

"Uh huh. I got caught. Putting it to her. In the Biology lab."

"God, how wonderful! Love among the specimens. Was it beneath the pickled foetus?"

"What pickled foetus?"

"Never mind. Any news of the other gringos? Doreen maybe?"

An ember of mirth in Dickie's burnt-out eyes. "Don't act so innocent. Word gets around. Everybody knows who blew the whistle on Charlie. And who got that film on TV."

"Whistle? Film?"

"I don't know what you're afraid of — you're a national hero. But if you don't want to talk about it, that's your business. So — news? Doreen's hubby, Raul, is in the slammer. Maybe even sharing a cell with Charlie."

"Bloody splendid. And the Whale herself?"

He coughed. "Why you interested in her?"

I shrugged.

He said, "They destroyed her house. And not only because of Raul. That's where they flushed out Charlie."

"No!"

"I saw it, Mac."

"You were there? That night?"

"With this whore from Philadelphia." Remembering, he seemed to revive, as if the recollection was a tonic. "I'll skip to the good part. I smelled smoke, and whores started screaming everywhere. Except for Mili. She started laughing for some reason. We grabbed our clothes and beat it. The yard was full of soldiers. I stood on the sidewalk among the half-naked whores — the johns didn't hang around. Black sheets of smoke were crawling up the walls. Mili gives me a little punch on the arm, says 'See ya in the funny papers,' limps on down the street."

"Charlie — they tried to arrest him?"

"Sort of. He came out fully dressed. Nice pink sweater. Not coughing, not blinking. Davy Crockett . . ."

"Of the fucking Andes."

"With this hysterical whore wearing a sheet. One or two of

the soldiers points a gun in Charlie's direction. The rest just sort of twitch and shuffle. Charlie doesn't even seem to see them. He takes his whore by the hand and leads her down the walk. No one tried to stop them. He led her down the block, they got into a black limo, and *hasta luego*, Charlito."

"Now why didn't Mili tell me any of this."

"You know Mili? I thought you didn't approve of whores."

The train stopped — some problem with the tracks. I could see that Dickie's account had tired him. "No matter," I said, "It's all in the past now."

I let him rest.

Miracle Stylists: A one-chair beauty parlour in a Philadelphia mall; Milagro Ulloa, proprietress. Mili had suggested a blow job to go with my blow-dry. I, in no mood for pleasure, had declined. No mention of that night at Doreen's. Fine. Mili knew about rags and bones of the heart, and had chosen wisely to let the past rest in peace.

Before Philadelphia there had been an aimless peregrination through Central America and Mexico, of which I remember nothing but lying on my back in hotel beds with air conditioners roaring, desperate for alcohol.

And in Fort Lauderdale I looked up Ms. Nieves' sister, Engrácia, who lived alone in a stucco bungalow with a palm tree in the front yard. She gave me coffee and said that Ms. Nieves had stayed for a few weeks and then had returned to South America to take a job on President Moncayo's personal staff. Ms. Nieves, Moncayo can look into the face of what has to be done until he goes blue in his own face — he'll never look down a kindlier bosom than yours.

And later, in Montreal, when I tried to speak to the bank clerk in French it came out Spanish. But they gave me my drug money anyway and, as in the song by my compatriot, I went down to a place by the river where, among garbage and flowers, I made a bonfire of the bills.

Soon the sun slid behind the mountains. There was not much

more twilight here than there had been in Esperanza. A gauze of darkness began to accumulate between Dickie and me. I felt I had to reach into it, to feel around in it for what I still wanted. Because, unlike Mili, I could not let the past rest peacefully. The train began to roll again.

"After that? No one else came out of the house?"

He had been resting with his eyes closed. Still, when he spoke again his voice was weak and rough. "Yeah, one more person came out."

"Doreen?" My heart thumped.

Dickie sat up. "I don't know if it was the smoke or what was happening, but she was crying. She just stood there on the step. Looking bewildered. As if she didn't have a clue where she was."

"What was she wearing?"

"What?"

"What was she wearing?"

"Jesus, Mac . . ."

"Just tell me. What was she wearing?"

Dickie looked at me through the thickening dusk for a minute. Finally he decided not to ask my why I wanted to know. "If my memory serves me correctly, I think she was wearing a loose dress. Made of some kind of flimsy material."

"Colour?"

"Red. I remember the red, and I remember the tears."

"And what happened?"

"There was a soldier. At the bottom of the steps. He was holding a jerrican of gas. He said, *'Ballena!'* and held the can between his legs and wiggled the nozzle around as if it was his cock. Doreen screamed and ran down the stairs and out to the street — fucking fast for a fat woman — but the soldier was right on her tail, calling, *'Ballena! Ballena!'* Threatening to douse her with the gasoline."

"And did he?"

"I don't know. I got out of there."

"All that fat," I said. "She would have burned for a long time."

"Burning still, for all I know."

I let him rest again.

Outside, the rice plain had darkened, but I saw Doreen there, running along beside the train, burning like a campfire marshmallow and giving off a satisfying heat. What, no lecture on economics?

"And you, Mac? You could have stayed there — your man came out number one. You could have been king of the whole shitaree. What are you doing alone in this land of whores and smiling sons of bitches?"

"Dickie, I am learning to have no desires and no regrets. Eastern wisdom."

He coughed.

"Also, I am still learning how not to want a drink. But most of all I am not hurting people. And at this at least I believe I am being successful."

"Yeah, you look successful as hell."

We rocked along without talking.

After a spell he said, "Did you know I was a father too? There was a girl. Before you came to Esperanza. A student. Pilar. She went away to the States, and she's bringing up my son there. I never saw her again, and I have never seen my son. I never wanted to. Until . . ."

"Look, I'd rather not . . ."

"And now it's too late."

"Damn you! I just wanted to be left alone." I half stood and looked around the car to see if there was an empty seat, but it was too dark to see anything.

He said, "I know where your wife and your son are. I know how to get hold of them."

"Don't you understand? I don't want to know!"

He gasped, "Time out, okay?"

We said nothing for about half an hour. Dickie coughed

occasionally. When I saw ahead the lights of my destination, I said, "Anyway, I'm not alone. There is a woman. Her name is Supattra. I call her Soupy. When I come home from the Council every night she bathes me, and then we make love, and then she gives me my supper, and for dessert she fixes me a pipe of opium. She never asks for anything. Especially love."

Dickie leaned forward. There was something terrifying about the way his face floated toward me. He was like a shadow. His hand lifted. A finger touched my chest.

"This thing," he rasped. "Some eastern trinket?"

We both rose, because it turned out we had the same destination. We got rooms and then walked on the beach. Dickie admitted that he was dying, that he had a Disease, that he had picked it up from a woman, or women, that he would die probably within a year of what they called opportunistic infection. But maybe he could stick it out longer — in the City of Grinning Procurers there was more and cheaper medicine than anywhere else in the world. It was dark on the beach. We could not see the beauty of the dead fish we walked among.

As I'd had from my apartment in the City of Hope, here too I had a view. But there were in it no volcanoes, nor even mud shacks. Rather, there were other apartment buildings as ugly as my own, on the far side of a marshy field. "Do not walk through that field," my landlady had said once in a kind of quacking English, "because there are cobras."

Patrón, revenge had gained me nothing. And I had nothing I cared to call my own except for the trinket I wore around my neck, and a book with some photographs — two of my dead family, two of my living one. So every afternoon on the way to the Council and every night on the way home I took what I told myself was a shortcut through the field, kicking at the grass and muttering, "Come on, you little bastards, just try it."

And of course there was no woman called Supattra or Soupy or even Sioux City Sue.

The rains came. I pretty much gave up going in to work. As well as lying in bed I spent a lot of time wading through the streets with my pants rolled up above my knees, grimacing into the downpour and, whenever I thought no one would hear me, howling. So much for no desires and no regrets. Sometimes there would be a deep pothole, and I would plunge out of sight.

I did not have a phone, so often I would wade to the corner store, where the proprietor wore a yellow robe and a shaved head and lounged on a raised wooden platform and let his wife run the place. I would call Dickie — needing the comfort of a face from long ago, and surely now he too would want company. As he sank with his red crest and his regrets toward the end of all pain. But there was never an answer.

Once I bought a bottle of vodka, but on the way home I dropped it unopened into the mud. Before I slept that night I sat on the edge of my bed and stared at the bare wall and wondered if I would after all follow in Jock McKnight's defeated footsteps.

And that night I dreamt that Jeff was painting a portrait of his grandfather. As Jeff worked Jock recited. *"Yeats and Poe and Stephen Crane Had a go at the shit quatrain. Stephen Crane and Yeats and Poe Knew it was shit but had a go."*

God. Even in dreams. His Glasgow accent. "You got it, Grampa," said Jeff.

I felt like going to work the next day. In the middle of my last class I stopped as I was writing a sentence on the board, turned and looked one by one into each pair of dark eyes. "What are you doing, *ajahn?*" asked someone.

I said to the class in general, "Do you like me?"

There was a melodious response, resembling, it seemed to me, the tankle of an enormous wind chime. "Yes, *ajahn*, we like you very much!" And there was happy laughter.

When I got home that night there was a manila envelope in my mailbox. I examined it as I climbed the stairs to my apartment. American stamps. On the back a return address in

Boston. And a name. McKnight. I did not make it to my apartment but sat on the stairs and, with trembling hands, as Poe might have said, opened it. There was a familiar handwriting.

Dear Mac,

Dickie Pendergast wrote to us. I was really surprised. He got our address from someone in Esperanza. I got the impression that he was kind of desperate, not like the Dickie I remember, is he alright? He said that I should write to you. You needed to hear from me he said and so, Maquito, I am writing. I would have before but I did not know where you were, I can understand why you did not want to tell me but you should have because Ken never stops asking about you, when you are coming home etc. I have never been able to tell him that you did not want to come home. Because you love him so much, don't you, and I did not believe you would stay away forever even though you were disappeared for all this time. And maybe still you love me a little to? I have had much time to think about everything that happened in Esperanza and I have learned the truth about my father which is sad but I have to accept it and I understand why you did those things. I am living alone with Ken and my mother and there is no other man, how could there be after my strange McKnight. This is hard to say but I will say it. Please come home and we will start again. I will be so sweet to mamita and persuade her what a nice man you really are. Here is also a small letter from your son, I helped him to write the words.

Your wife who still loves you,

Montserrat

And there was a phone number.

And now, this other rather wrinkled piece of paper. With big wiggly letters made by the combined hands of my wife and my son. I fingered Montserrat's little golden man, which Dickie had thought might be some eastern trinket. And I read.

Hi Daddy,

I can't write yet so mommy is helping me. When are you going to come home. We have an apartment. Not like our big house that we had before but there are more kids here to play with. I have that big picture of you that my brother in Canada painted in my room. And I miss you and please come home.

Love,

Ken

There were some Xs and some Os. And a PS from Montserrat: *He wrote his name by himself and the hugs and kisses to.*

And there was yet another folded sheet of paper. Upon this one, a crayon drawing of stick people. A woman with circle breasts and a triangle skirt and black hair. A small person with yellow hair and a smile and round eyeglasses. *Eyeglasses?* And a tall man with shaggy grey and yellow hair and glasses and a beard. The man's hand was holding the boy's, and the boy's other hand was holding the woman's, and there was a stripe of blue at the top of the page and a gold sun beaming.

Though they say there are no longer crocodiles that escape from the canals into these thoroughfares, how can you be sure? Especially at night. As my shins go *swish swish* through the water. And I see that I have forgotten to roll my pants up and remove my shoes. Never mind, the cloth and the leather will protect me against the teeth. Of whatever. This night, *patrón*, I wish to be careful. For one has decided that to continue living is both necessary and desirable. By now I know where the potholes are, and will not do the plunge number. Not long ago, quite recently actually, I lived in a lofty town and made jokes about plummeting. But tonight I divest myself of irony, and will henceforth be a simple man possessed of a simple faith. Perhaps soon I will start to speak like a normal person — nice day, eh? Wadja thinka the game last night? — and not like some jaded aristocrat. Perhaps I have not been well all my life. But tonight I start. Being well. Or, really, is it just waking up? For does not all this now seem like a dream? Voices coming out of that restaurant door with its English name, *Eat Happy*. These amber streetlights reflected on the water like half-real fingers. Going kitchy-koo, wake up, Gussy. When I went to see the Reclining Buddha I was astounded that they had written sutras on the soles of his feet. Ticklish business, this enlightenment. And under a tree in the yard outside the temple I paid a monk to open the door of a bamboo cage. Good actions, to clean the soul, he said. Of course they catch the same sparrows again with a few grains of rice, but if those birds can carry away with them up into that dusty tree even one particle of my past, then I will pay to set them free till the cows come home. On the sidewalk beside my apartment building there is on a pedestal a sort of doll's house, to accommodate and appease local spirits. Whenever I pass it I see images of false teeth flying and hear shots and the Woman's voice. *Mate-me*. And Jeff's voice, saying *clay*. So into the spirit house I shout, "Fuck you, spirits!"

Those clouds up there brown with the light of this corrupt city. Those few stars between. But stars are stars everywhere and so part of no dream. Shine down, okay? — and show me how to stay alive until I wake up forever from this thing I have been until now. Up finally onto this dry bit of sidewalk, and I hope they don't mind a little more water on the floor of their store.

I pushed open the glass door, then shut it behind me, to block any mosquitoes that may have caught my scent. The air was thick with incense, maybe for the proprietor's spiritual benefit, or maybe to keep the mosquitoes away. Beside the counter the pigshaven gentleman rested, as always, on his platform. Instead of his usual little smile and bow and the prayer thing they do with their hands, he slid tonight to the edge of the platform and stepped down into his sandals, as if we were keeping an appointment. Except for the shaven head he looked uncannily like Humphrey Bogart. But he came up only to my chin. He thrust his hand across the counter to his wife, a wiry woman with bobbed grey hair and a fierce demeanour, and she placed between his fingers a cigarette she had been smoking. He took a drag, exhaled with a hiss, tilted his head back and said, "I have been meaning to talk to you for ever so long."

"Not to help with your English, obviously."

"You are so kind. No, I am merely curious. You are an American gentleman?" His voice was like a boy's.

"Canadian. But nevertheless a gentleman."

His giggle. "Someday I hope to learn the art of irony."

"It does not befit a monk."

"I am only a monk for one week longer."

"I am sad to say I won't be able to teach you. I am giving it up in order to be a simple man possessed of a simple faith. Anyway, irony is best practised in isolation, emotional if not physical."

"If you cannot teach me irony, perhaps you can teach me your simple faith."

A crisp twinkle in his eye. I laughed. "Well, I wish we had talked before now. We could have been friends. God knows I needed one."

"But you are not going away?"

"I am."

"This is ever so sad. When we have just met."

"As a man not only of the spirit but also of commerce, would you possibly know what time it is in Boston?"

"I would guess, sir, that — let me just calculate — yes, dawn is about to break in Boston. But will you not leave me with at least a word about this simple faith of yours?"

I opened my fist above the counter. A quantity of coins crashed down and rolled everywhere. The hands of the man's wife darted and, when she had corralled them all, she shoved toward me a red pay telephone.

I winked at the monk. "Shmile, shweetheart."

Then into the slot of the phone I slid a tarnished coin with the face of a king, and dialled the international operator.

And soon a voice said, "Go ahead, sir."